Praise fo

“Adriana Locke creates [illegible] captivating characters. She’s a go-to author if I want to escape into a great read.”

—*New York Times* bestselling author S. L. Scott

“Adriana Locke writes the most delicious heroes and sassy heroines who bring them to their knees. Her books are funny, raw, and heartfelt. She also has a great smile, but that’s beside the point.”

—*USA Today* bestselling author L. J. Shen

“Adriana Locke is the master of small-town contemporary romance. A one-click author for the masses, her perfect blend of wit, sexy banter, and well-developed characters is guaranteed to leave readers satisfied. A book by Adriana is sure to be the romantic escape you’re looking for.”

—*USA Today* bestselling author Bethany Lopez

“No one does blue-collar, small-town, ‘everyman’ (and woman!) romance like Adriana Locke. She masterfully creates truly epic love stories for characters who could be your neighbor, your best friend—you! Each one is more addictive and heart-stoppingly romantic than the last.”

—*USA Today* bestselling author Kennedy Ryan

“Adriana’s sharp prose, witty dialogue, and flawless blend of humor and steam meld together to create unputdownable, up-all-night reads!”

—*Wall Street Journal* bestselling author Winter Renshaw

The Sweet Spot

OTHER TITLES BY ADRIANA LOCKE

The Exception Series

The Exception

The Connection: An Exception Novella

The Perception

The Exception Series box set

Landry Family Series

Sway

Swing

Switch

Swear

Swink

Sweet

The Landry Family Series: Part One

The Landry Family Series: Part Two

The Gibson Boys Series

Crank

Craft

Cross (a novella)

Crave

Crazy

Dogwood Lane Series

Tumble

Tangle

Trouble

Carmichael Family Series

Flirt

Fling

Stand-Alone Novels

Sacrifice

Wherever It Leads

Written in the Scars

Battle of the Sexes

Lucky Number Eleven

Like You Love Me

The Sweet Spot

ADRIANA LOCKE

Montlake

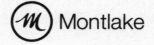

Published by Montlake, Seattle

www.apub.com

ISBN-13: 9781662504006 (paperback)
ISBN-13: 9781662503993 (digital)

Cover design by Letitia Hasser
Cover photography by Regina Wamba of ReginaWamba.com
Cover images: © Haoxiang Yang / Getty; © Evgenii Emelianov / Shutterstock

Printed in the United States of America

To my children, Alexander, Aristotle,
Achilles, and Ajax.
You will never know how much I love you.

CHAPTER ONE

Palmer

"You've been warned."

I plop on a barstool across from my best friend, Val. She wipes her hands on a white dishrag and side-eyes my situation. Because I'm clearly *a situation.*

My mascara doesn't look as neat as it did when I applied it . . . yesterday morning. But that's what happens when you stay up late matching socks and wake up to a hungry twelve-year-old who's already missed the bus. Still, it might've been okay if I hadn't rubbed my eyes during a bout of allergies after bebopping through the bus yard at work like I own the damned place.

I sigh.

Early-afternoon sunlight streams in the windows of Fletcher's, the only restaurant in a ten-mile radius. The aroma of my favorite Friday lunch, open-faced beef manhattan sandwiches, perfumes the air. Before I can order one to go, I notice the line drawn through it on the menu board.

Of course.

"I'm afraid to ask . . . ," Val says, handing me a glass of tea. *God bless this woman.*

"If I didn't enjoy my job so much, I'd quit."

"No, you wouldn't. You need the money, and Kirk pays you too much to walk away."

"Fine." I sigh, swirling the straw around the glass. "If I didn't enjoy my job so much *and* Kirk didn't pay me well, I'd quit."

Val giggles.

"I had a customer call for a radiator surge tank today," I say.

"A radiator what?"

"Surge tank. I'll spare you the details. It's a very specific bus part that we usually keep in stock. That's all you need to know."

"Okay. Noted."

"So, I get the order for the tank, and I call the shop to see if we have one. Burt insisted we didn't. Like, he was ready to fight me over it. But the whole time we were talking, I could hear the little farming game he plays on his phone mooing and clucking."

"Ooh, this isn't going to end well," Val says, her eyes sparkling.

"I have two choices, right? I can take Burt's word for it, since he *is* the shop manager, and just call the customer back and relay the information. *Or* I can do what's right by Kirk, since I am the assistant general manager, and go see if there's a bus with the tank in the yard—because I know there is. *I know it.*"

Val bites her lip. "You had one, didn't you?"

"Three!" My blood pressure shoots up again. "I wasn't going to go look. I was just going to call the customer back and tell them we were out of stock, but it *ate at my soul.* So I put my boots on and marched into the bus yard—through the mud from the last five days of rain—and found them my damn self." I take a quick breath and blow it out. "I then proceeded to have a brilliant come-apart worthy of a night in the hospital, but we're not talking about that."

She laughs. "This explains the mud on your jeans." She leans toward me and peers at the side of my head. "And on your ear. Come here."

I tip my head toward her, and she plucks a glob of gunk off my right earlobe.

"You just . . . sit there, drink your tea, and calm down. I'm going to go wash my hands," she says. "Be right back."

I take a long, cold drink and feel the sugary sweetness slide down my throat. The tea helps settle the tornado roaring inside me. But that's what life always feels like these days—a giant natural disaster.

There's beauty in the storm. I know that and I appreciate it. I even start my day off by listing things that I'm grateful for out loud. It's supposed to help build a pattern of positive thinking—at least that's what the TikTok influencers say while I'm scrolling in the middle of the night.

But it's still a damn storm.

I'm lifting my glass to take another sip of sugar when a shoulder brushes against mine. I'm two seconds from turning and giving someone a warning . . . but stop.

My body stills as a set of large, calloused hands presses against the laminate countertop next to me.

Thick, muscled wrists attach to forearms the size of my biceps. The space around me is impregnated with a very heady, very *masculine* vibe.

A bubble of curiosity blooms in my stomach. The intrigue grows as a rich, balmy scent licks at my senses. It's the kind of cologne I love—the type that makes the person smelling it feel better, more confident, more attractive by proxy.

That is not a harbinger of good things, though. I know from experience.

I ignore the warning bells dinging in my head like the seasoned expert I am and twist to the side . . . and nearly fall off my stool.

Holy. Man. Candy.

His hair—thick and wild, lying to the side in an errant wave—is the color of tobacco. It's a stark juxtaposition to the chips of sapphire sparkling in his eyes. A sharp jaw is dusted with more than a day's worth of stubble, finishing the glorious package with a sinful edge.

"Hey," he says, his voice smooth and inviting.

"I'm sorry," I say, finding my voice. "Do I know you?"

He grins. "Not yet."

Damn it. My insides tighten, and I squirm in my seat.

"That's actually why I sat down," he says. "I was hoping that you'd give me your number."

What?

He laughs at the look on my face. The sound is warm and effortless—the audible version of his cologne.

"And why would I give you my number?" *Because you're gorgeous.* "I don't even know your name."

"That's an easy fix."

His smile blurs the chaos of the restaurant bustling around us. It's as if it's just us in the room, and he doesn't notice anything but me.

"Knowing your name is not a good enough reason to give you my number," I say, lifting a brow.

"What if I told you that my buddy sitting at the round table by the window bet me a hundred dollars that you wouldn't give it to me?"

"I'd say one of two things. Either this is a big joke, and I look like a sucker in my dirty jeans and old Florida State sweatshirt," I say, remembering that I barely finger combed my hair this morning before tossing it up on my head, "or he knew that you'd say that and was trying to toss me a red flag so I'd blow you off."

He grins.

"And that was *not* an innuendo," I say, pointing a finger in his direction.

His grin turns into a chuckle. I find myself smiling right back at him.

"This isn't a joke," he says.

"So then it's a red flag." I narrow my eyes playfully. "But what kind of a red flag? *Hmm.* Maybe you're a mass murderer as your side gig. You could be a Dexter, for all I know."

He laughs. "Nope. I haven't killed anyone."

"Maybe you don't like puppies?"

His shoulders tremble as he chuckles again. I can't help but notice how broad they are.

"I love puppies," he says. "I'll be honest—not a huge kitten guy. But puppies are awesome."

I lean back and study him. "Then are you the guy that doesn't clear the remaining time off the microwave? It must be that."

His chuckle turns into a full-blown laugh. "That's it—you got me. I open the door with a few seconds left and just leave it."

"I'd almost prefer it if you were a mass murderer." A grin kisses my lips. "But I suppose it's better for mankind this way."

Val comes by and asks him if he wants anything else. Their interaction is breezy. His charm cuts through his presence and puts Val at ease. She's normally a tougher nut to crack.

But I realize something else—he's put me at ease too.

"Do you want to order lunch?" Val asks me. "Or did you just come by to say hello?"

My stomach growls, but nothing sounds good but the sold-out lunch special. "I'm good."

Val takes a quick look at the guy before sliding her gaze back to me. "I think you are." She winks before strolling toward the kitchen.

"What did you say your name was?" he asks after Val walks away.

"I didn't."

He rests against the counter with his body angled toward mine. A black and gold baseball cap is pulled low on his forehead. "Well, my name is Colson Beck. You can call me Cole."

I study him for a moment. Besides being ridiculously handsome and delightfully alluring, he also seems . . . nice.

It's just a little banter. One conversation. What can it hurt?

"I'm Palmer Clark. You can call me Palmer."

He smiles. "Are you from around here?"

I lean against the bar and angle my body toward his, mimicking his posture.

"Yes," I say. "And obviously you are not."

"True. I'm a California boy, lover of sunshine and salt water."

"Oh, are you a surfer?"

He laughs. "No. I'm terrible on a surfboard."

"Probably safer. You know, sharks and all."

"That's what my mother says. I lie to her every time I go to the ocean just so she doesn't worry."

I gasp. "You lie to your mother? That's awful."

"It's better than her thinking I'm going to die all afternoon," he says, his voice tinged with a laugh.

I can't help but grin at Cole. "Okay. Fine. That's true."

He fiddles with a napkin on the counter. His fingers work the paper back and forth in the same tempo as his boot-clad foot tapping against the floor. The entire thing is so casual and disarming that my frustration from Burt and his ridiculousness drifts away.

"Who are you, anyway?" I ask. "Why are you here?"

"My parents moved here six months ago, and I came to visit them. Perks of retirement."

"Not judging or anything, but aren't you too young for retirement?"

The question pleases him. A slow smile slips across his face.

"The average age for retirement in professional baseball is thirty," he says. "I am—*was*—the catcher for the San Diego Swifts. So, short answer is no. I'm right on target."

Professional baseball?

What?

He leans back and runs his hands along his thighs. I make a point not to watch the movement. There's no sense in torturing myself.

Besides, I'm still wrapping my head around the fact that a professional baseball player is in Bloomfield, Ohio.

"Maybe we could have dinner or something while I'm in town," he says, his words measured more carefully than before.

My stomach flip-flops at the invitation, and my insides war with how to respond.

I need to decline. For so many reasons, I should give Cole a smile and send him on his way. But needs and wants are two totally different stories, and right now, the line between them is muddy.

"Dinner?" he asks again. "Or lunch? I can even do breakfast, if you'd rather."

My face flushes, and I move around in my seat. I'm about to give in, to say yes to dinner, when my gaze lands on the tiny tattoo on my wrist. The delicate lotus flower reminds me every day that beautiful things can come from the dirtiest waters. I just have to keep growing.

"Thank you," I say, forcing a swallow. "But no."

His brows shoot to the ceiling. "No?"

I shrug. "No."

"There's a word I don't hear often."

Instead of it coming across as cocky, it borders on self-deprecating. It's surprisingly adorable.

"Fish is never going to let me live this down," he says, his words teasing.

"Fish?"

"My friend that's sitting back there."

I glance over my shoulder at a large blond man sitting near the window. *Also handsome.*

"Who cares?" I say, turning back to Cole. "He shares his name with an aquatic vertebrate."

He laughs. "He's a big deal, you know."

I bite my lip to keep my grin from growing too wide. "*Ooh.* I love that."

"What?"

"I love when a man can admit that he's not the biggest deal in the room."

He stills, pulling his bottom lip in between his teeth. "I didn't say *that*, sweetheart."

Nice try, Mr. Baseball.

"Maybe since he's such a big deal, he'll let you keep your hundred bucks," I say, hoping my cheeks aren't as pink as I think they are.

"You don't know Fish. He'll have me forking it over before we get out of here."

My lips part, but no words come out.

I struggle to breathe from the brightness of his blue eyes. The warmth in his irises is so comfortable that I fail to object to the way his gaze holds mine. It's not until he starts to smirk that I shake out of my reverie.

Val slips my tab from the past week under my glass. I groan, having forgotten that it was due today.

"I guess I'll go pay Fish and get it over with," he says with a sigh. There's an opening embedded in the words, a last chance to take him up on his offer.

I glance down at my bill and gulp. "Or you could give me seventy-five dollars."

His brows rise to the ceiling. "What?"

It's a wild idea and not well thought out, but I'm too far in to back out now.

"Give me seventy-five dollars of the hundred you'll win. Sounds fair to me, considering it's my number," I say.

He wasn't expecting my offer. Hell, I wasn't expecting it, either, but here we are. And it's not a terrible idea. It'll give me twenty dollars after I pay this week's tab, and twenty bucks never goes astray as a single mom. Besides, I'll never have to answer his call.

Cole's features twist into amusement, and then, much to my surprise, he pulls out his wallet.

"You have money?" I ask.

He lifts his head just high enough for me to see his smirk. "Yes. *I have money.* Quite a lot of it, actually."

"No," I say, my cheeks flushing again. "I mean *cash. You have cash.* No one ever has cash anymore."

He hands me three crisp twenty-dollar bills, along with a ten and a five. "I do pride myself on being prepared for all occasions."

"I see you also brought your humility with you." I shove the money in my pocket. "Thanks for that."

"No problem." He lifts his chin expectantly. "Your number?"

"Yeah. *My number.*"

I pull my attention away from his eyes as they try to pierce mine. I study his leather boots instead.

How am I going to swing this? Just as I'm about to hand his money back to him, Val laughs. *Bingo!*

"Let me just . . . put it in your phone for you," I say.

He hands over his phone without hesitation.

My heart thumps in my chest. His readiness to go along with this befuddles me.

While I don't know much about him, I know enough to know that I need to not give him my number.

He might be gorgeous and charming, but he is not what I'm after. Damn it, anyway.

It has to be a *no* for me. But for Val, it could be a total win.

I bite the inside of my cheek and enter her number into Cole's phone. Thankfully it's one of the very few that I actually remember these days because I made my son memorize it in case of an emergency. Then I hand the phone back.

"There you go," I say, relieved to have this over with. "I'm a little richer, and you win your bet."

He nods, then looks at the screen with tugged brows as Val walks over to us.

"Do you need more tea, Palm?" she asks. "I'm going on break."

"Nope. I'm good."

I give her a little wink. *You owe me, and you don't even know it yet.*

She starts to speak but stops as she pulls her phone out of her pocket. Jacinda, the waitress covering for her, bustles by.

"I got you," Jacinda says, stutter-stepping for a moment as she spies Cole. "Go ahead. Take your break now."

Val looks at her phone. "That's a weird prefix."

"Probably about your car warranty," I say, laughing. "Those assholes call me at least once a day."

"Yeah, probably so."

I look back at Cole. His eyes pin me to the spot. He holds his phone between us as Val's continues to ring.

My name is displayed on his screen.

Val ends her call, and then my name disappears from Cole's phone.

Oh shit.

Cole raises a brow. "Really, Palmer?"

Whoops.

Val turns back around and looks frazzled. Slowly, reality unfolds in front of her face.

She laughs as she puts her phone in her pocket. "You gave him *my* number? Not that I mind," she says, looking quickly at Cole. "But that's freaking hilarious."

My cheeks burn as Cole's eyes dig into mine. There are a myriad of emotions playing out across those irises, and I pluck the one I can handle the easiest—hesitancy—and try to explain myself.

"I must've . . . gotten confused," I say. "It's not like I ever call myself."

"Sure." He rolls his tongue around his mouth. "Here." He hands his phone to Val. "Put Palmer's number in here for me."

"Val . . . ," I warn, but she completely ignores me.

She happily taps my name into Cole's phone, her bright fingernails drumming against the screen with every digit pressed.

My insides twist as I scramble to figure out how to stop this mess from proceeding. But by the time I get it together, it's too late. He smiles like the cat who ate the canary.

"Thanks, *Val*," he says without ever looking at her.

"You're welcome."

His gaze lingers on me. "I'll talk to you soon, Miss Clark."

No, you won't. "Can't wait."

I lift a brow in some ridiculous form of defiance as he stands. He waves his hand through the air as Fish appears at his side.

Cole gives me a lingering smile, pausing just long enough for his cologne to serenade me one final time. Then, after my insides are nice and melted, he turns casually on his heel and exits Fletcher's.

CHAPTER TWO

Palmer

Val whistles through her teeth. "Wow."

"Wow" is right.

My gaze stays affixed to the door for longer than I care to admit. Cole's unexpected handsomeness has made me sweat. I paw at the counter until I find the napkins. I pull one out of the dispenser and wipe my palms.

Why couldn't I have been casually cool?

"He was okay," I say, tearing my eyes from the door and swiveling around to face Val.

She snorts. *"Right."*

"What? He was altogether forgettable."

"What are you talking about?" she asks. "He was *not* forgettable, and he had a very definite thing for you. Will you stop it?"

Jacinda walks by and stuffs a twenty-dollar bill in Val's waist apron. "And he was an excellent tipper."

"Stay out of this, Jacinda," I say.

Her laugh is light and airy as she enters the kitchen.

Val holds her arms out to her sides. "Are you that oblivious? Did you not sense the pheromones in here?"

Yes. "No. I sense a heavy dose of friend failure since you didn't save me a beef manhattan."

She rolls her eyes. "Only you would focus on beef and mashed potatoes when a whole freaking snack just walked out of here with your phone number."

The reminder makes my tummy somersault again. But I don't give in. That would only encourage Val.

"Of course I would. I've eaten chicken nuggets and macaroni for a week. I'm hungry."

She tries to keep a straight face. Her lips curl toward the ceiling a little more with each second that passes.

"It's not funny," I say, laughing. "You don't even know the life I live."

She smirks. "I know you're going to be living a life of missed opportunities if you don't answer the phone when he calls."

I hate it when she's right. And she *is* right this time. I feel it deep in my bones—the parts of my bones that haven't been touched by a man like that in way too long.

"Regardless of the life I'll lead when I send him to voice mail, I can't do it, Val."

"And why the hell not?"

My body screams in agreement with her. I ignore them both.

"Why?" I ask, repeating her question. "Because . . . because you're taking tai chi classes for the hell of it on Thursday nights, and I've never done that."

She blinks at me. "Say what?"

I sigh.

"What does *my* tai chi class have to do with *you* not answering Cole's phone call?" she asks, like I've officially lost my mind.

And maybe I have.

Cole Beck is the man I would create if God handed me modeling clay and said, *Go for it: create the man of your dreams, and I will make him into reality.* Tall, lean body. Perfect smile. A heavy dose of wit with a hint of naughtiness that promises a good time in bed.

But the reason that option isn't available to me must be because every time I get a man close to that, he wrecks my heart. My joy. *My life.* And if the fact that Cole is a walking sculpture of my design isn't bad enough . . . he doesn't even live here.

Done.

That was easy.

Why bother investing time in a man, even for a quick bout of fun, when there is simply no future with him?

"I just need a minute," I say, hoping that it will be enough to suffice.

It's not.

"A minute for what, Palm? You're always talking about wanting to live life again—well, live it. With him. In bed, preferably, but if you want to get fancy, try a table. Or a boat."

I roll my eyes. "I'd be thrilled to have sex with Cole if it was just that—sex."

"I'm sure that can be worked out."

"Val . . ." I give her a pointed look. "Do you really think that I can have sex with him and not think about it the next day? Or the next week, probably? I'd be doing laundry and fantasizing about him and the rinse cycle."

"Be honest. You'd probably relive that for the rest of your life."

I sit back on my stool and sigh. "That's my point. That's what I've done my entire life. I've never, not once, done myself any favors, and I'm trying to change that. I'm on Team Palmer now." I shake invisible pom-poms. "Go, me!"

She's not entertained.

"No offense, but I think screwing the daylights out of him would be doing yourself an *orgasmic* favor."

I can't help but laugh at her. "I'm sure it would be orgasmic. Hell, I nearly had an orgasm sitting beside him."

She laughs too.

"But sleeping with him—or having dinner with him, for that matter—is not what I need to be doing right now." I level my gaze with hers. "It'll be a total waste of time, and I've wasted enough of my damn time on the wrong men."

As right as Val was earlier, *I'm right now.*

I've spent so much time waiting on guys who promised me the world—men who took everything that I had to give and gave nothing in return.

First, there was Jared, Ethan's dad. I spent six years biding my time and hoping he would grow up and decide to trade the video games for vacations. Never happened.

Then it was Charlie, the cutie I met at work. That bastard cost me almost a year of my life that I can't get back.

Now I'm thirty-two years old, a single mom, with no happily ever after on the horizon. Yes, I could be happy on my own, but I don't want to be. I want someone to share my life with.

I don't want to have to substitute a golden retriever as my lifelong companion, but I'm getting to that point.

"No, you're right," Val says, shaking her head. "You've dated some real champs."

"Gee, thanks."

"Hey, you know it. I'm not stating new facts here. But keep your options open because I think he could be a real champ, if you know what I mean."

Our eyes lock, and together we laugh.

"We'll see," I say, hoping my concession will end the conversation.

But instead of accepting my remark at face value and moving on, she snorts. "You just mom'd me," she says.

"What?"

"When a mom says, 'We'll see,' that means it's never happening." She looks over her shoulder. "Hang on. I need to help Jacinda for a second."

I exhale. The release relaxes my shoulders, and I lean against the counter.

I watch Val laugh with Jacinda near the coffeepots, nearly spilling a gallon of tea onto the floor. The two of them are so free and happy, and I wish, for just a moment, that I had a little bit of that in me.

They know what styles of jeans look good on them. Neither of them worries that she's too old to go back to college, despite being nearly my age, and Jacinda has a kid. Heck, they both can probably tell you their favorite colors.

Me? I know nothing about myself. Not really.

I want to be able to pick a red lipstick out with confidence. What's my 5K time? I don't know. I also want to be able to pick out a man with long-term-material vibes.

Unfortunately for me, that's not the sweet-talking visitor from California.

Ugh.

"Are you okay?" Val plants her hands on the counter. "You have a weird look on your face."

Her voice snaps me out of my head. "Yeah. I'm fine." I glance at the clock on the wall. "I need to get going, though."

"Are you headed home already?"

"Ha." I reach into my pocket. "I have about four hours of paperwork left at the office and then a million loads of laundry at home."

"Is Ethan home this weekend? Or does Jared have him?"

I whip out some of the cash that Cole gave me and hand it to Val. "Jared is picking him up from school and keeping him until Sunday evening. Or so he says."

"Want to go out? Do something fun?"

"Depends on how you're using the word 'fun.'"

She grins. "I'll keep it tame for you. Maybe we could drive over to Forest Falls and do some shopping?"

"I'm sorry—did you just use 'shopping' and 'fun' in the same sentence?"

"My apologies." Val laughs and walks to the end of the counter. She inserts my cash for the tab amount into the register and then brings me a receipt. "How about if I bring some pizza to your house, and we watch *Fried Green Tomatoes* tomorrow night?"

I down the rest of my tea. "Deal."

Val hands me a small slip of paper and my change. I plunk a nice tip on the counter and shove the remaining money in my pocket.

The door chimes as a new customer walks into the restaurant. Val welcomes them and tells them to have a seat. Then she turns to me.

I start to smile before she even says a word. I don't know what she's about to say, but I can see her forming the thought.

"I'm not answering if Cole calls," I tell her preemptively. "If that's where you're going mentally, save it."

She gives me a sigh that's laced with a growl. "Why do you hate me?"

"Hate you?"

"Yes, *hate me*. When is the next time either one of us is going to get to go out with a professional baseball player that looks like he stepped off the cover of *GQ*?"

"I hope for your sake that it happens again soon."

"Oh, it won't. The dating spirits chose you, and you don't even care."

I laugh. "Stop it."

"The world just handed you an oyster, and you aren't even going to crack it open."

"There's a pearl joke in there somewhere . . ."

Val grabs an order pad and giggles. "At least call me if he calls you."

"He's not calling me, Val."

"Call me. Promise."

We look at each other with the comfort that only best friends can exchange.

"I promise," I say. "I'll call you if he calls me. I'll even screenshot the missed call just for you."

Her shoulders fall. "You're so mean."

I laugh and head for the exit. "Talk to you later, Val."

"Bye, Palmer."

I push open the door and step into the fresh spring air. The breeze is laced with the scent of pine and rain. I pause to fill my lungs with the loveliness.

Spring is my favorite season. It always has been. It has such a promising vibe, with its colorful blooms and longer days with a brighter sun. But it also signifies something deeper: hope.

It signals a fresh start—a clean house, new flowers, a new chance at life.

"Let's hope this turns out to be the best season of my life," I say as I head to my car.

I'm almost to the driver's-side door when my phone vibrates in my purse. I can feel it against my thigh.

A slight chuckle escapes my lips as I imagine Val jumping to conclusions. She would be sure Cole is texting me.

Me? I doubt it.

The bet is over. He got my number. End of.

That's fine with me. It's great, actually. Because after six years with Jared, almost a year with Charlie, and enough time with other men who were complete wastes of energy, I'm done. I'm making choices on a long-term basis and not a *you're cute* one.

It's now or never. And I'm not getting any younger.

I smile.

This is going to be my best season, and no drop-dead-gorgeous, honey-tongued, retired baseball player is going to change that.

Period.

CHAPTER THREE

Cole

"Good work today, boys." Dad claps my shoulder with one hand and Fish's shoulder with the other. "Never would've gotten this fence fixed without you."

The final rays of the day's sunshine filter through the tall pine trees. The rays cast a warm amber glow across the backyard.

I don't know what I expected their new place to look like, but it wasn't this. Instead of the spacious, stucco-style home in Arizona, they chose a cozy ranch layout in a verifiable forest. It's so different and unbelievably quiet.

In the limited time I had today to explore Bloomfield, that's what I learned. It's quiet here. That and people are nosy.

"You wanna stay for supper, Fish?" Dad asks. "We'd love to have you."

"I would, but I have meetings all day tomorrow in Cincinnati. I better get my ass back to the hotel tonight."

Dad gives our shoulders a final squeeze before releasing them. "Well, suit yourself. But I hope you'll come back and see us before you head back to California."

"Oh, for sure," Fish says. "Me and Cole haven't even had time to cause trouble yet."

"That's true. We still need to light this little town all the way up, Pops," I say, elbowing my father in the side.

He gives me a stern look. "I thought you'd grown out of all of that debauchery."

Fish cackles as I try my best to look innocent.

"Me?" I point at myself. "Debaucherous? *Dad.*"

He ignores me. "Thanks for your help tonight, Fish," Dad says.

"Hey." I look at my father. "What about me?"

"What about you?"

"Do you think I wanted to spend my vacation out here fixing fences?" I joke.

"I don't give a rat's ass. You're retired now. These are the things you do in retirement."

Ouch.

I know he's kidding. I was too. But that jab felt like a knife twisting inside an already ripe wound.

There's no way for Dad to know that, though.

He smiles at me, nearly beaming. Why wouldn't he? His only son—his only child, for that matter—is home. Retired from the major leagues. Living the dream that he's always wished for himself.

And here I am bitter about it.

I toe a rock, kicking it across the lawn. It comes to a stop near a picnic table that my mom painted magenta.

"Yeah," I say when I realize that both Dad and Fish are waiting for me to say something. "That's me. Retirement guy."

Fish studies my reaction in the same way he has ever since I told him that I was walking away from the game. His response to the announcement has been measured. He's done all the things—offered support, congratulated me. He even threw a party for me in Vegas.

But I know Fish . . . and Fish knows me.

The party was for appearances. It was the natural thing to do, to celebrate a hell of a career and go out with a bang. And strippers, naturally, because it's Fish.

The event hushed any whispers around the league that I was exaggerating my injury. I must've really gotten whacked when Tyson Balmby slid into home plate and ran his helmet straight into my shoulder. Why else would I retire at the top of my game?

"You know," I say, kicking another rock. "I think I'm more of a hiring guy."

"What do you mean?" Dad asks.

"I think instead of being the handyman, I'll hire someone to come and do those things for me."

"Nah." Dad waves a hand through the air. "You have to do it yourself. It's a part of the process."

I make a face. "Or maybe I'll just contribute to the local economy. Why do a job when someone else knows how to do it better and probably would appreciate the business?"

"Because you're a Beck, that's why. Besides, I'll give you six months, and you'll be desperate for a project. Every retiree needs a good project to work on. Hell, maybe we can do them together someday."

Fish grins. "I think your boy found a *project* today."

I smirk.

Damn, that woman.

I *felt* Palmer walk into Fletcher's this afternoon. I don't know any other way to explain it.

The air changed as soon as she stepped foot into the restaurant. The hair on the back of my neck stood up, and I was compelled to turn around.

And there she was, walking into the room like a beautiful storm.

Her clothes were slightly baggy, skimming over curves that I could barely make out. A wild mess of strawberry-blonde hair was piled on top of her head, and the irritation on her pretty face was so adorable that I laughed out loud.

I've never been pulled to a person like I was today. I *had* to talk to her. Usually, if a woman piques my interest, I sit back and wait. They come to me. They always do. But relying on that strategy seemed too risky. Fish, always observant, gave me the excuse I needed and goaded me with his stupid bet.

Stupid, but it worked. I needed a reason to talk to her and didn't have time to come up with an opening.

I slip my phone out of my pocket and reread the text I sent her earlier.

Hey, it's Cole. It was really nice meeting you today. If you change your mind about dinner, just let me know. I'll be in town for a few days.

She hasn't texted me back.

For some reason, that information stretches my grin from ear to ear.

"I need to get going," Fish says as he shakes my father's hand. "Call me if there's anything else your boy here can't manage—oof!"

He leans forward, holding his stomach like the punch I just threw at him jokingly hurt.

"Get out of here before I don't pull the next punch back," I tease.

Fish walks backward. "Call me tomorrow, Cole. Good to see ya, Lawrence. Give Casey a kiss on the cheek for me."

We say our goodbyes as Fish turns and walks around the house and out of sight.

I wipe my brow with the back of my hand.

"Well, what do you think?" Dad asks, sitting on the edge of the picnic table.

"About what?"

He shrugs.

I blow out a breath and sit across from him.

The evening sun is warm despite the cool air beginning to lick at my skin. I adjust my Swifts baseball cap to shield my eyes from the final rays of light.

"What did you and Fish do in town today?" Dad asks, folding his hands in front of him.

"Grabbed some lunch at Fletcher's, like you suggested. The beef manhattans are excellent, by the way. Played some golf at Fairgreens. Oh—we stopped by Bud's Sporting Goods. That guy is a gem."

Dad's chest rumbles as he laughs. "He is, isn't he? He's one of my favorite people in town. Good guy—great guy, actually. He helped me cut up that tree out front when a storm took it down this winter."

"Yeah, he seemed pretty nice. He was super friendly."

"I bet he appreciated you and Fish coming in. Two real athletes in a small-town sporting-goods store." Dad's eyes shine with pride. "Bet it made his day."

"We signed a bunch of shit." I laugh. "He was getting our input into the fall ball draft he set up for the Little League. It was hysterical but smart."

Dad nods, tapping his hands against the table.

The sun shifts. It dips behind the tree line, casting a plethora of shadows across the lawn.

The levity in Dad's face drifts away, and in its place is a soberness that winds my stomach into a knot.

"We haven't really had a chance to talk about your retirement," he says.

Fuck.

I look down to see that I've laced my fingers together just like his.

"What about it?" I ask.

He shrugs. "I'm happy you called it quits when you did—and not just because I hope to see more of you now. There's something to be said for walking away when you're at the top of your game."

Yeah. It's called being out of your fucking mind.

"But I will also say that I'm surprised," he says, his voice thick with caution.

Same, Dad. Same.

"What's surprising about it?" I ask. "This shoulder is done. I could've maybe played another season or two, but I couldn't have pulled off what I managed the last couple of years." I shrug. "Better off to call it quits after a season where I lead the league in home runs and won a Gold Glove, right?"

The words, phrases that I've memorized ever since I started prepping for the announcement, taste sour. I don't know how anyone believes me. It doesn't even sound realistic. Yet they do.

Maybe I could have a second career as an actor.

Dad bows his head, nodding slightly.

"What?" I ask.

He sucks in a deep breath. "You're all right, aren't you?"

"Well, yeah." I force a swallow. "Why wouldn't I be?"

He shrugs.

"I'm living the life, Pops. I have tons of money—more than I'll ever need. I'm great looking."

Dad half grins.

"I'm definitely going into the Hall of Fame at some point," I say, continuing on. "And now I have all the time in the world to do whatever the hell I want—which does not include projects. Just for clarification's sake."

He unfolds his hands and leans back, grabbing the edge of the picnic table. He watches me closely. "And what is it that you want to do, Cole?"

Fuck if I know.

I stand and stretch my arms over my head. My right shoulder pulls from the injury I sustained on national television last year—a high throw to home and Balmby needing to score . . . and me in the way. At least I got him out.

But what do I want to do? That's easy. I want to play baseball. Live the life I've always lived.

I want to get up in the morning, go to the field, work out, play ball. Then go home, have dinner, call a woman if I'm feeling that kind of way, and go to bed.

Wash, rinse, repeat.

Except I can't. And I never will again.

My stomach twists so tight that I think I might puke.

"What do I want to do? Are you trying to get rid of me already, old man?" I ask, biting back bile.

"You know better than that."

"I've only been here two days. I couldn't possibly be driving you crazy yet."

Dad gets to his feet. "You know that having you here is the best thing to happen to me and your mother in years. We've missed you. We've not gotten to see you nearly enough, but it was a sacrifice we all had to make and we made it happily. Hell, you could move in, and your mother would be over the moon." He smirks. "But if you hear something in the middle of the night, close your ears."

"Dad!" I make a face. "What . . . no. *No.* That's my mother."

He chuckles, amused with himself.

"I'm definitely not moving in with you. I'm retired, not desperate," I say, physically shaking the idea out of my head.

"So, are you staying in San Diego?"

"Maybe." I pace around Mom's bright-yellow tulips. "It'll probably depend on what offers come in and what my agent thinks I should do. There's lots to consider." I hope.

"Makes sense."

I blow out a breath and shove my hands in my pockets. I stop walking.

The knot tightens like it does late at night, when there's no way to distract myself from reality. I hate thinking about all this. There is no great solution.

There's also no one to talk to about it. Not really. Not without making it a big deal . . . and making it real.

"What's Mom making for dinner?" I ask, desperate for relief.

"Your favorite—chicken-fried steak and mashed potatoes."

I smack a mosquito on my arm. "Well, let's go in and get cleaned up before it's time to eat. I'm a mess from that fence."

Dad wraps his arm around my shoulders, and we head toward the house. "You know what, Cole?"

"What?"

We stop at the base of the stairs that lead to the back door. Dad turns to face me.

"We love this little town," he says. "I hope you find some of the magic that your mom and I have found here."

He walks up the stairs. As if he knows I need a moment, he disappears into the house and leaves me standing alone.

I face the backyard and breathe in the fresh evening air. It's crisp and clean. It's nice.

It would be so easy to get overwhelmed, to spin out of control with the decisions I have to make. A part of me wants to sit down and just get it all sorted, no matter how hard it is. But another part of me wants to do what I do best—ignore it as long as I can.

"Who are you, anyway? Why are you here?"

"Aren't you too young for retirement?"

My lips twist into a smile. *"Palmer Clark. You can call me Palmer."*

Ignoring it is even easier when I have a distraction readily available. And distractions don't get any better than Palmer Clark.

I take my phone out of my pocket and find her name. My text from earlier today is still unreturned. There are no missed calls either.

I consider texting her for the second time since I walked out of Fletcher's but decide against it. There's no sense in looking thirsty. This is a small town, after all. We're bound to run into each other again soon.

My phone goes back in my pocket.

"I hope you find some of the magic that your mom and I have found here."

A smile tickles my lips as I take the stairs to the kitchen.

I don't know about magic, but I think I've found the perfect diversion. And that's all I need right now.

CHAPTER FOUR

Palmer

"Oof."

I set the laundry basket down with a thud. One of Ethan's sweatshirts tumbles off the pile and lands on the floor. I pick it up, smiling at the wild tie-dye design that he's suddenly become enamored with.

The shirt was a few dollars at an off-price retailer in Forest Falls. He's worn it so often that the drawstring has been pulled out of the hoodie and a little hole has formed in the right cuff. He'll probably wear it until it disintegrates in the washing machine.

I smile.

Ethan is such a mix of me and his father. Like me, he doesn't care about designer labels. He wears whatever he feels best in—even if that's a hoodie so bright I pray it fades every time I toss it into the dryer. Like his father, he doesn't care what anyone thinks of him. He says *I love you* in front of his friends without a care in the world.

Not that Jared ever did that. *I love you* doesn't generally come out of his mouth to anyone.

I sit on the sofa and grab the remote. With the push of a button, the romantic comedy I've been keeping half an eye on for the last hour starts playing again. It's not a bad flick, but it's not great either. I mainly keep it on to prevent the house from being too quiet.

I turn up the volume before folding Ethan's hoodie. Then a pair of joggers. Then a Nirvana shirt he sleeps in because someone on social media told him Nirvana was cool.

I'm about to reach for a pair of shorts when my phone rings. I glance down and see Skoolie's office number.

"Hey," I say, expecting to hear my boss, Kirk, on the other end.

Instead, I get Burt.

"Palmer?" he asks, his tone gruff.

"Yes?"

"Where is the title for the bus we're sellin' to Agnello?"

"It's in a file on my desk. Why?"

"'Cause he's here to pick it up."

I spring to my feet, the top of my head so hot that I think it might blow off.

There's no way he did this.

"Agnello can't pick it up. He hasn't even paid for it yet," I say, moving my hand around in front of me. "We had this conversation on Thursday."

"And *I told you* that he'd be here today."

I grit my teeth together and try not to see double.

"Have you called Kirk?" I ask, my heart beating in the side of my neck.

"No," he says like I'm a child. "I'm calling you because I need the title. Kirk doesn't have the titles."

"No," I say, using the tone he used with me, "but he might like the money."

His sigh is mixed with a growl.

You're irritated? Me too, asshole.

"What do you expect me to do?" he asks. "Tell Agnello to come back on Monday? Tell him that he drove all the way here from New

York and he'll have to stay a couple of extra nights because you won't tell me where the fucking title is?"

Nope.

I'm willing to overlook Burt most days. He's never my favorite person, but I bite my tongue for the good of the business. Besides, he's generally just a dick, and I don't waste my energy on getting mad.

But this? No. We aren't going to pretend he's not talking to me like I'm a child. He can shove his farm game where the sun won't shine on his crops.

"First, change your tone. *Now,*" I say, standing up straight. "You will not speak to me—"

"Just get me the title."

It's amazing how loudly someone can hang up a cell phone.

My hand trembles as I toss my phone on the couch. *What a jerk!* I eye the stack of laundry and wish I could go back three minutes ago and fold in peace.

But that's over. I'm pissed now.

I pace the room and consider my options. This isn't my problem. I know that. Rationally, I'm aware that Burt making side agreements with customers has nothing to do with me. But I also know . . .

My phone rings.

That I'm going to get roped into going in on a Saturday.

I clench my jaw and scoop up the phone. This time, it's Kirk.

"Hi," I say, my voice soaked in a faux sweetness.

Kirk picks up what I'm throwing down. I can almost hear him grimace.

"I'm sorry," he says.

"Well, that would be great if the apology was yours to deliver."

"I'm going to talk to Burt. I got his version of the events . . . in a manner that has me driving to the office right now to lay down the law, so I can only imagine what actually happened in your conversation with him."

"I'm done when it comes to him, Kirk. I take his mouth and language day after day and ignore it because he's not worth me getting worked up. But when he talks to me like I'm a child, like . . . like I don't have value to our company and as a human being? *I'm done.*" I pause to let the point hit home . . . and also to catch my breath. "I'm telling you right now that I'm not having it. I can't beat him up, but that doesn't mean that I won't square up with him."

Kirk laughs.

"I'm not joking!" And I'm not. Exaggerating? Maybe. But I'm not going to be belittled by the oversize five-year-old who bullies me because he's bigger. And a man.

Nah, fuck that.

"I know you're not." He clears his throat. "But it won't come to that. I told you—I'll handle it."

I blow out a breath, relief washing over me.

"But about Agnello . . ." Kirk takes a breath. "He wired the money late yesterday. We're good on that front."

Agnello's failure to send the money on time—it was due by the end of the day Wednesday—irritates me. But knowing that Burt went behind my back and promised him a Saturday pickup pisses me off even more.

Why can't everyone just follow the processes? And why do I always have to bend over backward to fix their fuckups?

I sit on the edge of the couch and mute the movie. "Just say it."

"Is there any way you can come to the yard and get the title and tags for him? I know it's Saturday, and you have every right to say no and I can't even get mad about it. This is all Burt's doing. I get it. But . . ."

My gaze fixes to the television. Either the movie is better without sound or it's a better alternative to this conversation.

As I watch a woman get swept up from behind by a dashing prince who failed to divulge his royal roots—*and somehow she was mad about that*—I wonder when someone is going to make a movie about a life like mine. A tired woman with no ball gown at her disposal, just a monotonous life—sleep, work, cook, mother, rinse, and repeat—and an empty social calendar that would preclude her from meeting an available, handsome prince if one actually existed.

There should really be a prince shortage in the movie if they want to get it right.

I cup my chin as the dramatics play out on the screen.

"Palmer?"

I want to say no. I don't want to go all the way to Skoolie's because Burt is a dick. But I also don't want to cost Kirk a deal or a customer. That would do no one any favors, and I like my job—minus Burt.

"You know what bothers me about this?" I ask, my mouth moving awkwardly in my hands.

"No. Tell me. I mean, I'm sure I can guess, but I want to hear what you have to say."

I get to my feet. "Do you know why Burt went behind my back and moved it to today?"

"No."

"Because it was convenient for him."

Kirk sighs. "He's selling Agnello one of his personal cars, isn't he? I'd forgotten about that."

"Yeah, he is, and he wants the cash for that this weekend. So when I told Burt that Agnello was set up for Monday, it infuriated him. So fuck professionalism or respecting me and my job—Burt gets what Burt wants. He just rescheduled Agnello so it fit his agenda. If I go in today, he wins, and *that's* what bothers me."

"*He doesn't win.* Trust me."

"I kind of have trust issues, but thanks."

A gentle pause drifts between us.

Kirk knows what I mean—at least vaguely. He watched my relationships with both Jared and Charlie burn to the ground. He's heard me complain about not being in a situation to have more children and about going home to an empty house when Ethan's at his dad's. If anyone knows my frustration with never being taken seriously, it's him.

But he always has treated me that way.

He could've fired me so many times for coming in late or looking like a swamp monster held together by ungodly amounts of dry shampoo. And heaven knows that I've had to leave work early multiple times to pick Ethan up from school, since Jared lives in Forest Falls and routinely doesn't answer his phone.

So Kirk knows what I mean when I say that I have trust issues. But I also know that he means it when he says to trust him.

"Fine," I say, my voice void of all enthusiasm. "I'll go in. But I'm doing it for job security, and I'm still pissed about it."

His laughter is a mix of relief and amusement. "Your job isn't going anywhere. We'd fall apart without you."

Don't I know it.

"And you better deal with the moo man or I will," I say.

"The moo man—oh! Because of that damn game." Kirk bursts out laughing. "That's gold, Palm."

I grin. "I'll be there in thirty minutes, and I'm bringing my boxing gloves just in case."

"Palmer—thank you. For real."

"Yeah, yeah." I end the call. "You're lucky you are one of the few people that I like, Kirk." As I say those words aloud, I think about the other people I didn't necessarily dislike this week.

Like the sexy baseball player from Fletcher's.

His simple, four-lined text message kept me up late into the night.

Hey, it's Cole. It was really nice meeting you today. If you change your mind about dinner, just let me know. I'll be in town for a few days.

It's sad that the fact that he came through on his word shocks me. Men never follow through with promises like that.

"I'll talk to you soon, Miss Clark."

Or threats. I grin. *It was more of a threat.*

I wrestle with myself about how to feel about this situation. I know that sending a text is literally the least you should expect from someone . . . but I didn't expect anything at all. And without giving him a star for effort, it's still nice. *He* was nice.

What would I do with a nice guy?

I laugh, then put the phone back down and pick up another shirt. *I'd do all sorts of not-nice things to that nice man.*

My laughter grows louder, and I'm sad that Val isn't here to appreciate that line.

I fold the rest of Ethan's laundry, making quick work of the hoodies that are in the bottom of the basket. All the while, my mind sticks on Cole.

Not returning his text took a monumental amount of self-restraint. My phone's been a rock in my pocket ever since yesterday, begging me to deal with it.

But I haven't, and it's almost been painful.

There's no use in starting a conversation with Cole. *Why bother?* You go out on a date with someone to test the waters, to see if you're compatible. Our compatibility simply doesn't matter.

I want a man with a good LTR score—someone who exudes the potential for a *long-term relationship*. Anything else is a waste of time. And Cole Beck screams *waste of time*. He needs to stay firmly in the forbidden, red-flag territory.

Red flag one: by all accounts, he's nearly perfect. Handsome, sexy, charming—he's the whole package. Men like that get way too much attention to settle down. Are there exceptions? Probably. But I've never met one . . . and I have met Charlie, who was about an eight compared to Cole's ten, and he strung me along for eleven months.

Red flag two: He got my number from a bet with his best friend. If that doesn't scream emotional immaturity, I don't know what does.

Red flag three: He's a professional athlete, which still feels hard to believe. His definition of a "diamond" is probably much different, and much dirtier, than mine.

Red flag four: His life is based on the other side of the country. *"I'm a California boy, lover of sunshine and salt water."* Ohio doesn't have much sunshine and has no salt water. Plus, I'm not about to even entertain the idea of moving Ethan away from his father, even if Jared is invisible most of the time. My boy loves his dad.

I just need to delete that message and forget about Cole Beck.

I blow out a breath, my shoulders tired, and stack Ethan's clothes back in the laundry basket. I swipe my phone off the sofa and start to shove it in my pocket. But before I can, it rings.

My heartbeat picks up as I answer it. "Hello?"

"Hey, Palm. You busy?"

"What's wrong, Jared?"

He never calls unless something is askew. Ever. It's one of the only reasons we're able to coparent—our lives are absolutely separate, and we don't talk unless we have to. There's surprisingly very little we have to discuss.

My breath shakes as I exhale, mentally hurrying him along. The fact that he doesn't sound panicked helps. But then I remember that he didn't panic when I nearly sliced my finger off with a sewing machine either.

Come to think of it, maybe that was a sign.

"Jared?" I say again.

"Oh. Yeah. So, is there any way I can bring Ethan home? Or, even better, that you could meet me in town and take him?"

I stand still. "Why?"

"Well, Robbie needs a ride to Cleveland, and—"

"And you want to cut your weekend short with your son to take your friend to Cleveland?" I bark.

"Aw, Palm. Come on."

I throw my free hand up in the air. "*Jared.* You haven't seen Ethan in two weeks."

"I know."

"And you're going to just shuttle him back home because Robbie needs a ride? What . . ."

I catch myself before I say what I'm thinking. I don't ask him what kind of father pulls this shit because that would only add fuel to a fire already starting to burn.

I take a deep, cleansing breath and will the fury coursing through me to steady.

God, give me grace.

"Will you please reconsider?" I say as calmly as I can.

"Robbie doesn't have anyone else."

Either grace isn't bestowed on me or it isn't enough.

"So?" My voice rises. "Robbie's probably heading there to do devious things anyway. You'll spare him a headache. Also, *your son* wants to spend time with his father. He doesn't have anyone else *as his father* either."

"Look, I'll pick Ethan up tomorrow afternoon, and we'll go throw the ball around or something."

I roll my eyes.

Jared sighs. *He knows he's full of shit too.* "So, can you meet me or not?"

I'm not you. "What am I supposed to say?"

His voice switches. It turns softer, more manipulative. "You say that you'll meet me at the bowling alley in ten. Please, Palm."

My shoulders fall forward. "Fine. Don't be late. I have to head to work, and I'm supposed to be there in twenty minutes."

"Great. Thanks so much."

"Whatever."

I press the red button so hard that I'm surprised the phone screen doesn't shatter.

And this is another reason why I can't go to dinner with nice men. I. Don't. Have. Time.

I grab my keys off the counter by the door and storm to the car.

CHAPTER FIVE

Palmer

"Oh, little Palmer. You've made some bad choices in life, sweetheart," I whisper to myself as Jared comes down the street toward me—ten minutes late.

Good thing I warned Kirk that I would be delayed.

A sign reading King Pin Alley hangs on the front of the building on my right. The letters glowed in bright neon colors back in the eighties. They haven't worked since then.

Jared's car pulls into the parking lot a few spaces down from mine, leaving a trail of dust behind him. I wonder if he left a few empty spots between us randomly or if he knows I want to throw my Coke all over his windshield.

Probably the latter.

My heart sinks as my gaze meets Ethan's through the passenger-side glass. He flashes me a brief, sad smile before unbuckling himself. His cowlick in the front, just above his right eye, makes his twelve-year-old self look younger . . . and more disappointed.

I open the door and swing it shut with a little more force than necessary. *Hey, it's the little things.*

"Hey, Mom," Ethan says as he climbs out of Jared's car. "I thought Dad and I were going bowling. Then I saw you."

He makes a face that I think is supposed to be a smile but resembles a frown just a bit more.

Once again, Jared lets me clean up his mess. He couldn't even tell Ethan the truth.

Damn it.

I pull my son into my side and kiss his cheek. My eyes flutter closed as I breathe in the body spray that somehow fills our entire house in the mornings.

How can I make this better?

Suddenly, I remember the extra cash I have left from Cole's bet yesterday.

Bingo.

"I told your dad to meet me here so *we* could go bowling."

Ethan pulls away, his eyes lit up. "Really?"

I nod. "We have to run to my work for a minute first. Kirk just called. But then we can come back and bowl a game. Maybe grab a corn dog. How does that sound?"

"That sounds awesome."

"Good." I kiss his cheek again. "Go get in the car. I'm going to talk to your dad for a second."

Ethan presses a baseball and glove into my chest. "Do you want this?"

"What do you want me to do with that?"

"Dad signed me up for baseball." He stares at me like it's the worst idea in the world. "I don't know how to play baseball."

I push the glove and ball back at him. *This is going to be my problem. I know it.*

"Put it in the car," I say. "Let's . . . We'll deal with that later."

"Fine."

He turns toward my car. I turn to his dad's.

Gravel crunches under my sneakers as I march to Jared's window.

"Hey," he says after the window is rolled down.

"Hey."

He takes in my face for half a second. "I'm sorry—"

"Don't." I stop inches away from his door. "Don't tell me you're sorry."

"Then what do you want from me?"

He looks at me with a practiced pout—one that used to work. Those days are long gone. I no longer find his puppy-dog eyes cute, and his droopy bottom lip makes me want to pull it off his face instead of kissing it better.

Easy, Palmer.

"I'll tell you what I want from you," I say, struggling to keep my voice low and even. "Consistency. Reliability. I want you to make Ethan a priority. I want you to make a lifelong commitment to Ethan—one like you couldn't make to me."

"I do."

My eyeballs nearly fall out of my head.

"What?" he says, frustration thick in his tone. "I do, Palmer. Just because I don't baby him all the time—"

"Jared!" I say before catching myself and lowering my voice. "You don't see him with any regularity. You don't pay child support. You don't—"

"I signed him up for baseball."

"*Oh great.* Another thing for *me* to manage. How kind of you."

He scoffs. It's not the sound that snaps something in my brain. It's the face he makes.

No, it's the familiarity that I have with the gesture that breaks me.

I've seen him do this so many times—for years, even. I hated that he did it to me, and I hate even more that he does it to Ethan. No one is more important to Jared than Jared himself.

And nothing I can do or say will change that. I've tried.

"You know what?" I say, backing away slowly. "Run Robbie to Cleveland. Have a great rest of your weekend."

"Really?"

I shrug. "Sure. I'll take care of it because I *always* take care of it."

He pops the transmission into drive, ignoring my dig at him. "Tell E that I'll get him tomorrow."

"Sure." *I won't because I won't let you disappoint your son twice in one weekend when you don't turn up tomorrow afternoon.*

"Great. Later, Palm."

He makes a wide turn around me in the direction away from Ethan. *Naturally.*

I growl, my irritation exceeding a healthy level, and start toward my car. And then stop.

My eyes zip immediately to the figure jogging down the sidewalk. Cole's eyes are already on mine as my gaze connects with his. He grins, switching his trajectory toward me instead of across the road.

Oh, good grief. Not now.

His hair is damp, his muscles taut as he moves smoothly across the parking lot. His sun-kissed skin glistens with perspiration, and his sweatpants cling to his body in a way that should be illegal.

A gold chain with a round gold emblem bounces on his delicious pecs as he comes to a stop in front of my car.

I'm not strong enough for this today.

"The benefits of living in a small town." He wipes his forehead with the back of his hand, grinning from ear to ear. "Guess it makes up for the lack of cell service."

The text.

I'll ignore that.

"Are you all right?" he asks, the gold chain catching the sunlight. "You seem kind of pissed."

"Because I am pissed."

"Anything that I can help with?"

The question catches me off guard. I blink rapidly and try to pull my thoughts together.

"No. Just an ex that decided to be a total douchebag today—which really isn't unlike the other days of the year. Today just has a little special sauce on it."

A drop of sweat drips from the ends of his hair onto his shoulders.

Ethan steps gingerly out of the car. "Mom?" He looks back and forth between Cole and me.

Crap. I don't have time for this.

"Hey, buddy," I say, motioning for him to join me. "Ethan, this is Cole Beck. I met him the other day at Fletcher's. Cole, this is my son, Ethan."

"Hi," Ethan says, standing beside me.

Cole points to the baseball glove on my son's hand. "You play?"

Ethan holds the leather mitt up in the air awkwardly. "Um . . . kind of."

"Kind of? Do you have a ball?"

Ethan releases a ball that's tucked into the webbing of the glove and holds it up in the air.

Cole's eyes light up. "*All right.* Let's see what you got."

I open my mouth to protest—to tell Cole that I need to get to Skoolie's—but the excitement in Ethan's eyes stops me in my tracks. He seems surprised that a stranger is interested in spending time with him. Playing with him. *Oh, Jared. I hate that you've done this to our son.*

"Hey, Ethan," I say instead. "Did you know that Cole is a professional baseball player? He played for the San Diego Swifts."

Ethan turns to Cole with a mixture of awe and joy on his face.

Let him have this moment.

"I'm not very good," Ethan says, tossing the ball underhanded to Cole like a baby. "My dad just signed me up for a spring league. I've never actually played before."

If Cole picks up on the tension that fills my body or the sadness in Ethan's voice, he keeps it to himself. Instead, he moves away from us with the ball.

Cole points toward a big pothole in the parking lot. "Stand over there."

Once Ethan is situated, Cole tosses the ball to him.

I should be focused on my son and how he manages to catch the ball. The delight in his eyes should flood me with pride and hope. The way he tries to throw it back to Cole with a self-confidence that I don't expect is heartwarming . . . if I'm paying attention.

I'm a terrible mother.

My mouth goes dry as Cole's muscles flex in the sunlight. The breadth of his shoulders. The way the cotton fabric clings to his ass when he leans into an exaggerated throw to show something to Ethan.

Oh. My. Gosh.

I reach for the hood of my car to steady myself.

"You okay over there?" Cole grins, holding the ball at the bend of his hip. His fingers cover the leather laces as he swirls it around his palm.

"Yup," I say through the cotton lining my throat. "All good."

Ethan hurries over to me. "Can I, Mom?"

"Can you what?" I look down at him. "What are you talking about?"

Cole snickers as he joins us at the front of my car.

"Can Cole give me some lessons? I mean, he is a professional baseball player and he offered. *He offered*, Mom."

"Oh." *Crap.* "But, buddy, he doesn't live here, and right now, we need to get to Skoolie's. I'm very, very late."

"What about later?" Ethan asks, not willing to let an opportunity that I missed in my daydream go.

I sigh. "I thought we were going bowling later?"

"You're going bowling?" Cole tosses the ball back to Ethan. "I was thinking about bowling later too."

I glare at Cole. He ignores me.

"Come with us," Ethan says before I can stop him.

"No, Ethan. He's busy, buddy," I say, trying to stop the mayhem before it gets completely out of control.

Cole pins me to the spot with his gaze. A smirk threatens to break out across his lips, but he fights it.

"I'm really not," he says.

The me a year ago would've given in. I would've been certain that the universe had dropped Cole into my lap as a gift. But that was the me then. I'm not her anymore.

I'm not sure how to get out of this situation, and I don't have time to figure it out. I have to get to work.

"I'll text you," I say before I think twice about it.

"Really?" He lifts a brow. "That's interesting."

"Why is that interesting?" Ethan asks.

I turn and face my boy.

"Can you wait in the car, please?" I ask him.

"Mom."

"Ethan . . ."

He sighs with all the dramatics of a preteen. *"Fine."*

"Thank you," I call after him.

"I'll see you soon, Ethan," Cole says.

"Yeah. Okay." Ethan climbs into the car and slams the door shut. *Just like his mama.*

I turn back to the glorious man in front of me. My heart thumps as a wave of what can only be described as testosterone hits my senses. It rushes over my skin and pools in my core . . . right where I don't need it.

His grin is delicious and borderline criminal. He licks his bottom lip as if he knows he's driving me nuts.

"You are a pain in the ass," I say, plucking my gaze from his mouth.

"I've heard that before. But it usually comes just before someone agrees to something they've been fighting."

"Don't tell me that I get to be the first woman to break that streak too? I get to tell you no and then not follow up the ass comment." I make a face of surprise. "Wow. That's two cherries."

He narrows his eyes playfully. "Don't get ahead of yourself, Miss Clark."

"I'm already ahead of you."

"Is that so?"

Maybe. "Yes."

Cole wants to say something. I can see it on his face. But after a few seconds, it becomes clear that he's not going to share whatever's on his mind.

That's probably for the best.

"I hate to cut this interesting little rendezvous short," I say, "but I do need to go."

"Is everything all right?"

"Yeah. I have to go to work for a bit."

He makes a face. "On a Saturday?"

"It's a long story involving a bus, New York, and a middle-aged man with a penchant for mooing livestock. But, yes, I have to go to work on a Saturday."

"Sounds like a great story," he says, his eyes sparkling with humor.

"It's not. Unless that middle-aged man gets cocky with me when I get there." I throw some punches into the air. "It might not end well for him. He'll be the one mooing if he doesn't watch it."

Cole bursts into a fit of laughter. "Wow. Okay. I didn't realize that I had a boxer on my hands."

"That's right." I throw another punch into the air. "Don't judge a book by its cover."

He grins. "Fair enough. But what about judging a woman that ignores my texts?"

I drop my hands.

"I didn't agree to text you back, you know," I say. "I just said that I'd give you my number."

"And technically you didn't even do that. Val did."

"Oh yes. My traitorous best friend." I sigh, the stress of knowing that the Agnello situation is still hanging out there weighing on me. "Look, I don't know why you're doing this, but it's . . . Let's just let it go. Okay? I have a kid, and my life is just really, *really* busy."

"As people's lives are."

Despite the fact that it makes it harder to walk away, I do appreciate his determination. Most guys bail when it's clear they'll have to put in any work at all.

Ethan honks the car horn. The sound makes me jump.

I sigh, walking backward toward my door. "It was good to see you. Thanks for throwing the ball with my boy."

"Anytime."

I give him a small smile and grab my door handle.

"Do you want to grab pizza later?" he asks.

"No."

"Come on. Bring Ethan. It would be fun."

Bring Ethan? No one has ever suggested I bring my son on a date before.

But then I recall the joy on Ethan's face from Cole's attention—letting Ethan develop a relationship with him would be even stupider than me falling for him. I know better. Ethan does not. My son is already smitten with him. I can't set him up for heartbreak too.

"You're sweet," I say, still touched by the offer. "But no. Thanks anyway."

"Okay."

He stands in front of the car until I'm in the driver's seat. Then, slowly, he starts jogging across the parking lot again.

What a freaking day.

I buckle up, check Ethan's buckle, and then pull onto Main Street.

"Well, that was interesting," Ethan says, poking around for information.

I laugh. "Ethan."

"What?"

I look at his smirk-y grin.

"Hush," I say, laughing.

He laughs, too, and for a moment, all is right in my world.

CHAPTER SIX

Palmer

"You need to get to bed," I say, ruffling Ethan's hair. It's the same color as mine—a soft reddish hue layered over a warm gold. "It's getting late."

He stays focused on the video game in front of him. "Well, technically, I'm supposed to be at Dad's this weekend. So, technically, I should get to go by Dad's rules."

"Oh, okay. Yeah. That's gonna fly."

"It is?"

"No."

"Oh." His fingers glide across the controller in his hands—the one with the green cover that I paid an extraordinary amount for at Christmastime because it was the one thing he wanted. "Darn it! I died."

"See? Even the game knows it's bedtime, kiddo."

He rolls his eyes and switches off the game.

"Did you shower after we got home?" I give him a quick once-over because I know he'll lie to me. Coats and showers are his nemeses. "Nope. You didn't. Same clothes."

"Ugh."

"Your shower is going to give you another twenty minutes. Now, up." I pat the underside of his arm to encourage him to stand. "Go shower and brush your teeth."

Ethan stands. The top of his head is nearly level with mine. He looks into my eyes, and for a split, fleeting second, I see the little cherub face that used to look up at me in a milk coma.

Time flies.

"Go," I say, ruffling his hair again before heading for the door. "I'll be downstairs with Val if you need anything. Come tell me good night before you go to bed."

"'Kay."

I make a left in the hallway, and he turns right toward the bathroom.

My feet sink into the carpet as I make my way down the steps. A thin layer of dust bunnies is starting to accumulate against the wall, and I make a mental note to run the vacuum at some point before Monday. I'm not even sure when I ran the vacuum last. That's a problem.

I get to the bottom of the stairs and find Val on the sofa. A bowl of chips rests against her side. Her phone is in her hand.

She looks up as I come into the room and watches me collapse into the recliner by the window.

"Have you bothered to check out Cole on social media?" she asks.

Really, Val?

I sigh. "No, I have not."

"Well, you should. I'm not sure if he posts these things as thirst traps—like if that's the actual point—or if he's really trying to give legitimate baseball advice, because I don't know a damn thing about baseball. But I'll tell you what—if this is what baseball is, I'm in. Big fan. Let's go get some Cracker Jacks or whatever they say in that song."

I slip my hands under my butt to keep from reaching for the phone.

"Good," I say to Val. "You can be the baseball-loving pseudo–Aunt Val when Ethan starts baseball this week."

She furrows her brows. "Ethan is playing baseball? I thought the kid turned into sand if exposed to fresh air and sunlight."

I roll my eyes. "Jared signed him up."

"Oh." She takes a chip and crunches it in her mouth. "And Ethan is going along with this without a fight? Remember when you tried to sign him up for . . . what was it?"

"Basketball."

"Right. And he had a meltdown because he was going to be a professional video gamer when he grew up, and you were sucking his life force out of his soul or something equally dramatic." She grins. "I have no idea where he got the dramatics."

I roll my eyes again. "Ethan seems to be going along with it as of now. I don't think he's thrilled about it, by any means, but he's not protesting too heavily. Yet."

"Maybe he's looking forward to spending time with Jared."

"Oh, come on," I say. "You don't really think Jared is going to have anything to do with this, do you?"

Val shrugs.

"This will be one more thing that I have to take care of because I don't have enough on my plate."

The back of my neck grows taut. I grimace at the discomfort.

"You know," I say, "on one hand, I wish that Jared spent more time with Ethan so Ethan had a strong role model around to lean on when he had boy questions and stuff."

"Yeah, but you and Ethan have a great relationship. I'm sure he knows he can come to you with anything."

"For sure, and I'm thankful for that. But I remember when I was a little girl, and not having a mom around really fucked with me. I mean, I couldn't go to Dad because I'd be talking to Jim Beam, not Tim Clark. I remember just wishing I had an aunt or grandma to talk to about starting my period and needing a bra, you know?"

Val shifts on the sofa. The bowl of chips nearly falls to the floor.

"Yeah," she says. "But what you're describing is a responsible adult. We need to be honest here that Jared was never one of those."

"Exactly. Which is why, on the other hand, I think it's better off this way. I mean, even if he was consistent about coming around and following through on promises . . . he's still Jared. He's still not the best role model in the world."

My spirits sink because, somehow in the land of mom guilt, that feels like my fault too.

Val puts the chips on the floor and levels her gaze with mine. She's ready to defend my honor because that's what Val does . . . and why she's my best friend.

"Don't go there," she warns. "You started dating him at, what—nineteen? You likely expected that he would grow up. Mature. Get a job. You had no way of knowing that he would fail to launch."

No, but I wasted over half a decade of my life believing he would.

"Can we talk about something else?" I ask.

"Sure. What happened at work today?"

I make a face at her. She holds her hands to her sides.

"You said to change the subject," she says.

"I was thinking to something happier."

"Okay. Let's talk about how my nails look bomb today." She holds her fingers toward me and wiggles them. "This color is Decadent Peach, and I really think it's the color of my aura."

I snort. "I totally agree."

"But do you?" She drops her arms to her sides. "I sense a bit of sarcasm there, Miss Yellow Aura."

"Do you want to know what I think?" I grin at her. "I think you chose that color based on the name because it lets you think of Shane Kensington every time you see it. It gives you an excuse."

Her cheeks flush, which feels like an accomplishment on my end. Val doesn't blush.

"He did say my ass reminds him of a juicy peach," she says, flipping a long lock of red hair over her shoulder.

"That could mean that you need an antibiotic."

We laugh as the water heater kicks off. Soon after, Ethan's footsteps pound across the ceiling, and he appears in the doorway.

"Going to bed since you're being mean," he says, the words tempered with a smile. "Love you, Mom."

"Love you, buddy. I'll come up and check on you in a bit."

"Heard you're playing baseball," Val says. "Chicks love baseball players."

Ethan grins. "It's the only reason I'm playing."

"Ethan!" I say, my jaw dropping. "No chicks for you, sir."

He laughs. "Good night, Mom. Night, Val."

"Night, stud," Val hollers after him. She winks at me. "He's so ridiculously cute. Don't you wish you had another one?"

Every day.

My back presses harder into the recliner as I blow out a breath.

I've always wanted a houseful of children. Probably because I know the loneliness of growing up alone.

My dad's alcoholic benders were long and emotional. I'd be forced to sit in the kitchen for hours and listen to the tragedies of his life—and be expected to convince him, a drunk adult, that the terrible things that had happened to him weren't his fault. I had to do this when I barely understood the situations. And because he'd rail on me if I gave the wrong words of solace, I tried remaining silent.

That backfired in the worst ways.

I was always walking on eggshells with Dad. And then he'd sober up for a couple of days and be the nicest guy anyone had ever met. It was such a mindfuck. It made life completely backward. I never got to be a child, blissfully ignorant of real life.

I paid the utilities out of his disability check at the age of eight, forging his signature on the checks. I was responsible for cooking the canned vegetables and deer—which he poached all winter—by the time I was ten. And when I was twelve, I knew exactly what lies to tell so no one would know that my black eyes were from my father hitting me. After all, I couldn't let us get separated. No one would be around to take care of him.

I would go to bed at night and dream of having a full, warm house filled with laughter and food and hugs. But that's never happened for me. And the older I get, the more I think it might not.

That's sad . . . for me and for Ethan.

"Sometimes," I say, answering Val's question. I'm afraid to be totally honest. I'm afraid my voice will break. "I've checked into adoption a few times, and it's too expensive."

She pulls the chips back to her lap and eats one, studying me all the while.

"What about you?" I ask her.

"Someday. One or two. I'm in no hurry."

"Well, if I'm going to, I need to get on it," I say. "I don't want to be too old, and I'd rather not have twenty years between Ethan and his sibling."

"I get that. Totally."

I pop the lever on the side of the recliner. My legs rise and my back reclines just enough to feel moderately relaxed. I settle back and feel myself melt into the chair.

"You know," I say, rolling my head to the side so I can see Val. "If Kirk wasn't sixty-five and married to the best woman ever, I might just marry him."

Val coughs, choking on a chip. She pulls a water bottle from between the couch cushions and takes a long drink.

"Sometimes I think you're basically my child," I say, laughing. "Did you really have that drink wedged in my sofa?"

"Don't mom me. I was trying to keep it upright so it didn't leak out everywhere."

"You do realize that you're almost thirty."

"Rude." She makes a face and eats another chip. "Kirk is pretty handsome, though. The salt-and-pepper hair really does it for me."

I chuckle.

Val picks up her phone again. Immediately, she's engrossed. She licks the salt from the chips off her bottom lip slowly as she brings the screen closer to her eyes.

"What are you looking at over there?" I ask, curiosity piqued.

"Cole's feed. It was still pulled up."

I groan.

Val lays her phone in her lap and cocks her head to the side. "Okay, real talk."

"What?"

"I've been approaching this Cole thing with you as if you're just embarrassed by the attention or having a hard time believing that it's real. Or you're just flustered because he is a flustery kind of guy."

I laugh. *He is a flustery kind of guy.* I wish it were only that. "I saw him today when I picked up Ethan."

"Really? You've been holding on to that little nugget for hours. Totally unfair."

"Very funny."

"And?" She motions in front of her, prompting me to divulge whatever secret she thinks that I'm withholding. "What happened? Did sparks fly? Did you realize that you need to take a swing with his big, hard bat?"

"Will you stop it?" I giggle. "You're . . ."

"Right on the money?"

I roll my eyes. *Kind of.* "Hardly."

"You're the worst best friend in all the lands."

I snort. "Fine. He asked me out again, and I turned him down again."

"What?"

"I know. He even said Ethan could come."

She moves around on the couch until her legs are tucked up beneath her. "No. Not that. I was *what-ing* the part where you said that you told him no."

Val is never going to understand my perspective.

"Okay. I'm starting to think that you're serious. And if you are and you're not into him for whatever reason—maybe you're just not into blue eyes the color of gemstones, and that's okay—then I want to respect that." She lifts her chin. "See? I'm capable of empathy."

My chest shakes as I chuckle at her ridiculousness.

The corner of her mouth twitches. "So, are you going to screw him or not?"

"Val!"

"What? It's just a question. I'm just trying to help you *live*. You're tired of the same old decisions and results, right?"

This is technically true. But it doesn't mean that her suggested choice is the right one, because it's ultimately not.

"Pardon me for stating the obvious," she says, "but I'm pretty sure that sexy baseball player could take you to third base, if you get what I'm saying. Use him to get on base, and then let someone else hit you home."

I laugh. "Stop with the baseball analogies."

"I've been looking them up. This is fun!"

I act like she's ridiculous because she is. But I also get what she's saying.

Therein lies the problem.

At least I know my weaknesses—in this case, giving other people the benefit of the doubt. I have the wherewithal to double-check myself before I wreck myself this time, thank God.

I can easily see myself having dinner with him, laughing, having fun. It would be a great distraction from work and Burt and dealing with Jared and the overall crisis of my life. Opening that door with Cole would be like handing the steering wheel over to him for a while. I can't say the break from the chaos wouldn't be appreciated. But I also can't say it wouldn't just be digging the hole deeper for me to climb out of later.

The truth is, Cole is a nice guy. I'm sure he would be a good time. Even stranger is the fact that I think he would be good with Ethan, and that's much harder to find than it should be.

Cole is a Milky Way that you zap in the microwave and let get all melty and gooey. And then, when you eat it, it gets all over your face and fingers, and you wind up in a blissful sugar coma. It feels wonderful at the moment, but you have to work those calories off later—that or live with the added weight, which is what I usually do.

And I'm tired of doing that. I just want the salad.

Proverbially. I hate salad.

I look up at Val. "Yeah, I'm sure. I'm also sure that I'm done talking about Cole tonight."

"Cool. I'm here to help you live your best life."

My stomach squeezes. I'm not sure why I suddenly feel so antsy, but I do, and I need it to stop.

"Let's do something," I say, sitting up. The end of the recliner snaps down again. "Let's reactivate my dating apps and see what we can find."

"*Oh yeah.* This is the way to find a serious, committed man." She snorts. "But what the hell. If you want to do some Cole Avoidance this way . . . sounds fun. I'm in."

I laugh and make my way to the sofa. She's right. This is an attempt at Cole Avoidance. It seems like the only way to distract Val—by giving her other men to focus on.

The tightness still twists in my gut as I get settled, but it's a bit lighter. I'll take it.

Val helps me get my accounts live again, and we slide through the matches. As we flag the ones we like and wait to see if we're a hit, it takes my mind off the baseball player who, in the right situation, could have been a total home run.

It's too bad that I'm a strikeout queen.

CHAPTER SEVEN

Cole

"Do you have everything?" Mom tosses her mustard-colored bag over her shoulder and looks at me like we're headed to the World Series. *Pure excitement.*

I hold my hands out in front of me. In one of them is my wallet and the keys to Dad's truck. In the other is a travel tumbler that she filled with coffee while I took a quick shower.

"If we're running errands in town, I'd say that I'm good to go," I say. "But if the look on your face means anything and I was mistaken, now is the time to tell me so I can prepare."

She squeezes my biceps as she walks by. "Nope. Just running to town with my son for the first time in years." She holds the front door open for me. "I'm just excited to show you off."

I stop on the threshold. "Then you better make sure you never open a door for me again, young lady. That's my job. Do you want Dad coming out here and kicking my ass?"

She laughs.

I reach over her head and press my palm over the door. "After you."

"Thank you."

We make it to Dad's truck and climb in. Mom settles herself in the passenger's seat, then buckles up while practically bouncing around the cab. I get strapped in and then get us backed out onto the gravel road.

The rock crunches under the tires as we roll quietly away from the house. Trees line the road with bright-green leaves. Flowers bloom in the ditch and under the trees, just starting what my parents promise is a show from Mother Nature in the spring.

"What do you think of it here so far?" Mom asks as casually as a woman amped up on caffeine can.

"I haven't seen a whole lot of it yet."

"Didn't you go for a jog yesterday?"

I nod.

"And to Fletcher's. And Bud's?" she asks.

"Yeah."

"Then you've seen Bloomfield." She smiles. "It's so lovely, isn't it?"

I stop at the stop sign, turn on the blinker, and then make a right turn to town.

"It's a nice little town," I say.

"Oh, honey. It's better than a *nice little town*. The people here are so friendly, and the weather is unreal. You get all four seasons, and sometimes you get all four in a day!" She laughs as if this is the funniest joke ever.

I ignore her nudge toward a discussion about my future.

"Fish is going to come up next week and hang out," I say. "I told him you wouldn't mind."

"Of course not. We love Fish." She pauses. "What does he think of it here?"

"Well, he's from a town like this on the other side of Columbus. So it's normal to him."

She shifts in her seat. "Do you think it could be normal for you?"

Nothing is normal for me anymore.

I blow out a breath and feel my spirits sink.

"I don't know, Mom. This all happened pretty fast, and I didn't have much time to plan out what I wanted to do."

"That stupid shoulder injury," she says, shaking her head.

Yeah. That stupid shoulder injury.

I regrip the steering wheel. "I had a phone call with my manager this morning. I've had a few offers come in that we need to take a look at when I get back to California."

"Oh, really?"

"Yeah. One is for a baseball program on one of the streaming channels. Another is a cohost for a podcast. That might be fun."

"You'd be great at that."

I look at her and smile. Although that's not what she wants me to do, I appreciate her encouragement.

"Mom?"

"What?"

"I love you."

"Oh, honey." She pats my arm. "You'll never know how much I love you and how proud I am of you and how happy I am to have you around."

Her words are sweet and, more importantly, genuine. They make me feel like a little boy, but I've learned in life that it's okay to let your mom baby you. I don't particularly understand it, but it's where she seems to get her joy.

"Hey. I think we need to stop at Bud's." Mom twists in her seat and peers into the truck bed. "Yes. Pull in there, please."

I do as instructed.

"Your dad put his golf clubs in the back. I can't remember what he's having done to them, but I remember him asking me to drop them off. Maybe he's having them cleaned. Do people get golf clubs cleaned?"

I just laugh at her.

There are four cars in the parking lot. I take a spot between two other trucks.

"This place is always pretty busy, huh?" I ask as we climb out of the cab.

"Yes." Mom shuts her door. "Bud does so much more than sporting-goods stuff. He organizes the Squash Festival in the fall. He does all the fundraising for the church. I think he's the head of the tourism board too."

I snort, grabbing Dad's clubs out of the bed. "Bloomfield has a tourism board?"

"Well, I think it's two or three people. But they get a lot of traffic through here, really. People come this way to hunt and fish and hike. The board helps them all know that we have Fletcher's and Bud's," she says, waiting on me to get the door for her. "And the little market on the other end of town."

The door makes some kind of animal call when I open it. Mom laughs at the ridiculous sound and marches right up to the counter.

A circular desk is placed in the center of the main room, and a graying Bud Winters stands in the center.

"Good morning, Mrs. Beck," he says, the corners of his mustache moving. "Did Lawrence send you in with his clubs?"

I hold them up in the air.

"I'll take those from you," he says.

Bud comes around the corner, and I hand him the strap.

"It's good to see you again, Cole," he says.

"Did you get your baseball program all figured out?" I ask, leaning against the counter.

He looks at the floor and shakes his head. "You know what? I didn't. The guy that always coaches . . ." He looks up at Mom. "You know Ted from the butcher shop?"

Mom nods.

"Well, he had a dual hip replacement this winter. The doctors said he'd be back to good by spring, but he's not. The man can barely walk.

His son has been running the butcher shop since October because he can't even stand for long periods of time."

"That sucks," I say.

"It does suck," he says, as if he doesn't say that word very often. It comes out of his mouth clunky. "Things aren't looking good for the team. They're looking awful, actually. My backup option took a welding job in Pennsylvania and can't do it. And Lord knows that I can't do it with all the other things I have on my plate. I'm still waiting to hear back from the Forest Falls gym teacher to see if she can step in and help. Hopefully she'll know enough about baseball to make a difference."

I can see the grief that this causes Bud. It's written all over his face.

My heart tugs. It's nice to see someone care so much about something that's not themselves—especially kids' sports. Most people blow athletics off like a place for adults to live their childhood dreams through their offspring, but they're more than that. They can give kids a place to go after school and a reason to say no to bad behavior.

I'm opening my mouth to say something when a coyote howls behind us. I look over my shoulder, and my eyes immediately lock with Palmer's.

Her cheeks flush as the door closes behind her. I give her a tentative grin and am relieved when she returns it—even if it is a bit wobbly.

"Hey, Cole!" Ethan smiles beside her.

"Hey, Ethan," I say, smiling back at him. "Whatcha doing here?"

"Getting cleats."

"Makes sense." My gaze slides over to his mother. "Hi, Palmer."

Her eyes are wide, clearly surprised to find me at Bud's. She licks her lips. "Oh, hi, Cole." She clears her throat. Her gaze lingers on me for a long moment before she flips it to the man behind the counter. "Hi, Mrs. Beck. Hi, Bud."

"What can I help you with today, Palmer?" Bud asks.

"Cleats for the big guy here." She wraps her arm around her son. "Jared signed him up for baseball. Are they over by the fitting rooms?"

"Sure are," Bud says with a wide smile.

Palmer directs Ethan toward the cleats display but doesn't immediately follow him. Instead, she turns to face me.

"I'm going out on a limb here, but are you stalking me by any chance?" she asks, biting her bottom lip to keep from grinning.

"Ooh, fun thought, but shouldn't a stalker come in after you?"

She laughs. "I guess technically, but not if you were spying on me and heard me tell Ethan we were coming here. Maybe you just beat us in."

If I were spying on you, Miss Clark, you wouldn't be such an enigma.

"I'm not sure if I should be proud that you think I'm so capable or concerned that you've thought about this so much," I joke.

She wrinkles her little button nose. "I'll leave you to think about that." She starts her trek to the back of the store but calls out to my mother, "Keep your eye on him, Mrs. Beck."

My mom laughs. "I will, Palmer. I will."

Palmer shifts her eyes over me and then heads toward the back of the store.

Why is she so friendly and then . . . not?

I run a hand down my jaw as I watch her with her son. They're adorable together in a genuine, real way, and it takes everything I have not to walk to them and get involved in the cleat-selection process.

But I don't. I resist, mostly because she keeps telling me to.

Damn it.

I rip my gaze from her back and settle it on Bud.

"Do you know Palmer?" Mom asks.

"I met her a couple of times," I say, switching my weight from one foot to the other. "Do you?"

Mom laughs easily. "Everyone in this town knows Palmer. She's a pure *delight.*"

I'm glad my instincts aren't off.

"They have this drive-in picnic every month for the nursing home residents over at Pickaway Park," Mom says. "The community makes dinner and delivers it like a picnic. It's so much fun, and they love my cherry crisp."

I look at her. "They're in a nursing home, Mom. That doesn't mean they can't taste food anymore."

Bud chuckles as Mom swats my shoulder.

"Anyway," she says, getting back to her story. "Palmer helps more months than not. Sometimes she'll chip in a dish, and other times she's there with that darling little boy of hers, passing out trays and helping with the cleanup. Everyone loves Palmer."

I can't help it. I glance over my shoulder at the two of them. It reminds me of the time that my dad took me to get my first cleats. I remember the smell of the store that day and how the carpet was a thick brown shag instead of the turf stores have today. I was so damn excited and promised Dad that I would make his expense worthwhile.

I grin. *I was such a cocky little shit.*

"She is a good person," Bud says, his eyes on Palmer. "I really hate that she has to deal with that Jared character."

My ears perk up. "Why?"

Bud sighs. "I don't like to talk about anyone in this town—or in other towns, to be clear. But that guy makes it really hard to have much good to say about him. He's put that poor girl through hell. Pardon my language, Mrs. Beck."

"Bud, I'm married to Lawrence, for goodness' sake." She laughs. "I've heard a curse word a time or a dozen."

I lean against the counter and get comfortable. "He signed his kid up for baseball. How bad could he be?"

I'm prying, and I think Bud knows it. Mom is oblivious as she sorts through a stack of old postcards by the cash register.

Bud grins. "Sure. He signed him up. But we'll never see him."

I raise a brow.

"Jared Doughtry isn't gonna show up. Are you kidding me?" Bud scoffs. "I'll bet ya a dime to a doughnut he never sees a practice or a game. Mark my words."

Marking them as we speak.

"When will Lawrence's clubs be done, Bud?" Mom asks.

They get into a conversation about Dad's golf set. I tune them out. Instead, I angle my body in a way that lets me keep an eye on Palmer and Ethan.

My body aches to walk across the store and help them—to make sure Palmer has Ethan try on the cleats before she buys them.

She takes the pair that Ethan obviously has his heart set on, a pair that's not worth the price. Her face falls. The smile she gives him is strained.

My heart dips in my chest.

It's not my business. Stay out of it, Cole.

"Are you ready, Cole?" Mom taps me on the shoulder. "We're finished here."

"Oh. Yeah. Sorry." I run a hand through my hair. "It was good seeing you, Bud."

"Same here. We'd love to see you at the fields this year for the teams we're able to have."

I open my mouth but close it just as quickly.

My breathing picks up as I sneak another look at Palmer and Ethan.

"How many teams did you say you're canceling?" I ask.

Say a bunch of them. Make this easy to walk away.

"One. It's such a shame."

Fuck.

I take a slow breath to give myself a second to opt out, but as I exhale, I still feel the same way.

"Can I see the roster of the kids whose team doesn't have a coach?" I ask.

Bud fights a smile. "Absolutely. Sure can." He reaches under the counter and pulls out a giant binder. He sorts through the pages until he lands on a purple tab. "Here you go."

I feel the weight of his gaze as my eyes move down the list. I'm also fairly certain that Mom is holding her breath.

My finger trails down the short list of names until it lands on the one I was searching for—Ethan Doughtry.

Shit.

"Yeah, that's Palmer's boy," Bud says quietly. "I don't know whether to tell Palmer before she buys the cleats that he might not be playing or just let them buy them and hope for a miracle."

I look up and see the hope in his eyes. I don't even attempt to look at Mom.

My stomach twists into a tight knot, and I'm hit with a shot of adrenaline.

I'm not sure if this is a ridiculous idea or if I'll hate myself either way I go. But as I think about what I'm going to do for the next month or two . . . I don't know. Nothing productive, I'm sure. Just sitting around and worrying about what's to come.

"How long is the season?" I ask.

"It's a spring league, mostly to gear the kids up for the big summer league. The kids that excel usually don't participate. So we just have a bunch of kids that are looking to learn the game or sharpen their skills."

I nod. "So, four or six weeks?"

"Exactly." He nods enthusiastically. *He knows he's got me.* "It's four weeks of games and then a tournament in Forest Falls. Nothing big or fancy."

Four to six weeks? I can do that. With no other commitments and nothing but time on my hands, I could spare a couple of months, and it might do me some good.

If I go back to California with nothing to do, there's a chance that I'll turn into the one thing I loathe most—a burden.

The thought makes me sick.

One thing I love most about baseball is the teamwork spirit. Each person pulling their own weight. Everyone contributing to the common goal. No one being a drain on the system, and if a mishap occurs, someone is there to pick up the slack. It's the key to success.

The idea of heading home and being a load on Fish's time because I'm bored disgusts me. Making my parents worry because they think, not incorrectly, that I'm having some sort of crisis? Irresponsible. And I know that my agent thinks I'm just sucking his energy while piddling around aimlessly, and I hate that he thinks that of me.

If I stay here and coach this team, none of that would happen, *and* I'd be helping out the community. I could even spend more time with my parents and pay them back for all they've sacrificed for me over the years.

"Let her buy the cleats," I say.

"Who?"

"Palmer."

Bud forces a swallow. "Why?"

I force a swallow too. "You just found yourself a coach."

"Oh, Cole," Mom says, her voice on the brink of tears.

Bud grabs the back of his chair. "Are you sure?"

"Yeah." I pick the binder up to hand it back to Bud. It slips from my hands and hits the counter with a soft thud. "I'll come by this afternoon, after I finish carting Mom around, and you can fill me in on logistics."

I push the binder across the counter and into Bud's hands.

"I'll have a packet ready for ya. This is . . . wow. This is really something. A real pro teaching the Bloomfield kids," he says.

"Hey, just because I can play doesn't mean I can coach."

"Are you kidding? You're going to be a fantastic coach, Cole." Mom grabs my arm. "It was good seeing you, Bud."

"You too, Mrs. Beck."

Palmer's laugh catches my attention and pulls it across the store. I look up just in time to see her pull Ethan into a one-armed hug.

"Jared Doughtry isn't gonna show up. I'll bet ya a dime to a doughnut he never sees a practice or a game. Mark my words."

I dig into my wallet and pull out two one-hundred-dollar bills. Discreetly, I slide them across the counter.

"Tell Palmer that the cleats are on the house," I say, my voice low so only Bud can hear.

His eyes go wide. "Really?"

I nod.

"This is too much," he says. "The most expensive pair I have aren't even this much."

"I'll get the change when I come back." I glance at Palmer quickly again. "But don't tell her that I paid for them. Got it?"

Bud smiles from ear to ear. "Got it."

Mom and I make our way to the exit.

A frog croaks when I pull the door open. Mom jumps, then laughs, before walking through the doorway. I pause and take a chance and look back at Palmer.

She's watching me, and I love seeing her blush when I catch her. My insides still as our gazes lock together, and then, before I press my luck, I give her a nod and walk out.

Palmer is gorgeous and funny. There's no doubt about that. *But why am I so drawn to her?*

I have no idea. But maybe, hopefully, I *will have* the opportunity to figure it out.

CHAPTER EIGHT

Palmer

"I don't know why I love this weather so much, but I do." I pull the drawstrings of my sweatshirt, tugging the hood tighter against my head. "There's just something so rejuvenating about the gray sky and bright sun—"

"And the way the cold and wet flares up your arthritis?" Kirk grins. "Getting old is for the birds."

"Who are you kidding? You're not old. You get around this bus yard better than anyone."

He groans as he hops from the bottom bus step to the ground.

"Do you have the list?" I ask.

Kirk holds up the clipboard with the inventory list we've been building. It's something we've done together every spring for the last ten years.

"Got it," he says.

"Good. Do you remember the one time we left it wedged between a bus seat and the wall?"

He makes a pained face. "Good grief, yes, I do. How we ever found it without flashlights, I'll never know."

We start the long trek from the back of the bus yard to the offices at the front. Our boots slosh in the mud with every step.

"I've always had an affinity for this time of year, even if it hurts me," he says, hunkering his shoulders against the wind. "My mother and I used to sit in front of the fire and plan her gardens in March. She'd get so excited, almost giddy. I found her so entertaining when she'd pull out her sketchbook and make her seed list. She was like a little kid when it came to growing things."

"You know something? I don't think I've grown a thing in my life."

"You grew a child. That's the hardest thing in the world that there is to grow."

"Good point, sir."

The apples of his cheeks are rosy as he grins. "Thinking that's working out better for you than that aloe vera you tried to keep alive when you started for me."

"I forgot about that." I laugh at the memory of that poor plant and my futile attempts to keep it from dying. "What happened to that thing?"

"I think Burt took it home to his wife."

Poor lady. She had to deal with a struggling plant and Burt. Each is as prickly as the other.

I pause to work a boot out of a particularly thick vein of mud. As I free it from the hole, I look around.

This part of the bus yard—the back corner of the ten acres—has always been my favorite. If it's foggy, the elevation has a magical vibe. If it's clear, you can see all the way to Forest Falls. I always feel a touch removed from the world when I'm here, and sometimes that's what I need.

"Did I tell you that Ethan is starting baseball today?" I ask Kirk as I catch up with him.

He chuckles. "Listen to all of that enthusiasm dripping from your voice."

"Very funny."

He shakes his head. "What spurred this, anyway?"

"What do you mean?"

"Well, I've never had Ethan pegged to be a sports kind of guy."

I can't discount this observation. I'm not sure Ethan would either. This proves two things. One, Jared doesn't know his son very well, and two, he doesn't respect me even a little bit. Otherwise, he would've had a conversation with me about baseball before signing him up.

Ugh.

"Jared signed him up," I say with a shrug. "I'm sure you guessed that."

"I did."

"I don't know what to think about it, really. I mean, it's good for Ethan to get away from his video games and get some fresh air. And I love the teamwork aspect of it because he's an only child."

Kirk laughs. "As the father of three children, having siblings does not mean you learn teamwork. Just manipulation."

I grin at him.

"What's your holdup?" he asks.

"What do you mean?"

"Well, you said you didn't know what to think about it. What is the other side of the coin, so to speak?"

I blow out a breath and watch the heat billow from my mouth.

There is something about the baseball situation that feels off in my stomach. I can't explain it to myself, let alone to Kirk.

Jared doing anything that can remotely be described as parenting is so unusual. But baseball? Jared didn't even play baseball, so it's not a "my kid has to do what I did" kind of thing—not that Jared cares about that anyway. I'm happy when he remembers he *has* a kid.

So that's weird. But what's even stranger is that Ethan has never once, in his twelve years on the planet, mentioned an interest in anything with a ball. He didn't even like balls as a toddler. I know Jared wasn't prompted by something Ethan said.

It's so random and out of left field. Pun intended.

"I guess what it is," I say, walking around another mud hole, "is that I can't decide what to make of it. It feels like this whole baseball thing just got dropped in my lap, and it's so heavy."

"What do you mean by 'heavy,' Palmer?"

"I mean that it just landed in my life with a thud."

He chuckles. "All right."

I know that was a pitiful response, but it feels accurate.

"I just . . ." I look at the cold, gray sky. "I was sure that I was going to have to tell Jared to get his fee back because Ethan wouldn't play. And then we ran into Cole Beck in a parking lot, of all places."

Kirk looks at me, his brows pulled together. "Lawrence Beck's son? The baseball player?"

"Yes, he just retired, apparently."

"I didn't know he was in town. I bet Lawrence is thrilled."

How the heck would I know? "I bet he is."

"Huh." Kirk shakes his head. "Anyway, you ran into Cole . . ."

"Yeah. We did. And Ethan was surprisingly receptive to the whole thing. He tossed the ball around with Cole, and . . . Ethan *wasn't my kid*. He seemed excited about an outdoor sport with a ball."

Kirk laughs.

"Then I take him into Bud's to get some cleats, because apparently you can't go to one practice to make sure you like it without the proper footwear." I roll my eyes. "And Bud said that there was some kind of rebate on them and they were free."

"Really?"

Kirk believes that line of crap about as much as I do, but I don't know how else to explain it. Bud isn't one to give things away, so I'm not sure what to think. He wouldn't take no for an answer, and we walked out of there with a pair of baseball shoes for free.

"Really." I shrug. "It's like this whole thing should've been called off at every turn, and yet, with every turn we lean more into it."

Our pace slows as we start down the steepest part of the hill. Kirk chews on his bottom lip like he does when he's thinking.

I think, too, but on a slightly different trajectory.

My thoughts slide easily—too easily—from baseball to Cole.

A puff of a breath whispers into the air as I give up the fight. Because that's what it's like—a constant struggle not to think about him.

My mind is made up when it comes to Cole. Nothing is going to change that. But I'm not having an easy time switching my brain patterns back to last Friday, before I met him.

It's bizarre.

I've thought a lot of men were handsome over the years, but I was able to forget their names. Charming guys are few and far between, but they do exist. And I'm able to move along from our exchanges.

So what is it about Cole? I'm not sure.

He's easy and fun to talk to. I secretly adore his persistence. Watching him be so kind to my son—taking time out of his day to play catch with him for a moment—doesn't hurt. And I'd be lying if I didn't admit that seeing him and his mother interact at Bud's softened my heart a little bit.

But none of that explains the immediate comfort that flows through me as soon as his name comes up in a conversation or his face pops up in my mind. Sure, I'm frustrated, too, but there's a very clear wash of warmth, like a giant exhale, that accompanies my irritation.

It's so, so baffling.

"Have I ever told you the story about how my father started Skoolie's?" Kirk asks.

I shake my head and stomp in the middle of a puddle. Water squishes out both sides of my boots.

"Dad was a mechanic," he says. "He worked for a guy in Forest Falls but also did work on the side, as mechanics do. A man contacted him one day to see if he could work on his bus because he wanted to convert it into a mobile home, like they do now. But this was back before all of that was cool."

"I love that you use the word 'cool.'"

He smiles at me. "So, Dad did it even though he wasn't a bus mechanic, but he knew enough to help the guy out. And, as things happen, Dad's name started to float through the bus community that he was the guy to do quality, cheap work."

Our boots crunch through the gravel as we hit the driveway that leads from the storage sheds to the offices. A deep slate–colored cloud barrels across the sky, and I wonder if we're going to get caught in a rainstorm.

"I remember overhearing a conversation between my parents," Kirk says. "Dad was saying that he didn't think that working on buses was worth the time, and Mom said that the universe was leading him that way for a reason. I suppose that's why he kept at it. And the skill he learned and the connections he made looking for parts and that sort of thing—he changed his life and mine too."

"Can you imagine what would've happened if he didn't open Skoolie's?" I grin. "I probably never would've met you. Or Burt."

Kirk laughs. "Before you get off on a tangent, let me make my point."

"Then you better hurry because I'm ready to tangent."

He shakes his head at me. "The point is that you can't force fate, Palmer."

"With all due respect, I'm not sure that baseball is my fate." I make a disgusted face. "Let's hope not, anyway."

"Maybe it's not baseball. Maybe . . . maybe it's what baseball will lead you to."

Kirk pauses and lets me take the steps first up to the trailer we use for offices.

"I think baseball is going to lead me to a bottle of wine," I joke. "And probably a headache."

We step inside the office and change from our boots to tennis shoes.

"I'm going to make a couple of phone calls," he says, grimacing as he stands up straight.

"I have a few emails to return, and then I'm leaving right at four. I need to get to the Bureau of Motor Vehicles on my way home before they close."

He nods. "Sounds good. Have fun at baseball."

I head to my desk and feel a spark of energy rush through my veins. "I'm sure I won't. Hopefully Ethan will."

"Just be open to it. Who knows? Maybe you'll become a baseball mom. You can keep the book for the coach and bring snacks."

"Ha." I sit at my desk. "I'm many, many things, Kirk. But a baseball mom isn't one of them."

"You don't know that. The universe is leading you to the ball diamond for a reason."

I reach for my water bottle. "I'd definitely like to be led to a diamond, but not that kind."

Kirk laughs, waving a hand through the air like he's done with me, and closes his office door.

I get to work, happy to have something to take my mind off this new thing in my life that I'm going to have to manage.

Ugh.

CHAPTER NINE

Palmer

"Oh crap."

Ethan glances at me while continuing to pound his right hand into his baseball glove. "What's wrong?"

"Tell me you grabbed your water bottle." I squint into the rainy sky and wish I'd had time to stop at the Quick Stop and squeegee the windshield. There's an oily residue coating the glass from following a semitruck to work this morning. "You got it, didn't you?"

"Which do you want me to answer?"

"What do you mean?"

"Do you want me to tell you that I grabbed it, even if I didn't? Because that's what you said—'Tell me you grabbed your water bottle.' Or do you want me to answer your question—"

"Ethan." I throw him a look so pointed that he flinches. "Did you get it or not?"

"Yes, Mother. I got it."

I'm *this close* to telling him to watch his mouth, but I don't. I can't quite read between the lines. His words didn't actually sound sarcastic, even though that's how I heard them, and the entire exchange wears on my already gray mood.

I lean forward and peer at the darkening sky. Secretly, I prayed for rain this afternoon. There wasn't a line at the Bureau of Motor Vehicles, and I managed to renew all of Skoolie's business-vehicle tags in about ten minutes. That would've left me with a long evening at home to pay bills, run the damn vacuum on the steps, and make a homemade dinner that doesn't involve chicken nuggets.

But we have baseball.

The only thing dissolving my irritation is the sparkle in Ethan's eye.

Bud promised me when we checked out last night that spring baseball is more of a learner league. He assured me that Ethan will be in great hands and will have a lot of fun.

I hope so. I hope there aren't a whole heap of kids who are already experienced and make Ethan feel bad for not knowing how to play. I worried about it all night.

I pilot the car onto Cardinal Lane toward the baseball complex.

Maybe this will help him form a framework of men he can go to for help and advice.

It's the one thing in life that I really can't give him. That drives me nuts.

"Mom . . ."

I slow down for a set of speed bumps leading into Cardinal Park, named after the local high school mascot, and then look at Ethan.

"What's up?" I ask.

"Um . . ." His chin dips. "Do you think there's any chance that Dad will be here?"

Fuck you, Jared.

I regrip the steering wheel and try to keep my features as smooth as I can. "I know that you'd like him to be."

He doesn't say anything, just lightly shrugs.

My heart sinks. "You won't be alone, kiddo. I'll be there."

"You're *always* there."

He gives me the sweetest, saddest smile that I've ever seen. Tears pool in the corners of my eyes as I try to figure out how to protect my ninety-pound heart sitting beside me.

"I don't want you to think that I don't care that you're there," he says. "But I . . . You know, the other kids probably have a dad there, and I . . . It might feel weird, you know?"

"It might. I don't know how you're going to feel. But I do know this—I'll play catch with you in the evenings. I'll even get a sparkly shirt with *Ethan's Biggest Fan* on the back like a proper fangirl."

This brings a smile to his face. "Don't do that. Thanks, but don't do that."

His smile lifts mine.

I park my car on the end of a long line of pickup trucks and kill the engine. I don't make a move for fear of rushing him into something that he doesn't want to do.

If he blurts out that he wants to go home, we're gone.

Ethan sits in the passenger's seat and stares onto the wet, brick-red field. Boys his age toss balls to one another, while some walk around in little duos or trios and talk.

"You know anyone out there?" I ask gently.

"Yeah. I know all of them."

"Are they nice kids?"

"Yeah." He opens and closes his glove with his eyes glued to the boys on the field. "I know why Dad signed me up."

My throat squeezes together. Before I can come up with a response that won't put him on the spot or bring me to tears, he speaks.

"He did it to make himself feel better about not being a good dad." He turns his head to me. "I'm not a stupid little kid anymore. I understand things."

"Ethan . . ."

"This is his way of pawning me off on someone else but getting to say he signed his kid up for baseball. It gives him a good line to tell everyone."

My heart breaks into pieces as I look into the eyes of a little boy who knows too much.

Instinctively, I want to lie to him and tell him he's wrong. It would make him feel better if he thought that Jared had any plans whatsoever to show up at a game or practice and watch him play. But it would be a lie, and by the look on Ethan's face, he knows it.

Even though my heart is in the right place, and all I want to do is protect him, I need him to trust me. And that means being honest.

My mouth goes dry as I struggle to find the right words for this situation.

"Your dad means well," I say because I can say that and mean it. "He doesn't wake up in the morning and think about hurting you or—"

"No, because he doesn't wake up thinking about me at all."

Damn it.

I let my eyes flutter closed for a moment to help settle my nerves.

"Ethan, I can't explain his behavior because you are the first thing I think about in the morning and the last thing I think about at night. You are my *whole entire world.*"

He lifts his chin, but his eyes give him away. They remind me that inside that tall body that's starting to smell funky if he doesn't shower . . . he's still a little boy. *My little boy.*

"I'm sorry that Dad makes you feel that way. It breaks my heart because I want you to be the happiest little boy in the world."

He lunges across the middle console and wraps his arms around my shoulders. The suddenness of his movement takes me aback.

His face buries in the crook of my neck for a split second before he pulls away.

I search his face. "Do you even want to play? Did I even ask you that?"

"I don't know. I'm pretty sure you just trusted me to tell you if I didn't."

"And you do or don't?"

He bites his bottom lip. "What do you think I should do?"

"I think . . ." I study his face again. His freckles shine across the bridge of his nose. "I think you should do whatever makes you happy. It would be good for you. Fresh air and activity are positive things. But if you think baseball isn't your jam, then we can find something else." I muss his hair. "You're old enough to know what excites you."

"Girls. And *Fortnite*."

I bop his shoulder as I pull my hand away, making him laugh.

"Yeah. I do want to play." He puts his glove on his lap. "Want to know why?"

"Why?"

"Because I told Dad I would. I want him to see what it's like for someone to follow through on their promises."

Sweet, strong boy.

"How'd you get so mature?" I ask.

"I think it comes with getting pit hair. I have three strands now."

"Ew." I laugh, wrinkling my nose. "That's more information than I need, kiddo."

My disgust fills him with a prepubescent joy, and his laughter fills the car.

"Okay." He nods in an exaggerated motion. "It's time I go out there and show 'em what I got. *Which is not much.*"

We exchange a grin that warms my heart.

"You may not have much now, but you have to start somewhere," I say.

"True. And I have an invitation from Cole to help me, remember?"

Men are the bane of my existence.

"I do, and that was super nice of him. But he'll probably be on a plane back to California soon, so I wouldn't put too much into that invitation, okay?"

Ethan rolls his eyes. "Mom."

"What?"

"Just because you have a crush on him—"

My jaw drops. "Ethan Wayne!"

"What?" He giggles. *"You do."*

"I absolutely do not."

He puts his glove on again and punches it in the webbing with his other hand. "What is it that you tell me?" He taps his chin with his glove. "'You can talk to me about anything. Nothing is off limits between us.'"

His grin is smug as he watches my reaction—one that I try desperately to keep in check but fail.

"First of all, nice imitation of my voice," I say, getting my footing. *Although I don't sound anything like that.* "And second of all, that's a one-way street, little boy."

"No offense there, Ma, but I'm pretty sure that you'll get better advice from me than Val. And who else do you have to talk to?" He shrugs. "Think about it."

I have no idea what is happening in this conversation, nor why my baby all of a sudden seems like a grown-ass man. Whatever it is, I don't like it. Not even a little.

Even though he's right.

I point at the field. "You need to get your behind out there before you're late. That's no way to make a good first impression with your new coach."

"What would you say to me here? Let's see . . . 'This conversation is not over.'"

"Ethan," I say, laughing. "Get out of my car."

He wrinkles his nose, chuckling at his own ridiculousness, and opens the car door. The cab fills with damp, cool air. I shiver.

"Zip your jacket up," I tell him.

"I just gave you adult advice, and you're acting like I'm a child."

"You just overstepped your bounds, and you're twelve. So, yeah, zip it up. Now."

"Mom."

"I'm not paying for a hospital bill when you get pneumonia because you won't listen. Now zip it, kid."

"Ugh."

He slams the door shut. Then, while glaring at me from the other side, he jerks the zipper up his jacket with a flourish.

"Thank you," I mouth at him through the glass.

He rolls his eyes and storms off toward a dugout where the kids are congregating.

I sink back in my seat and turn off the ignition. The car cools down almost immediately.

Ethan marches right up to a group of kids and joins their conversation. His shoulders are relaxed, his head falling back as he laughs at something one of the boys says.

I spot a set of bleachers behind home plate. A few mothers are sitting with blankets around them and travel mugs beside them.

Overachievers.

But as I look at Ethan and see how bravely he's trying new things—*maybe I need to step out of my comfort zone too.*

I blow out a breath and grab a plaid blanket from the back seat. Then I fold it over my arm.

I'm still not going to be a baseball mom.

My eyes flip ahead of me as I start to climb out of my car. Then I stop.

Hand hovering over the door handle, body twisted to the side—I sit and return Cole's stare.

He's standing behind the dugout with a whistle around his neck. A clipboard is tucked under his arm, and the word COACH is printed on his black hat in bright-white lettering.

Coach?

I lift a brow. He lifts his too. Then a slow, hesitant smile slides across his lips.

Fuck.

CHAPTER TEN

Palmer

There's no way.

I don't move, despite my awkward position. Instead, I sit frozen in a half-twisted arrangement like the car yogi that I am not. Hell, my back will probably be sore from this in the morning.

The corners of Cole's mouth turn higher and higher until they're a mixture of dubious and smug.

There's a half a car between us—metal, glass, and various viscous fluids—not to mention ten feet of gravel and air, and I still feel like I'm being pulled toward him.

My breath hitches, hitting such shallow depths that my watch warns me to breathe. The delicate chime alerting me to take a breath breaks the near trance of shock. *What the heck?*

Cole is Ethan's coach?

Too many thoughts fly through my brain to grab ahold of any of them. I should sit back in my seat and refuse to deal with this until I can get a grasp of the situation, but that would be a very adult decision. I'm too fueled by adrenaline—and excitement and annoyance and annoyance at my excitement—to act responsibly.

I fling my door open and step into the brisk air. Forgetting all about my blanket, I cross my arms and cling to the opposite elbow in a poor attempt to keep warm.

Cole faces me head-on. He shifts his clipboard from under his arm to his hands and lets it hang at his side.

"Where's your jacket?" he asks me.

"That's what you lead with?"

I think if I were appropriately dressed, he would laugh.

"Seriously, Palmer. I expect to fight middle schoolers about wearing jackets, but not you."

I stop a few feet in front of him and do my absolute best to avoid his cologne. That sure as hell won't help anything.

"Tell me that the word emblazoned on your hat doesn't mean what I think it means," I say.

"What word?"

He takes off his hat, and I immediately regret prompting him to make this movement.

His hair is wild, with soft, thick waves. It's tousled and sexy and does absolutely nothing to help me keep my head clear.

"Oh," he says, twirling the hat in his hand. *"Coach?"*

He presses his lips together as if the word is a kiss. *A kiss of death, maybe.*

"I'm going to go out on a limb here," he says, grinning. "You weren't expecting to see me today."

"Cole, what are you doing here?"

He slides his hat back on, shoving his dark locks up and under it. "Turns out that the league didn't have anyone to coach this team."

So?

I squint as I try to make sense of whatever is happening. "So you're filling in? Is that what this is?"

"Yup. I'm the new coach."

"For the whole season?"

The baseball moms on the bleachers turn toward us. I recognize some of them from Ethan's school—the PTA moms who seem to have infinitely more time, energy, and money than I do. They've formed a group bound together by Pinterest secrets. Either they know I don't have that app or they've heard me lament "farmhouse chic," but something has prevented the natural progression from a simple hello in the hallway to group monogramming-our-towels night.

I'm never getting that invitation now.

"Does it bother you that I'm the coach *for the whole season*?"

Cole sweeps my gaze up in his. His eyes are so bright that I can nearly see my reflection in them.

For a moment, everything around us stops. The baseball moms and their overt gawking don't exist. The boys' chatter on the other side of the dugout ceases. My anxiety about staying impervious to Cole's charm for six damn weeks slinks away, and in its place is . . . *calm*.

I hate that he can do this to me, that he can take my breath away with nothing more than a steady, sturdy look. I hate it even more than I like it.

But of course I like it. I always like it from men who are inaccessible.

"Does it?" he asks, prompting me to answer his question.

"I thought you were headed back to California?"

"That was the plan."

Was?

I shift my weight from one foot to the other.

"No, that *is* the plan," he says, correcting himself. "I'll just wait until this is over."

Oh.

He grins. "That's the beauty of retirement, right?"

I don't realize how quickly my mood's shifted until he puts things in the present tense. The gray skies hide the sun in my soul that was starting to peek out from behind the clouds.

Don't. Don't do it, Palmer. Don't set yourself up for failure. Again.

I find my footing—this time, steeped back into reality.

"I don't think I'll ever retire," I say, shivering. "I'll probably add on a greeter job at one of the big-box stores when I'm seventy."

"You say that like it's a dream of yours."

"Okay. Fine. I actually want to be the person that checks receipts before people exit. You know, when you have unbagged items and they make sure you're not stealing."

His smile stretches across his face.

"It's really a twofer job," I say. "You get to see all the little things that the store sells that you maybe didn't know, *and* you get to call thieves out on their bullshit. Does it get any better than that?"

"Well, while I see the perks you described, I happen to think coaching might be a bit better. Think about it—you don't even have to work. You just get to play baseball the whole time."

He shrugs. I'm awash in the warmth of leather in his cologne.

Save me.

My knees wobble, and in case he notices, I make a point to shiver again.

"But you have to consider the weather," I say, gritting my teeth against the cold. "At least a door greeter works inside."

His eyes narrow. Before it registers in my head, he reaches for my shoulder. Then, gently, he presses on the corner—effectively guiding me in a half circle.

"I can't have a conversation with you when you're literally freezing to death," he says. "And I don't have a coat to give you."

He presses so gently, so lightly, on the back of my shoulder to guide me back to my car. I move one step at a time, with my attention fixed on the exact spot where his fingers press into my sweatshirt.

The contact is just enough to get the job done—get me back to my car. But it's also just enough to frazzle the connection in my brain.

He reaches around me, brushing the side of my arm with his, and pulls open my car door.

"In you go," he says.

"I was going to make a joke and say, 'Thanks, Daddy,'" I say as I collapse into the driver's seat. "But two things—one, I don't think my dad ever did anything that thoughtful for me, and two . . ." My cheeks flush. "You know, the obvious."

He turns his body, angling it toward the street and away from prying eyes.

"You know," he says before biting his lip. "It's going to be really hard to go coach a bunch of twelve-year-olds with a hard-on."

My eyes flip to the crotch of his black workout pants. Sure enough, a bulge causes the fabric to press away from his body. His hand reaches down and adjusts it, and it's only then that I realize that he's watching me watch him.

The heat in my face goes up exponentially. I'm glad I can't see myself because I probably look like a beet.

"If it helps, and it probably doesn't," I say, "I didn't think that through before I said it."

"It doesn't. I'll be replaying that in my head all night now. Thanks."

He groans, situating himself while staring over the top of my car. Pointedly *not at me*.

I glance at the field, where two men are playing catch with the boys. My heart squeezes until I find Ethan in the mix of the chaos . . . smiling.

My shoulders fall in relief.

"You might get lucky," I say, pulling my gaze back to Cole.

His eyes shoot to mine, and I realize where his brain just went.

"*I mean* that it looks like you have a couple of dads out there ready and willing to take the team over," I say, grinning.

"You're mean, all right." He takes a step away from my car and glances at the field. "Those two have never thrown a ball in their lives. Look at their mechanics—or lack thereof, I should say."

He makes a face of disgust that makes me giggle.

"Don't do that either," he says.

"What?"

"Giggle. I'm still extracting my thoughts from the ones you planted earlier."

I sigh, amused by his antics, even though I don't want to be. Even though I shouldn't be. "Come on, Cole. Stop it."

He looks down at me. His features read sober. "See? Nothing you can say will sound normal now. You ruined it."

"Is that all I had to do?"

I lift a brow, my cheeks aching from all the smiling I'm doing. And the cold. *Probably the cold.*

"For what?" he asks.

"To get you to stop chasing me everywhere."

His eyes twinkle, sparkling with mischief as he huffs an exhale.

"I'm glad that I found the key to keep you from asking me to dinner," I say. Although I mean it—because I'm not going to dinner with him—I hold my breath.

"You think talking in innuendos is going to stop me from asking you to dinner?"

My insides quiver. I worry my voice will, too, so I don't respond.

"I will ask you to dinner until you give me a good reason why I shouldn't," he says.

"I have."

"No. You haven't." He glances over his shoulder and then back to me. "But right now, I have to go show this group why baseball is the greatest game in the world."

"I thought that was *Super Mario 3*?"

He laughs. "Let's continue this conversation after practice."

Then, as if he hasn't scrambled me enough for one day, he goes in for the kill. He winks. The bastard has the audacity to wink at me.

I take in his nice round ass as he jogs to the boys.

The plan was to take my blanket and join the women on the bleachers, but after a quick assessment, I decide against it. Instead, I close my car door and turn on the ignition to warm up.

On the outside. My insides are already ablaze.

Cole steps onto the field, and everyone—kids and adults alike—stops. They turn toward him like he's some kind of baseball god. Maybe he is. *I should look into that.*

I smack my thighs with the palms of my hands and groan.

No. No, I shouldn't look into that.

I rest my head on the seat front and sigh.

How many times a week am I going to see this man? And will I be just as flappable with every interaction?

He motions for the kids to circle around him, and they do it happily. Ethan stands near the back of the group with another kid's hand dangling over his shoulder. His cheeks are red from the cold as he watches Cole with rapt attention.

He's how I'm going to endure it.

Ethan deserves it.

My heart swells as I watch my son nod at something Cole says. I smile when Ethan's head falls back and he laughs right along with the team. I sink into my seat and give a whisper of thanks when he looks my way and beams, joy rolling off him in waves.

I'll do anything for that kid, even if it means avoiding a rendezvous with Cole Beck.

CHAPTER ELEVEN

Cole

Dinner was great, Mom." I put the last plate back in the cabinet and toss the towel on the counter. "You're spoiling me."

"Some things never change," Dad jokes as he takes his cup of coffee into the living room.

Mom dries her hands on the edge of her apron. "I'm probably going to pull back from it just a little bit since I know I have you for another month. I need to pace myself."

I laugh.

"When are you having practice again? I'd love to come watch you in action. Mary Beth Goheen said you were a natural," Mom says.

"Why was she there? I know she doesn't have a little kid."

"Well . . . she might have been walking by and saw you out there."

The twinkle in her eye tells me enough. I don't want to know if my mom's sixty-year-old friend has the hots for me.

It's happened before. It changes the dynamic when I see them at the post office.

"I'm giving them tomorrow off. Don't want to burn them out right away," I say. "It's supposed to be warmer the day after anyway."

"This weather is crazy. Warm one day and cold the next. That's Ohio for you."

"That's one thing I won't miss."

Her smile falters. "Yes, well, let's not talk about that. I don't want to think about you not being here."

I give her a smile that's supposed to make her feel better but I think only makes her feel worse. So I do the only other thing I can and pull her into a tight hug.

She pats my back and then presses her palms into my back like she did when I was a little kid. Despite her five-foot-one-inch height and her feather-like weight, her embrace calms the center of my body, which has been buzzing all day.

I don't let go because she doesn't.

"I heard through the grapevine that you had a pretty animated conversation with Palmer Clark today," she says, finally pulling away.

At the sound of Palmer's name, the fog in my head clears.

"A grapevine named Mary Beth Goheen?" I ask.

Mom laughs.

"What did she say?" I ask.

"Nothing," she says too breezily.

I lower my chin and give her a look.

She waves a hand through the air and turns toward the sink. "Oh, she didn't say much. Just that you two looked pretty comfy with one another."

"I told you that I knew Palmer."

She hums, the tune painting a picture that she has her mind made up about whatever Mary Beth said.

"Her son plays on my team—which you already knew," I say. "So don't start humming at me."

She spins on her heel. The apples of her cheeks are pink and bunched up just beneath her eyes as she smiles.

"Don't . . ." I shake a finger at her. *"Don't do that."*

"Don't do what, Cole?"

"Don't look at me like that."

"Oh. I thought you meant not to presume that you had a thing for Miss Palmer. Because Mary Beth sure thought Palmer had a thing for you."

I wish. Especially now that I'll be in town for more than a few days.

I could have weeks with the presence of pretty Palmer Clark.

If she'd only say yes to me.

It requires a mental war with myself not to replay Palmer's innuendos. They're right there on the tip of my brain, but I will myself to keep them just out of reach. *I don't want a chub in front of my mother.*

"You can rest assured that if Palmer had a thing for me, I'd tell you," I say. "I've asked her to dinner more than once, and she's turned me down every time."

Mom's jaw drops.

"I know. I'm shocked too."

She rolls her eyes. "I think you're perfect, but that doesn't mean every woman will."

"Right. Because there's one holdout, and her name is Palmer Clark."

This should, by all accounts, discourage my mother. But it does not. Instead, her eyes light up as if I've just set a gift in her lap and told her to open it.

"Did you . . . you know, hear what I just said?" I ask. "Or do you need hearing aids?"

"Heavens, no. I don't need them. Your father, on the other hand . . ."

"Good. Because I don't want you thinking—"

"That Palmer likes you." She smiles from ear to ear. "Got it."

I look at her warily. "It doesn't seem like you got it."

"Oh, *I do*. And I know there's no way that Palmer doesn't think you're handsome."

"Clearly not." I snort. "I didn't say that. She's not blind."

Mom laughs. "Should I ask her to dinner?"

A heavy dose of dread begins to sink in my stomach. "Mom, no."

"What about if I say I'm your baseball helper and I pretend to twist an ankle? I could—"

"Mom." I laugh, more out of disbelief than amusement. I am not a gangly teenager here. I do not need my mom's help with women. "What are you doing right now?"

"I'm trying to help."

"Help me what?" I hold my hands out to the sides. "You realize that you're planning a fake injury to help a woman that has turned me down—multiple times, at that—to . . . I don't even know what you were trying to get her to do. It doesn't matter because this whole thing is ludicrous."

She pops a hand on her hip. "'Ludicrous' is a little much."

"Funny, because I was going to go with 'insane' and backed off of it a little out of respect."

She sighs and reaches into the cabinet for a mug. "Want some coffee? It's decaf, so it won't keep you up."

"No. I'm good."

"Suit yourself." She pours herself a steaming cup of joe. "I didn't want to say anything. You know how I don't like to get involved in your personal life. I don't want to be *that mom*."

"Clearly."

She fires me a warning look just in case I'm being sarcastic. Which I am.

"But I do think you and Palmer could be a very good couple," she says.

She sips her coffee while wishing me with Palmer.

My lips part to argue with her—to tell her that I disagree or that I've seen enough of Palmer to know that it wouldn't work out. But both would be a lie.

The truth is that the more I see of her, the more enchanted I become. She's great. Palmer is the kind of woman I would settle down with if I were so inclined to make such commitments. Actually, she's the prototype I was looking for just a year and a half ago, when playing the field—both literally and figuratively—got to be too much.

She's beautiful and funny. Charming and playful. Responsible and nurturing, and watching her with Ethan? It makes me respect her so much.

And if I'm being honest, it makes me consider what it would be like to have her as the mother to my children.

That leads to a million other thoughts. *What does she look like when she wakes up in the morning? Does she listen to music on her way to work? What's her guilty pleasure?*

How does she like to get fucked?

"What do you think?" Mom asks, pulling me out of my reverie.

I snap out of my daydream about bending Palmer over the hood of her car and come back to my mom's kitchen.

"About what?" I ask.

"Do you think the two of you could be a good couple? I know you said you asked her to dinner, but dinner and a relationship are two vastly different things."

One hundred percent.

"Getting into a relationship would be silly, don't you think?" I ask. "Considering the obvious."

She narrows her eyes. "Well, maybe if you were in a relationship, *the obvious* wouldn't be necessary."

I stretch my arms over my head, more to avoid replying to her than anything. I quickly evaluate my right shoulder as I pull it higher in the air. *Not too bad.*

When my arms are back to my sides, my mother is still looking at me.

Shit.

I don't want to get into this tonight, and even if I did, now isn't the time. That's not why I'm visiting—that, and I'm not mentally prepared for that conversation. I need to be solid about what's going on before I off-load that onto my parents. God knows I'm nowhere near close to being comfortable with it myself.

"You know I'm going to have to get a job at some point, and there's nothing for me to do around here," I say.

She scoffs. "Don't bullshit me, Cole."

Well, okay.

It's not that I haven't heard my mother use profanity, because I have. But I've never heard her just throw one out there in conversation with me until now.

I expect her to recant her vulgarity and backtrack. But the only thing she does is lift her brows in challenge.

"You do *not* have to get a job," she says. "Your last contract alone was three years, fifty million dollars."

Excellent point.

"And you save money like it's nobody's business." She presses her lips together in a suppressed smile. "You're driving your father's truck instead of getting a rental."

"Don't throw that at me," I say with a laugh. "What happened to, 'Your dad's truck needs to be driven, or the battery is going to go dead'?"

"What can I say? Sometimes I like to pretend like you still need me."

She smiles, but it doesn't quite cover the way her bottom lip trembles. I don't dare hug her because that will definitely set off the waterworks.

My heart swells as I adjust to this new dynamic between us—the one where I'm the adult child of aging parents. I don't know when that happened. I guess I was too busy before to notice how much older she seems and how many more wrinkles line her eyes.

She turns away, then grabs a piece of paper towel and dabs her face. She doesn't let me see her cry.

I hold my breath and close my eyes as my mind drifts to a place that I try to avoid.

My life has changed so much in the last two years alone—in ways I never anticipated. I'm left with a ton of questions and few answers, and I wrestle with what the future will look like for me in so many ways.

But as I watch my mother toss the paper towel into the recycling bin, it hits me that my parents are in a similar spot. Their lives look different, too, just not in the same way.

I don't know what to do about that.

"I guess you at least came home," she says, facing me again.

"What's that supposed to mean?"

She leans against the counter and wraps her arms around her middle. "I know something is wrong, Cole."

And that's why I love you, Mom. You always know.

"And I'm glad you came home," she says, lowering her voice. "I've always hoped that we raised you to know that no matter what you go through in life, wherever we are—you have a place too."

I smile at her.

"Even if you have all that money and expect me to cook every night," she teases.

"Fine. We're eating out every other night I'm here."

"No, we are not."

I laugh. "Yes, we are. I'm hiring a catering company now. Do you want Thai tomorrow night? Or seafood, maybe. Dad loves seafood. I'll have some lobster flown in from Maine. Fuck it."

"Don't you dare."

"You want to get mouthy with me, I'll put my money where my mouth is. What about you? Can you take the heat?"

She swats my shoulder.

I laugh again. "Keep it up, and I'll tell Mary Beth Goheen you buy your gooseberries from the Amish."

She gasps. "You wouldn't."

"You're right." I grin. "I wouldn't."

She leans her head against my biceps. "And you wouldn't forget that you can talk to me about anything in the world, right?"

I lean my head on top of hers and sigh.

Someday, Mom. Someday.

"I know," I say.

She sighs too. "Good." Her head pops up and she smiles. "Now, let's figure out how we're going to fix you up with Palmer."

I lift my chin to the ceiling and groan. "Mom."

"So the fake injury is out, but what about a picnic at the park . . ."

Her voice trails off as I walk out of the kitchen and up the stairs.

Maybe I should use some of that money in the bank to get a hotel room.

CHAPTER TWELVE

Palmer

"How can I have two hundred channels and not be able to find one thing to watch?" I mumble.

I flip through the selections once again, scrolling the entire list of movies, shows, and sports programs before giving up.

It's probably not the menu of choices that's the problem. I'll bet that it's more likely a mix of exhaustion from a day of walking all over Skoolie's yard, avoiding Burt like it's my actual job, and mentally avoiding all thoughts of my son's baseball coach.

Why?

According to the chatter behind the bleachers after practice, having Cole coach the twelve-year-old team is basically a gift from heaven. The Blanket Brigade, the nickname I've given the six moms who have formed a Cole Beck fan club, has decided that this is the best thing to ever happen to Bloomfield. And it might be the best thing that has ever happened to them, too, if they play their cards right—or so they imply.

"Which is fine with me," I say to the dark room.

The only light in the living room comes from the television. It's not that bright since I left it on the menu and not an actual show. I yawn, my eyes watering as I stretch and feel a pull in my tight muscles, and I know I should just go to bed. But if I do, I'll just lie there awake. There's nothing worse than lying in bed with your eyes open.

I might as well stay out here.

I'm reaching for the remote again when my senses pick up movement from the doorway. There's a soft outline of a body in the shadows.

A cold blast of fear nails me square in the chest as my fight-or-flight response kicks in. Just before I hurl the remote at the doorway and spring off the recliner for the knife that I used to cut an apple earlier, the person takes a step forward.

"Val!" I pant, throwing myself back into the chair. My heart pounds so hard that it takes me a second to get it under control. "What the fuck?"

"You gave me the key." She bounds over to the sofa and throws herself on it. "I couldn't sleep and saw that you were on social media a few minutes ago, so I came over to cuddle."

My hand splays over my chest. "And you didn't think to shoot me a text?"

She shrugs as she pulls a throw blanket off the back of the couch and over her body. Then she nestles down into the pillows.

"What's keeping you up? You're never up this late," she says.

"Life." I toss the remote to her. "I can't find anything to watch."

The remote lies untouched at her stomach.

"What's keeping *you* up?" I ask her.

"Generalized insomnia."

"How generalized?"

She presses her lips together. "Basically, it's generalized into three main categories. One is guilt about things I said to my mother when I was a teenager."

I laugh at that because Val and her mother have an amazing relationship. I guarantee her mom isn't thinking about any of those things tonight.

"The second category is actually a question. Where are my birth certificate and Social Security cards right now?"

"Seriously, Val?"

She raises her head a couple of inches off the pillow. "*Yes, seriously.* What if I need them? Do you know how sucky and hard it would be to try to get those things replaced? I don't even have the documentation to get them replaced because I don't have either one of them. It would be mission impossible!" Her head drops like a rock back to the pillows. "I should know where these are, and I don't. I don't have a clue. Hell, have I ever even had possession of them? I don't know."

I giggle. "Why are you this way?"

"Beats me." She sighs dramatically. "And the third thing is that I need to find affordable housing that's not over a funeral home."

I make a face.

"Yeah," she says. "That probably should've been reason number one."

"You think?"

"I didn't think it would bother me," she says. "Like, the people that come in there are already dead. They're not going to haunt the place that put them to rest. They're going to go torment their husband that's now fucking their best friend or the woman that killed them. Right?"

I lift my shoulders up and down. "I don't know. I don't want to think about it, to be completely honest with you. And may I just say that I pointed all of this out before you signed that lease last year?"

She frowns. "Well, the four-hundred-dollar-a-month rent with utilities included was too hard to pass up."

"Because it's a funeral home!"

"I mean, good point . . ." She chuckles. "But that lease is almost up, and I have to figure out what I'm going to do."

She reaches for the remote and picks a cooking show. As the redhead on the screen babbles about shrimp and grits, my mind drifts off.

There are virtually no rentals around Bloomfield. The few available are sketchy—like the funeral home. Val has played with the idea of moving elsewhere as soon as she finishes her nursing degree, and I do my best to talk her out of it. But if she can't find somewhere to live now, I might lose her.

And, really, she's all I have besides Ethan.

"I'm not going to leave you," she says, rolling her eyes.

"I didn't say a word."

"You don't have to speak when I can read your face, friend."

This is why I love her.

"I'll find something," she says. "Don't worry about it."

"Sure. Right."

She lowers the volume and flops from her side to her back. From that angle, she's looking directly at me.

"We could move somewhere together," she says. "Me, you, and Ethan—the three amigos. We could get the hell out of this weather and go somewhere warm. Or somewhere cold and magical. Or somewhere with both but more temperate."

I grin at her. "You know I'd love to get out of here. But I'll never leave Bloomfield until at least Ethan is an adult, and probably not even then if he sticks around this area."

She frowns. "Because Jared is here."

I take in her tight lips and narrowed eyes. "Yes. Partly."

"Fuck him."

"Val . . ."

I sink back into my chair and try to figure out how to explain this to someone who doesn't know what it's like to be a single parent with a child in a grown-up's body as the coparent.

"Look—my job right now is to give Ethan every advantage that I can possibly give him in the world. I believe it's beneficial for Ethan to be able to foster some kind of a relationship with Jared. And, honestly, he's the only male figure he even has right now."

"That doesn't mean a shitty figure is better than no figure."

I consider that. "Okay, true, but Jared isn't evil. He's not mean. He's not abusive. He's just not . . . around."

"You're a bigger person than me. You literally center your whole life around that kid and expect nothing from Jared."

I don't have a choice.

"Trust me. One day when Ethan's an adult, I'm going to go wild. I'm going to blow up on Jared, buy gratuitous things from social media ads, and . . . I don't know. Go to Vegas or something."

She barks a laugh. "You've lived such a sheltered life. You don't even know how to have fun."

"One day. Right now I'm trying to give Ethan the stability and love and structure that I didn't have growing up." The levity of the moment passes, and a shadow falls across my soul. "Only I'm afraid that I'm failing at it. I'm continuing a cycle, albeit a variation of it, that I promised myself my whole entire life that I would break."

"You are an *excellent* mother."

She says the words with gusto. It's as though she delivers a stamp with each syllable to make sure they etch onto my heart.

Both sets of words—hers and mine—hang in the air between us. *I hope she's right.*

"Ethan knows he has you in his corner. That's the biggest thing, Palm."

"Yes, but . . ."

I pull the lever on the side of the recliner and sit upright. My exhale is long and strangled. I don't know why I'm going here—getting all philosophical about life—but I blame it on the hour. Things always feel heavier at night.

"I've had to raise myself alongside raising Ethan. I look at some of the choices I made now, and I see what I did wrong—I see the errors of my ways."

"You make it sound like you sold heroin on the street corner."

I snort. "Obviously I didn't do that. I'd have more money."

Val throws a pillow at me, barely missing the side of my head. The action makes us both laugh.

She turns the television back up, but I can't get into the shrimp on the screen. I also can't seem to get away from the thoughts in my head.

I should've done a lot of things differently in my life. My relationship with Jared went on far too long, even though I was convinced that it was the right thing to do. Of course, him telling me that we would get married and he would settle down *as soon as he got a job (or a promotion once he had a job)*, or *once we'd saved enough for a house*, or *right after the holidays* didn't help. But I let that continue when I should've been making moves for our future—mine and Ethan's.

And my choice to date Charlie wasn't much better, really. It was a variation of the Jared game plan—*I just need a bit more time,* he said—but at least I was able to cut the cord on that much faster. So I did grow . . . in some ways.

Therapy helped me to see that I was picking essentially the same man over and over again. I was subconsciously picking men like my father. Men who were emotionally unavailable. Men who wouldn't commit. Men who had an out. Men who abused my trust, just in different ways. Men who wouldn't support me or love me or give me faith in a future—and I did that because it was what I knew.

I have to give myself grace for it. I didn't know any better.

But now I do.

Now I have no excuse. I have to do better for me and my son.

"He really liked baseball yesterday," I say, my heart warming as I remember how he slept with his glove last night. "He talked all day about how much it stinks that they don't have practice until tomorrow."

Val presses against the couch until she's sitting up. "Speaking of baseball, the word at Fletcher's this afternoon was that Cole is the coach. I'm assuming not Ethan's coach because you definitely would've called me about that. Right, best friend?"

I slink back in my seat.

"Palmer!"

"What?" I laugh. "I . . . forgot."

"No, you didn't. As a matter of fact, you avoided me when I texted you last night and said you were doing laundry. You could've told me then. And your phone was off all afternoon."

"I was in the shop yard with Kirk, and my battery died."

She makes a face. "I would've been pissed if I left here tonight and forgot to bring it up. Man, I'm slipping or something."

"No, you just know that it's not a big deal."

Her jaw drops. *"Okay."*

I can't deal with her, so I pick up my phone.

A rush of excitement at Cole's entrance into this conversation is difficult to ignore. So I open my favorite social media account. It's always good for a solid distraction.

But when the screen loads, the flow of adrenaline peaks instead of recedes.

"What?" Val asks.

"Nothing."

She rips the blanket off herself and springs toward me. My phone is in her hands before I know what's happening.

"Cole friend requested you." She looks at me with wide eyes. "Are you going to accept it?"

Am I? I don't know.

"I need a second to—"

"There." Val holds the screen toward me. "I made the decision for you."

"Val!"

"He's your son's coach. He might need to talk to you about . . . baseball stuff." She grins, her eyes sparkling. "Now come to the couch, and let's scroll his profile."

"Val . . . no," I whine. "What have you done?"

She whistles through her teeth and walks backward to the sofa. "I've just found a spank bank, that's what."

I get to my feet and let out a fake cry. "Now I wanna see but I don't want to wanna see."

"Oh, trust me. You wanna see."

I sit beside her and gaze at the tanned, muscled flesh on my screen. *Damn.*

There are pictures of Cole running in the surf. Images of him in board shorts on the beach with a bandanna tied around his head. There's another of him at the top of a rocky incline with the ocean at his back. In every one of them, he's nothing short of perfect.

I'm not sure what I like most as Val scrolls his profile. *Is it his chiseled abs? The beautiful setting? His easy smile?*

Or is it the way everyone around him seems to be having just as much fun as he is in every single picture?

"Oh, go back," I say, ignoring Val's amusement at my sudden interest. "No. The one before that. The one where he's by the fire."

She stops at a picture of Cole sitting in a backyard next to a bronze-colored firepit. The flames dance in warm, orangish hues.

He sits on the far side of the fire in a cream-colored sweater. His hair is a bit longer than it is now, and his face a bit sharper. He appears to be midlaugh, the lines around his mouth and eyes crinkling as he smiles so wide.

He's glorious.

"That's a good shot, huh?" Val says.

"Yeah. I wonder who took it?"

She looks at me out of the corner of her eye. "I don't know. A friend, probably."

"Yeah." My throat goes dry, and I fight an odd sense of jealousy trying to erupt inside me. "Let's keep going."

I point at the screen at the exact moment that Val moves the phone closer to her. The simultaneous movement causes my finger to hit the little heart sign.

"No!" I hit it again, removing the red from the shape. "That won't register anywhere, will it?"

Val laughs. "Yup. Sure will."

I fall back to the pillows. "No. Tell me it won't. I unliked it so fast. Maybe it'll never show." I look at her with fear. "*Tell me it'll never show.* Lie to me, Val."

"You can't erase the notification on his end."

I grab a pillow and cover my face. I feel heat pooling in my cheeks as I try to figure out how to make this all go away.

Val laughs louder. "And that picture was from three years ago!"

This time, my whine is real.

"He's going to know you were trolling deep, Palm."

"I'm blaming it on you," I say, my voice muffled in the pillow.

"You're like the Adele song, but 'trolling' instead of 'rolling.'" She laughs. "That was funny. Come on."

Val tugs on the corner until I finally give in. She takes in my flushed face and laughs a third time.

"You are a terrible best friend," I say. Then I get up from the sofa and head to the stairs.

"Where are you going?"

"To bed."

"But I'm still here."

I stop at the top of the staircase. "You let yourself in. Let yourself out."

"What about your phone?" She grins and dangles it in the air. It looks like a bomb about ready to explode. That's what it feels like, at least.

I turn away from her and walk away. "Keep it. It's your problem now."

A knot forms in the pit of my stomach as I walk down the hallway. That might cause even more problems. *Val, with my phone, and my login, and Cole's photos.*

Shit.

But the bigger problem? If only I believed, even for a second, that Cole won't call me out on "hearting" his photo.

From. Three. Years. Ago.

Do I have a hat that can completely hide my face for practice tomorrow?

I sigh and climb into bed.

CHAPTER THIRTEEN

Palmer

Have fun—"

My words are cut short by the door slamming shut. Ethan starts to jog across the outfield, where I parked behind the fence to put some distance between myself and the coach, but then he stops. He turns around in a wide circle and races back to the car.

I roll down my window and squint into the evening sun. "Did you forget something?"

His little eyebrows pull together. "You're not gonna sit in the car the whole time, are you?"

Yes. "Well . . ." I bend my hand over my forehead to block the sun. "I'm not sure what moms are supposed to do. I figured it was best to stay out of the way. You know how I like to yell helpful advice to you that's not actually helpful." *Please accept this and carry on.*

He grins. "You do that."

"I know."

"But I see other moms. See on the bleachers? And there are a couple by the fence, I think. And at the last practice, there was a mom in the dugout trying to keep the kids organized. She said she was never coming back."

I laugh. "I'm smarter than that. I already know how messy one twelve-year-old can be. I want no part of . . . how many of you are there? Fifteen? Sixteen?"

I shudder, making him laugh.

"Still. You should get out and get some fresh air." He nibbles his bottom lip. "Weren't you the one telling me how fresh air is good for you?"

My response is on the tip of my tongue—I got fresh air at work today. But as my mouth opens to release my excuse into the air, a flash of the truth bolts across his eyes.

He wants his parent there too. And I'm it.

"Okay," I say around the heaviness in my chest. "Get over there and warm up. I'll . . . walk laps around the field or something." And avoid Cole.

His face lights up, rewarding me with a megawatt smile. "Great!"

I really ought to be thankful. He's not embarrassed by my presence and wants me there. With him. Part of his world with his friends. I know how lucky I am to still have a kid who wants Mom around.

I slip on my jacket and pointedly avoid acknowledging anyone or anything on the field except Ethan. He waves at me from right field before tossing a ball with slightly better "mechanics" to a boy with bright-green socks. As my gaze sweeps back to the outfield, I spot Cole near the pitcher's mound next to a man wearing a visor.

The air is slightly warmer than it was this afternoon when Kirk and I walked to the shop office to see Burt. Burt had approved an invoice that was $300 too high and wasn't too keen on his mistake being out in the open.

He was even less happy that I was the one to catch it.

I carry some of that weight with me as I walk next to the outfield fence. I wish there were a way to let the frustrations of work go when I clock out. But I find myself worrying about Kirk and the business more than I'd like.

"I wish I didn't care so much," I mumble as I step over a dandelion.

My steps come quicker as I find what I call a "worry rhythm." When I finally look up, I'm nearly to the visitors-side dugout. My head is still at work, replaying Burt's excuses, and doesn't have time to scream at me to not look at the pitcher's mound.

My gaze collides with Cole's somewhere along the third baseline.

I stop walking. Stop moving. Nearly stop breathing as I get my bearings.

I'm sure he's both used to my reaction—as he must get it wherever he goes—and wondering if it means I'll say yes to his dinner invitation.

But what he can't see is the knot in my stomach that refuses to unwind.

Maybe he didn't notice that I liked his old post on social media. He might be the kind of guy who doesn't check those things. I bet he has a million notifications anyway. It could've gotten buried.

The line of thought that I finally settled on around three this morning rolls through my brain. Not an hour has gone by today that I haven't rested on this—the one plausible way out of the potential humiliation.

Cole says something to the man in the visor. The man nods and goes back to raking the dirt around the pitcher's mound . . . and Cole walks toward me.

He saw it.

A smirk develops. It starts as a twitch of his lip and settles so deeply that I'm sure if I leaned too close to him, I might fall in.

Damn it.

I shift my weight from foot to foot, knowing I'm about to be called out for my mishap. My cheeks flush before he even gets off the field. There's time to flee. I could absolutely walk back the way I came or even power walk behind the concession stand, where I might, if I'm lucky, be out of sight.

Before I can choose, his arms are draped over the fence and we're three feet apart.

My focus immediately goes to his hands. I shiver at the mere thought of how his fingers felt pressed against my back at the last practice.

"Hey," he says, his voice thick and gooey like warmed-up Nutella.

"Hi."

Our gazes lock. Together, our lips pull toward the bright sky and into full smiles.

"How have you been?" he asks. "Busy?"

"Me? Always. You?"

"Never." He stretches his arms over the top of the fence, wincing ever so slightly as he rolls his shoulder around. "Had a lot of time on my hands, actually."

"Tell me what that's like."

I don't know what shit I've stepped in, but I know I have. His eyes grow dark and fill with mischief.

"Well, let's take last night, for example," he says.

Oh no.

"I was lying in bed," he says, grinning. "And I thought I'd check my social media to see if there was anything that I needed to respond to."

No. No, no, no.

My insides wither like a flower during a freeze, and although I don't do it intentionally, I find myself a couple of feet farther away from him.

This does not deter him. It only encourages his behavior.

He pulls his arms back over the fence. "Do you know what I found lurking in my notifications?"

"Couldn't tell ya."

"Someone by the name of Palmer Clark liked a photo of me from *three years ago*." His chest puffs out with an apparent shot to his ego. "Can you believe that?"

"I bet she has a friend named Val that probably used her phone to snoop. I mean, that seems entirely possible to me."

He hums in agreement. "It is entirely possible, but at almost midnight? *Eh.*" He rocks his head from side to side. "I don't know."

"Well, I couldn't tell you because . . . I mean, I didn't even know this happened until now."

I bite my lip to keep from smiling. His eyes are glued to my mouth as I let my bottom lip pop free.

I'm aware of his attention. I feel the heat of his gaze and the way it flips a switch inside me and makes me feel . . . desired.

It's intoxicating to feel wanted by Cole. He's so handsome and charming and freaking sweet. His pictures online get thousands of likes and so many thirsty comments that you could scroll through them for hours.

Men have wanted me before. I've known that. I've felt that. But it was nothing like this.

I take a step backward, a stumbling kind of movement, and nearly run into Bud.

"Oh," I say as I jump to the side and press a hand over my heart. "I didn't see you."

"I'm sorry, Palmer. I was too busy looking for Katie Evans and didn't see you either."

Cole frowns. "Who is Katie?"

"She has a son on the six-and-under team. She volunteered to reorganize the supply shed for me and has been missing all week. Not answering her phone, not showing up." He sighs. "I'm going to have to come down here Saturday and do it, I suppose."

I leap at the opening to put some distance between Cole and myself before I go all gaga over the man.

"Hey, I don't claim to know anything about baseball, but I can organize like it's no one's business," I say.

Bud's eyes light up. "Palmer, that would be amazing. Are you sure?"

"Yeah. I'm here anyway. Besides, Ethan would love for me to be more involved."

I mentally pat myself on the back. *Good work.*

"I didn't know you wanted a more participatory role," Cole says, rolling his tongue around his cheek.

Bad work. Very bad work.

"I think the shed will fulfill that need," I say.

"You know that your team doesn't have a team mom," Bud tells Cole. "I don't know if I mentioned that to you or not."

Cole's brows lift. "Oh, really?"

Bud nods enthusiastically. "You really need to find one, Cole. Last year, we had a kid get bopped in the head with a bat because we didn't have anyone minding them. It really is a safety issue."

My jaw drops open as I look between the two of them. I don't know what's going on, but it certainly feels like I'm the one out of the loop . . . but being pulled right into the middle of it.

"What do you say, Palmer?" Cole asks. "Will you be our team mom?"

I don't know if his thoughts go back to my "Daddy" comment from earlier this week or if it's just mine doing that. But as soon as a chuckle falls from my lips, he follows suit.

I should say no to this impromptu offer, but I'm weak. *That, and I owe Bud for those free cleats.* Besides, Ethan really would love my participation.

"Only if I get a whistle," I say over my shoulder as I head to the supply shed.

Bud catches up with me after saying something quickly to Cole. Together, we make our way behind the concession stand.

"This is great of you, Palmer," he says. "Thank you for helping us out. This year has been pure chaos."

"It's fine. I'll, um . . ."

I pause at the doorway, presumably to let Bud go in first. In reality, I stop because it hits me that I'm the team mom and Cole is the coach. That means I'll be collaborating with him.

Oh shit.

Even if my brain rebels against the idea, my body does not. It hums with appreciation and forces my mind to visualize situations that have no business being anywhere near a baseball field.

"See the mess?" Bud sweeps his arm around the compact building filled with baseball gear. "If you could just get it in some semblance of order—so the coaches can find the baseballs and bases, things like that—it would be so helpful."

"Oh, sure. I can try."

Bud smiles. "I owe you one." He starts to leave. "I have to get back to the sporting-goods store for a bit. We got a shipment in today, and I haven't even started to go through it. I'll come back and lock up in a couple of hours."

I look around at the mayhem around me. "Sure."

The shed creaks as Bud steps off the step, and I'm left alone.

There's no good place to start, so I grab all the errant baseballs that I can find and load them into empty buckets. Then I set them in the back corner until I can formulate a better plan.

My hands are dusty and white with chalk as I peer into bags, relocate bases, and try to figure out what to do with catcher's gear that was probably bought before I was born.

"This organization needs a fundraiser or something," I say, taking in the state of the equipment.

I need to pull things off the shelves and start to make sense of them, but a massive pitching machine is in the way. I try to push it to one side, to no avail. Then I grab the back and try to drag it deeper into the shed, but that doesn't work either. So I heave a breath and grab it from two sturdy pieces of metal in the front and push.

Nothing.

I rock it from side to side, wondering if it's stuck to the wooden floor.

It's not.

"Just move," I groan, grabbing the metal brackets again.

I squat, feeling my butt cheeks stretch the fabric of my yoga pants, and lean back on my heels. Then I pull with every muscle fiber in my body.

I pull until my face feels like it's going to burst. I give the machine another jiggle, hoping it will break free. But the only thing that breaks free is *me*.

"Ah!" I yelp as my movement propels me backward. My sneakers slip, my arms flail, and—*"Umph!"*

Suddenly, I'm not flying through the air but being scooped up and hauled into a hard chest.

Cole's deliciously hard chest.

I would've been more prepared to smash my face into the sharp end of a cleat, bang my head off a base, and then fall face-first into a bag of brick dust than to land in Cole's arms.

He turns me to face him. His hands lock against the small of my back. I'm not sure if it's to steady me or to hold me close, but I'm in no state to start assessing that kind of damage.

My nostrils fill with the scent of leather. A spike in my body temperature has me teetering on the edge of passing out. The contact of our bodies—chest to steel chest—makes my insides turn to mush.

"What the hell are you doing?" he asks, a chuckle in his tone.

The levity in the words is what lets me shuffle myself back into some semblance of a grown woman not in the throes of a lust-fueled breakdown.

I push away from Cole and then make a show of checking for injuries—mostly so I don't have to look at him.

"I was trying to move the pitching machine so I can organize around it," I say, dusting off my knees even though I didn't land on them.

"Where do you want it?"

He means the pitching machine. *Clearly.* I blame it on the fact that I was touching my knees and he was looking at me like he wanted me *on my knees* that my brain goes . . . elsewhere.

I look up and realize he's thinking the same thing.

He smirks. "The pitching machine, Palmer?"

"Oh. Yeah. Just . . . put it wherever it fits best." *What? Oh shit.* "I mean, just push it to the side."

This doesn't help.

I roll my eyes as he laughs.

"I'll help?" I say to avoid stumbling over more words that lead us both to the gutter.

"I think we're both safer if you just stay back."

My hand goes to my hip in defiance. "Like you can move it yourself. I can't even budge it."

He flips me a look, and then, as casually as reading the Sunday paper, he glides the machine to the entrance.

"I must've loosened it for you," I say.

"Sure." He crosses his arms over his chest. "So . . ."

"Don't you have a team to coach?"

He grins. "I do. And someone is hitting them pop flies. They can manage without me for a second."

"Are you sure? Because damage can happen in the blink of an eye."

"Yes. I think you just proved that."

I try not to smile at the cheeky bastard, but it's impossible.

"I actually came in here for another bag of balls," he says, looking around.

"They're in the corner. I just gathered them."

He steps toward me—likely toward the balls, but it's the same direction. So I take a step back. He moves closer. I retreat again. All the while we're performing this dance, our gazes are swimming in a dance of their own.

My breathing is ragged as he closes the distance between us. I lose focus on anything and everything but Cole and the circus in my chest.

I stop just in front of a tall shelving unit. Cole stops inches in front of me. His irises are pools of oceanic blue just before a storm.

Heaven help me.

My shoulders are back. My chin is lifted. Even though I'm nervous about whatever is about to happen, I'm also weirdly confident.

How can I not be? Cole makes it easy to be me. He makes it easy to like him. He makes it easy to do everything but breathe.

The air between us grows into a tizzy. I can almost hear the snaps and crackles of the electricity bolting between his body and mine.

He doesn't touch me. He doesn't even try.

And I wish he would.

The thought—spelled out in bright, wild letters flickering through my brain like a neon sign about to fizzle out—is impossible to miss.

I want him to touch me.

A surge of anxiety swamps me as I stare into his eyes, then across his chiseled jaw, and down his thick neck. My lips part and I drag in a breath, hoping it will still my energy.

You can't do this, Palmer. You have to be smart here.

"The answer is no," I say, sliding a swallow down my parched throat.

The corner of his lip quirks. "I didn't ask anything."

"You didn't have to."

It's there, right in front of me—an invitation to dinner. Or to *be* dinner, maybe.

My knees wobble.

It's been so long since I've been touched by a man. And despite my hands-off vibes, this man is still edging closer. In his unique, sweet *yet so fucking sexy way*.

"I know you feel this," he says, licking his bottom lip. The moisture left in its trail is enough to nearly make me whimper.

"I don't know what you're talking about."

My words are barely a whisper as my gaze fixes on his mouth.

"Then please explain the picture you liked at midnight from three years ago."

"My friend Val did that," I say, my tone surprisingly calm. "She has a thing for you."

His grin is decidedly alluring. "She does, huh?"

"I don't get it, but whatever."

"Right."

He moves his arm. I take a quick, rushed breath and hold it in my lungs. My body flexes, waiting on the contact . . . which never comes.

His eyes narrow as he twists his jaw back and forth. Finally, after working through something in his head, he relaxes his mouth.

"I'll make you a deal," he says.

"What?"

He widens his stance, his feet straddling mine. I'm perfectly capable of walking around him if I choose to. But I don't.

"Look me in the eye, right here, right now, and tell me you don't want me to kiss you," he says, his voice barely above a whisper. "If you do that, I'll believe you. We'll never be in this situation again."

What?

This was never about not wanting to kiss him.

My resolve slips. Slowly, second by second, my mind starts making excuses.

You can't waste too much time on him. He won't be here.

You're stronger than you've ever been. You can handle this. It's a measure of strength to go for what you want, and you want this.

You'll regret not saying yes.

I take a deep breath and fly the white flag.

Fuck it.

I cup his face in my hands and bring my lips to his. He's surprised for a split second before moving his mouth against mine.

He tastes like heat and peppermint, need and desire. There's a tenderness mixed with an urgency that nearly burns me and this stupid shed down.

His hands dig into my waist, his fingers pressing into the space just above my hips. I'm held in a frustrating, heady position between *holding me in place* and *pulling me into him*.

Every stroke of his tongue, each movement of his lips, is intentional. Measured. If I didn't know better, I might think he's been mapping this kiss out for days. *Just like I have.*

"*Wow,*" he says, pulling back with a smile.

I pant, catching my breath. Heat pools in my cheeks as I let my hands fall from his face.

I can't believe I just did that.

My head spins, relief washing over me with the finality of my decision. But in the second wave that comes around, I feel a surge of anxiety at how this might play out.

He takes a step back, pressing a finger to his lips as if he's sealing in the taste of my mouth.

"Cole . . ."

"I'm not about to press my luck," he says, backing away toward the door. "So I'm going to go back to my team."

I nod, gulping. "Yes. Do that. Please."

He stops, moves forward again, and grabs a bucket of balls. His gaze lingers on me, silently making promises that feel like threats, before he turns and walks out of the shed.

And I clean faster and with more energy than I ever have in my whole entire life.

CHAPTER FOURTEEN

Cole

"Okay. Let's gather around for a minute." I motion for the kids to join me on the pitcher's mound.

Fourteen boys scramble toward me. One has his shoes untied and nearly trips over his own feet. Another is carrying his friend on his back. A third has taken off his shirt. Again.

"Hey, Braylon—get your shirt back on," I say as he approaches. "It's not warm enough for that. Your muscles will get cold, and you'll pull something."

I added the last bit to make him feel like an athlete. It works. Thank God.

"I saw a lot of hard work today," I tell them. "Did you have fun?"

Their heads move up and down.

"Good. There's no sense in being out here if you aren't having fun. That doesn't mean that I'm not going to ask you to work hard and hustle—because I am. Everyone understand?"

They nod again.

"Hey, Coach," Braylon says. "When do we get to practice hitting dingers?"

"What's a dinger?" The boy who nearly tripped over his own feet wipes his nose with the back of his hands. "I don't get it. A dinger? Like . . . a wiener?"

The group laughs, much to the delight of the jokester.

"A dinger is a home run," I say once the laughter subsides. "And you can't hit one if you don't make contact with the ball. Right?"

I wait until they all nod or mutter their agreement.

"So we practice hitting the ball, using good mechanics, making contact. The dingers will come," I say. "But baseball is about so much more than home runs, guys. It's about working together to move the runners around the bases. Backing each other up. Communication. The little things like that are what makes the game both fun and successful."

I can see that I'm losing them, and I don't want that. The last thing I want to teach unintentionally is to tune me out.

"We'll meet here again on Monday at five thirty," I say.

"Not until Monday?" Ethan asks.

I smile at him. "The field is being used until Monday. It stinks, I know, but we have to use what we have."

"Okay," he says, kicking at a rock on the ground.

"All right. Let's get in here and give me 'Team!' on three." I hold my hand in the air and wait until a gaggle of gloves meet it. "One, two, three—*team*!"

We all drop our hands, and the boys mosey away.

I glance at the dugout to find the two fathers who have situated themselves as my co-coaches instructing the boys to get their stuff. They're nice guys, and I'm happy for the help, even if Dad said that they're name-dropping me all over town. Comes with the territory.

"Thanks for the help," I call out to them as they guide their own kids toward their trucks. They wave.

I'm turning toward home plate to gather the balls when I notice Ethan walking across the outfield. I follow his line of sight until I see Palmer waiting for him by the fence.

She kissed me.

A warmth blooms in my chest.

She tasted like cinnamon and sugar—like the top of a cake doughnut. Her lips were like pillows, soft and silky, and it took everything I had to pull away when I did. Because, if I didn't, I would've touched her body, and it would've been game over.

I walk toward her, knowing I can use the team mom excuse to talk to her if she balks.

And I have half a notion that she might just do that.

Ethan reaches her before I do. He hands her his stuff before hopping the fence.

"Hey," I call out, even though she sees me coming.

She smiles like we share a secret. Because we do.

"Hi," she says. "I'm glad you came over here."

I smile. "Really?"

"Yeah. I was going to ask you about the shed." Her lips press together, hiding a smile. "Bud said he'd be by to lock it up, but he hasn't come back. I don't want to just leave it open so someone breaks in, but I can't lock it up either."

"I'll take care of it."

"You sure?"

"Yup. I got it. No worries." I look at Ethan. "You did great today."

His eyes light up. "I did?"

"You sure did. Let me see your glove, though."

Palmer hands me Ethan's glove. I work it around, bending it in my hands.

"Do me a favor, okay?" I ask Ethan. "Get some glove oil. Bud's has some. It's pretty inexpensive. Then put it on your glove and work it in with a sponge."

"Okay," Ethan says as if I'm giving him the secret to curing cancer.

"Then I want you to take a ball and put it in the pocket of your glove where the webbing meets the palm. Wrap some rubber bands around it and leave it overnight. That'll help you break it in and make catching a little easier, okay?"

He looks up at Palmer. "Can we do that?"

"Absolutely."

"But I don't think we have a ball at home," he says. "I lost the one we had."

I point at the field. "Go grab one from out there. There are a dozen behind home plate."

"Are you sure?" he asks, bouncing on his toes.

"Yeah. I'll replace it. No worries."

"Thanks, Coach!"

Ethan springs over the fence and makes a mad dash toward home plate.

"Smooth way of getting me alone," Palmer says, leaning against the fence.

I lean against it from the other side so we're face-to-face.

"Happy coincidence," I say.

"Sure." She smiles at me. "I'm glad because we need to have a little conversation anyway."

Her smile falters just enough to make me concerned. *This is not where I thought this was going, I don't think.*

"What's up?" I ask, hoping it sounds as cool as I intended.

She takes a long, deep breath. "I kissed you—"

"And I loved it."

Her shoulders fall. "It was impulsive."

"It was spontaneous. That is, unless you've been thinking about it for days like I have. I've basically walked through that kiss a hundred times, so it was less spontaneity and more dream-to-reality for me."

"Cole."

"Why are you saying my name like a whole damn sentence?"

She sighs, glancing toward the field before focusing her laser-like attention on me. "I got caught up in the moment. For honesty's sake, I *have* been thinking about it for days, and that's probably why I did it."

"I don't see the problem here, Palmer."

"The problem is . . . I'm too old to be doing this. I've played around enough in my life—kissed enough boys behind sheds. Now I'm thirty-two and have nothing to show for it except the best kid in the world that I'm fully and solely responsible for."

I hold up a hand. "Whoa. Slow down. You're getting way ahead of yourself here."

She stands up too. "That's what I'm saying. I'm way ahead of where *this thing* between us is going."

"You do realize that I asked you to dinner and not to marry me, right?"

"Yes!"

I make a face because I'm confused as fuck. "Also, we kissed *in* the shed, not behind it. Surely that means something."

My attempt at levity goes unnoticed. That or ignored. Either way, she doesn't bite.

"Look, Cole. I'm not looking for a 'friends with benefits' thing or a one-night stand or even to bide some time with a guy because we're bored or have nothing better to do with our lives."

"Okay."

She hesitates, and I think she's going to clam up and change the topic. I fully expect her to crack a joke and then tell me she has to go.

But she doesn't.

"I want . . . *more*, Cole. I want to find a guy that I can settle down with. That will truly and actually love me. That will commit. That won't leave me hanging."

I don't know what to say to that. It's . . . a lot.

"I have a twelve-year-old son that deserves a family," she says. "And I keep picking guys that don't give a shit about that. They like having someone around to pick up after them or help them get off after a shitty day, but they aren't wanting to blend their lives and say 'This is us' to the world."

"No offense, but why would you want to be with a guy like that anyway?"

"Right?" She holds her arms out to her sides. "Excellent point. I don't. It was explained to me like this: my expectations for a male relationship are very low due to the experiences I had growing up. So me picking a partner is like going to the grocery store on an empty stomach and not knowing how to read the nutrition labels. I pick the lowest-hanging fruit that resembles the foods I know."

"Okay, that . . . that's going to take me a minute to process."

"You don't even have to process it. Basically, I've screwed up, and I'm trying to do better. My kid deserves for me to do better. A part of doing better is not picking men that are in the same food group that I choose—no offense."

I draw back, baffled. "I am offended, actually. Not that I know of whatever food spoilage you've consumed in your life, but I'm a full-on nutritional package."

She snorts.

Slowly, what she's saying starts to make sense. *I'm like the other guys she's dated, and they're all losers.*

I should keep my mouth shut and go on about my night because I have no interest in being *the one*. Hell, I can't be anyone's everything. I can't promise anyone shit—not even myself.

But I also don't understand how she's associating me with any man who had her and blew her off. *Fuck. That.*

She sighs. "I'm sorry. I shouldn't have lumped you in with them in such a general way."

"Or in any way, but thanks."

"I just meant that you're unavailable. You don't live here. You don't even live in a place that's remotely accessible to a girl in Ohio unless I hop on a plane for a half-day trip."

This is true. Completely true.

"You told me that you're a California boy. 'Sunshine and salt water.'" She half smiles, half frowns. "Kissing you was a big mistake. *Huge.*"

"Well, I mean, I wouldn't go that far."

She crosses her arms over her chest. "You, Mr. Beck, are a slippery slope. I think you know this."

I grin. *It's a compliment.*

"I'm going to have to relive that kiss for days now. Weeks, even," she says. "And that's not . . . that's stupid."

I *hear* what she's saying. I *understand* what she's saying. I *agree* with what she's saying.

But after a few moments of letting her words settle in my psyche, I'm still not convinced that she's right. The two of us spending time together, kissing—*or more*—does logically seem like a waste of time and a potential disaster when I go back home.

Because I *am* going back home.

So why does that logic, that common sense, fail to make me not want to see Palmer again?

"I'm not going to try to convince you to do something that you don't want to do," I say. "And I'm not going to lie to you and paint a picture that isn't real."

But as I lay the words on top of the fence between us, she recoils.

"But I will say this . . ." I take off my hat and run my fingers through my hair. "I think honesty cures a lot of miscommunications and problems in life."

"True."

I plop my hat back down on my head. "You don't want a relationship with me any more than I want one with you."

Her face falls, and it causes an uncomfortable blip in my chest.

"But two adults can be friends and have fun together and know that it's not going anywhere. Right?" I ask.

She nods slowly, like she's unsure.

"I have a helluva lot of fun when you're around," I say. "You make me smile and laugh, and you're so fucking beautiful."

Her whole face lights up.

"I don't want to cause you any problems," I say. "I just like being around you, Palmer. So if you change your mind and decide you want to hang out—"

"I picked them all up!" Ethan hits the fence like a train. The entire fence line shakes as he climbs it like a tree. "They're in the bucket."

"You got all the balls picked up?" I ask.

He hops off the top of the fence and lands on his feet. Then he spins around and grins from ear to ear. "Yup!"

"Thank you, buddy. That's super helpful."

"Sure!" He tosses a ball up in the air and catches it in his bare hands. "I'll be in the car, Mom."

"Okay. I'll just be a second."

Palmer turns to face me. She takes a long, deep breath. As she exhales, the shakiness is evident.

"You make me nervous," she says quietly. "Like, I hear what you're saying, but I don't know if I can be that much of an adult and remember . . ."

"Remember what?"

She grins. "I don't know if I can see the stop sign that we just plunked down at the end of baseball season. That's when you're leaving, right?"

I nod.

"So this is just . . ." Her voice trails off.

"It's whatever you want it to be. It's fun. It's friendly. It's killing some time until I go to Cali and you find your Prince Charming."

She levels her gaze with mine. The intensity, the soberness, buried in her eyes lights a fire in my core.

Fucking hell.

"If Val will watch Ethan for me Friday night—*and that's a big if*—maybe you could come over and we could order a pizza."

I grin. "Can't wait."

"Oh."

"Did you think I wouldn't take you up on that offer?"

She walks backward toward her car. There's a hesitation in her eyes, and I hold my breath to see what she says.

"I'll let you know what Val comes back to me with," she says, grinning. "But she might refuse because I'd get a meal with the guy she was trolling last night."

I let out a loud chuckle. "That was you, and you know it!"

She shrugs, as if that's all there is to say, and climbs into her car. Ethan waves as they pull out onto the street.

I wave back. Because that's all I can do besides wonder if I've just made the right decision.

The point Palmer made was valid. Can I respect the stop sign? Can I ignore how much she turns me on? Stirs something soul deep?

I have no fucking idea.

CHAPTER FIFTEEN

Cole

"Hey, Scott."

My agent asks me to wait a moment and then puts me on hold.

I walk along the tree line of my parents' property and breathe in the fresh air. The scent of pine and soil, still wet from the sudden rainstorm after yesterday's practice, fills my lungs and helps settle the frazzled state of my soul.

My body aches. My right arm is so tight from practice that it feels like it might snap like a recoiled rubber band. I work my shoulder in small circles like the physical therapist taught me, ignoring the scream of my muscles and the fire that bites down my spine.

I stop moving to catch my breath.

"Sorry about that," Scott says. "It's good to hear from you, Cole."

Right. Scott Canelo is full of shit. There's no way it's good to hear from me after our last conversation ended in a standoff. His frustration with the perceived lack of cooperation on my end makes him feel like I don't take the process seriously and that I don't appreciate his hard work. But I do.

Scott works his ass off to secure me postcareer opportunities. I absolutely respect his efforts and am grateful to have him on my side, even if my actions don't always match my appreciation.

"I just wanted to check in with you and see how things are going," I say, breaking the ice. It seems a better way to start the conversation than admitting that my feelings haven't changed and I still need time.

"Things are looking good here," he says. "We still have the streaming opportunity on deck. The network sent a proposal over this morning, but I don't think my secretary has forwarded it to you yet."

"I haven't checked my email since this morning, but I didn't see it."

"Yeah, she was pretty swamped today. Give her a day or two, and I'm sure she'll have it to you. By the middle of next week at the latest." Papers shuffle in the background. "We still have the podcast deal sitting here, waiting on a response. Have you given that any more thought?"

I hang my head and walk aimlessly around a large pine tree.

"I have," I say honestly. "But I'd like to give it a few more weeks and really think it through."

Scott sighs. "Cole, I understand that you have a lot going on and a lot of decisions to make in this new season of your life."

You have no idea.

"But, like I've told you since we first discussed your retirement—which, I will remind you, happened practically overnight, with no forewarning—your chances of securing something lucrative are highest in the immediate days and weeks following the announcement. Cole, we're already going on month three here—"

"I know. As you said, we've discussed this several times, and you've made it clear that I need to pull the trigger on something."

Like I pay you to do.

"But there are a couple of things still up in the air that affect my decisions, and I just don't have all the information yet."

"And you still choose not to fill me in on those pieces of the puzzle?"

"That's correct."

My jaw pulses as I think about those puzzle pieces and how fucking helpless I feel. It's like standing in the batter's box, amped up and prepped to hit a home run, and having to wait as the opposing side changes pitchers. All I can do is wait.

How is this even my life?

My stomach sinks. A fire boils in my gut, threatening to spew the negativity that simmers just below the surface. I can't deal with all this—the questions from Scott, the uncertainty of my life, the what-ifs that come to meet me every night as the sun dips below the horizon.

It's not like me to take this approach to problems. I've always met challenges head-on, armed with information and preparation and a game plan to slay the beast, whatever it may be.

But this time? This time it's not up to me.

"I understand that, Cole. I really do," Scott says. "And I want you to take your time. I want you to make the right choice for you and your family. Well, you don't have a family, so that should make your choice that much easier."

What the fuck?

"You know that I never want you to rush into a decision," he says, continuing on like he didn't just toss a dig at me. "But, as your agent, it is my responsibility to get you the best deals that I can. I'm going to be honest here and take the blanket off the baby—the offers will dwindle if we don't jump on something soon."

"I know."

"We can even just enter into official negotiations, but we're going to have to shit or get off the pot, for a lack of a more professional term."

"Yeah."

My eyes fall closed and I stand still, recentering my breath and heartbeat. I lift my chin to the sky and blow every bit of air in my body out into the world.

I'm fine. It's going to be fine.

"Let me reiterate something," I say. "I'm not just interested in the money. There's a lot more at play here."

"I'm aware. You have a lot in the bank. I get that. But think about it. If you're going to do something—let's say, get on a podcast—I'd rather you sign for five million now instead of waiting and getting one or two million in a couple of months. It doesn't make any sense to leave that kind of money on the table."

The meaning, or at least part of it, is squeezed in between the lines. Scott gets a pretty percentage of all my deals. He wants to get paid too. But he also doesn't understand anything outside of himself. He's one of the most selfish people I've ever known.

My spirits drop because I know my indecisiveness is costing him too. But it's not like I'm dragging my feet over nothing.

"Your pause is making me pause," he says.

I run a hand down my jaw and over my chin. "A couple of weeks. Let me work through a few things and have some conversations, okay? I'll get back to you as soon as I can."

"Okay," he says as if it's not okay at all.

I wish I could explain. I wish I could tell him why this is so fucking complicated and why I announced the end of my career during a seventy-two-hour window.

It would feel so good to blow up and let my emotions explode into the world and not have to keep them cooped up inside me anymore. *And not have to hide things from my parents.*

Scott would understand. How could he not? It should be blatantly obvious why I bailed and retreated to Ohio and then have hesitated to commit to anything for the time being. But that conversation isn't one I'm ready to have—not with Scott, not with Fish, and not with my parents.

Not yet. *Which makes this side of retirement pretty fucking lonely, if I'm honest.*

Sharing anything with the people in my life at this point would be selfish. I don't have enough details. I can't answer the questions I'm sure they'll have. All I would do is unload my fear onto them and make them carry that around—on top of their own shit.

I'm not that kind of man. I carry my own weight in relationships, whether personal or professional. Period.

"Should I continue to feel out opportunities on your behalf?" he asks. "Because I don't want to court relationships if you're not interested."

"Yes. Please do. I'll make a decision before I leave Ohio in six or eight weeks."

"No offense, but what the hell are you doing in Ohio for six fucking weeks?"

I grin. "I'm coaching a kids' baseball team."

"You're fucking with me?"

"No. It wasn't on my to-do list, but it's actually a lot of fun so far. Who knew?"

He laughs. "All right. I have five calls to make before I can leave the office, and I'd like to get home by midnight so my wife stops threatening to divorce me. Get back to me as soon as you can, and I'll make sure my secretary gets you the streaming offer, if she hasn't already."

"Awesome. Thanks, Scott."

"Take care."

And the line goes dead.

I turn back toward the house. The kitchen light is on. My mother's shadow sneaks across the window as she moves around, probably making dinner. I stand in the field and watch her like I'm casing the joint when, in reality, I'm trying to steal a piece of her peace.

Even in my wildest dreams, I never expected to be in my thirties and feeling so uncertain about my life. I'm Cole Beck. I'm a baseball legend. And here I am, at my parents' house, under the guise of spending some time with them because they need it. In reality, I'm the one who needs it.

Fuck Scott and his remark about not having a family to consider in my long-term plans. Sure, I'm single—*happily*—but what the fuck? That doesn't mean that I don't have a family. And it doesn't mean that I don't have priorities and dreams. Maybe someday I will have a family, and whatever decision I make could affect that.

I'm walking toward the house, giving myself a mental pep talk, when my phone buzzes in my hand. I look down, expecting it to be Fish, but am pleasantly surprised that it's not.

Palmer:

I didn't handle any of that very well, did I?

I grin, my fingers flying across the screen.

Me:

So, you do know how to text. 😈

Palmer:

Very funny.

Me:

I have no complaints. At least you figured it out.

I stop walking and stare at my phone. Finally, her response pops up.

Palmer:

I didn't mean to come across as so hot and cold. I know that I've done that and it's embarrassing. I'm not playing games with you or anything like that. I just have a hard time bridging the gap between what I want, what I need, and what I need to want.

Me:

I appreciate that. But you have nothing to be embarrassed about. You aren't the only one that feels that way about things in their life.

Palmer:

Thank you. It's just so frustrating.

Me:

Believe it or not, your frustration came through in your above text. 😉

Palmer:

Very funny. 😆

Me:

What's going on? Boil it down for me.

Palmer:

Okay. It's simple. I'm attracted to you. But I need to stay focused on what's best for me. Long-term. For Ethan too. I need to want what's best for me, which has always been my Achilles Heel.

Me:

I feel like my best bet here is for me to focus on the you being attracted to me part.

Palmer:

That's the part that I'm having a hard time not paying the most attention to.

My shoulders ease as I relish the simpleness of the exchange. The banter. This amusing, intriguing woman. Even though she's rejected me—a few times—this is the only easy thing in my life at the moment.

It occurs to me as I stand beside the picnic table that this is precisely why I can't shrug this woman off.

She's the only thing that feels right to me right now.

Me:

So, about the pizza—what kind of pizza do you like?

I asked not because I care about what pizza toppings she prefers but because ending this conversation feels lonely. And besides, she reached out to me. Maybe she's lonely too.

Palmer:

Anything but olives. You?

Me:

I've never met a pizza that I didn't like.

Palmer:

I was afraid you were going to pull some California pizza thing on me with cauliflower crust and a broccoli Rabe topping.

Me:

I mean, to each their own but that description does not equal a pizza to me in any way, shape, or form.

Palmer:

Thank God. Also, now is a good time to tell you that Val set aside her frustration that you chose to have dinner with me and not her after her overt picture-liking and said she'd be happy to watch Ethan on Friday.

Me:

That's the second-best thing to happen to me this week. 😉 😙

I watch with bated breath for another message to pop up on my screen. Just when I'm scrambling to put together a message to keep the banter flowing, my phone dings.

Palmer:

🙈 I've got to get this kid to bed. But, before that, we're going to have a battle about taking a shower. What is it about preteen boys not wanting to shower? I just don't understand.

Me:

I think it's less about the shower and more about being able to exert control over your own body. I've actually never thought about this until now but that's what came to mind as I remember being his age. I wanted to decide what I could do with my body. I didn't want my mom telling me.

Palmer:

So you fought your mom about taking a shower too?

Me:

Yes, ma'am.

Palmer:

Did you also fight her about wearing a coat in the winter?

Me:

No. I didn't want to be cold. But I do recall someone *coughs* you *coughs* that didn't wear a jacket to practice.

Palmer:

😬

Me:

😄 I will see you Friday unless I run into you before that.

Palmer:

Sounds like a plan. And thanks for everything you're doing with the boys. Ethan talks about baseball constantly. We stopped and got the glove oil you mentioned. It's really nice to see him so excited about something.

Me:

He's a nice kid. It's my pleasure.

I wait for a long time to see if she responds, but she doesn't. I wonder if she's also staring at the word "pleasure" and comparing that with the taste of our kiss earlier today.

Me:

Good night, Palmer. Say good night to Ethan for me.

Palmer:

Good night, Cole. I will.

I slide my phone into my pocket, but I don't move. Instead, I stand in the stillness of the country evening and think about the wild-haired woman who has captured my attention.

It occurs to me that I really know nothing about her—way less than I usually know before I have a meal with someone. Interestingly enough, I've had *more* conversations with Palmer than I usually have before a first date, but I actually know *less*.

Our chats are more generalized and about nothing and are less set up. Maybe that's why I think about her all the time. This *thing* between us is more authentic, more organic—all happenstance.

I blow out a breath and look up. Mom is standing on the back porch, waving her hand to tell me it's time for dinner.

Nothing is fixed and nothing is better. But the ball in my stomach is somehow a little less raw.

CHAPTER SIXTEEN

PALMER

"Why does he do this?" I growl at the computer. "He does this intentionally."

Burt's company credit card is on the screen. The charges are half-legit and half-bogus—I know Kirk didn't authorize a one-hundred-dollar dinner at Texas Roadhouse.

I sit back in my chair and rub my eyes. I'm not sure if they burn from irritation or from staring at the computer all morning. Either way, they're so dry that I think they might combust.

My gaze slips across Burt's online statement. "Why do you do this?"

Sadly, I think I know the answer. I think he does it to see if he can get away with it. There's a twisted part of the old man that I think gets off on costing me time and making me have to email him to explain the charges.

"Not today, buddy," I say, scooting my chair up to the computer. "Today is the day I copy Kirk directly on the email."

I should've done this before now. Instead of just handling it myself and clueing Kirk in later, I should've dragged Burt in front of our boss and let the truth be told. I yawn. *I'm so done making do.*

I'm about to open a new email and attach Burt's statement when my cell phone buzzes on my desk. Jared's name flashes on the screen.

My heart leaps in my chest, and I mentally calculate the time and Ethan's location. *It's eleven in the morning. Ethan is at school.*

"Hey, Kirk," I call out. "Jared is calling. I'm going to take it outside, okay?"

"Go. I hope everything is okay."

Me too.

"Hey, Jared," I say, pushing the office door open. A blast of cool air smashes me in the face. "What's happening?"

"Hi, Palm. What are you up to today?"

I roll my eyes. "I'm at work, like I am every other day of the week from six a.m. to five p.m.—except Saturdays." But I often have to show up then too. "What are you doing? Why are you calling me?"

"Easy there, Palm. You're awful testy today."

His laugh fuels my irritation.

"I've dealt with idiots all day long. Please do not add to the tally."

"Cool. I'll make it quick then." He takes a deep breath. "I'm getting evicted. Well, I got evicted. I just made it easier on them and went ahead and left."

All the oxygen rushes out of my body as I stare at the bright-blue sky. *You've got to be kidding me.*

A hundred thoughts cross my mind, but I boil them down to one.

"Why?" I ask, even though it's really none of my business why he got kicked out of his house. The only part that's any of my business is how it will affect Ethan.

"I got behind on my rent, and the landlord's wife told me I would be okay if I just added a little cash each month to catch up. Well, the landlord apparently didn't agree and wouldn't honor the deal. He tacked a thirty-day notice to the door a couple of days ago. Nice, huh?"

"Honestly? I'm less concerned about their manners and more concerned about where you might be living when our son visits." *When you have him all of one day a month.*

He takes a deep breath. "Well, here's the thing . . ."

I don't know where he's going with this, but I know that I'm about to hate it.

"You know I don't love it when you start sentences like that," I say.

"Robbie got a job in Cleveland, and he was basically telling me that he can hook me up with something too. I know it's a little far, but I could really turn shit around fast and be back down here in a new place. You know, it can all work out real easy."

Are you fucking kidding me?

I struggle to keep my frustration with this man contained. He's just moving to Cleveland like that? To work with Robbie, no less—a man who couldn't make a legal living if he had to.

My throat pulls together. I march across the parking lot away from the office in case I need to scream.

Or cry. Who knows?

"You know, Jared, I'm not your mother and I'm not your girlfriend. But I am the mother of your child, which makes me somewhat inclined to not want to see you dead or end up in prison."

"That might be the nicest thing you've ever said to me," he jokes.

I roll my eyes. "I'm reading between the lines here, and I'm not sure what you're going to do up there, but it doesn't feel like a great solution to the problem at hand."

He breathes heavily into the phone. His frustration that I'm not rolling over and cheerleading his next bright idea pisses him off.

I brace myself for his retaliation—because there will be retaliation—but I can't let this go.

"What do you suggest, then? Huh?" he asks. "Because that's what you do, Palm. You're so quick to point out fucking problems and never have a fucking solution."

"This is my fault? Oh, wait. Of course it is. Why wouldn't this be my fault?"

My temples pound with a rush of blood flow as I grit my teeth and try to stay calm. I lean back against the trunk of my car. The cold metal bites into my skin, but I'm too riled up to register it.

"My solution to the problem would've been not to get into the situation in the first place," I say with all the calmness I can muster.

"Hindsight's twenty-twenty."

"So is foresight. If you don't pay your rent, they're going to evict you. And you know as well as I do that the landlord's wife pocketed whatever cash you paid toward your rent. You were fooling yourself to think that was going to go over because this nearly happened six months ago, and you didn't learn your lesson!"

"You love it when I have to learn a lesson, don't you?"

"No. I don't, actually," I say, rubbing my forehead. "I don't even care. I only care about Ethan, and right now I'm trying to figure out what this looks like for him."

Our son's name hangs in the air.

"I'm worried about him too," Jared says, his voice dripping with anger. "That's why I'm doing this. That's why I'm going to Cleveland and—"

"No. It's not."

I can't take it anymore. I can't let him walk out of Ethan's life, again—because that's what this is—and pretend like everything is fine and Jared is some kind of father of the year.

"What the fuck do you mean?" he asks.

"Let's be honest here since we're fighting anyway. You're going to Cleveland because it's the easiest decision for you and seems the most fun. It has nothing to do with Ethan or what's best for him because you don't even factor him in your life when you live here."

The line goes eerily silent. I'm sure Jared is shocked that I've broached this topic because it's one I usually avoid to keep the peace.

But my filter has broken. This man has hurt my son over and over, and I can't be silent anymore.

This is so fucking unfair for Ethan. Again.

I pull the phone away from my face so I can catch my breath without breathing into the line. My heart pounds, and my mind races through a million scenarios about how this will end up.

"I'm sorry that I'm not parenting to your standards," he says.

"See? That doesn't make sense because I don't hold you to any standards. Clearly. I let you do what you do and try to be happy that you can fit him into one weekend a month, at best. I mean, I do think it's fucked up that you don't prioritize your one child into your life, but that's on you. Not me."

"I signed him up for baseball, didn't I? Isn't that what dads do?"

"No. Dads play baseball with their kids. They play catch. They—"

"I bought him a fucking glove. Do you know how much that fucking thing costs?"

"Oh, I'm sorry," I say, shoving off my car. "I'm sorry for not acknowledging that sixty, seventy dollars that you spent on a baseball glove. Do you know how much it costs to feed Ethan? To clothe him? To keep him warm? Or to buy the batting helmet that I'm going to have to buy this week so he doesn't get head lice? Because you know what's expensive? Head lice treatment."

Jared doesn't say a word, so I keep going.

"I don't ask you for a dime because all child support will do is get you in a bind, and I'd rather you not give me a penny and stay out of jail than the reverse. And I don't bring that up. Wanna know why? Because he's my kid. I'm his mother. That's what mothers do. We take care of our children, whether the fathers step up or not."

"Well, aren't you just a peach?" He spits the sentence at me. "You know, I was hoping we could work something out, and I could, I don't know, meet you one weekend a month and take him to Cleveland with me—"

"No. There is no way in hell that you are taking our son to Cleveland to live . . . where? Where would he stay? With Robbie?" I laugh out loud—louder than I anticipated. "No. You are welcome to come and see Ethan anytime. I'll even let you stay in my guest room to facilitate it because I do want him to have a relationship with you. But I will not let him go to a place with people I don't trust in a situation that I don't think is safe for him—or you, for that matter. But that's neither here nor there at this point."

"You're going to keep him from me?"

I half laugh and half sigh. "That's what you took from that?"

"That's what you said. You just make damn sure you tell him that this is your doing. I offered to see him."

My heart sinks in my chest as reality collapses around me. I slump against the trunk of my car again.

"I'll do what I always do, Jared. I'll make sure this is as easy for Ethan as I can. I don't know what I'll tell him this time. Maybe I'll paint it like you actually have a job and are getting your shit straight. But just know that I don't do this for you. I do it for him."

"You do it for you because you get that little ripple of being the hero, don't you?"

I ignore him. There's no sense in arguing with someone who will never even acknowledge that you have a point or opinion that should be considered. But then I think about Ethan's take on Jared's absence.

"He doesn't wake up thinking about me at all."

And how my heart crashed when Ethan told me why he was playing baseball.

"I do want to play. Want to know why? Because I told Dad I would. I want him to see what it's like for someone to follow through on their promises."

"I'm going to say one more thing," I say. "Ethan is getting older, and there will come a time soon that I can't smudge reality for you. He's going to see right through it, and that's going to be on you. Not me."

"It's always on me. I'm always the fuckup. Just ask you."

Even though he can't see me, I shrug. It's all I can do.

"Make it right while you can," I say.

"Ha. There's a solution. You're finally offering a solution." He laughs angrily. "I think this is the first time that you've ever actually proposed a problem and then a potential solution. Of course, it's because I'm a loser, according to you. But it's a solution nonetheless."

I sigh. "Are you done here? Like, do I need to come by and pick up anything of Ethan's at your place? Or do you want to swing by and tell him goodbye?"

"I'm already on the road. I cleared everything out last night. He didn't have anything there."

That's telling.

"He's at school, right?" he asks.

"Yeah."

"Okay. Well, tell him his dad loves him. Thanks for making me feel like a deadbeat, Palm."

"Jared . . . whatever."

The line goes dead.

I sink against the car and close my eyes. The corners of my world start to shrink. My insides constrict like I'm being strapped back into the same roller coaster that I keep finding myself in and can't seem to avoid.

Please don't let this break Ethan's heart.

I press off the car and head back toward the office with a slower pace than I walked out here with. I have too much work to do to stand in the cold and ruminate over Jared's ineptitude.

But the fact that Ethan has been so happy lately does dull my gloominess a bit and gives me hope that maybe he'll have something to distract him from the news that his dad has left without saying goodbye.

The image of his little face as he wrapped the rubber bands around his glove last night boosts my spirits.

Maybe Jared signing him up for baseball was a gift, after all.

My brain makes the quick, natural transition from baseball to Cole. That's the final shot of adrenaline to my heart that I needed. Cole might not be a solution to anything, but at least the pizza night tonight is something to look forward to.

I touch my lips as I remember the taste of Cole's. I shiver as I remember the way his hands felt as he caught me from landing on my ass. It was a brief moment, part humiliation and part foreplay, but it's a moment in time I won't forget, because for that split second, I felt something that I've never felt before.

I was safe.

Even though I know the feeling is fleeting and I can never find permanent safety with a man who doesn't reside in my world, I relish it. I recall the warmth and the support and strength . . . and then let it go.

There's no use getting too comfortable in that memory. He's not a permanent fixture in my life . . . or Ethan's.

My heart sinks as I slip back to reality.

Ethan has already formed an affinity for Cole. I have to be very, very careful. I can't set him up for heartbreak either.

CHAPTER SEVENTEEN

Cole

"That's it," I say to myself.

I steer Dad's truck into the narrow gravel driveway beside the bright-blue mailbox. The address matches the one my mother gave me when I realized that I don't know where Palmer lives.

That was probably a mistake.

Mom's *entire being* lit up at my inquiry. She was far too willing to assist. My repeated lines of *It's for baseball*, *She's the team mom*, and *Don't read anything into this* were intentionally ignored.

That's a conversation that will have to be continued another day.

Rocks crunch against the tires. I drive around sedan-size potholes and cringe as tree branches scrape the top of the truck. I pass a barn that seems to be holding on by sheer will. A basketball hoop hangs lopsided just above the doors.

I park next to Palmer's burgundy compact car and cut the engine. The silence is deafening.

The truck door squeals as I open it. My shoes hit the soft earth with a thud. I look around and breathe.

I've heard people say they can feel oxygen fill their bodies. Fish says it every time he visits the mountains. The only time I've ever experienced anything like that is when I'm getting oxygen as a part of the recovery process after a game or training session—and now.

Leaves flutter above my head as I take in Palmer's house. It's a mossy-green, two-story home with reddish-hued wood trim. A light glows beside the deep-brown door, inviting me onto the porch.

A swing hangs off the rafters, moving gently in the breeze. I make my way past it and to the door, then knock twice.

My mouth goes dry as I stand on the welcome mat and wait for Palmer to answer. A thought, a brief one, races through my mind and asks me if I should be here.

Should I be? My heart pounds. *I don't know. But I'm not about to get back in the truck and leave.*

Palmer catches me off guard when she opens the door. I turn toward her, shifting my gaze from a row of pine trees to the stunner in the doorway.

Holy shit.

She's wearing a pair of camouflage pants that look soft to the touch. A cream shirt that has four tiny buttons at the top, three of them undone, skirts her curves. Her hair is half-up, half-down, and I immediately think of kissing her on the exposed piece of skin just behind her ear.

"Hey," she says, leaning against the door. "Did you just realize where you were or what?"

"No." I chuckle. "Sorry. My mind was wandering."

"I mean, there's no pressure if you'd like to leave."

She pretends like she's going to close the door in my face. Or maybe that's what she is going to do. But I reach out and catch the corner with my hand and grin.

Her pupils widen as a small, soft grin spreads across her lips. "Okay, then. Come on in."

"Thank you."

I step inside her house, and a thought hits me instantaneously. *This isn't a house. It's a home.*

I'm not sure what I expected, if anything, when I showed up at Palmer's. But this? This isn't it.

The air is lightly perfumed with citrus, as if love and laughter take place here often. The walls are suffused with the aroma of home-cooked meals. It's not really a scent but a warmth. I know because my mother's house has the same vibe, and no matter what I do in my own house, I cannot duplicate it.

I've tried.

Books pepper the room in front of me. On all available surfaces sit spines with topics ranging from the wildlife of Ohio to the benefits of essential oils. Pictures are propped up on a small mantel above a fireplace that's seen better days, and a painting of what might be a dog with the words LOVE, ETHAN hangs in the corner of an oversize mirror by the front door.

"Welcome to my humble abode," Palmer says as she shuts the door behind me.

"I love it."

She blows me off. "It's not the greatest thing ever, but it works."

I consider telling her what I was thinking only a few seconds ago, but I don't. I don't want her to think I'm pandering to her.

"Do you mind if I look out the window?" I ask, motioning toward the large picture window directly across from me.

"Sure. Go ahead."

She steps to the side and allows me to walk by her. I avoid my natural inclination to touch her. Instead, I march on by to the glass that promises a view of green.

"It's not salt water," she says, coming up beside me. "But I like it."

"This is really spectacular."

She laughs. "It's a lawn and woods. It's more common, less spectacular, but thanks."

The backyard is bright and green, littered with a multitude of kids' toys. A swing set sits next to a haphazard square filled with sand. Weeds poke through the beachy material, and I wonder how long it's been since Ethan played in it.

A bike is propped up against a tree beside a bright-orange circle that I think is a sled.

A sled in the spring? I have so many questions.

"I keep thinking that one day I'll get a hammock and stretch it between those two trees," she says, pointing to a couple of large tulip poplars near the bike.

"Great idea. Have you not lived here long?"

She laughs again. "I moved here shortly after Jared and I broke things off. My boss, Kirk, actually owns this place and gives me a great deal on the rent. Otherwise, we'd be living in a box somewhere."

I'm not sure what my face does, but Palmer bumps my shoulder.

"I was kidding." She grins. "I'd at least be able to live in one of the buses at Skoolie's."

I'm not sure why she thinks that's funny. Maybe because she knows she's joking. But I really don't find much amusement in it.

She walks out of the room, talking to me over her shoulder. "Do you want a drink?"

"Yeah. Sure," I say, following her.

She leads me into a bright-white kitchen. The counters are black and gray, made out of some kind of laminate, and the floors are the same hardwood as the living room and foyer.

"I have pop, water, and milk," she says, peering into the fridge. "But I wouldn't trust the milk."

"Pop?"

Of course I know what she means. I've traveled across America enough to know that some parts of the country use the word "pop" instead of "soda." But hearing it out of her mouth is adorable.

"Coke. Coca-Cola, to be precise. In the Midwest, it's just pop. Order a pop, you'll get a Coke."

I smile. "I'll take a pop."

She goes to work getting two glasses and then filling them with ice.

"Tell me about Skoolie's," I say, keeping the bar in between us. "What do you do there?"

"We sell buses and bus parts. I know it sounds kind of off the wall, like how big could that market possibly be, but it's huge." She hands me a glass and a Coke. "We sell to customers all over North and Central America."

"Thanks," I say, taking the drink. "That sounds really complicated."

Her eyes shimmer. "Oh, it can be. There's a ton of red tape and logistics, and it can be a total nightmare. But, secretly, I love it."

I knew that before you said it.

We carry our glasses back into the living room and then down a set of stairs. Pictures of Ethan in various stages of his life are hung on the walls down the staircase.

Palmer turns to me. "Wanna sit down?" She nibbles her bottom lip. "It's more comfortable down here. The furniture upstairs is way too stiff, and we never sit up there."

Even if I couldn't hear the wobble in her voice, I could see the apprehension on her face. It makes me want to hug her, to tell her everything will be all right, but I don't reach for her because something tells me that might be what she's worried about.

I take a seat on the end of the gray sofa. She moseys around before sitting on the opposite end.

"What happened to your friend . . . Fish?" she asks. "Wasn't that his name?"

"Yeah. He's in Cincinnati right now. He grew up not too far from here. He supports a lot of small businesses around southern Ohio and has his hands in all kinds of cookie jars, so to speak."

"Oh."

"I think he's coming tomorrow, maybe. Just to say hello before he heads back to San Diego."

She taps her fingertips against the glass. "Do you guys live close to each other?"

"No. Not really. We see each other at work—*saw* each other at work," I say, correcting myself. "And then in the off-season, Fish usually comes back to Ohio."

"So you have other friends there you hang out with?"

It's a straightforward question, but it's super awkward in my soul.

"Actually, not really." I chuckle in surprise. "I mean, I have a group of friends that I vacation with in the off-season and might grab a dinner with during the season, but there wasn't time for that kind of stuff late February through October."

Her eyes go wide as she sips her drink.

"It's one of the trade-offs you make to play pro ball," I say, as if that should wash away her surprise.

But it doesn't.

She takes a long drink and then sets her glass on the coffee table. "So what happens now for you? You get to just reinvent your life?" She leans back into the sofa cushions. "That actually sounds pretty amazing."

I mirror her posture and lean back too. "I mean, I guess that's what I'm doing. I haven't thought about it like that."

"It has to be a little nerve racking. You've done one thing your whole life, and now you have to fill your days with something else. How do you feel about it?"

How do I feel about it?

No one, not one single fucking person, has asked me this. Everyone always makes assumptions about my retirement. The Swifts management assumed my shoulder was torched. My agent figures I want to make easier money. My parents are closest to the truth and think that there's something I'm not saying, but even they haven't asked me how I feel about things.

But Palmer did.

My heart squeezes in my chest so tight that I squirm. "I'm okay."

"Do you want me to take that at face value, or do you want me to push?"

I laugh. "I told you I'm okay."

"'Okay' is such a nondescript word. It's what I would say if someone asked me about my relationship with Jared and I didn't want to spew the truth. 'It's okay.' That's what I'd say."

"Let's go there. What's he like?"

She rolls her eyes and sighs. "He's *not* okay."

"I sense a little anger."

"You're wrong." She levels her gaze with mine. "There's *a lot* of anger there. He moved to Cleveland today. Didn't even say goodbye to Ethan. Just called me and dropped the news—managing to toss some blame my way for his failures in life, per usual—while driving."

My jaw hangs open. "He just left your kid?"

She nods.

"Wow," I say, running a hand down my thigh. "That's . . . yeah."

"*Yeah.* Which brings me back to what I was saying earlier about you getting to create something new for yourself. There's an excitement about that."

I don't know if I'd say "excitement."

I sit up and take a drink of my Coke. "It's a lot to figure out. Don't get me wrong—I'm very, very lucky to be in the situation that I'm in. I don't take it for granted for a second. But figuring out the rest of your life . . . it makes me feel like a teenager again. So many choices and not sure what path is the right one. The fear of choosing the wrong one."

Especially with all the unknowns.

"You must have some idea about what you want to do, right?" she asks.

I wrap my hand around my glass. "It's not as easy as you think."

She grins. "Oh, I disagree."

"Fine, Miss Clark. You get to reinvent your life today. Right now. What are you doing?"

She sits up and folds her hands on her lap. "What are the parameters?"

"What do you mean?"

"Like, how much money do I get? Do I have to consider Jared in this fake world? Do I have a passport?"

"You don't have a passport?"

She laughs. "Don't judge me!"

"Not judging," I say, my lips parting right along with hers. "Sorry. Carry on."

"Can't. I don't have the parameters."

"Oh. Right. Sorry. You have infinite money, forget Jared, and you definitely have a passport."

She squeals, then shifts her weight around until her legs are pulled up beneath her. The carefree, relaxed look that's painted on her face makes her look even prettier than before.

I wish I could keep it there.

"What would I do?" She looks at the ceiling. "Damn. This is harder than I thought."

"See?"

She drops her chin and looks at me like I've lost my mind. "It's not that hard. First-world problems, buddy."

"I'm aware of that."

She takes a long, deep breath. "You know what I think I'd do?"

"What's that?"

Palmer shakes her head and shrugs, sprinkling a light, bright laugh through the air like pixie dust.

"I don't think I'd do anything differently," she says. "How weird is that? I mean, I'm a thousand times more likely to tell Burt to fuck off,

I'd never cook again, and I'd take a vacation every other month. But I think that's it."

She reclines again, pressing her lips together. Her brows pull together, and I can't quite read what she's thinking.

"Should I ask you how *you* feel about it?" I ask, laughing. "You seem perplexed and on the brink of a crisis."

She turns her head toward me and smiles. "I'm always on the brink of a crisis."

"You play it off so well."

We chuckle. Our voices mix together, dancing around the room in a comfortable familiarity that feels *nice*. If only she knew that I think I might be on the brink of a crisis too. I just hope I play it off as well as she does.

She opens her mouth but is interrupted by the ringing of the doorbell.

"Pizza," she says, getting to her feet. "If you want to wait here, I'll bring it down."

"I'll come up and pay."

"I got it."

"No," I say, shaking my head. "I'm not letting you pay for dinner."

"Well, I foresaw this conversation and paid for it when I ordered. Already tipped the driver too." She winks. "Be right back."

I watch her take the stairs two at a time, wishing I had her energy and joy.

"You know what I think I'd do? I don't think I'd do anything differently."

How do I get that? How do I get to that place of contentment?

Maybe if I had a home to come home to, I'd be the same. But I'll have to file that under *Things I'll Probably Never Have.*

CHAPTER EIGHTEEN

PALMER

"No," I say, patting my full tummy. "You're wrong. He was the one that slept with her sister and knocked her up."

Cole's brows pull together. He points at the screen. "Him? Are you sure? Isn't that the other dude's twin?"

I laugh and roll my head to the side. "Are you even watching this?" I pause the television.

Cole is sitting on the opposite end of the sofa with his legs stretched out across the ottoman. His feet dangle off the end. He removed his shoes at some point before we started the movie we found by flippantly scrolling through the television channels and discussing what kinds of shows we like and dislike.

The last few rays of the evening sneak in the window. They cast a warm, snuggly glow over his handsome face. Coupled with how relaxed he looks and how comfortable I am . . . it's a dangerous, if not welcome, combination.

I stretch, wiggling my toes and enjoying the pull through my muscles. It's an odd sensation to just sit and be. Typically, if Ethan is gone, I'm tackling chores or feeling guilty about all the time I'm wasting not doing something on my never-ending to-do list.

But this? It wasn't on my to-do list, and I don't feel guilty about it.

Actually, I'm enjoying it. *Profusely.*

"Can I ask you a question?" Cole asks, breaking my concentration on the sweet smile on his lips.

"Sure. What?"

"Why do women like these movies?"

"What kind of movies? Like the one we're watching?"

"Yeah. I mean, you know that they're going to end up together in the end. They tell you that in the opening credits."

"So?"

He laughs. "So—where is the excitement?"

"Oh, Cole," I say, sighing with enough dramatics to rival the actress on the screen.

"That's your answer?" he teases. "*Oh, Cole?* That sounds more like what I expect will come in the movie in about another ten minutes."

I giggle as I sit upright and pull my knees toward me. "And that's the reason women—*I*—like these kinds of movies."

He pushes up with both hands and swivels his body to face mine.

I add, "It's . . ." I try to think of a way to describe it without sounding like a dork. "It gives people hope. You know, take our heroine in the movie. She's a single mom. Her husband impregnated her sister—"

"On a yacht."

I roll my eyes. "That's the fantasy factor. There's more than one element at work here."

"Clearly."

"There's the fantasy part of it that takes you out of your reality. You can live through the heroine on a yacht and forget for a few hours that you just opened your cabinet doors so the water pipes don't burst overnight." I sigh. "And then there's hope that things will work out. Like, if Gina, the maid at the motel, can find lasting love with a prince from a small country in Europe, then maybe I can too."

I laugh. I'm not sure what I'm laughing at more—the ridiculousness of the analogy or the idea of finding love in my personal life—but I laugh, nonetheless.

"Life is too much of a shit show to go into a movie and not be sure if she gets the guy or not," I say. "Sometimes, you just want to know that it's going to end well for a change."

He nods approvingly. "I get it. Do you happen to know of any movies where the baseball god retires unexpectedly and lands with both feet on the ground, a solid trajectory, a wife, and maybe a dog?"

I grin. "I don't know of one offhand, but I'm sure it's been done."

He leans his head back on the sofa. "Maybe that's what I can do with my life now. I can make movies."

"We lead such different lives."

"Why?"

"Because I've never, in my entire life, thought, 'Ah yes, I'll just go make movies now.'" I smirk. "Well, I did hear you can sell foot pictures online, and I might have considered that once or twice."

He drops his jaw.

"What are you looking at me like that for?" I ask. "It's easy money."

"Tell me you haven't done that."

I shrug. "I mean, I haven't, but I do like the entrepreneurial spirit of the whole thing."

He runs a hand over his face while his chest rises and falls.

"And I do have cute feet." I hold a foot up just to screw with him. "I bet that I could get fifty bucks out of this."

"You've lost your mind."

I pretend like I'm considering that. "Definitely. Fifty bucks a pop might be on the cheap side."

"Stop it," he says before taking a pillow and tossing it at me.

I catch it and laugh. "At least I have a backup plan. Well, you do, too, but your whole making-movies thing sounds a lot more involved than mine."

"I'm not actually going to make movies."

"Why not?"

He holds his hands out. "I don't know. Because I don't know how. It doesn't interest me. There's a plethora of reasons."

"Okay. What interests you, then?"

He crosses his arms over his chest. "Baseball."

"You can't say that."

"Why not?"

"Because that's obvious."

He blows out a breath. "Surfing, even though I'm terrible at it."

"I already know that."

"Are there any other rules that I need to know?" He laughs. "Damn."

"No," I say, grinning. "I just want to know *new* things that interest you. Things that I don't know."

He shifts his body so that he's leaning on his side. He looks longer, more muscled, as the sunlight rakes over the lines of his figure.

I shiver and hope that he doesn't notice.

"I like to cook, I think," he says.

"You think?"

"Yeah. I haven't actually done it too much, but I kind of enjoy being in the kitchen and fooling around with spices and stuff. It's fun."

I'd like to fool around with you.

"What?" he asks, smirking. "Your face just turned red."

"Nothing." I clear my throat. "Cooking. What else?"

He narrows his eyes like he's not going to let it go. Slowly his features return to normal, and I'm able to exhale.

"I like teaching," he says. "I thought at one point in my life that I might be a teacher if the whole pro ball thing didn't work out."

"I could never do that. I don't have the patience."

"I'm not saying I could actually be a teacher in a classroom, but I find it calming to break down a bigger task—like hitting a ball—into smaller, more manageable chunks." He rolls his tongue around his mouth. "Okay. What about you? What do you like to do?"

"Oh, I got this." I move onto my side, facing him. "I like sleeping. Taking long baths without answering questions. My favorite thing of all is *not* doing a science project the night before it's due. You haven't lived until you still have twenty-four hours left, and it's sitting on your kitchen table, completed."

I clutch a hand to my heart and close my eyes, relishing the one time that actually happened.

Cole chuckles. "Wow. What a life."

"I know. Be jealous."

When my eyes open, Cole is looking into them. A softness radiates from the watery blues, and I feel myself drifting away on the current.

"Would you believe me if I said that I *am* a little jealous?" he asks.

"No."

My voice is barely above a whisper. If I speak too loudly, he might flinch and the moment between us could be lost. Although I'm not sure why that feels like it would be a loss, it does.

"I've lived a big, bright adventure," he says, his voice just loud enough for me to hear. "Not a day goes by that I'm not humbled and appreciative of the opportunities I've been given and for the hard work that my parents put in to get me where I've been."

I nod, not sure where he's going with this.

"But my life and all of its dazzle hasn't had any of the things you've talked about," he says.

"So you've managed to sleep, and you're complaining?"

He grins. "I meant more of the interpersonal connections. The relationship that you have with Ethan. Your relationship with Jared, even though I don't really know what that entails."

"No. My relationship with Jared, or a lack thereof, doesn't deserve an honorable mention in this conversation."

"You're missing my point here," he says.

"Well, you had to go start taking turns and falling off of bridges. Stay on track."

Cole laughs. "What I mean is that . . . I've had these big moments in my life and none of the small ones."

"And I've had all the small ones and none of the big ones."

"Right. But what if some of your small ones are really the big ones? I've been thinking about these kinds of things lately. What if having the kid and falling in love—"

"There you go again. Off the bridge."

He smiles. "You know what I mean."

"I get what you mean in theory. I've never actually been in love."

He sits up and drags himself to the center of the sofa. I struggle to sit upright, too, because reclining beside him feels too vulnerable.

"I think that's the big thing for me," I say, forgoing all jokes. "That's my World Series, if you will. The one thing that I can do and then feel accomplished. I only want to find someone and fall spectacularly in love with them and have them actually fall just as hard for me."

My gaze hits the sofa before the words have finished falling from my lips. My face flushes as my brain screams at me to stop talking.

Why am I saying this to him?

He reaches out and presses the tip of his finger below my chin. Gently, he lifts my head far enough for his eyes to capture mine.

The honesty, the genuineness, in his baby blues steals my breath. I wait for him to speak because there's no way I can think my way out of this moment.

"I bet," he says, his eyes never leaving mine, "that you've had a hundred guys in love with you."

"Not true."

My throat is hot and my voice is wrapped in cotton. I fear looking too deeply into his irises in case he can see my wounds.

I don't want Cole Beck to see the ugly inside me—the parts that other men see and then retreat as far away from as they can. Emotionally, anyway.

But whether I want him to or not, he searches my face, and I can't hide.

"That's why I didn't want Ethan here when you came over," I say, my voice betraying me with the slightest vibration.

"Why? I don't understand."

Much to my dismay, Cole drops his hand.

I struggle to ignore the flash of coolness on my chin and stay focused on the question he asked of me.

"Ethan is at the age where he needs a male role model. He's craving it. And his dad, well, you know, just took off to Cleveland without a second thought. And I don't want Ethan latching on to anyone—because I'm afraid that's what he would do—who isn't into the two of us long term. And that's clearly not what's happening here with us."

Cole's brows pull together, and he licks his lips. "So that explains the hot-and-cold thing you've been doing."

"Partially." I take a deep breath and feel my spirits sink a bit. "I also want something more for me—something real and tangible. Something that I can believe in and just . . . I don't know. Rest, I guess, knowing it'll be there tomorrow."

But then you came along, and I still want those things . . . but I want you so much. I don't know what to do.

"Palmer?"

"What?"

He smiles. "Don't ever apologize for doing what you have to do for you or your son."

My insides fill with a light and warmth—a sensation of being understood.

I didn't need Cole's validation. I know I'm doing what's best for my family. But Cole is the first man to listen to what I have to say, to hear it, and then acknowledge it in a positive, thoughtful way.

It feels damn good.

"Thank you," I say.

"What are you thanking me for?"

"For listening."

"Well, thank you for opening up to me." He looks at the plates on the floor. "And for the pizza."

My gaze follows his to the stack of pizza crusts. I swing my legs over the side of the ottoman and bend down. At the same time, Cole moves to grab the plates off the floor.

We collide midair and fall into a heap next to the plates—Cole on his back and me halfway across him.

Our laughter breaks through the silence in the room.

The heat of his body radiates into mine. The movement of his chest as he laughs fills me with an energy that I needed.

I press a hand against his chest, his heart thumping beneath my palm, and start to press off him. But before I can, his hand wraps around my wrist.

My mouth goes dry as I peer down into his handsome face. Slowly, he raises up. Less slowly, I bend down.

A hundred million thoughts race through my mind. Some of them tell me to kiss him. Others scream not to. Another segment has me ripping my clothes off and straddling him in some kind of sexual-aggressor mode that I didn't know I possessed.

Cole's breath is hot as he grows closer. My heart beats so loud that I'm sure he can hear it. He's right in front of my face when he stops, hovering just inches from me.

He blinks, his beautiful blue eyes as clear as the sky on a summer afternoon.

"Are you sure?" he whispers. "Because I've heard what you said, and I don't want to put you into a situation that you don't want to be in."

Am I sure?

My body trembles, needing the next moment to happen without me thinking about it. I want him to kiss me—I want him to kiss me so freaking bad. I want to lose myself in his arms and forget about logic and what might be right and what's probably wrong.

But should I?

My phone buzzes with a very specific tone on the sofa behind me.

I pull away and fall onto my heels.

"I'm sorry," I say, the connection between us broken. "That's Ethan."

"Sure. Get it."

Cole falls back to the floor with a thud.

I grab my phone and read Ethan's text.

My stomach hurts. Can you come get me?

My phone buzzes again.

Val:

I think Jared called Ethan's cell. I was in the bathroom and I'm not sure what happened, but Ethan's acting kind of weird.

Me:

I'm on my way.

I get to my feet. "I'm really sorry, Cole. But Jared apparently got a hold of Ethan, and God knows what he said . . ."

Cole is on his feet just as quickly. "Can I do anything? Want me to come back later and play catch or take him for some batting practice?" He glances over his shoulder. "Well, it's dark. But we could—"

"Cole?" My heart swells. "Thank you. I got this but . . . honestly. Thank you."

We stand face-to-face for a long moment. I'm not sure if he's going to hug me, kiss my cheek, or pat my shoulder like a friend. Any of them would be welcome. But none of them are probably a good idea.

"If whatever his dad said was too bad, call me," Cole says, smiling. "I have many talents."

I wish I could hug him. My fingers itch to pull my body into his and let him shield me from some of the shit of my life.

But I don't.

What I said before is true—my life is often a shit show. I have no one but Val, on occasion, to pull me out of it. And I have a son who needs me right now. Ethan trumps everything, even Cole Beck.

"That's nice," I say, walking around him and leading him upstairs. "Way to paint my imagination in a rainbow of colors just as you're leaving."

He laughs as we climb the steps and go back to reality.

Damn it, anyway.

CHAPTER NINETEEN

Palmer

"Are you hungry?" I watch as Ethan kicks off his shoes and slides them inside the shoe rack by the door. "There's some pizza downstairs, but I could heat up the chicken-fried steak from last night, if you'd rather have that."

He hums. It's not an answer so much as him blowing me off—just like he's done ever since I picked him up at Val's.

I haven't asked him what his dad said, only if he contacted him. A simple nod was really all I needed to know.

If I close my eyes and think too much about it, I'll step outside and call Jared and let him have it. So I don't. It wouldn't help. It wouldn't change Jared's behavior, nor would it help Ethan. And that's all I really want to do.

My chest burns as I watch my little boy war with the emotions building inside him.

"Did you know Dad left?" he asks.

The question catches me off guard, even though I know it's what he's thinking. It's the clarity, the boiled-down, cut-through-the-shit inquiry that knocks me back a couple of steps.

"Yes," I say.

"Why didn't you tell me today? Why did you send me to Val's and not tell me that my dad moved to Cleveland?"

His gaze pierces mine. It's guarded, with a look of pain mixed with fury, and it breaks my heart to see it so obvious in his sweet green eyes.

My mouth goes dry as I try to formulate the correct response. *How do I be honest and protect Ethan at the same time?*

I shift my weight from one foot to the other.

"I found out just before I picked you up from school," I say. "He called me late this afternoon."

"But why didn't you tell me?"

"Because, Ethan, I didn't know how. I don't want to tell you one thing and then be wrong about it. How many times has that happened? How many times has your father told me, *told us*, one thing and then turned around and did something else?"

The anger in his eyes softens.

"I figured that if he really did go, then fine. What did it matter?" I ask. "He'll be back. He *always* comes back, and he'll probably return before it was time for him to see you again anyway. Why risk upsetting you if there's a chance that he shows up here tomorrow?"

His gaze drops to the hardwood floor.

"Look, buddy, I was going to tell you. I promise. I just . . . It's hard sometimes to know how to handle your dad, and I don't want you having to figure it out. I want to do the hard stuff and let you just enjoy being a kid."

His eyes lift to mine. "I told you the other day that I'm not a kid. I understand way more than you think I do."

"I know—"

"And it felt really bad to have to hear it from Dad when you already knew."

My chest squeezes. "Ethan, I'm sorry."

He hangs his head and walks toward the steps but stops. Then he raises his chin and looks at me with the clearest, most vulnerable look that I've ever seen him serve.

"I don't even care that he left, Mom. I mean, I do. It would be nice if he lived here and he remembered that he had a kid, but that's not going to happen."

My fingers itch to reach for him, to pull him into my chest and cuddle him like I used to when he was a baby. But that reaction would be *for me*. I need to be here *for him*.

"I wish you would've told me so I'd know I can trust you," he says.

He doesn't waver. He doesn't blink or smile or soften his words so they won't puncture my heart. My twelve-year-old son just looks at me like the man he isn't and makes me feel about two inches tall.

"You can trust me. You know that," I say. "Don't say things like that, Ethan."

"It's always been me and you. We haven't needed anyone—not Dad or his mom or even Charlie."

"That's right."

"So don't let me find out crappy information from Dad when you already know it. It's not fun to feel like there are secrets going around and I'm the only one that doesn't know them."

"I didn't mean to do that. I was trying to protect you."

His shoulders fall. "I know. But I'm not six years old anymore. I'm almost thirteen. I get stuff. I understand. I'm not in the other room watching cartoons and not thinking about things."

"I don't want you to have to be thinking about things, Ethan. I want you playing baseball and having fun with your friends. Going to Val's and skateboarding with the kids in the parking lot, like you love to do. Did you do that today?"

He nods, giving me a small grin.

I sigh, the relief evident in my exhale. "Good."

He starts down the steps. I give him a couple of seconds' head start before I follow—both for him and for me.

The pictures of his life along the staircase hit a little harder than they usually do. I remember the way he smelled like baby lotion in the first picture and how, shortly after the fourth image was snapped, he choked on a strawberry. He wore the rain boots in the fifth picture for a solid six months, fighting me when he had to take them off for baths and bed.

"What did you do today?" Ethan asks.

"I had to work late."

I watch the now preteen enter the living room below me and wonder how time can possibly move this fast.

He faces me with a quirked brow and a smug smile.

"What?" I ask.

"Looks like someone had a guest over while I was away."

My breath catches in my throat as I do a quick sweep of the room. The throw pillows are a mess, not propped up in specific places like I usually keep them. There are two plates on the coffee table and two glasses of pop that I didn't take to the kitchen in my haste to get Ethan.

Shit.

"Now I see why you had to 'work late,'" he says, using air quotes like some kind of grown-up when he is not.

"Listen here, child . . ."

His laughter is quick and loud. I'm not sure what to make of it, so I just stand there frozen in place.

"Not that I have to defend myself to you," I say, keeping an eye on him while I gather the dishes, "but I *did* work late." *You little smartass.*

"Okay."

"Ethan!"

"What?" His grin would be wide and adorable . . . if I weren't on the verge of both irritation and humiliation. "So, you had a date? You don't have to—"

"It wasn't a date." *I don't think. Ish.* "And it doesn't matter anyway. I'm not discussing this with you."

He shrugs. "Fine. I'll ask Cole if the pizza was good at practice on Monday."

I drop a plate. This amuses my son to no end.

"So it *was* Cole," he says, picking up both the pizza and the crust that fell to the floor.

"It's none of your business."

He plops down in the recliner and gets comfortable. "I don't want details."

I start to take the dishes upstairs—partly because that's where they need to go and partly because I don't want to have this conversation—but then I stop.

Maybe we need to have this conversation.

If Ethan is right, he's astute enough to realize that there's a connection between his coach and me. And if I'm being honest, I'm going to have a hard time trying to fight it.

Like I haven't been struggling already.

So maybe the right answer is just acknowledging that in some way and blaming it on my team mom duties. That way Ethan doesn't get the wrong idea.

I place the dishes on the coffee table again.

"Fine," I say, blowing out a breath. "Cole was here."

Ethan grins.

"I'm the team mom now. I don't know if he told you that. We had some things to talk about, and I ordered a pizza because I worked late."

Oh, well done, getting the "work" part in there.

"I thought you weren't discussing this with me?" he asks.

"I'm not."

"You know he has a thing for you, right?"

"Ethan!"

He laughs. "Well, he does. He watches you when you walk around the field. So do half the boys on my team, so it's not like a new thing. It's gross, but not a new thing."

They do?

My cheeks flush. I can't tell if he's making this up or telling the truth. Not that it matters one way or the other, but I'm not ready for this conversation.

"And obviously you like him," he says.

"I do not."

He sits up in the chair and laughs. "Look, Mom—if Cole Beck, the catcher for the San Diego Swifts, likes you, and you don't like him back and ruin the potential glory that I could get out of this in school . . ." He makes a face. "I'm moving in with Dad."

"Over my dead body," I say with a laugh. "Cole is a nice guy. I enjoy talking to him." *And kissing him.* "But whatever you're thinking in your head? It's not going to happen."

"And why not?"

Are we really having this conversation?

"Yes, we're really having this conversation," he says, as if he can read my mind.

I scramble to stay on top of this exchange.

"I know you think that I try to protect you too much when it comes to your dad," I say.

Ethan nods.

"But it's not just with your dad. It's with everything," I tell him. "And how irresponsible would it be if . . ." It's hard to even say the words. "If I did date Cole or see him in some kind of way, and then he left."

His eyes sparkle. "That would be the best story ever. My mom dated a professional baseball player. That's at least three extra cool points in high school."

I snort, shaking my head.

"I love you," he says, getting to his feet. "I love you so much. But stop babying me. Okay?"

"Never."

He rolls his eyes. "I know that I thought Charlie was going to be my new dad there for a minute. But I was a kid."

"You're still a kid."

"No. I'm not. And if you hang out with Cole, I'm not going to lose my mind when he goes back home. I'm going to think it was really cool that he hung out with you, and maybe me if you're willing to share the fun with me. I'll have some great stories for high school."

I don't know what to say to that. It's *so* not what I was expecting. So I pull the kid, who's taller than I am now, into my chest and hug him tight.

"Can you let go now?" he asks, squished against me. "I'd like to have some pizza and then go play a game."

I release him and muss up his hair as he pulls away—much to his dismay. He takes two slices of pizza and starts up the stairs.

"Ethan?" I call after him.

He stops on the landing. "Yeah?"

"You know, you're right. I should've told you about your dad. I'm sorry." I smile at him. "It's always going to be me and you, kid."

His grin is brilliant and warms my heart. "You better believe it."

I collapse into the recliner, too exhausted from the conversation to even pick up the dishes right away. Instead, I close my eyes and listen to the faint sound of Ethan yelling into his mic in his room.

As if on autopilot, I pull my phone from my pocket and send two quick texts.

We're home and he's fine. Love you, Val.

I smile as I type out the other.

Sorry that I had to cut that short. All is well now. (Mostly.)

The response comes back instantly.

Cole:

I'm glad to hear it. Been wondering.

Me:

A mom's duty never ends. He also saw the pizza and plates and put two and two together. 😳

Cole:

Shit. Is everything okay?

Me:

He just thinks I'm SUPER COOL now.

Cole:

He's right. 😉 How'd he take me being over there? I know you were worried about that and I feel guilty for not picking up the evidence now.

Me:

He took it well. He's upset he wasn't involved.

Cole:

Well, my mom is making her famous roast and potatoes on Sunday. She would think that I'm SUPER COOL if the two of you joined us. (No pressure at all.)

I take a deep, shaky breath. *Eating with his family?* I already know his mother vaguely, and she seems nice. But wouldn't eating with them . . .

Cole:

You're overthinking things.

Me:

How'd you know?

Cole:

Because you're breathing.

Me:

Ha.

Cole:

Just think about it. Let me know tomorrow. No rush.

Me:

Okay. Going to go clean up this mess now. Talk to you tomorrow.

Cole:

Thanks for having me over.

Me:

Thanks for coming.

Cole:

ignores the joke on the tip of my tongue

Me:

ignores the joke about the tip of your tongue

I turn my phone off before we banter back and forth all night. And then I get up, gather the pieces of dinner, and take them upstairs.

CHAPTER TWENTY

COLE

Saturdays aren't as exciting as they used to be.

I stretch my arms overhead. A *pop* sounds loud enough in my shoulder that I lie perfectly still and wait for the pain.

A burst of fire streaks across my shoulder and down my arm. It burns across the top of my back and bleeds into my spine. The pain radiates into my ribs. I cringe, holding my breath, and wait for relief.

"Fuck," I groan, hissing through my teeth. The discomfort worsens before it gets better. *"Ugh."*

I focus on my breath. My chest rises and falls, unsteadily at first. But as I concentrate on the rhythm, it evens out.

"There you go," I whisper as the ache dissipates. "That's better."

It's my own fault that the throbbing is back. I haven't been to a therapist since I got here. Granted, I thought I would be home by now, but I've really made no effort to rehab myself in a couple of weeks.

What's it matter if I go to rehab or not?

I shake my head, shifting the thought aside.

Of course it matters. It matters if I want to be able to do normal things. It matters if I don't want to be a selfish prick and have to ask someone to take care of me.

This time, the pull across the back of my neck is from not my injury but stress.

I grit my teeth and sit up. But as soon as my legs touch the ground, the left one goes numb. The only sensation in the lower-left half of my body at all is a tingle just above my knee. It's as though a hundred knives are being pushed into my skin repeatedly.

"Fuck!" I stomp my leg to try to wake it up. "Come the hell on."

It takes a full minute for the spasms to stop. I get up as soon as I can bear weight on my leg and walk around my room, limping for the first little while.

Needing a distraction, I grab my phone and pull up my email for the first time in a couple of days—and instantly regret it.

A red exclamation point sits boldly beside one subject line: Urgent—YourChart Update.

I stand in the middle of the guest bedroom, holding my phone like a ticking bomb. I don't know whether to throw it or try to defuse the situation.

My breathing is shallow as I stare at the subject line. A bead of sweat breaks out across my forehead. My legs are weak and threaten to give out as I try to make sense of the message.

Do I click on it? Do I ignore it?

Ignoring it won't make it go away.

But it could stop the uncertainty and let me fucking breathe again.

Or not.

"Damn it," I say, squeezing my eyes shut.

The pit of my stomach—the dark, raw abyss that pools every fear that I've been too scared to admit—churns with this information.

The results are in.

I toss my phone on my bed. It's as if somehow losing the weight of the phone will release me from the burden of the message.

My skin is too tight. My clothes too clingy. I need a shower and a run and to vomit—preferably not in that order.

I run a hand down my face and talk sense to myself.

Just open the message, read the report, and then it'll be done. You're still here, which is a blessing. You can sit down with Mom and Dad and go over things with them.

I drop my hand to my side as a bubble of bile creeps up my throat.

How will I tell Mom?

I'm getting ahead of myself. I know that. *I need to calm the fuck down and wait and see what the email says.*

Instead of doing that, I pace to the other side of the room and sit on a wicker chair that Mom restored from a garage sale.

The room is much bigger than it was a few minutes ago. It's spacious and cold and altogether lonely.

I'm lonely.

I'm lonely because I'm alone. And it will probably always be this way.

The bitterness of that fact washes over me like a cold rain.

I close my eyes and see Palmer's sweet smile.

Last night plays out like a movie—one that's infinitely better than the comedy we watched at her house. I can taste the cinnamon on her lips and feel the heat of her breath. I melt into the familiar energy of her home and the comfort of her gaze.

Why can't all that be real?

I open my eyes and sigh.

Palmer Clark is a unicorn. There's substance behind her beauty, a humbleness behind her swagger. She's kind yet confident and has a vulnerability that eats at me in ways that it shouldn't. She's funny and also fierce, and watching her with her son pulls at something soul deep.

She triggers something inside me that makes me want to protect her. *Hell, I volunteered to coach a bunch of kids just to be near her.*

I'm not sure what I thought this was going to be. *How did I think it was going to end up?* Did I expect that the woman who captured my attention from the moment she walked into Fletcher's was going to lose my interest?

Surely I wasn't that stupid.

But what do I do now?

I tug at my hair and let the war raging inside me continue.

Do I try to walk away from Palmer? I don't want to. I have no interest in doing that. The thought of walking away makes me want to call her, just to prove to myself that she's still there.

Do I open that fucking email and then decide? I'm not sure that it really matters. Sure, it would matter if Palmer and I were serious, but we aren't. And she's made it very clear that she wants something long term. How can I be long term if I'm in California? And how can I do something with my life in Ohio should I get a wild hair up my ass and decide to relocate?

I can't do that.

Or do I just keep on with how things are going and let it be?

A slow wash of acceptance covers me, and I know the last option is the right answer. No one gets hurt. Everything is on the table that needs to be on the table. There are no lies or miscommunications.

Lord, I wish I were with her now.

I'm starting to stand up when my phone buzzes on the bed. I get to my feet and reach for the device.

Palmer:

So, on a scale of 1-10, how much can I trust you?

Me:

10.

Palmer:

Quick answer. Makes me suspicious.

Me:

Odd question and even stranger response. Makes me doubly suspicious.

Palmer:

🙄 Ethan mentioned you this morning . . .

Me:

Too bad it wasn't you thinking of me . . .

Palmer:

I didn't say I wasn't. 😉

I laugh out loud.

Me:

Awesome. Continue.

Palmer:

Right. So, I might have mentioned having dinner with your family tomorrow and he might have been really into it.

Me:

I'm really into it too.

Palmer:

So you still would be okay if we came?

Is she out of her mind?
I can't type fast enough.
Me:

YES.

Palmer:

And your parents won't care?

Me:

NO. I will apologize in advance for my mother's behavior. I'm not sure what she'll do to embarrass me and put you on the spot, I just know she will. Also, if she has a preacher here to marry us tomorrow, I had nothing to do with it and will help you escape.

Palmer:

Whoahhhhhhhh.

Me:

It comes from a good place. I swear.

Crickets.
I furiously type again.

Me:

I'll tell Mom you're coming around 2. Does that work?

Palmer:

Yup.

Me:

Great. Tell Ethan to bring his glove.

Palmer:

It's on his hand as we speak.

Me:

That's where it should be.

Palmer:

We are going to sweep the steps and do some otherwise boring chores today. I hope you have a fun Saturday!

Me:

You too. See you tomorrow.

Palmer:

Bye.

I watch the screen for a long time just in case she says something else. Finally, I stick the phone on the bedside table.

My shoulder is still sore. I work it in small circles like my therapist showed me and try to get my head straight. The email is heavy on my mind, but I push it out and focus on the day.

I'll get to the email . . . later. Right now, I want to focus on tomorrow.

CHAPTER TWENTY-ONE

Palmer

"Use your manners." I watch Ethan bounce around the passenger's seat, held vaguely still by only the seat belt. "'Please.' 'Thank you.' Don't talk with your mouth full."

My anxiety is spiraling the closer we get to Cole's parents' house. I've second- and third-guessed myself about this plan all morning and have arrived at the conclusion that I must be out of my mind.

I'm going to see Lawrence and Casey Beck when Cole goes back to California. *Won't that be awkward? "Hi, yes, I'm the girl your son fiddled around with when he was in town. Don't mind me. Would you like to cut in line?"*

Oof.

"Mom?"

I glance at my son. "What?"

"No offense, but if you're having to remind me as we're pulling in the driveway to use my manners, it's probably a lost cause."

He flashes me the cheesiest grin, which zaps me back to center. *Thank God for this kid.*

"That might be true," I say, slowly pressing the brakes on the gravel road. "But I'm your mom. It's my job to remind you."

"Cool. Then, as your son, it's my job to remind you to be happy about this."

"Why wouldn't I be happy?"

He rolls his big green eyes. "I have no idea, but you look like you just sucked on a lemon."

Do I? I quickly inventory my face and realize . . . I do. I must look constipated. My brows are furrowed, my lips pressed into a thin, tight line as I consider every possible thing that might go wrong today.

"When is the last time we were invited anywhere to dinner?" Ethan asks. "Besides Val's, but does that really count when she just brings home leftovers from Fletcher's and we eat on top of the morgue?"

"It's not a morgue. It's a funeral home." I glance at him and grin. "But point taken."

"See? It's fun to do something different for a change. Not that I don't like it being just the two of us, because I do, but it feels happy. Right?"

My stomach clenches. I try to shake it off. "Right. But remember that—"

"*I know.* I'm the one that explained it to you, remember?"

I flip on my turn signal and pull into the driveway of the Becks' home. "How did you get so mature?"

"Well, it wasn't from you or Val. Or Dad." He scrunches up his face. "Actually, I don't know. Good question."

I'm laughing as I park the car, which is a step in the right direction. It allows me to ignore the sudden urge to pull back out, probably spin the tires because it's gravel, and then drive as quickly as I can back home.

Ethan and I climb out of the car. A giant yellow dog races across the front lawn, its tongue hanging out the side of its mouth, and makes a beeline for my son.

"Ethan! Be careful," I call out just as the dog leaps the last few feet and crashes into him.

"It's the neighbor's dog."

I look up to see Cole standing on the porch. Dressed in a white long-sleeved shirt, black fitted joggers, and a Swifts hat sitting backward on his head, he looks like an athletic ad heading my way.

I'm not prepared.

My legs weaken at the sight of him—at the smile he displays just for me. He pats Ethan on the shoulder as he struts across the yard toward me.

"Hey," he says, stopping just inside my personal bubble.

I want to kiss him. Everything inside me wants to feel his breath against my lips again. My fingers itch to touch him, and my mouth goes dry just thinking about being covered by his.

Cole must read my thoughts because his smirk deepens.

"Hi," I say after an awkward and obvious pause.

He chuckles. "I'm glad you came. I was starting to think you were going to bail."

"She was!" Ethan shouts from his wrestling match with the dog.

His voice snaps me back to reality.

"Ethan, let that dog go. You're going to be filthy, and we haven't had dinner yet." I step to the side of Cole. "Ethan, *now*."

He releases the dog with more than a little disappointment. "It's just a dog, Mom."

"I know and I'm sorry. But we have to go into these nice people's house and sit at their table, and you don't want to smell like a dog."

"It's better than what Cole used to smell like after a game." Cole's mother stands on the porch, practically beaming. I recognize her from around town. She wipes her hands on a white dish towel. "Hi, Palmer. Hi, Ethan."

I heave a nervous breath. "Hi, Mrs. Beck."

She waves the towel through the air. "I'm Casey." Her attention shifts to Ethan. "Do you like cookies?"

"Uh, yeah."

Casey looks at me quickly for approval. I nod. After a quick wink, she turns back to my son. "Well, follow me, and we'll wash your hands and spoil your dinner." She smiles. "How does that sound?"

"Awesome!"

Ethan runs across the yard and up the stairs without a second thought, leaving me alone with Cole.

"Is that why you're so rotten?" I ask Cole, grinning.

"What do you mean?"

"Your mom spoiled more than your dinner, didn't she?" I laugh. *"She spoiled you."*

He feigns surprise, making me laugh harder.

I'm relieved that things are so easy. My shoulders release some of the stress and worry they've been holding for, well, basically my entire life, and I breathe in the tranquility of the Beck homeplace.

"It's so nice out here," I say, taking in the trees and grass. "It's like a nature reserve or something."

"It's very different from how I grew up, that's for sure."

"Why did they move here? Ohio seems so random."

He shrugs. "They do a lot of boating and hiking—outdoorsy stuff. And they like the slow life here, I think, and the seasons. I hear a lot about that."

"They're overrated."

He grins. "I don't really know how they picked Bloomfield specifically, but they seem really happy here."

We begin to walk slowly toward the house. Our hands brush against one another's, but neither of us pulls away. I sense him looking at me out of the corner of his eye, because my senses flood with a warmth that I wish I could bottle up and keep forever.

"What about you?" he asks out of nowhere as we ascend the steps to the porch.

"What about me?"

"Are you happy here?"

I stop at the top of the stairs and look at him. There are so many ways to answer that. Am I happy in Bloomfield? Yes. Am I happy at his parents' house? So far, yes. Am I happy that I'm here with him?

Also yes.

He stands next to me, facing me, with the scent of roast beef floating through the screen door. Ethan's laughter and Casey's voice tickle my ears. I hold my breath, afraid to breathe because, if I do, something could go wrong.

Cole touches the side of my face, peering into my eyes. "Breathe, sweetheart," he whispers.

I part my lips and let the warm air fill my lungs.

"Do you hear that?" he asks softly.

"What?"

He pauses as Ethan laughs again. Then Cole smiles. "You overthink things," he says.

"I have to. I'm every line of defense between the world and that boy."

He lowers his face closer to mine. "And between the world and you."

Cole is right, of course. I am the only person to protect me. But the fact that he knows this makes my vulnerability flare.

"What are you saying?" I ask.

"I'm saying that when you're with me, here, or anywhere else we are, I want you to trust me. You can relax." His fingers reach for mine and toy with them at my side. "I admire how strong you are and how much you love Ethan. But I want you to know that I'm on your side, okay?"

Damn it.

Tears pool at the corners of my eyes as my brain repeats his last words over and over: *"But I want you to know that I'm on your side, okay?"*

No one has ever been in my corner. Not even for a day. How can he say something so sweet, and mean it, I think, without really knowing us?

Who is this man? And why is he pursuing me?

"Stop it," he says, wrapping his fingers around mine long enough to give them a gentle squeeze. "I didn't mean to make you cry."

"Then don't be nice to me."

He laughs. "Being nice to you makes you cry?"

I tap my eyes with the back of my hand. "I have a hard time with nice emotions, okay? I don't know how to process them. Just say something mean to me, and I'll snap right back."

"Yeah, silly woman. Not happening." He opens the door and props it open with his shoe. "And don't cry, because then my mom will cry because no one cries alone in her presence."

I close my eyes for a moment and then open them. "There. I'm over it."

"Just like that?"

"Yeah, I just pretended like you said I couldn't have a whistle at practice, and it recentered me."

He shakes his head as I walk past.

Cole leads me into a small living room filled with enough collectibles to fill a small mall. There are baskets and candles and a clock on the wall that's stopped telling time. Little pink hearts hanging off a rope that's dangling around the neck of the Swifts mascot. Pictures dot the space—most of them of or including Cole.

"Hi, Palmer," Lawrence says, rising from a recliner. "Welcome. Glad you could come for dinner."

"Thank you, Mr. Beck."

He gives me a look that reminds me of Cole when he's adorably irritated. "It's Lawrence."

I smile at him.

"Are y'all ready to eat?" Casey shouts from the dining room.

"Coming," Cole calls back to her.

He presses his hand lightly against the small of my back and leads me into a dining room that's open to the kitchen. Ethan is at the stove with Casey, holding a bowl as she scoops mashed potatoes from the pot into the vessel.

"Get yourself settled at the table," Casey says. "Ethan and I will be there in just a second."

"Don't expect your boy to eat much," Lawrence says, chuckling. "I think Casey gave him a dozen cookies."

"Don't be a snitch!" Casey shouts from the kitchen. "Mind your business, Lawrence."

I laugh and sit in the chair that Cole pulls out for me. My heart soars, but I don't have time to really register it as Cole sits at the head of the table beside me. Lawrence sits across from him.

Casey and Ethan join us. They place the bowl of potatoes and the salt and pepper shakers on the table before sitting down.

"This looks wonderful," I say, in awe of the spread in front of us. It's nothing short of a small buffet with the roast and vegetables cooked around it. There's also the bowl of mashed potatoes, ears of corn on the cob, green beans with ham chunks, and sliced tomatoes and onions.

"Yes, Mom. It does," Cole says. "Thank you."

"It's an awful lot of starch," Lawrence says.

Casey hushes her husband with a look. "We didn't know what you liked, and everyone likes a starch."

I laugh.

"Well, there's probably ten desserts in there that are full of it." Lawrence stabs a green bean with his fork. "She's been cooking for two days."

"I don't see you complaining right now." Casey lifts a brow. "And don't you eat that bean until we've said grace." She looks at Ethan. "Do you want to say it?"

He looks at me with wide eyes. I'm about to come to his rescue when he shrugs.

"Sure," he says and then bows his little head.

I drop my head and look at my plate—pretty white china with butterscotch-colored designs near the rim.

Ethan clears his throat. "Dear God, thank you for this day. Thank you for letting us come to this house and have this nice meal made by this nice lady, even if it is a lot of starch."

I smile as Lawrence chuckles softly to my right.

"Thank you for . . . um . . . letting Cole be retired so we could meet him and for my mom letting me play baseball. We are really grateful, God. Amen."

I press my lips together to keep my emotions from spilling all down my cheeks. When I lift my head, Ethan is looking at me.

"Perfect," I mouth at him.

He smiles.

"That was an awesome job," Cole says. "I get so nervous when I have to speak like that, but you did it like a rock star."

"You get nervous?" Ethan asks.

Lawrence laughs. "One time, Cole had to give a speech in high school. What was it for, Casey? Do you remember?"

"Honor Night, I think."

Cole groans. "Do we have to tell this story?"

Lawrence ignores him. "So he gets up there in front of his whole school and all of their parents. The bleachers were full. It was packed to the brim. And do you know what he did?"

Ethan shakes his head, riveted by the story. "No. What did he do?"

"Well, he gets up there and stands at the microphone and—"

"I puked, okay?" Cole passes me the bowl of potatoes.

Ethan laughs. "You puked in front of everyone?"

"Yeah. But Dad made chili the night before, and I think he poisoned me."

Lawrence tips his fork at Ethan. "We've never had chili since."

"That would be so gross," Ethan says, laughing. "I bet no one let you forget that."

Cole lifts his drink and grins. "Thankfully, they didn't."

"Why are you thankful for that?" I ask him. "That seems embarrassing."

Cole takes a sip of his tea and then settles his gaze on me. "Because I survived, and I'm stronger for it."

"Can I have another piece of roast?" Ethan asks Casey.

I try to tear my eyes away from Cole's, but I can't. They're locked together, entwined in a conversation that I can't hear.

In the distance, Casey laughs at something Ethan says and Lawrence teases my son. It's the first time in a very long time that I truly exhale.

My foot reaches out until it finds Cole's. He grins as he extends his leg toward mine.

And that's it. That's all it takes to understand what he meant earlier.

"I'm saying that when you're with me, here, or anywhere else we are, I want you to trust me. You can relax."

I don't know what this means, but I think I believe him.

"You go to Cash Cave?" Ethan's question draws me back to the conversation around us. "I love it there. Mom took me once."

"It's one of our favorites," Casey says. "Lawrence and I were just talking about going there this weekend."

Lawrence rolls his eyes, grinning, making it clear that there wasn't a prior conversation.

I blush and stab a bean with my fork.

"Maybe," Casey says carefully, "your mom would let Lawrence and I take you after we eat."

"Mom!"

"Ethan," I say, resting my fork on my plate. "Indoor voice. *Wow.*"

He squirms in his seat. "Sorry. But can I go with them? Please?"

Cole nudges my foot with his, making me smile.

"I mean, if they're going and don't care . . ." My voice falls off as Casey presses her hands together in front of her.

My chest tugs as I watch Casey and Ethan banter about the cave. I can't help it—*I miss my mother.* I imagine her like Casey—sweet, kind, and nurturing. I wonder if Mom's house would've been full of knick-knacks and snacks like this one. I imagine what it would be like to watch her love on my son.

With my bottom lip trembling, I look down at my plate.

"Perfect. It's settled then," Casey says. "Let's eat so we can go!"

Thank you for this moment. Thank you so much.

CHAPTER TWENTY-TWO

Palmer

The door closes with a soft thud.

Footsteps clamor down the porch steps, and the laughter from the trio going on a hike gets farther and farther away. Cole and I stand at the kitchen island—in the middle of what looks like a food war zone—and look at each other.

The afternoon light shines in the window over the sink and highlights the angles of Cole's face. I now know that his jawline comes from his father, and his slightly crooked nose comes from his mother. I'm not sure why that makes me like his features even more, but it does.

"Your parents are really sweet," I say. "I can't believe they're taking Ethan to Cash Cave."

Cole grins. "That was all my mother's doing. She was willing to feign an injury to set us up."

"What?" I laugh. "You're making that up."

"No, I'm not. Sadly. She's a bit of a . . . well, she'd say a romantic, but I think she crosses some lines in her quest for love."

I can't help but feel a small sense of satisfaction at the idea of Casey thinking I'm worthy of her son. As a mother, I know how prickly I'll be someday when my child enters the dating realm.

But Cole and I are not in that realm. Right?

"I need to clean up a little bit of this mess," I say, turning toward the pots and pans strewn about the kitchen.

Cole captures the crook of my arm with his hand and holds me in place. "No. You heard Mom."

"Just a few things. Just let me pick up the trash and rinse the dishes."

"If I let you do that, she will kill me."

"Cole . . ."

"She explicitly said to leave them there." He releases my arm. "My guess is that she knows you clean up messes every day, and she's trying to give you some time off. Let her."

"I . . ." *She's trying to do me a favor? That's what this feels like.* "Are you sure? We could make quick work of it."

He rolls his eyes and motions for me to follow him out of the room. I begrudgingly follow, the idea of leaving a mess for the woman who fixed the meal eating at my conscience.

Cole picks up the remote out of his dad's chair and mutes the news station on the television. I mosey around the room and check out Cole at various stages of his life.

"You were a cute kid," I say, pointing at a photo of him with a big, toothy grin.

He comes up beside me. "Ah, third grade. I hated that year."

"Why?"

"I was really fast and bigger than most of the kids in my grade. So I could throw harder and swing the bat with more speed than the rest of them. I took a lot of shit. It wasn't the best time of my life."

I frown. "The thought of this little guy getting teased or whatever happened to you makes me sad."

"And that's why you're a good mom."

I smile to myself as I walk to another cluster of pictures. "What about you? Do you want to be a dad?"

When he fails to answer me, I look over my shoulder. He's standing next to the coffee table, looking at me like I've just asked him to solve world hunger.

"Cole?"

"I don't know," he says, running a hand over his chin. "I've always thought that I would be."

"You're great with the boys on the team."

"I just . . . I'm in a very strange part of my life right now."

"Well, just so you know, your childbearing years end." I pick up another image of him. This time, he has a football jersey on. "Although men can have kids longer than women."

"Do you want more kids?" he asks.

"Yes." My answer is quick and unequivocal. "It's a part of the reason why . . ."

I don't want to say that I'm averse to wasting time again. Cole knows this. He knows I want a future with someone who wants Ethan and me long term. But do I want more kids? *Yes.*

I set the picture back down. "It's partly why I don't date."

And yet . . . his mother thinks we need this time alone, which isn't necessary since he's leaving.

"I do want more kids. Obviously, I can do that without a man. I'm doing that now. But I want to raise a child with someone—really have a family."

Cole sits on the arm of the sofa. "What was your family like growing up?"

My heart sinks in my chest as I think back on my life with my father. It always surprises me how I can go back to the little house on the road by the park with a simple flip of a mental switch.

I can smell the cigarette smoke, taste the vodka hidden in the orange juice. I can hear the train blasting its horn one block over and feel the floors creak as my father goes back and forth from the garage to the kitchen to get more to drink.

"I think the word 'family' would be an inaccurate choice," I say, turning away from him. "My mother died in childbirth. My father . . ." *How do I paint this picture accurately but also fairly?* "I don't know. He did his best, I suppose, but his best was shit."

Cole's gaze is heavy on my back. I don't turn around to face him, or else I won't be able to talk about my father. I can't say these things and look him in the eye. It's embarrassing and definitely not flattering, but he's leaving anyway. *So what does it matter?*

"My father loved me, but he loved vodka a little more," I say, distancing myself from the memories to save myself the pain. "His disability check from a back injury brought in just enough to cover our bills but not enough to cover them and his increasing bottle habit. So, by the age of nine or ten, I was figuring out if we were going to have water or electricity that month. It's a tough call for a kid to make."

"Palmer." The sofa whines as Cole stands. "That's terrible."

My cheeks flush. I keep my eyes averted from him. "Well, it's my truth. And, like you said earlier, I survived and I'm stronger for it."

I jump as his arms wrap around me from behind. My breath catches in my throat. I still as he pulls me slowly into his chest and rests his chin on top of my head.

My body sinks back, using him for support. He's a steel wall of a man but also soft.

Damn this man.

He doesn't move or speak, just holds me in his arms.

"I used to blame my dad for a lot of his mistakes," I say softly. "And they were his doing and they were his mistakes. But, in a way, they prepared me for the rest of my life. And I—"

"No child should ever be prepared for life like that, Palmer. Ever."

My heart warms. "You're right. But—"

"No buts." He spins me around and bends down so that I'm looking him in the eye. "Don't make excuses for shitty decisions that other people make."

I stare at him, taking in the mixture of ferocity and tenderness in his eyes.

"He wasn't preparing you for life," he says, lifting my chin with the tip of his finger. "He was surviving. And if you don't want to blame him for that, don't. I wasn't there, and I'd like to think that any father in the world wouldn't intentionally hurt their child. But don't give him the credit for your strength. *You* prepared you. *You* learned and fought and rose above. *Not him.* Don't get that twisted."

My head spins as it sorts Cole's words.

No one has ever said this to me before.

I've heard things like *Look for the silver lining* and *His choices weren't about you*. I've had teachers and therapists use my experiences to rationalize my subsequent behavior: *"You're a people pleaser because that's the survival instinct that worked. Now, let's work on trying to not use it in our adult relationships . . ."*

But no one has ever told me to look at things this way—to be proud of my resolve. The focus has always been on the past—on my trauma—explaining Dad's behavior and how *that* affected who I became. No one ever consoled that little, desperate girl and told her "well done" for everything she was able to do despite her age. And that, even though that little girl never felt what it was like to hide within the arms of a father who loved her more than anything else, she grew. She fought. She blossomed.

It prepared me to be the resilient adult that I am.

But I accepted those responsibilities and made them mine. The focus has never been on the present and who I'm responsible for—the woman I am. It's so much more powerful to think of it like this.

I try to look away, to put some distance between us so I can ultimately change the subject. This is a little more vulnerability than I'm ready for. With vulnerability come the rough edges and the bruised parts of my heart and soul, and I'm not prepared for Cole to see those.

But as I squirm, working my way into another place both mentally and physically, Cole holds me tight. He looks at me so deeply that I have no choice but to live with his words for a moment.

Is he right? I know I learned and fought and rose above the shitty life that I had with my father. But have I twisted who did what? Should I not attribute my strength to Dad's weaknesses?

There's no judgment in his pretty blue eyes. He's not prying or poking or digging in to somehow twist things back on me like I've had done before. Instead, he just sees me standing in front of him and accepts it.

"If only you could see yourself from my perspective," he says. "You're smart and strong and protective. You're a survivor. You're beautiful and funny."

I'm not sure how to respond to that . . . because I think he might believe it.

"You think I'm funny?" I ask, grinning.

He laughs. "I think you're so many things, and the more I learn about you, the more interesting I think you are."

"And here I thought you knew all kinds of women. But you must not if *I'm* interesting."

"Want me to give you a list?" He smirks. "I could detail all of the women I know—"

"No."

The abruptness of my response catches us both by surprise. While my eyes go wide, his smirk deepens.

"You sure? I could compare and contrast you with your predecessors . . ." He leans closer to me. "And tell you how you beat them all in every category."

Whether he truly believes that or not—and really, *how could he?*—I'm not in a position to argue with him. I don't *want* to argue with him about it. I'll take the sensation of walking on air over bickering with him about my flaws any day of the week.

Or, at least, I will right now.

His smirk dissolves into a grin as his hands reach for my face. He nestles my face in his palms, stroking my cheeks with his thumbs.

It's magic. Standing in this cozy little house with Cole Beck looking at me like I'm the main character in the story is nothing short of marvelous. There hasn't been a moment in my life when I've felt this *steady*—confident and valued. I'm standing a little taller than normal. My thoughts aren't racing. I'm doing something that I normally can't, and that's a state of just *breathing*.

"I'm not sure you're real," I say, smiling up at him.

He smiles back. "Why would you say that?"

"You're too much. Too handsome, too kind, too smart. Definitely too charming."

"I am pretty charming, aren't I?"

I snort.

His fingers move against my skin. It's a light tapping, a smooth brushing of the fingertips against my cheeks, but it ignites a fire inside me that burns in an instant.

"Cole," I say, forcing a swallow down my throat.

"Yeah?"

"I didn't know that my cheeks had a line connecting them to my libido, but it seems that they do."

His face splits into a wide grin. "Now *that's* interesting."

He widens his stance. He boxes me in, sandwiching me between him and the wall.

Shit.

I'm not sure what I'm doing here. I know what I'm doing *here*, at the Beck house, but what am I doing in this particular situation?

It's clear where this is headed. And damn it if I don't want it. *Bad.* I want it so bad that I think I need it if I ever want to function without sex brain again.

But is giving in the right choice? Is it the right answer? Is there even a right answer at all, or am I going to be screwed, one way or the other, regardless?

I drag in a lungful of air and will myself to stay calm. *At least attempt to keep a handle on your emotions.*

I'm opening my mouth to speak, to tell him what I want, when my phone rings in my pocket.

CHAPTER TWENTY-THREE

Palmer

I still.

Cole drops his hands from my face and watches me with muted disbelief. "Do you ever turn that thing off?"

"No. Someone might need me." I tug the phone out of my pocket and spot Val's name. By the time I see it, the call has ended and she's sent a text to call her later. "It was just Val."

"You realize that you don't have to be on call for every person in your life all the time, right?"

"Yeah. Kind of."

"Do you ever just . . . I don't know. Turn your phone off?"

"No. What if Ethan needs me?"

He shifts his weight. "Ethan is with my parents right now. I assure you, one million percent, that if anything happened to him, they would call me. Send the National Guard. Hell, Mom would release carrier pigeons if she had to—the woman is unstoppable."

I laugh.

"Palmer," he says, lowering his voice a couple of octaves, "I can't promise you everything you deserve or want."

"I know, Cole—"

"But fuck, *I want you*. Right here. Right now."

Holy shit.

My mouth goes dry, both from his words and the heat in his gaze. I can feel my heart pound, pulsing blood through my veins at a tempo that probably isn't conducive to staying upright.

My resolve weakens to the point that it breaks altogether. I've made the choice to be with men far less tempting or deserving many times before. *So why not Cole?*

I know the answer. *It's because he's dangerous.*

While that might be true, I'm in control of this relationship or situation or whatever it is between us. Unlike with Jared or Charlie, I'm not going into this with any hopes or dreams. There are no promises—only the guarantee that he's not going to be around forever. That's a fact. It's on the table. I already know how this ends.

And while this ending would be a terrible movie, it does make it easier.

I just won't get my emotions involved, and it'll be fine.

I'm tired of fighting this. There's no false pretenses. I can trust myself . . .

I hold my phone in my palm. And turn it off.

A slow, sexy smile splits his cheeks as I toss the device onto the sofa.

"Is that your way of saying you want me too?" he asks, grinning.

"No." I smile. "That was my way of saying *I need you*. Right now."

He grins. "Are you sure?"

"Well, I mean, I said 'right now.'"

The words are barely out of my mouth before his lips find mine.

The contact disintegrates the invisible barrier between us. It's as if the red flags I initially saw in him have all switched to green, and now we're racing toward the checkered flag waving in the distance.

Cole cups the back of my head. His fingers lace through my hair, and he holds me still so he can kiss me.

His mouth moves against mine with a lazy thoroughness that drives me crazy. I part my lips. His tongue doesn't miss a beat, tangling with mine as my hands curl around his neck. He walks me back two steps until my back hits the wall. A giant basket filled with fake flowers hits my shoulder and then topples to the floor.

I pull away, laughing. He buries his face into the crook of my neck and sweeps me off my feet—literally.

"The flowers!" I say, pointing to the chaos on the floor as he carries me through the room. My legs dangle over one of his arms. The other arm supports my back.

"What about them?" The words are pressed into the space just below my ear. "Fuck the flowers."

I laugh again, dizzy with the endorphins flooding my brain.

He hums against my lips as we head toward a set of stairs. The vibrations carry through my body and pool in my core.

I lean my head back, exposing more of my neck. It's not intentional, but I'm not mad about it because Cole uses the opportunity to plant kisses across my jaw.

The scent of his body, sweet and warm, invades my senses. The pressure of his lips and fingers against my skin is almost too much to bear. The anticipation of what's next, *what's to come*, has me ready to crawl out of my skin.

"Where are you taking me?" I ask. "And why is it taking so long to get there?"

He chuckles, kicking a door open.

The room we enter is flooded with light. Before I can get my bearings, he tosses me onto a bed. The mattress recoils with my weight.

Cole stands next to the bed and smiles. "Was that fast enough?"

"No. I said I needed you, like, three minutes ago." I smile back at him. "You're giving me time to back out."

His grin wobbles. "If there's any chance of you backing out, we shouldn't do it to start with."

My shoulder blades dig into the mattress as I stare back up at him. *How is this man even real?*

I get on my knees and hold his gaze. Then, with courage that I didn't know I possess, I lift the hem of my shirt over my head.

The cool air wraps around my bare skin and through the lace of my bra. It's quite the juxtaposition to the heat building inside me. The contrast makes me light-headed but not unsure. So, under the weight of Cole's unbelieving watch, I undo the button of my jeans.

His Adam's apple bobs in his throat. He doesn't move.

I hold his gaze and undo my zipper, then slip out of the denim and discard it onto the end of the bed.

My curves are on full display. My cellulite and the cesarean scar across my belly from having Ethan are visible. The stretch marks across the top of my breasts and at my hips are there for him to see.

Typically, those elements that I consider flaws make me nervous, and I hide them if at all possible. But not today.

Cole's lips twitch as he takes his fill of me visually. "*Damn*, Palmer."

"This is me." I hold my arms out to the side. "If there's any chance of *you* backing out, we shouldn't do it to start with."

He grins at my words, the same ones he just gave me. "Backing out isn't an option for me, sweetheart. I've wanted you since the first moment I saw you."

His fingers find the edge of his shirt, and he rips it from his body.

My eyes nearly pop out of my head.

Cole must've been molded by an artist because his body is nothing short of a work of art. The lines in his abdomen are thick and deeply cut—practically carved out of the muscle in his torso. His shoulders raise from his body in heavy peaks that make me whimper. And his sides? *Kill me now.* They form an inverted triangle and narrow to his trim waist, which looks as powerful as it does lean.

I haven't fully absorbed the glory of his body when he removes his pants and boxer briefs.

I gulp.

His cock is rock hard. A bead of precum glistens at the head, and while I've never thought a penis was attractive, I'm into this one. Or, rather, hope this one is in me. Soon.

"I've never felt so ogled," he says, laughing.

"You know, the baseball people aren't doing a great marketing job."

"Why is that?"

The sun shines in the window, highlighting him as if it agrees with me.

"Because if they want to up their viewership, all they have to do is show some of that." I point at his naked body. "I'd tune in, and, being honest—I hate baseball."

He moves toward me. His hands hit the bed, and he crawls toward me. I scramble backward and lie on my back as he gets closer.

"How can you tell me you hate baseball?" he asks, positioning himself between my legs and hovering over me.

My body is *on fire*. Blood pours to my groin. My clit pulses, begging for stimulation to end the throb that's nearly painful.

His breath is hot against my skin. The skin-on-skin contact of our lower bodies frazzles my brain, and I can't think of anything but *him* and how if I moved the right way, I could probably find some relief.

"I don't know what you were saying," I say, almost panting.

He snickers. "You hate baseball."

"Yes," I say, shifting my hips in a desperate attempt for contact. "I also hate talking."

"Since when?"

"Since now."

He pops up on his hands in some kind of push-up that raises his body off mine. Just when I think he's going to roll off me, he lowers himself again.

His arms shake as he stays suspended inches above me and kisses me like he has all the time in the world.

I melt into the bed, draping my arms over his shoulders and lapping up the attention he bestows on me. He kisses me slowly, leisurely, nibbling at my bottom lip before pulling away.

He starts to get up, but I stop him with a palm to his chest. His brows furrow, unsure what I mean, but he stops moving all the same.

My heartbeat thundering in my ears, I take his hand. I hop off the bed and tug him to the edge.

"Palmer . . ."

His voice is laced with a warning. His tone is gruff. The sound scuffs against my skin, and I kneel in front of him.

I hold his gaze and slide the elastic off my wrist. My hands go to my hair as I fasten it high and out of the way. Cole watches my breasts move with the motion and licks his lips.

He sucks in a hasty breath, drawing the air in through clenched teeth.

I take a deep breath of my own and then, like the vixen that I am not, I lick the head of his cock.

He shudders, leaning back and catching himself with his hands. *"Fuck."* His hips flex forward as I situate my palm over his thick girth.

My thighs are coated with a wetness, sticking together as I get comfortable. I pump him in my fist and watch another bead of arousal form at the tip.

My tongue darts out, licking it as if I'm taking the top off an ice cream cone. The liquid is salty and hot, and I lick the residue off my lips.

He hisses.

"Do you like that?" I ask, squeezing him from base to tip.

He groans in response.

"Aw. Since when do *you* hate talking?" I ask, teasing him.

His eyes flash a darkness that causes my stomach to clench. "You're pushing it."

I grin up at him before putting him inside my mouth again. I swirl the head around, the softness stretched over the hardness of his shaft winding up my libido even more.

"No, I'm sucking it, actually," I say, the end of my ponytail brushing against his leg.

Cole laces his hands in my hair and tugs, as if he needs relief as badly as I do.

I reposition myself again and lick him from top to bottom.

"Palmer . . . ," he warns. "Damn it, Palmer."

But before he can say anything else, I take him in my throat.

"Shit."

It doesn't take long to discover what he likes. The rhythm is automatic, the pressure of my hand immediate. With each flick of my tongue, he tenses a little more.

My nipples bead into painful buds. I massage the base of his cock, holding his balls gently in my free hand.

And that's what does it. That's what has him removing himself from my clutches.

"I can't," he says, pulling me to my feet. "I'm not coming in your mouth."

"Why?"

He presses a long, wet kiss to my mouth. "Because you're coming first. And the first time I come, it's going to be inside you."

Fuck.

My knees go weak as I watch him dig through a dresser. He turns around and rips the corner of a condom with his teeth. It takes him a quick moment to roll it over himself.

I shiver as he nears.

Everything is heightened. The prickliness of the hair on the top of my head. The heaviness of my legs. The weight of my breasts and the throb in the apex of my thighs.

"Will you ride me?" he asks.

Suddenly, despite the events and confidence of the last little while, a nervous energy spreads through me like a warm summer breeze.

He rakes his gaze over me like I'm some kind of dream. It's confusing and dizzying and altogether lovely.

"Don't do anything that you don't want to do," he says softly. "But I really want to watch you come. I want to see your body and feel your curves. I don't want any of it hidden from me."

He unfastens my bra and lets it fall to the floor. His thumbs hook beneath the waistband of my panties, and he draws them down my legs. I kick them to the side.

Cole takes my hand and gently leads me onto the bed. He lies on his back and guides me on top of him.

I straddle his body, blocking out the way I think I look hovered over him, and focus on the happiness in his face.

He grabs his cock and positions it at my opening.

The sun fills the room, dousing us both in bright-yellow light. It's warm against my skin . . . just like Cole's mouth against my nipple.

"Oh *shit*." I moan the words as I lower myself inch by delicious inch onto his cock.

He tenses, lifting his chin and growling, before falling back to the mattress.

Watching him enjoy me is the most euphoric thing that's ever happened in my whole entire life.

"This feels so good," I say, my eyes rolling back into my head.

"You have no idea."

I try to laugh, but I'm too preoccupied with the fullness of my sex to offer more than a slight chuckle.

"Move," he commands, flexing his hips. "Come on. *Move*, baby."

I rock against him, nearly yelping at the contact with my swollen bud. Cole's fingers bite into the dip of my hip, urging me on.

We move together, finding our rhythm until we're in complete sync. It's a dance, and the steps feel like we've done them a hundred times. We fit together like a puzzle as he slides in and out of me with a perfected motion.

I open my eyes and look down to see him watching me. I start to look away.

"Hey," he says, gripping me tighter.

I return my gaze to his. He smiles and moves one hand to my breast. He rolls my nipple in between two fingers, and it's all I needed.

It's too much.

It's all too much.

The looks, the touches. The sweet words and sexy phrases. The way he makes me feel like I'm both not me and completely me at the same time.

It's all way too much.

"I can't . . ." My eyes roll back in my head. "Cole, I'm . . ."

The rest of the sentence comes out on a sigh.

"I'm almost there too," he says, the words caught in his throat.

The sound of his desire puts me over the edge, and I begin a free fall off a climax that's so high I think the crash might just kill me.

"Cole!" I scream, the explosive ecstasy spreading like wildfire through my veins. "Oh. My. *Shit!*"

My words are strangled, barely audible through clenched teeth. I shake from the pressure of the release.

His fingers are fire on my skin as he sinks into me one last time, holding himself as deeply as humanly possible inside me.

Finally, I collapse. My shoulders fall and I roll off the side—completely kaput.

The room is suddenly cold and not as brightly lit. Everything is more muted.

Everything except him.

I lie still, unsure what happens now. It wasn't something that I had time to think about beforehand. But before I can lose myself in the questions and drive myself mad, he surprises me.

He pulls me into his side and holds me against him.

"Don't," he whispers in my ear.

I pause, confused. "Don't what?"

His body shakes as he chuckles. "Don't start thinking too much."

"How did you know?"

He leans back and brushes a strand of hair out of my face. "Because I think I'm starting to get to know you."

Oof. "Oh."

He's still breathing heavily, and even that turns me on. *I did that to him.*

I nestle against him, growing sleepier with each passing second. He strokes my back lazily, as if we have all the time in the world.

But we don't.

"Palmer?"

"Yeah?"

He looks deeply into my eyes and whispers, "That was fucking incredible."

Oh. I like hearing that.

I blush. *It's true, though. It was incredible.* He *is incredible.*

"Let's get you cleaned up and presentable before they get back."

"Solid plan."

He grins and presses a kiss to my forehead.

And out of all the things that have happened today—that's the one kiss that I won't forget.

CHAPTER TWENTY-FOUR

Cole

"Be safe." I pat the roof of Palmer's car and back away. *Call me when you get home.*

Palmer gives me a smile, pulling the corners of my lips up with it, and then backs the car behind Dad's truck. Then, before I'm ready to see them leave, dust flies behind their tires as they head down the driveway.

I reach in my pocket and turn my phone back on.

My body buzzes with adrenaline from the afternoon. It's hard to stand still. I need to move, go—*do*.

I want to be with her.

Today was the easiest day that I've had in a long fucking time. I didn't worry about job offers, retirement speculation, or the numerous potential land mines in my near future. Not once did I consider what I was going to do with myself now that I'm a free man. And, somehow, I made it a whole day without side-eyeing my email and voice messages.

The last few hours were an alternate reality—one that I desperately needed. But that worries me too.

Do I just like spending time with Palmer and her son because I need the distraction? Or is it because I like them?

"Do you want dessert?"

I didn't realize that Mom has come outside. I glance over and spot her on the porch.

"I'm good," I say.

"I packed most of the chocolate pie and peanut butter bars up for Ethan to take home. But there's a bit left."

Her kindness makes me smile. Perhaps Palmer was right—I have been spoiled by my mom. But it also felt right watching her spoil Ethan. He's a good boy, and it hurts to know he doesn't have more people in his life to spoil and love him.

"I'm good, Mom. Thanks."

"Suit yourself." She starts to turn back to the house but stops. "It's funny, huh?"

"What's funny?"

She grins. "How . . ." She shakes her head. "You know what? Never mind."

Then she turns and goes back inside without another word.

I heave a sigh of relief as the door swings shut, grateful that she didn't go where I think she was going. Because I do know what's funny—how you can open your eyes and find yourself in a place you didn't know existed and with people you've never met . . . and feel at home.

I've done it once before. I knew the moment I walked into Swift Stadium that I was meant to be there. The feeling was unexplainable. Instead of being more anxious as I entered the locker room, I was soothed. I instinctively knew how to operate in the space and where things were. It felt like home. And if I allow myself to really analyze my time in Bloomfield—and more specifically, my time with Palmer—I might be inclined to feel the same way.

My heart tugs in my chest. Whether I've mentally processed the idea or not doesn't matter. I'm afraid that the rest of me has already sorted that shit and come to a conclusion. *Palmer Clark is fucking incredible.*

I jump as my phone vibrates against my thigh. I yank it from my pocket. *Fish.*

"Hey," I say, clearing my throat.

"Hey, what's happening over there?"

I suck in a lungful of air. "Not much. You?"

"Enough to keep me from heading down there to see you guys." He laughs. "I woke up this morning to water pouring into my kitchen from the apartment above me. You could've floated around if you had a raft."

"Doesn't sound good."

"Been waiting around on building maintenance all day. They got the water stopped upstairs and most of the standing water down here sopped up, but they're sending some professional crew to come dry it out or something. I don't fucking know."

"That sucks." I mosey around the lawn, tilting my face toward the sky. The final rays of the sun stream through the tree branches and warm my skin. "When are you heading back to San Diego?"

"Supposed to be going back on Tuesday, but now I don't know. I'm getting sick of having three homes to take care of—I'm telling you that. If it's not the plumbing here, it's the lawn care at the Columbus house. And if it's not that, it's the fucking homeowner's association in San Diego. Why do I even have three places? Who let me make that decision?"

We laugh. *First world problems.*

"Speaking of places in different spaces, are you liking it up there? Haven't heard too much out of ya lately," he says.

I look at the darkening sky and laugh.

"What?" Fish asks.

It's a hard-and-fast rule that I never say too much to anyone—especially things that are personal. I tell Fish more than anyone else, but I still don't open up a lot to him. It's a lesson I learned early on. Everyone wants a piece of the most talked about man in baseball. *Me.*

So why do I have Palmer's name on the tip of my tongue? Why do I almost need to talk about her, as if getting her existence known will somehow relieve me of this pressure building in my throat?

"I don't hate it here," I say, wading tentatively into the unknown. "It's different from what I'm used to, but it's kind of nice."

"I've told you before that you'd like small-town America. It has its shitty parts, sure, but there's something to be said for knowing everyone in your zip code."

I chuckle. "Yeah, well, I think I've met half the people in this zip code already."

"You probably have. Hey, what about that woman from the restaurant? What was her name? Palmer? Have you seen much of her?"

My feet stop next to the driveway. I look up to see that I'm halfway to the road.

Our conversations since Fish went to Cincinnati have been quick and infrequent. Palmer hasn't come up. I wouldn't have had a ton to say about her anyway . . . until tonight.

I force a swallow down my throat. "I just saw her tonight, actually."

"Why do I feel like there's a story that you're not sure whether to tell me or not?"

I chuckle. It's laced with a warning—*don't push too hard.*

"She seemed like a nice one," Fish says, picking up on my hesitation. "And hot."

Palmer *is* hot. But hearing Fish say it, *hearing Fish state the obvious about her*, grinds something deep inside me. I'm not worried about Fish; he's committed to his girlfriend, Nicole. But it reminds me that every man Palmer sees undoubtedly thinks about her like that. They undress her with their eyes. I wonder how many of them try to manipulate her to their advantage.

I ball my fist at my side.

"Have you spent much time with her?" he asks—pushing.

My first instinct is to lie to him, to put some distance between him and what's happening between Palmer and me. But it instantly feels wrong to deny the truth. I don't want to.

Maybe because I don't know how to juggle this wobbly intensity inside me now.

"Fish . . ." I wince, knowing this might backfire if he's in the wrong mood. "I need you to be serious for a minute, okay?"

"Ooh. Yeah. Serious. Got it." He pauses. "This is going to be good, isn't it?"

"Forget it—"

"Sorry." He clears his throat. "I'm done. I swear. Talk to me, Beck."

This is a mistake.

I run a hand over my face and sigh. My shoulder tenses. I vaguely remember it screaming when I tossed Palmer on the bed. But even with the flames in my rotator cuff, I still smile at the memory.

"This is all hypothetical," I say.

"Sure."

"I mean it. I don't want you jumping to conclusions or asking a bunch of questions. Just take it for what it is and respond."

"Okay. Go."

"All right." I take a deep, steadying breath. But as I exhale, I change my mind. I don't want to talk about Palmer. *Yet.* Not when I can still taste her. "I . . . I don't know what there really is for me in California."

The words topple out of my mouth in rapid succession. It's like if they don't slip out fast enough, I'll change my mind.

It's probably true because the sound of those particular words in my specific voice is almost too foreign to be true.

"I get that . . ." Fish leaves his thought there.

"But there's not a lot for me anywhere else, really."

I don't expound on the subject because I'm not sure what direction to take it. Luckily, Fish helps me out.

"Well, if you take one of the deals Scott has for you, that'll help you decide, right?" he asks. "I mean, if you have to be in a studio or in a press box, then you can kind of go from there."

"Yeah, but Fish—I don't know if I want to do any of that."

The line goes quiet.

I've never verbalized this to him. I've never verbalized it to anyone. In fact, I've always held tight to the idea that baseball is my life. But as I think about Palmer's infectious smile, her honesty, Ethan, my mom's cooking and her ever-present comfort, Dad's solid, sturdy presence . . .

I used to believe that I'd have nothing if I didn't have baseball in some form every day.

But I don't think that's true anymore.

The idea, the acceptance of the idea, makes me shiver.

I walk to the backyard and sit on top of the picnic table. A breeze kicks up and drifts over my bare arms.

Fish stays silent. I can imagine that he's trying to figure out if I've lost my mind or if I need a second to get my bearings. He'd be right—maybe on both things.

"Scott keeps pushing shit because of the money. That's his job, and I've basically asked him to field offers, so I get it. But none of it appeals to me, and I just keep considering it because . . ." I throw my one free hand up in the air. "Isn't that who I am? Who am I without baseball?"

Fish takes a breath. "You're Cole Beck, the guy that was a hell of a baseball player and now is something else."

"But what? What am I without it? Am I a guy that lives in a small town in Ohio and coaches little kids and eats at a diner with bottomless coffee for a dollar?"

I stop myself when I realize what I've said. *Is that what I'm thinking?*

"You could be if you want to. I think it sounds like a great way to start the next season of life," he says. "Is that what you want?"

"I don't know."

"Are you wanting someone to tell you that it's a good choice? Because I will. I think it's a great one, actually."

Why?

I bow my head and sigh. "I don't need you to tell me it's a good idea. I just . . . I don't know. This is stupid."

"No, it's not. It's fucking normal, Beck. You're a guy at the top of his game that decided practically overnight to retire, and now you're having to walk on the other side without much of a thought. It's a lot, going from the rigidity of a baseball schedule to no schedule at all."

Even though he can't see me, I nod. *Although, technically, I didn't* decide *to retire.* And even though it doesn't help to think about the email sitting in my inbox—the one I've been avoiding for days now—I do.

That's the key to everything. All I have to do is open it and read it and make a couple of calls. But I don't. Every fucking day, I choose not to go there just in case it's not what I want it to be.

Because I know what it says. I feel it in my gut. And if I'm right, I need to get the hell out of here before it's too late. Before I become a burden to everyone.

"No offense," Fish says, "but I thought we were gonna talk about Palmer."

Her name makes me smile. "Yeah, well, I don't know what to say about her."

"Let's start with this—are you fucking her?"

"Fuck off," I say, shaking my head.

"So that's a yes. Good work, my man. I'd ask for details, but—"

"Don't."

He whistles through his teeth. "Enough said."

"I didn't mean it like that," I say, cringing. "I just don't . . . you know—she's not the kind of girl you . . ."

"Wow. All right." He gathers himself. "So is she a part of your sudden lack of interest in California?"

"No." *Maybe.*

She could be.

She would be.

If only . . .

I give myself a moment to consider the possibility of staying in Bloomfield with Palmer and Ethan. Having dinners with my parents. *Having a family.*

Throwing the ball around with Ethan after school—if he continues to love the sport. Going to the grocery store. Mowing my own lawn.

I smile.

Waking up with Palmer and tucking Ethan in at night . . . maybe even having kids with Palmer someday.

All that would be incredible if I could add value to their lives. If I could bat cleanup. If I could be a contributing member of their team.

My breath holds in my chest, burning my lungs, until I gasp for air and then blow it out slowly.

"Any chance Palmer would move with you to the West Coast?" he asks.

Hot, churning bile sloshes in my stomach. I grimace at the discomfort.

"I don't think so. She and her kid have roots here," I say, as if it matters. *Because it does matter.* "Besides, that's not gonna happen anyway."

My jaw pulses at the admission. *Because it's true.*

"Hey, Fish? I gotta go," I add, hopping off the picnic table. "I'll call you later this week."

"Beck?"

"Yeah?"

He sighs. "I don't know what's going on, and I'm not going to hound you about it. Just know that I'm here to listen whenever you're ready."

I close my eyes and nod.

"Talk to ya later, man." He hangs up the phone.

I'm starting to walk toward the house when my screen lights up. I stop and look down.

Palmer:

Remember when I asked if I could trust you?

My fingers fly across the screen.

Me:

Yes.

Her answer comes instantly.

Palmer:

I'm trusting you.

I reread her words over and over again. "I'm trusting you." Not sure what to say or how she means it, I text her a simple reply and put the ball in her court.

Me:

I'm glad.

Palmer:

Honestly, I'd be lying if I said that I didn't hope something would happen between us today. But I'd also be lying if I said that it didn't make me super anxious.

Me:

Why? Are you okay?

Palmer:

I'm great. 🙂 As you know, I just overthink things so now I'm sitting in my car after Ethan has already gone inside, worrying about how this might change things. So, I want you to know that I'm trusting you to be honest with me and to keep things safe between us.

My heart tightens.

This is one of the things that makes Palmer so different. Her frank honesty. It's something I so rarely see, and it's refreshing. *I'd never betray that.*

Me:

You're always safe with me.

Palmer:

I believe that or else I would've stayed away from you.

Me:

You have my word that I won't hurt either of you.

Palmer:

Good. ❤ I'm going to go inside now and fight with my kid about getting a shower.

Me:

Sounds fun. 😉 Thanks for a great day. I mean that.

Palmer:

I had a great time. I mean that too.

I have a million things I could say, a thousand directions to take the conversation, because with Palmer, it's so easy. Instead, I text her good night and then head toward my parents' house with a spring in my step and a craving for dessert. Not necessarily the one my mom made me, but it'll have to do.

CHAPTER TWENTY-FIVE

Palmer

"Hey, Palmer! Did you get that invoice about the Blue Bird buses over to Cutler?" Kirk shouts from his office.

"I did! Sent it first thing this morning. I called their office and asked them to expedite it to keep things moving. I'm supposed to hear back from them this afternoon."

He pokes his head to the side so I can see his smiling face.

"I'll let you know when they call," I say, returning his smile.

I go back to the spreadsheet on my computer. It's taken me most of the morning to add in all the functions, wrap the text, and enter the data to make it work. But it appears to be working, and that smells like a major victory.

"I don't know what's gotten into me, but I'll take it," I say, dancing in my chair. I'm not sure if it's the shaking of my hips or the words "what's gotten into me" that makes me think of Cole, but a sudden wash of warmth floods my veins.

The smile kissing my lips is unstoppable. It's been a permanent fixture ever since I left the Becks' house a few days ago.

My weight sinks back into the chair, and I swivel back and forth. Staring off into the distance, I let my mind wander.

I've been grateful that rain has canceled baseball practice and that I've been too busy at work to see Cole. The texts we've exchanged have been fun. Flirty. But they've given me a second to gather my thoughts about Sunday afternoon.

The fact that I had sex with him.

In the morning, I wake up thinking that I'm going to regret it. I lie in bed and close my eyes and wait for the gloom that I expect to cloud my head.

But it doesn't come.

I don't feel bad for having sex with Cole. There's not even a hint of dismay anywhere inside me for taking Ethan to the Becks' for dinner. If anything, I'm glad I did it—both things.

Ethan has been extra lighthearted lately. I heard him talking about going to the cave with one of his friends during an online gaming chat. The happiness in his voice made my heart sing. *How can that be a bad thing?*

And Cole . . . I wiggle in my seat.

I look forward to his texts. Sneaking outside to talk to him last night reminded me of a time in my life when I felt free. *Happy.* Like a whole person instead of one split into a bunch of roles that serve other people.

I love my life. Ethan is my world, and I adore my job and Val and the community events I participate in. But this thing with Cole is something just for me—even if it's only for a little while.

And that's okay. It has to be.

"Hey, Palmer?" Kirk asks, coming into the doorway.

"What's up?"

"I have a favor to ask of you."

Oh great. "Sure, Kirk. What's going on?"

A shadow ripples across his face. "There's a bus auction Friday in Parkersburg. There's no online apparatus for us to bid from here, and I was going to go, but the wife has a doctor's appointment in Columbus. I—"

"Do you need me to go?"

He nods. "I hate to even ask you, but Charlotte gets her biopsy results back from her breast scan. I'm sure it's nothing, but I really don't want to send her alone."

"You can't send her alone." I smile reassuringly at him. "Go with her. I'll go."

Relief settles on his features. "It won't cause you any problems?"

"No. I'll have Val grab Ethan from school, or he can ride the bus. It won't kill him. And I should be back in plenty of time to take him to practice."

And see Cole. I smile, ignoring the butterflies in my stomach.

"Thank you," Kirk says. "I appreciate you."

"Hey, no problem." I glance at my computer. "I'm going to finish this and then step out for lunch. Cool?"

"Absolutely."

He goes back into his office, and I make quick work of entering the last bit of data into the spreadsheet. The formulas work wonderfully, and I hit "Save," beaming at my handiwork.

I'm starting to get up and grab my keys when Kirk's voice fills the air once again.

"Palmer?"

"Yeah?"

"Hey, Burt said he can go on Friday if you don't want to."

His words hang in the air as I scramble to make a decision.

"Um, okay," I say, picking up my phone. "That would be easier for me, if you don't mind."

"Maybe it'll do him some good to get out of here. If he messes up down there, he'll have no one to blame but himself."

I walk across the room and stick my head inside Kirk's office.

"What a shame that would be," I tease.

He laughs. "Go take your lunch break and get out of here."

I laugh, too, and exit the office.

The sky is still dreary, but the temperature is warmer than it has been. The air tastes sweet and smells faintly of fresh spring flowers.

I head to my car with a renewed sense of optimism. Everything just feels . . . possible. Life seems doable.

It's just because it's springtime. That's it.

I climb inside my car and look at my phone. I have two missed calls from Val. It's unlike me to go more than a day without talking to her. *She's probably starting to worry.*

The phone rings three times before she answers. "I was getting ready to come looking for you."

I laugh. "I'm fine. Sorry for not calling you back. Work has been crazy today."

"And yesterday?"

"Yesterday too."

"Really, Palmer?"

I laugh again. "It's been a busy start to the week, okay?"

"That's great, but I get the distinct feeling that you're avoiding me. The question is *why*?"

It's immature and juvenile to feel the way I've felt since Sunday—like not telling anyone about Cole and me makes it special. *Because it's not special.* It's just a hookup, and I know that.

I think.

What worries me are the dreams that I have when I don't make an effort to block them. They come both in the day and night, visions of curling up against Cole in bed or making him dinner or hanging out with him and Ethan . . . like a family.

Don't.

"What have you been up to over there?" Val asks.

"Oh, nothing."

"You're lying." She laughs. "I'm trying to be a good friend and not push you to talk about things that you don't want to, but . . . *push, push*. Tell me."

A slow smile breaks across my face. "It's not much. Just that Ethan and I went to the Becks' house for dinner on Sunday—"

"You did what?"

I laugh.

"It's Tuesday, Palmer, and you're just telling me this? How do you even call yourself my best friend?" She huffs. "Oh, my gosh. Tell me everything."

My cheeks flush. "There's nothing to tell."

"That's it. I'm getting a new best friend that will let me live through her. That will share the sordid details of her life with me like a true ride or die."

I watch as Fred, the parts runner, approaches his car. He waves at me with a puzzled look, probably wondering why I'm just sitting in the parking lot. I shrug. He laughs.

"Cole invited Ethan and I over for dinner with his family. It was really nice," I say. "Then his parents took Ethan hiking, and Cole and I . . . you know . . ."

"You slept with him, didn't you?"

"Maybe."

She squeals. "I'm bringing wine over tonight, and you're telling me all the things. If you get into *those* kinds of details now, I'll get all flustered, and I have to go back into work."

I laugh.

"So, what's this mean?" she asks.

Her question is innocent. She means nothing by it, and if she had an inkling that her inquiry would throw me, she wouldn't have asked. If I get this far into things with a man, it usually means there's something there to build off. So it's a fair question.

But this time? There's nowhere to go from here.

My stomach wobbles. "It doesn't mean anything."

Despite my best attempt to keep my voice nonchalant, even I can hear the hollowness in the words.

"Oh," she says. "I just thought maybe . . . well, I don't know what I thought. You've just been saying that you didn't want to jump into things, and he . . ."

Yeah. I get it. This is stupid.

"I understand," I say, my spirits sinking. "I mean, you're right. This is going to be over before it really even starts."

"That's not necessarily a bad thing."

I strum my fingers against the steering wheel. My lips part for me to fall into old habits—to think the worst and start backtracking. But something stops me.

"No, it's not." My eyebrows rise. Even I wasn't expecting to say that. "I'm not going to lie. I like him."

The words burn as they slide out of my mouth. Admitting that—putting it into the universe—feels like I'm just asking for trouble. *But how can I be in trouble if I'm being honest? I can't be duped if I see it for what it is, right?*

"If Cole was a regular guy and worked at the Piggly Wiggly or the coal mine, I'd absolutely give him a shot," I say. "But he's not that kind of guy. So I have to take it for what it is, and right now, it's making me happy."

"That's great, Palm."

"I'm just going to keep a life jacket on, you know? Don't jump in too deep."

She claps, making me roll my eyes.

"Stop it," I say, shushing her.

"I like it. I like this Palmer. You go, girl."

"No one says that anymore."

"I just did. Besides, this is something worth celebrating."

"Why is that?"

She sighs. "Because you're living for you. You saw something you wanted and you went after it. You got it. You screwed it, apparently, and—"

"Stop!" I laugh. "Please. Stop."

"Fine. But I'll be over around nine, and you can tell me *everything*."

A grin kisses my lips. "I'll talk to you later. Bye."

"Bye."

I relax in my seat and feel the sun on my face. This feels like me—the me I want to be. *Fun. Hopeful. Exciting.*

Like there's something out there for me.

I close my eyes. My brain calms, the chaos in my head stills, and I find myself with one clear thought: if only this thing with Cole could be real.

You're always safe with me.

Thinking about the words typed on the screen from him floods my body with a calmness that I've never known. But that's the thing—Cole is all the things that I've always hoped to find in someone.

So of course he has to leave.

"No, you know that," I say to myself, opening my eyes. "You've always known that."

I'm looking down to reread his texts from last night when a new one pops up. It's from Cole to the parent group text for the baseball team.

Practice tomorrow night at 5:30 for whoever can show up. Last minute, I know, but we tarped the field and it doesn't look too bad. See you all there!

Then a separate text pops up just to me.

I have something for you. 😉

Me:

You do? Color me intrigued.

Cole:

I think you'll like it.

Me:

What is it?

Cole:

I can't tell you.

"Ugh," I say, my face aching from smiling.

Me:

Give me a hint.

Cole:

Well, it's hard.

Me:

Ooh. Do tell.

Cole:

I'll show you tonight if you're good.

I set my phone on my lap and look at the ceiling. My heart flutters so hard that I can barely breathe. I look at the screen again as it buzzes.

Cole:

Promise you'll blow on it?

Me:

WHAT ARE YOU TALKING ABOUT?

Cole:

Ha! Getting a call. Gotta go. See you tomorrow.

Me:

I wait to see if he replies, but he doesn't. He just leaves me hanging.

Instead of being frustrated, I'm intrigued. Also a little turned on. The rest of the day feels daunting, and not thinking of him and his *hard* present will be impossible.

Fucker.

Before I get out of my car and go back inside, I decide to even the playing field a bit.

Me:

They're pink.

His response is instantaneous.

Cole:

What is pink?

Me:

Oh, sorry, I didn't mean to send that to you.

Cole:

WHAT IS PINK?

Me:

My boss is yelling for me. Gotta go. See you tomorrow. 😉

I smile, turn my phone on Do Not Disturb, and head to Fletcher's for a sandwich.

CHAPTER TWENTY-SIX

COLE

"Whoa. Hold up just a second." I walk toward home plate from the outfield. "What are you trying to kill over here? You're swinging that thing like your life depends on it."

Braylon blows a snot bubble. "I'm trying to hit a dinger, Coach."

These kids and their dingers.

I take the bat out of his hands and refocus. "Hey!" I shout in a generalized way. "Everyone come in here for a second."

A dozen boys race toward the infield. Their cheeks are pink from the drop in temperature. Knees are dusted with grass stains and red dust from the field. They remind me so much of me.

I know the sparkle in their eyes from playing a game they love. The high from stretching your muscles and using your body is a power that I've chased all my life. But the camaraderie, the spirit of family they're experiencing with their teammates? That's the best part of all.

And that's the one thing I don't know how I'll replace in retirement.

"We have our first game in two weeks," I tell them. "You've really come together as a team. I've seen you supporting each other, cheering one another on, and working as a unit. I'm very proud of you."

A kid they all call "Sandbox" cracks his gum.

"So far," I say, "we've concentrated on the basics of fielding, base running, and a little hitting."

"We need to do more hitting," Braylon says. "I want to hit a homer in the World Series just like you."

I grip his shoulder and smile. "You can . . . *if* you practice the right way."

He slumps and sighs. *Not what he wanted to hear.*

"Listen up, guys," I say, giving Braylon's shoulder a squeeze before I release it. "Hitting is just as much about *how* you hit the ball as it is *how hard*. You have to have barrel awareness."

"I told them that!" Sandbox says from the back.

I smile at him. "You would be right. Does anyone know what this spot on the bat is called?" I point at the barrel and wait. Once it's clear that no one knows, I continue. "This is called the sweet spot."

"What does that mean?" Ethan asks.

"The sweet spot is the area on the barrel where it's most effective to hit the ball. It's the power source—the key to everything. We'll work on this at the next practice, but I want you all to be thinking about that," I say, glancing down at Braylon, "and not trying to kill flies when you swing the bat. All right?"

The team laughs as Braylon grins.

"Okay, Coach," he says.

I hand him his bat back. "Now, I want to make one more announcement before I let you leave."

My eyes flip immediately to Palmer. She's still standing by the fence, where she's stood ever since getting here late. Her late arrival made it impossible for me to chat with her before practice started, and the fact that she's been so close, yet so far away, has driven me mad. Every now and then I think I can smell a hint of her perfume in the breeze, and it makes me lose my concentration. I'd be annoyed if I weren't so turned on by it. *By her.* And I still sport a half-hard cock every time I think about her text.

It has taken everything in me not to drive to her house and call her repeatedly. I make do with an occasional text and a quick call here and there.

The thing is—I just like being around her . . . and Ethan. I find myself replaying our interactions when I'm alone instead of thinking about Scott's offers or the email that I finally read this morning.

> Dear Mr. Beck,
>
> Please call the office at your earliest convenience.
>
> Sincerely,
> Dr. Miigi

The world seems to slow down when I'm with them or think about them. My problems feel lighter. The future looks rosier. I don't feel as trapped in my own head, or my own life, like I do when I'm alone.

It's an odd sensation and one that I'm not sure what to do with. But I don't hate it. Not even a little bit.

I motion for Palmer to join us.

"Guys, I'd like to introduce you to Miss Clark—Ethan's mom," I say as Palmer gets closer. "I'm sure most of you already know her. She's going to be your team mom."

"Hey." She grins at the boys, then looks up at me with a hint of confusion. "Thanks for the introduction."

It's more of a question than an actual statement. It's also adorable.

"Miss Clark is going to be in the dugouts with you and helping you with the lineup," I say, ignoring the way Palmer looks up at me. "She'll answer your parents' questions and make sure you don't choke on your sunflower seeds, Sandbox."

Everyone laughs.

"I want you to treat her like you do me or any of the assistant coaches." I pull a whistle out of my back pocket. "Welcome to the team."

"Thank you," Palmer says, grinning. "I even get my own whistle?"

"Just don't use it a lot," I say.

She laughs, and it's music to my ears.

I place the whistle around her neck, trying my best not to touch her. She holds her hair off her neck as I lay the small lanyard against her. She smells warm, like coffee beans, and I want to bury my head in her hair and breathe her in.

"Before you guys go," I say, ignoring the fire in my stomach, "I want you to stop by and say hello to Ted. Do you guys know him?"

"Ted from the butcher shop?" Braylon says.

"He usually helps out with baseball," Sandbox says.

"That's right." I nod, shoving down the lump in my throat. "Please say hello to him. A big part of baseball is sportsmanship. He was supposed to be your coach this year but had a medical procedure. I know he misses being out here."

Sandbox looks up at me. "So, will he be our coach next year? Or do we get you again?"

"Please say you," Braylon says. "No offense to Ted, but you're swaggy."

"Swaggy?" I laugh. "Let's do this one season at a time, all right?" I hold my hand in the air at an angle. "Give me 'team' on three."

My hand is joined in the air by theirs.

"One, two, three—team!" we all say in unison before the group breaks.

Dirt is kicked in the air as the boys march off to say hello to Ted. I watch them shake the man's hand . . . and him beam.

I get it. They're a great group of kids, and coaching them has been entirely more fun than I ever dreamed. But they feel like my team now, and I'm trying to be an adult about it.

It's harder than I thought it would be.

"Thanks for the *hard* whistle," Palmer says, drawing me back to the present. "Really great description."

I wink at her. "What did you think it was?"

Her cheeks flush as she laughs.

Damn this woman.

"You did great today, Ethan," I say, needing a change of subject before my mind gets too carried away. "I saw that throw you made to your cutoff from center field. Nice job."

"Really?"

"Of course."

"I thought I got a little off with my mechanics." He takes a step and pretends to throw a ball. "I'm working on it."

"That's all you can do—work on it."

"I know how we can celebrate that," he says. "Wanna go get a corn dog with us?"

My gaze shifts to Palmer. She's smiling brightly. The reservation that I usually see in her eyes has weakened so much that I really have to strain to find it. *Thank God.*

"I could be convinced to have a corn dog for dinner," I say, giving her the space to bow out if she wants.

But me? What I want to do is wrap my arm around her waist and pull her into me. Kiss her forehead. Take her home.

"I think it would be fun." Ethan looks at his mother. "Instead of you two sneaking around and having pizza without me, you could include me this time."

Palmer gasps. "We weren't sneaking around, and even if we were, it's none of your business, child."

He laughs. "So is that a yes, then?"

"Maybe I don't want a corn dog," she says, smiling.

"Fine. I'll take Ethan, and we'll get one without you," I say, teasing her back.

Her hands find her hips. "Oh, no. You two aren't going without me."

"Then say yes," Ethan says, practically bouncing on his toes.

As if it pains her to acquiesce, Palmer sighs. "Fine. Go get your stuff, and we'll get a corn dog with Cole."

Ethan bounds for the dugout, fist pumping as he runs. I watch him and laugh.

"I'm getting him two corn dogs," I say.

"Why?"

I pull my gaze back to Palmer. Her hair is blowing in the gentle breeze, turning her cheeks the softest shade of pink. *Shit, she's beautiful.*

"Because I spent all practice trying to figure out how I was going to talk you into grabbing a bite to eat, and he did my dirty work for me," I say.

She laughs. "After the day I've had at work, I'm happy to do anything for dinner that means that I don't have to cook."

"Do you cook a lot? Is that a thing you like to do?"

"Well, no. Not really. And Ethan is so picky. It's macaroni and cheese and chicken nuggets and pizza way more than I really care to admit." She pauses. "But maybe I'd like to cook if I had more time to do it—to really prepare a meal and be thoughtful about it. Right now it's a mad scramble to get it done and cleaned up before I collapse onto the couch in a heap of exhaustion."

The scenario she's painted twists my heart. *Is that what her life is like? Does she not get to enjoy any of it?* It makes what my mom said mean even more. Palmer deserves more than a night off from cooking and cleaning up messes.

I mentally pull myself back as my mind jumps into action, trying to figure out how to make her life easier. How to make her happier.

That's not my place.

Is it?

Before I can think it through, Ethan joins us again.

"Got my stuff and said hi to Ted," he says, panting. "Are you guys ready to go?"

"You two go on. I need to clean up here and have a quick chat with Ted myself. I'll pick you up in twenty?"

Palmer nods. "Perfect."

We exchange a simple grin, and I fight the urge to kiss her. *Why does this conversation feel like it should end with a kiss?*

"See you soon," she says and then leads Ethan to her car.

I watch them go and feel a sense of satisfaction settle inside me. It's reminiscent of a constructive day or a holiday with family that didn't result in an argument about politics. It's a peacefulness that washes over me, and the fact that Palmer and her son are the ones who instigated it worries me.

"Hey, Beck!"

I look over as Ted, a staggering man in bib overalls, gets to his feet. A bright-red beard matches the short hair poking out from under a San Diego Swifts baseball hat. I wonder if he's always worn that hat or if he picked it up for this occasion. He wasn't wearing it the one time I met with him at Bud's.

"Ted," I say, extending a hand as I near him. "It's nice to see you again."

"It's nice to see you too. You're doing a hell of a job with the boys."

We shake hands.

"They're a great bunch of kids," I say.

He looks around. "Well, they try. Our really skilled kids play travel ball in the spring in Forest Falls, so these guys . . . you know. They aren't going to be our all-star players or anything."

The matter-of-factness of his tone strikes a chord inside me.

"These kids are twelve," I say. "They're just getting their coordination. Any of them could be an all-star in a couple of years."

He shrugs as if that's not a real concern . . . or possibility.

"Besides," I say, "I hope they have fun and make friends. That's the best part of this game."

"Sure it is. Sure it is," he says, nodding. "Well, the doctor cleared me to get back to doing stuff again. I have to take it a bit easier than normal—hit a six and a half or a seven instead of a ten like I usually do. But I got my boy working the butcher shop, and that helps a lot."

I get what he's saying. *He's ready to come back.*

"Oh," I say, stumbling around for the right words. "That's good news."

"Yeah. So if you need help out here, you just let me know. I know Bud turned over the team to you this year, but they always feel like mine. Guess it's because this age group has been mine for the last eleven years."

He laughs as if he's just being conversational and not confrontational. I'm not sure about that.

"I can add you to the group chat so you can see when we'll be practicing," I say with more than a small dose of caution. "It's been hit-or-miss with the weather, but we're out here two or three times a week at least."

"That'd be great."

"Great." I give him a forced smile. "I need to get this stuff picked up and get out of here."

"Sure thing." He takes a step back. "Nice to talk to you, Beck."

"You too, Ted."

I give him a final nod. I turn toward home plate and make quick work of getting things put in the shed so I can get to my girl.

CHAPTER TWENTY-SEVEN

PALMER

Hey, Ethan!" I poke my head out of my bedroom. "Will you call King Pin Alley and see how busy they are?"

"Why?"

His voice comes barreling down the hallway in a distinct tone that tells me he's already turned on a video game.

I tap my face with the towel in my hand and sigh. "Because I don't want to get down there and not have a table."

"You can't call?"

"I'm trying to get cleaned up! And I have to text Val not to come over!"

"Full box! Two hundred! On me! On me! I'm lagging!"

I hold my hands out in front of me. "What language is this child even speaking right now?"

"I lagged out!" Ethan yells from his bedroom. "Dang it! Why is our internet so bad?"

"Forget it," I mumble and then go back into my bedroom. I grab my phone and type a quick note to Val that our girls' night is postponed.

My jeans have been swapped for a cleaner pair. The tie-dye hoodie that I picked up at a garage sale with Val last year has been discarded for a black thermal shirt with a flattering V neck that gives the slightest glimpse of cleavage. I ran a brush though my hair and another across my teeth and refreshed my deodorant. All the while, I keep telling myself that this is not a date.

There are a ton of reasons why it's not. First, he didn't invite me. Ethan invited him. Second, my child is accompanying us, and while that's not a definite *not a date* indicator, it's close enough. Third, we aren't dating.

I sit on the edge of my bed with a pair of socks in my hand. Even though this isn't a date, per se, it's nice.

It's quite lovely to have something to look forward to tonight. And it's even better that it's with Cole Beck.

I enjoy being with him. But just as importantly, I enjoy being inside my own skin when I'm with him. I'm less stressed. I'm funnier. I feel prettier, even though being in his presence doesn't actually make me more beautiful. That's not how things work. But damn it if I don't feel a little rosier when I'm on the receiving end of one of his smirks or graced with one of his laughs.

I smile just thinking about it.

The doorbell rings, knocking me out of my reverie.

"Crap!" I toss my socks on the bed and spring toward the door. It takes only a few seconds to reach the foyer.

Cole stands on the porch with his hands in his pockets. He smiles. "Hey, good-lookin'."

I try not to beam but am pretty sure I fail. "Charmer." I step to the side and allow him in.

"I drove by King Pin on the way here, and it's a madhouse. Is bowling a big deal around here or what?"

"Yeah, I was afraid of that." I close the door. "It's Wednesday."

He furrows a brow.

"It's League Night. You know—when the league teams play."

"Oh."

I laugh. "Small-town entertainment."

He walks toward me and stops a few feet away. His chin dips. "Where's Ethan?"

Cole's voice is deep, husky. His eyes are pools of blue. They send a shiver down my spine.

"He's in his room," I say softly. "Why?"

The corner of his lip tilts toward the ceiling. "Because I've had this itch to kiss you all evening."

A flood of euphoria fills me from head to toe as I look up at him. *He wants to kiss me.* While I've had men want to kiss me before, it's not been like this. It's never felt so honest, so genuinely like they are so into me that they just want to kiss me. Not get me to bed, not manipulate the moment in some way. *Just kiss me.*

I smile. "That's funny."

"Why is it funny?"

"Because that's basically all I've thought about since I left you on Sunday."

His smirk melts me. My knees may no longer be attached to my body, but I can't take my eyes off his to check.

"That's all you've thought about?" he asks. "If that's all you've been thinking about, I didn't do a very good job."

The tiny sliver of air between us grows hot, amplifying every move that either of us makes.

"I thought you did a great job," I say, licking my lips. "But if you'd like a second chance to—"

"This internet freaking sucks!" Ethan's voice reaches the foyer moments before he does. "Mom?"

Ethan enters the room just as Cole takes a giant step back. Ethan grins.

"What are you guys doing?" he asks.

I look at Cole, my heart beating too hard to select words to respond with. Without missing a beat, Cole smoothly turns to Ethan.

"Hey, buddy," he says. "I was telling your mom that the bowling alley is packed. We can still go down there, but there was no parking when I drove by."

Ethan makes a face. "My friends are all online and want me to play with them." He looks at me. "Is that okay?"

"Well, you are the one that invited Cole for a corn dog . . ."

"Like you care." Ethan laughs. "I'll still eat with you. But maybe we can just hang out here and I can play my games? *Please?*"

I turn to Cole. "What do you think? This was a thing between the two of you."

He acts like he's warring over the decision. "I'll be a bit devastated, but I guess it's okay."

"Awesome!" Ethan fist pumps. "Holler at me when dinner is ready, okay?"

But before I can answer, he's already closing his bedroom door.

"He invites me over and then leaves me with you?" Cole laughs. "That kid is my favorite kid ever."

I laugh too. "I don't mind him myself."

"What do you want to do about dinner? You haven't eaten, have you?"

"No. I can just make something here." I head into the kitchen with Cole on my heels. "I don't know what we have, but I'll figure it out."

"Isn't there a place we can order from?"

I stop at the counter. "Sure. Um, there are a couple of pizza places and a Mexican place in town. And Fletcher's, of course."

"What's your favorite?"

"Fletcher's, I guess. We really don't eat out much."

A flash streaks through his features, but it's only there for a moment. Then he nods. "Cool. Want to order from Fletcher's, then?"

"Sure. Eating out on a Wednesday? Fancy."

He laughs at me like I'm being funny.

"I mean it," I say, sitting at the counter. "Midweek takeout is a fancy-people thing."

He sits beside me. "Well, you wouldn't believe how fancy I usually am, then. By the time I get home from practice, I'm not even thinking about making food."

"Well, I'd rather not think about it either. So no judgment here."

We share a smile.

"What did you do today?" I ask him.

He stretches his arms out in front of him. "I helped Dad finish a fence in the backyard. I now have a host of new topics to discuss with my therapist."

I giggle because I can tell he's joking. "It was that good, huh?"

"Turns out that I can swing a bat and hit a four-hundred-foot home run, but I can't properly use a posthole digger." He grins. "I can also swing a level bat, but my opinion of level for a fence is off. *Which might be true*," he adds, almost vaguely. "Anyway, it was a fun day. What about you?"

"I had a war with a shipping company today over a container of parts we sent to Panama. So that was a blast. And then Kirk told me that I didn't have to go to Parkersburg on Friday for a bus auction because Burt is going. That was fabulous on one hand because I don't want to go, but it also sucked because Burt makes *everything* harder than necessary. But that's all fine because he changed his mind at the end of the day, and now . . . I'm headed to the auction."

"Auctions sound fun."

I shrug. "I honestly don't mind them. It's exciting to bid on buses and decide which are worth the price and all of that. But when Val isn't around, it's trickier to get Ethan picked up from school and for someone to hang out with him while I'm gone." My spirits start to sink, so I shove them away. "Anyway, it's all good. Everything worked out."

Cole watches me carefully. "You really like your job, huh?"

"Yeah. I do."

The answer comes instantly. It falls from my lips without me thinking about it.

"I love the challenge of it," I say. "It's different every day. It's a constant spring of information. But more than anything, I like being a part of something."

Cole folds his hands on the counter. "That's a very natural thing. It's how I feel about baseball. How I feel about . . ." He shakes his head and stops himself. "It's how people feel about being with their families, in their communities."

That's not what he was going to say. I want to ask him about it but choose not to at the last second. Instead, I keep talking so it doesn't get weird.

"That's it," I say. "As much as I get annoyed with Burt and the guys in the shop, they feel like a family to me. And Kirk has been so good to me and believed in me and helped me when I was just a single mom begging for a job. I respect him more than anyone in my life, to be honest."

"Sounds like a great guy."

I nod. "I'm sure he'd give you a job, now that you're retired."

Cole laughs. "Hell, I might go see him about it. It would beat dealing with Scott."

"Who is Scott?"

"My agent." He sighs. "He's pressuring me to make a choice, but I don't want to choose anything on the table, if I'm being honest."

"So what do you want to do?"

It's a simple question, and I meant it as such. *What do you want to do with your life, Cole?* We've had this discussion to some extent too. But his reaction—the stillness of his body, the intensity of his gaze—makes me think he's internalized it in a much different, much deeper way.

"What do you want to do with yours?" he asks instead of answering the question himself.

Ah, deflection. He knows he tripped me up the last time, when he asked what I would change in my life if I could. So he knows my basic answer: a family. But I'm asking him to dig deeper, so I'll play fair and offer him my truth.

"I don't know." I shimmy around in my chair. "I mean, I'd like to find a rhythm to my life. I'd like to get married, have another child."

He nods.

"I want . . ." I try to find the right words. "I want a Christmas-movie life. Do you know what I mean? Like, I want traditions and routines. I want Ethan to be able to say, 'Oh, we have soup on Christmas Eve and open our matching pajamas, and we have dinner at six every night.' We do those things now, but it feels incomplete, in a way. Like there's a missing part of us, and I can't find it."

Cole sighs. "I know what you mean."

"You do?"

He takes a long, lingering breath. "Yeah. I do. All these options in front of me—none of them seem right. I feel like there's a piece of my life out there, and I can't find it either. I never noticed it before. Maybe it didn't exist before I retired. I don't know, but I certainly feel it now."

"We're just two lost souls."

He laughs. "That we are. So, dinner?"

It's not the most seamless transition, but I'm grateful for it.

"Cheeseburgers from Fletcher's?" I ask.

"Sounds great."

CHAPTER TWENTY-EIGHT

Palmer

"How did you know that?" I look at my son like he has three heads. "Who are you hanging out with?"

Ethan laughs. "I read books, Mom."

"You do?"

"Not by choice or anything. Teachers expect it."

"Oh."

Cole holds the remote control in the air. "Are we playing again?"

The closing credits of the third episode of an old game show roll across the television. I yawn, stretching my legs out on the ottoman in front of me.

"I'm not playing if Mr. Smarty-Pants over there is going to clean house in the astronomy category," I say, nodding at Ethan.

"I also swept the *Titanic* category."

"That you did."

Cole laughs. "I'm not sure I want to play with you two again. I thought *I* was competitive, but . . ." He whistles. "You two make me nervous."

Ethan rolls his eyes. "Mom is the least competitive person in the world until you turn on a game show. Then she's like a vulture."

"She actually did pretty bad in the bird category," Cole teases.

I throw a pillow at him. "I hate birds, so that was unfair."

"You also did terribly in mathematics," he points out.

"And mythology," Ethan chimes in.

I gasp. "Those are stupid categories. I killed it in nineties music and potpourri. Oh! And four-letter words. I nailed that."

Ethan looks at Cole and smirks. "Are those even real categories?"

"Yes, they are," I say.

Cole ignores me. "Compared to your astronomy knowledge and my deep understanding of world history and sports, I don't think potpourri really holds a lot of water." He glances at me. "She's cute, though."

I feel Ethan's eyes on me, but I can't look away from Cole. His grin is simple and adorable and makes me blush.

"Well, you're both cute too," I say, flipping my attention to Ethan. "And I'm super proud of your intelligence. You get that from me, you know."

"Clearly." Ethan gets to his feet and pretends to swing a bat. "You hit a home run with me."

Cole stands too. "Not with that swing. Come here."

I lean back against the sofa and watch the two of them delve into a baseball conversation that I can't follow. Or maybe I don't want to follow it. Trying to understand the mechanics of a baseball swing would take away from appreciating the two of them together.

My insides warm as Ethan shines under Cole's attention. *Again.* This has happened a number of times tonight. Cole will stop what he's doing to explain something to Ethan or listen to a joke or story, and Ethan eats it up.

But it makes sense. I do it, too, when Cole acts that way to me.

Cole Beck is one of the good ones.

I discovered tonight during dinner, when Cole stopped to look up the origins of hot dogs for Ethan, that Cole's attentiveness is my favorite thing about him. It's not his shoulders, which are fabulous, or the way he kisses me, which I love. It's not the way he smells or the sound of his laugh. It's the way he makes me feel like I'm the only person in the room.

It's even better when I know Ethan feels that way too. *He does that for my boy, like no one else but me has ever done.*

I'm treading into deep water here. I feel the depth licking at my throat. But I'm not scared like I thought I would be—like I should be. Maybe I'll regret this eventually, but right now the reward, even if for a bit, outweighs the risk.

"Yeah, just like that," Cole says. "Your power comes from your hips. Work on keeping your motion like that."

Ethan practices his swing a final time. Then he turns to Cole.

"Thanks for helping me," he says. "And for hanging out with us tonight."

This catches Cole off guard. He flinches briefly but recovers quicker than I expect.

"Of course, my man," Cole says, patting Ethan on the shoulder. "It was my pleasure. You're a cool kid."

Ethan looks at me out of the corner of his eye and grins a shit-eating grin. "A cool kid with a cool mom."

"A very cool mom." Cole looks at me over his shoulder and winks. "A pretty one too."

I laugh, shaking my head at them. "Why are you two being sweet?"

"Because I want him to like you so he comes back," Ethan says, laughing too. "Let's face it—he didn't come here to hang out with me."

"Ethan . . . ," I warn, but he keeps talking anyway.

"He's nice to you, Mom. *All the time.* Not like Charlie or the other guys you've gone out with that make you mad and frustrated. Or cry in the bathroom."

He knows about that?

"This is the kind of guy you should have around," Ethan says, his voice teeming with passion. "And I like him, too, and he doesn't think I'm just some punk kid in the way, like dumb Charlie."

Cole shifts, and his movement catches my attention. But my gaze is locked on my son.

I hold my breath, unsure about what to say. This is a revelation in a lot of ways because I didn't know he felt this way. I didn't know he was so astute about the guys I've dated or that I've been upset. I don't want to lie to him and discount the truth. *He should always know he can be honest with me.* But how do I address it correctly? And realistically?

There's so much to unpack, and I don't know that I want to do it in front of Cole.

I clear my throat. "You're right. Cole is the kind of guy that I should have around. I'm working on that. But you are *never* in the way. All right?"

He nods.

Cole pulls his attention from me. "It takes a lot of guts to do that, you know."

"What do you mean?" Ethan asks.

"It takes a lot of courage to be honest and tell people how you feel. Most adult men that I know can't do that."

Ethan raises his chin.

My heart squeezes as I watch their interaction. My instinct is to jump in and say something, to try to prevent the conversation from getting too serious. But the way Cole looks at him has me holding my tongue. *And my breath.* He's not backing away from the hard stuff. He's not leaving Ethan to wrestle with his feelings on his own.

Like Jared does.

"You and your mom have a pretty special thing going," Cole says. "It reminds me of me and my mom."

Ethan grins. "I like your mom."

"She likes you too. She told me that you are a lot like me as a kid."

"Really?" Ethan asks.

Cole nods. "It can be hard to be like us. We have a lot of fun on the outside but think about things too much. Sometimes that can be hard."

"*Yeah.* Especially at night."

What? I don't move, afraid that Ethan will remember I'm here and stop talking.

"Don't let your thoughts turn into worries." Cole grips his shoulder. "And never let anyone make you feel like you're in the way—especially when it comes to your mom. You're smart and kind and fun to be around. If anyone makes you feel any differently, that's on them. Not you."

I blink and hope the tears threatening to spill over my eyelids stop.

Ethan looks at Cole with a hope, a respect, that I've never seen on his face before. And the tenderness on Cole's face steals my breath.

"I'm going to go to bed," Ethan says, looking at me. "Good night, Mom."

"I'll come up and check on you in a little bit."

He grins. "Good night, Cole."

"Have a good sleep, buddy."

Ethan bounds up the steps and into the darkness.

As soon as he's out of sight, I draw in a lungful of air. *What just happened?*

Cole turns toward me slowly and sits on the end of the couch. He runs a hand over his chin and sighs.

"I d-don't . . . ," I stammer. "I don't know what just happened here. I feel gobsmacked."

He smiles. "That kid loves his mom."

"Well, his mom loves him, too, but I literally had no idea that he knew that I cried in my bathroom."

Cole twists his head to mine. A darkness filters through his blue eyes.

"Not that it happens often," I add in a hurry. "But I didn't know he worried about me like that. Here I am worrying about Ethan and how any man I date will affect him, and he's worrying about it too. What the heck?"

"He's not worried about that. His concern is *for you.*" Cole shrugs. "He wants you to be happy."

"I'm only happy if he's happy."

Cole starts to speak but stops. He runs a hand over his chin again.

"You were great with him," I say, my heart squeezing in my chest again. He listened in a way that showed Ethan his opinions were important. He validated him and supported him. *My gosh.* "Thank you for that."

He smiles. "I really had a fun time tonight. It's been a long damn time since I ate burgers and chips. And then played Uno and watched game shows while drinking milkshakes."

"We live a glamorous life over here," I say, laughing.

His smile remains, but he stills. "You've carved out a pretty neat little piece of the world for the two of you. I know that it hasn't been easy, and you're not where you want to go yet, but I hope you see how great it is."

I pull my legs to my chest and absorb the compliment. It fills me with pride.

"I have this house in San Diego," he says, his gaze drifting off into the abyss. "It's . . . very nice. I have nice cars. The ocean is in my backyard."

Wow.

"I've purchased paintings and rugs and dishes. I've hosted parties on occasion and had dinners with my friends in the kitchen. And no matter what I do, it doesn't feel like this." He looks at me again. "It doesn't feel like home."

My chest is the only thing that moves. My breaths, quick and shallow, are the only sound that I can hear.

I force a swallow. "Maybe you have bad taste."

It's a silly thing to say, but it's the first thing that comes to mind. The first thing except for the truth.

Maybe what he lacks is a family.

The mere idea of verbalizing that to Cole terrifies me. What if he thinks I'm suggesting it—as in, *Hey, we should be a family.* Because I'm not suggesting that. *Who would I be to think that he and I are on that level?* It's laughable. It's ridiculous.

It's impossible.

Cole grins. "I don't think that's the issue."

"Have you had an interior designer look at it?"

His grin gets wider. "I haven't. You think that will help?"

I shrug, my cheeks flushing. *Stop talking before you think.*

"Maybe I'll give it a try," he says.

"Great."

He laughs and stands. "I probably need to get going."

I scramble to my feet too. "Really? Why?"

He reaches for my hands. I place my palms against his. He pulls me closer—so close that our chests nearly touch.

Instantly, the vibe goes from slightly awkward to complete ease. He nestles his fingers together at the small of my back. The embrace, that really isn't one, causes all tension to exit my body. In its place is a comfort and peace that I wish I could bottle up for later.

For when he's gone.

For when I'm alone and needing to find this feeling that I'm afraid only comes with him.

"If I don't leave now," he says, his voice just above a whisper, "I'm going to have a hard time not kissing you."

I grin. "So?"

"And if I start kissing you, I'll want to touch you."

"And?"

He kisses my forehead. His lips linger against my skin. I lean toward him, closing my eyes, and try to take his advice. *Don't let your thoughts turn into worries.*

When he pulls away, I sigh.

"I have some calls to make early," he says. "And you have work tomorrow, right?"

I nod.

He takes my hand in his again and leads me upstairs.

I'm not sure what I expected tonight, but it wasn't this. It wasn't him leaving so soon—even though it's not *so soon*. It's already well after nine o'clock.

It's just that the night was so perfect, and I hate to see it end.

We get to the door and Cole stops. He turns around.

His eyes sparkle as he reaches out and brushes a strand of hair out of my face. "You really like it here in Ohio, don't you?"

My hands tremble as I loop my fingers in the waistband of his joggers.

I'm not sure what he's asking me or why—and I'm afraid to think about it too much.

"Yeah," I say. "My roots are here. This is my home."

Cole nods, biting his lip. "Okay."

"Okay."

He lowers his head. His lips find mine.

His arms wrap around me and pull me into him. I drag my arms to his neck and entwine my fingers through his hair.

The moonlight streams through the sidelights on either side of the door. Our shadows against the floor show a couple in a sweet embrace.

A couple in love.

His breath is warm, tinted with the chocolate from his milkshake. He presses his lips against mine as if with every movement he's telling me something.

I kiss him back, emboldened by the way I melt into his body and the tenderness with which he holds me. And I wish, for a fleeting moment, that this could be an everyday thing.

Cole breaks the kiss. He pulls back just far enough to look into my eyes.

"Good night, Palmer," he says.

I blow out a breath that's just as fueled by relief as it is disappointment.

"Good night, Cole."

He grins and then lets himself out.

CHAPTER TWENTY-NINE

COLE

"You're up early." Mom stops in the kitchen doorway and tightens her robe around her. "Is everything all right?"

I smile, even though I don't know if everything is all right or not. It feels better than all right, and that makes me wonder if nothing is actually right at all.

The thoughts that I've volleyed back and forth all night, the mental game of Whac-A-Mole that I've played over the last few hours, are nutty.

I've paced the floor. I went for a jog and nearly sprained my ankle in the predawn haze. I grabbed a shower, sent two emails to Scott, and then left a message at my doctor's office.

Finally.

But the movement has helped clear my head. The decisions that I've been so hesitant to make, the ones that I've felt so unsure about, have become obvious. I can't really explain why things are so apparent to me now, and I don't know what it was about spending my evening with Palmer and Ethan that really cemented how I feel and what I want for my future—but maybe it's not just one thing.

Maybe it's two things. Two very specific things. Two very specific people.

"Coffee?" I ask, reaching into the cupboard for a mug.

"Yes, please." Mom's voice is tinged with suspicion as she sits at the table. She takes the steaming mug I offer her. "You didn't answer my question."

I sit down beside her. "Everything is good, Mom. Great, actually."

She grins. "Are you going to make me press, or are you going to just tell me what's going on?"

"I don't know. Watching you not know is kind of fun."

She smacks my arm.

"I'm just kidding," I say. "I just had . . . let's call it a 'quiet epiphany' last night."

"Oh, I like the sound of that. May I ask what provoked this quiet epiphany?"

I purposefully ignore her question and skirt around it. "I made a decision this morning."

This is enough to redirect her attention. Her brows shoot to the ceiling.

"Don't do this to me, Cole. Don't make me suffer."

"A little dramatic, don't you think?"

She fires me a look. I laugh.

"Fine," I say, shaking my head. "What would you think about me sticking around Bloomfield?"

Her eyes light up, and she nearly squeals. She dances in her seat like a spring has popped beneath her and propelled her up. The whole scene is hilarious.

"Cole," she says, trying to contain herself. "I think that would be the greatest thing that you've ever said to me."

"I thought you might like that."

"So, what are your plans? What are you going to do here?"

I shrug. "I thought maybe I could spend some time with you and Dad. Help you out. Relax a little bit. I wanted to do that anyway, but then all of these offers hit the table." I nibble on my lip as a wash of nerves bubbles in my stomach. "But is that a bad thing? I mean, if I turn them down, that doesn't mean other offers will never come, right?"

Mom blows out a breath. "You're in your thirties. That's the third inning of your life."

I smile at the reference.

"You have over half of your life left, God willing, and just because you say no to a project now doesn't mean that others won't come along. Besides, you have to think about it from the other side of the coin."

"What do you mean?"

"Well, what if you say yes to one of those projects now, even though your heart isn't in it? Because it's not, Cole. I can tell."

I frown.

"And then what if something amazing comes along in six months, and you're already committed in this other thing?"

"That's true."

She smiles at me. "You should never make a decision because you're scared."

I sit across from her and think about that. She's right. I know it immediately. If I'd taken one of the offers Scott got for me, I would've been doing it because I was fearful. *What if I never get another one?* It certainly wouldn't be because it was the perfect fit.

The only thing that seems to fit is Palmer Clark. Well, not even just Palmer. Ethan too.

I wasn't kidding about what I said last night about the atmosphere in her home. It felt like home there. It's somewhere I want to fit, somewhere I want to belong because of the two of them.

Every time I realize that I'm thinking this way—that Palmer might be an endgame kind of woman—I'm more assured that I'm right. She is. Quite frankly, I think I'm falling in love with her.

I've never felt this way before, so I'm not totally sure. I just know that the depths of my feelings for Palmer are deeper than I've ever had for another woman.

Palmer is not just beautiful or a good conversationalist. She's not simply engaging or just fitting into my life conveniently. The thing with Palmer is that there's not potential to develop something more. *There just is more.*

I love her honesty and the way she takes care of Ethan. I adore her heart and how she tries to do the right thing, even when it's hard. She doesn't need me or my fame or my money—I don't think she even knows how much money I have. I don't think she cares.

"You're right," I admit, looking at my mother. "I have to look at things that way too. And there are some things that I will have to take off the table if I leave here and go back to the West Coast."

Mom stills and sets her mug on the table. "Are you talking about Palmer?"

A slow smile slips across my face. "Yeah. I am."

She falls back in her chair. A mixture of relief and joy spills across her face. "Cole, I am delighted."

"Well, temper that for a minute because we haven't actually cemented anything."

"Oh, like you have to cement things. You're the most handsome, most brilliant man on the planet." She looks around. "Besides your father," she says, a little more loudly.

I laugh.

"I had to add that in case he can hear us," she whispers, making me laugh even more. "But on a serious note, I'm not just happy about this because you'll be with us. I'm thrilled because I think Palmer is a great young woman, and her son is perfectly spoilable."

All I can do is shake my head. "Don't go wedding planning yet. I have a couple of things to work out before this is a thing."

"Well, you just go work them out because I've already committed to this."

"I . . ." My voice trails off as my phone buzzes on the counter, next to the coffeepot. I walk over to it and see Palmer's name on the screen. "Hang on, Mom."

"Sure."

I swipe the button and answer. "Hi, Palmer."

"Hey, Cole."

My insides twist. Something is amiss. I can hear it in her tone.

"What's wrong?" I ask.

"I . . . I don't want to do this," she says, her voice on the edge of breaking. "But I don't know what else to do. Val usually bails me out on stuff, but she can't today, and I'm halfway to West Virginia by now and—"

"Palmer, what's going on? Cut to the chase. You're starting to freak me out a little bit."

"No. Don't do that." She sucks in a breath. "I got to the office today and found out that the auction in Parkersburg is today, not tomorrow, and Burt's not here. Kirk's wife's appointment is also today, not tomorrow, so I'm not sure what the hell happened with the schedule, but all I do know is that I have to go to the auction, and Val is headed to Columbus because she thought—"

"Breathe." I inhale and exhale loudly for her benefit. "This is going to be okay. What do you need from me?"

A long pause settles between us.

"Palmer?" I ask gently. "What do you need?"

"I don't know," she says as if she's afraid to ask me for anything.

I replay what I know, what she just said, and try to grasp how I can fix the situation.

"I'll tell you what," I say, hoping this is the right answer. "I have nothing to do today. So why don't I run by your house whenever Ethan gets off the bus, and we'll throw some balls around. Maybe grab some dinner and hang out. Then you won't have to rush."

"Really?"

"If you aren't comfortable with me at your house, I can take him to Mom's. But if he comes home a spoiled little monster, that's not on me."

I glance at Mom. She's grinning.

Palmer sighs. "Cole, are you sure? I feel absolutely shitty about even calling you with this, and I know this is one hundred percent not your responsibility, and I—"

"Stop." I shake my head. "You didn't ask me to do anything. I volunteered. But if you want to feel shitty about something, then feel that way about not just calling and asking me outright."

I can hear her smile on the other end of the line. It makes me smile too.

"So, what time does Ethan get off the bus or need picking up or whatever?" I ask.

"He'll get home around three thirty."

"Cool. Is there anything I need to do or know? Homework? Picking up his room? Or would you rather me bring him to Mom's?"

"I'll check homework when I get home. I'm not asking you to do that."

"Are you saying I'm incapable? Because I'm pretty sure that I beat you in every category that wasn't pop culture."

"Very funny."

I laugh. "So, no homework. What else?"

"Nothing." She sucks in a breath. "Thank you for stepping in like this. Ethan has a key, and you're more than welcome to stay there. If you want to go to your mom's, by all means. Beggars can't be choosers."

"You don't have to beg me for anything."

The innuendo that I didn't plan on but that works perfectly hangs in the air. Palmer giggles.

"There's money in the cookie jar if you guys go get food or anything."

I laugh. "That's a relief."

"Shut up."

"Okay, you go do whatever you need to do today, and I'll hold the fort down." I glance at my mom. "I mean, it's better than hanging out with Mom. She was going to have me wiping down baseboards today."

"Oh, you'll still do that," Mom teases.

Palmer must hear her because she laughs. "Thank you, Cole. Honestly."

"Sure. But next time, just ask me when you need something."

I mean it at face value. But it's the insinuation that there will be a next time, and I'll be here for it, that hangs in the air between us.

"I'll call you when I'm on my way home," she says, avoiding the elephant in the room.

"Sounds great. Try to have a good day, okay?"

"Okay. Thanks again, Cole."

"Bye, Palmer."

I'm afraid to even look at my mother. And when I do, she's smiling like a loon.

"This is a sign," she says as if the angel Gabriel has just descended from heaven and handed her a placard.

"A sign for what?"

She shrugs. "I think this proves that you shouldn't take opportunities just because they're there. Sometimes what's in front of you can block you from things coming."

And then, like the philosopher that I didn't know my mother to be, she simply turns and walks out of the kitchen.

CHAPTER THIRTY

Palmer

Every cell in my body hurts.

I turn into the driveway. Even though I know that Cole and Ethan stayed at the house this evening, it still takes me aback that there are lights on. There are never lights on at the house when I get home.

The sensation tickles my heart. I know it's because my defenses are down after a grueling day at the auction—not to mention the two-hour drive home—but I'm still mulling over the idea as I park my car in the driveway.

Cool night air licks at my skin as I walk up the steps and unlock the front door.

The house is quiet as I enter. I set my keys on the table by the door and then peek into the kitchen. The light is on, but the kitchen is void of people but not scents. The air is tinged with the aroma of oregano and garlic. It makes my stomach growl.

I turn around and head downstairs. Cole looks up from the recliner as soon as I come into sight. He doesn't move anything except his lips. They form a delicious smile.

"Hey," I say, my voice soft so as not to disturb a sleeping Ethan on the sofa. "How did things go today?"

It's a rhetorical question. I was inundated with pictures and videos from both Cole and Ethan throughout the evening. There were images from their batting practice and short clips from the two of them unloading mulch from the back of Lawrence's truck. Every shot included wide smiles, and that helped me not be so aggravated about the morning's confusion, something Kirk apologized profusely about. The poor guy. He never makes these kinds of mistakes. He's been hiding his anxiety about his wife's appointment so well, but I know the strain and the unknown are eating him alive.

Cole brings a finger to his lips and gets to his feet. He walks to me and greets me with a sweet kiss. The stress of my day melts away as he wraps his arms around my waist. Oh, to be welcomed home in such a way every night. *That would be so lovely.*

"Come on," he whispers before leading me upstairs.

We hold hands as he leads me into the kitchen. He releases me and heads to the fridge.

"Are you hungry?" he asks. "Ethan wanted spaghetti from a place in Forest Falls. Limoncello? Something like that?"

I close my eyes and grimace. "Yeah. Limoncello." *Only the most expensive place we've ever eaten.*

"Great food," he says, completely unbothered by the fact that he paid thirty dollars for my son to have a plate of spaghetti. And I know he paid for it because there wasn't thirty dollars in the cookie jar. "I got you chicken fettuccine alfredo. Ethan said that was your favorite."

He takes a container out of the fridge and removes the lid. Then, as if he's operated in my kitchen a thousand times, he shoves it in the microwave.

I don't know what my face does, but it makes him laugh.

"What?" he asks.

"It's just odd seeing someone in my kitchen and having them wait on me."

"Sit down and I'll get you a drink."

What? I really don't know what to say, so I sit.

The microwave dings. He takes out the container and places it in front of me. Then he busies himself with getting me a fork and a glass of tea.

"How did Parkersburg go?" he asks.

I sigh. "It actually went pretty great, all things considered. I'm glad that I went. We got a number of buses that we desperately needed for inventory. I just started the day off so wonky, and it just set a pattern. I felt like I was off all day."

"Makes sense." Cole sets a glass beside my plate. "But the day is over, you kicked ass, and now you can come home to a hot and not-so-homecooked meal. Then I'll tuck you in bed."

Why are you so great?

I look into his eyes and wish I could just pause time. This feeling is everything that I've ever dreamed.

Supported. Appreciated. Wanted.

This man has taken care of my son—even helped him with his homework, which I know because Ethan sent me pics of them completing it—and is now heating me up dinner.

What is this?

I hesitate, unsure how to respond. This almost doesn't even feel real. And if it isn't, if I'm buying into something that I'm seeing because I want or need it, it could hurt in the end.

Tread lightly . . .

Cole rests his elbows on the counter and watches me carefully. "I had a great afternoon with Ethan."

I don't reach for my fork.

The moon glows through the window behind Cole and illuminates him. He's the most handsome that I've ever seen him in his T-shirt, sweatpants, and bare feet.

"Ethan texted me on my way home," I say. "He had a great afternoon with you too."

"I'm glad."

"Thank you," I say.

"You don't have to thank me for being a decent human being."

"That's not what I was doing."

He lifts a brow. "It is what you were doing." He stands and runs a hand around his jaw. "Look, I know this thing between us was just something we started because we couldn't avoid it. Right?"

I nod, unsure where this is going.

"But I think we're both cognizant of the fact that we've at least, at a minimum, developed a friendship."

I nod again. That's all I have at the moment.

"I know it was really hard for you to call me for help today," he says. "I can imagine that you've managed not to ask for help very much in your life, and it doesn't go unnoticed that you felt comfortable enough with me to reach out today."

My bottom lip trembles. I don't know why. Maybe because I'm so tired from the day of haggling over buses, or maybe it's that I'm worried about Kirk's wife, or maybe . . . maybe I'm afraid of where this conversation is going.

"And you know what?" he asks, his voice quiet. "I'm glad you did. I'm glad you reached out. Because I was having this conversation with my mother when you called, which she thinks is some kind of divine timing, by the way." He grins. "I was telling her about how I think I'm really starting to like it here."

It's his grin that gives him away. It's not on the verge of a smirk, and it's not prefacing a joke. He's not lining up a line to tease me either. It's simple and hits my heart in a way that none of his other smiles ever have.

"I thought you were a California boy?" I ask.

He moves aimlessly around the kitchen. It's not really a pace but more of a thoughtful kind of way.

"Do you know what I love most about baseball?" he asks.

Random. "No."

"Camaraderie. The teamwork. The way being a part of the team gives you a purpose and the satisfaction of working together toward a common goal."

"Makes sense," I say, although I'm struggling to follow along.

Cole stops moving. "That was the thing that I was missing ever since I retired. I wasn't sure that I would ever find that again."

His gaze penetrates mine. The intensity makes me shiver.

I grip the side of my chair and watch him. Breathing is a struggle. Surely he's not going to tell me that he's going to stay here. If he does, what does that mean?

I want to close my eyes and whisper a prayer that this is going the way I think it might. But I'm afraid to do either one—close my eyes or hope that hard. If I blink, this might prove to be a dream.

"We're just getting to know each other," he says. "But I think you feel the same way I do."

Oh. My. Gosh.

My brain screams. Who ends a sentence like that? It's like I'm being set up for failure. No matter how I respond, I could be wrong.

Crap.

"I feel a lot of things right now," I say carefully.

My answer makes him laugh. "Okay. Well, is one of those things that our relationship has shifted a little bit?"

"Yes."

Cole comes around the counter. I lean toward him instinctively. He wraps his arms around me, pulls me into his chest, and nestles his chin against the top of my head. I wrap my arms around his waist and curl against him, breathing in the comfort of his cologne and listening to the rhythm of his heart. Wishing *this* were my every day, not kissing Cole goodbye at the front door like last night.

What would life be like if I had him in it? If he was here to hold me, laugh with me, pick up dinner?

I twist my head until my forehead is against his chest and press a kiss into his abdomen. *I want so much with this man.* He pulls back just enough to look into my eyes again. This time, he doesn't have to say anything. I know what he's thinking.

The connection between the two of us steadies me. When I look at him, when I feel his touch, I don't feel alone in the world. Because I believe that if I needed him, Cole would be there. He cares—not just about me but about Ethan.

For the very first time, maybe ever, I have more hope than fear.

"Are you tired?" Cole asks.

"Yeah."

He runs a finger down the side of my face. "I want to have a conversation with you. Soon. But I want you to be awake and caffeinated and ready to argue everything so I can prove to you that I'm right."

I grin. "Sounds fun."

Instead of feeling a flush of nervousness, the deepest sense of calm settles over me. I have never known a man to be so . . . intuitive. He gets me. He knows I'm exhausted and cares enough to wait to talk.

"Ethan is going to Sandbox's house after school tomorrow," I say. "He's staying the night. Maybe we could talk then?"

Cole's face breaks out into a smile. "Great idea. I could come over after you get off work, and we could go out to dinner or something."

"Like a date? Like to Limoncello's?"

He laughs. "I'd take you to Paris tomorrow if you wanted to go."

I make a face. "Not Paris. Maybe . . ." I think. "Maybe Auckland."

"New Zealand? Random, but okay."

"Hey, this is my dream date." I yawn. "I wouldn't hate Paris, though."

He glances at my dinner. "How hungry are you?"

"I'm not as hungry as I am tired."

That's all it takes. He picks me up, draping my legs over one arm and supporting my back with the other. I curl against him as he carries me down the hall toward my room.

"You know there's a thirty-dollar plate of pasta spoiling on the counter," I say.

He laughs. "I don't think it was quite thirty dollars."

"Still. We should probably put it back in the fridge, and I'll have it for lunch tomorrow."

We enter my bedroom. I flip the light on as we pass the switch. Then he lays me gently on the bed.

"Damn it, you're beautiful," he says, climbing on the bed beside me. "I know you're tired, but it's hard to keep my hands off you."

I grin again. "It's hard for me to stop thinking about that pasta."

He shakes his head. "Is the only way I'm going to get your attention if I put the pasta in the fridge?"

"Yes. Or . . ." I tug at the hem of his shirt. "If you took this off, I'd probably be amply distracted."

He laughs, stripping his shirt over his head. He hops up on his knees and flexes his impressive abdomen.

Good heavens.

"Did it work?" he asks, like he doesn't already know.

I reach for him and grab the waistband of his sweats. Then I tug him until he's hovering over me.

"Did what work?" I whisper.

He leans down and wraps me up in his arms. He rolls me on top of him, then presses my body against his so hard that it's difficult to breathe.

But I don't mind. Not even a little bit.

Cole nibbles my bottom lip until I giggle and then slides his tongue in my mouth. He rolls me onto my back and kisses me like I've never been kissed before.

And I kiss him back. Of course I do. How could I not?

CHAPTER THIRTY-ONE

PALMER

"No. He left before Ethan got up," I say to Val. I wave at the trash-man as I pull into Skoolie's. "We thought it was best if he didn't do a walk of shame in front of Ethan."

I laugh at the idea. It doesn't seem like that is what it would be at all. But after spending the night wrapped around each other—and in and on and under each other, kissing and talking and laughing like teenagers—it seemed like the best solution for him to be gone before Ethan woke up.

Thank God Ethan is a very deep sleeper.

"So, now what?" Val asks. "You just see him when you see him or what?"

I pull into the driveway. A bubble of anticipation mixed with a dose of anxiety rises in my stomach.

"Well, no," I say. "He's actually coming over again tonight. Ethan will be gone, so we're going on a date, I guess, and having a conversation."

A conversation. I take a deep breath.

If I don't consider it too deeply, I think it's going to be fine. Maybe he just wants to clarify boundaries or check in on how I'm doing since he knows that this thing we've been doing wasn't necessarily on my radar. *Not with him, anyway.*

But who am I kidding? Of course I overthink it.

Tonight could go so many ways. In a fantasy world, I'd love for him to tell me he wants a real relationship with me. *He did mention having an affinity for Bloomfield.*

But is that even possible? Is it too far-fetched to hope for the conversation to go that way? Am I setting myself up for heartbreak?

"Why didn't you just do that in the middle of the night? What better way to have a state-of-the-relationship thing when his thing is . . ." She laughs. "Okay. I get your point. Probably better to do it tonight."

I laugh and park my car next to Kirk's. "For sure. We need a little time apart this morning to clear our heads."

"You mean *you* need some time to clear your head." Val sighs. "Don't do this, Palm. Don't overthink it."

"Too late."

I unbuckle my seat belt and kill the engine. Instead of climbing out of the car, I sit and stare into the beautiful morning sky.

"What if I lose my life jacket somewhere?" I ask, my voice hollow. "What if this gamble I take doesn't pay off, and I have to call you tonight in tears?"

And have to break Ethan's heart—because that's what it will be. He's fallen in love with Cole too.

The realization freezes me in my seat. *I'm in love with him.*

Holy shit.

I don't know whether to laugh or cry—to be amazed or ashamed.

I went and fell in love with him.

My insides push and pull in such a frenzy that I think I'm going to be sick. I hold a hand over my mouth and try not to puke.

"You haven't breathed in, like, a solid thirty seconds," Val notes.

I let out a rush of air. "I'm fucked, aren't I?"

"No, you aren't. As a matter of fact, I think what you're feeling is happiness, and you're afraid of it."

"I'm afraid of being happy?" I drop my hand. "I think that's impossible."

"Probably for everyone except for you." She laughs. "Every time you've been happy in your life, someone has made it their mission to destroy you. You have a fear of being happy because you expect the disappointment—the *destruction*—that always follows. It's not hard to believe. It's science."

Why does this make so much sense?

Val sighs. "You've been so happy lately. I've heard you laugh more than I've heard you laugh in your entire life. And you've basically been ignoring me, so the sex must be good."

I shake my head and smile.

"Give him a chance, Palm. Don't go into this conversation holding a match to burn the whole thing down just because you saw him at the gas station. Do you get what I mean? Did that analogy make sense?"

I laugh. "No, it did not."

"You know what I mean. Don't twist the happiness into something ugly just because you expect it. Give him a chance to surprise you."

He has surprised me. Every day.

I have been happy. That's what this feeling is. I wasn't sure that I would ever feel this way. The closest I've ever gotten to this was the day Ethan was born. But even that day was filled with an anxiety that Jared wouldn't be present. He said he would, but I already knew better than to put a lot of stock in the things he said.

But this isn't like that.

Cole has only ever followed through with his word. He's never made promises and failed me. He's been there when he didn't have to be and stepped up for Ethan's baseball team when he didn't have an iron in the fire.

He's a good man.

"He's nice to you, Mom. All the time. Not like Charlie or the other guys you've gone out with that make you mad and frustrated. Or cry in the bathroom. This is the kind of guy you should have around. And I like him, too, and he doesn't think I'm just some punk kid . . ."

"I really like him, Val," I say, my voice shaking. "I like him a lot."

"I know you do. And he seems like the exact kind of guy that you need, and I'm thrilled for you. Make sure you call me tomorrow and tell me what happens. I will refrain from calling you tonight, even though it might kill me, and I won't ask you to turn your phone on speaker mode and leave it in a fruit bowl so I can hear what happens."

"Oh, my gosh, Val," I say, laughing.

"God forbid you feel guilted into thinking you're a bad friend for making me wait to find out if my best friend is a taken woman."

We laugh together as I climb out of my car. "I love ya but not that much."

"Can't say I blame you. Anyway, I'm going in to work now. Have a great day and call me tomorrow."

"I will. Have a good day too."

"Bye, Palm."

I stick my phone in my pocket and climb the steps to the office. The wooden steps creak as I go up them. The handle is cold as I tug it open.

As soon as I step inside the trailer, I know something is wrong.

The door to Kirk's office is open. He's sitting at his desk. His face is unshaven, something I've seen only once in all the years I've worked for him. There's no smile waiting for me.

I don't walk to my desk, and I don't bother with greetings. I stand in his doorway and feel my soul sink to the floor.

"Kirk?"

He looks at me. His eyes have heavy bags beneath them.

"Kirk, what's wrong?"

He doesn't bow his head or make an effort to speak. He just looks at me with sad, tired eyes, and I know what's happened. *Charlotte's test results.*

I don't wait for an explanation. I walk around his desk, my heart shattering for the man I've grown to love, and I wrap my arms around his shoulders.

"Damn it, Palmer," he says, his voice breaking.

"I'm so sorry."

My words come out strained around the lump in my throat. I squeeze him tight, muttering a silent prayer for him and his family, before letting him go.

He motions for me to take a seat across from him, so I do.

"Well," he says, grasping for words that he obviously doesn't want to say. "It's . . . it's cancer."

"Oh, Kirk."

He looks at me with horror-struck eyes that are filled with as much disbelief as pain.

"It's not good," he says, barely above a whisper.

"I am so, so sorry," I say. "Can I do anything for you? Can I help?"

He shakes his head.

"Is she okay?"

"Right now, she's resting. I came by to grab a few things because I don't know how much I'll be around." He picks up a pen and moves it around his fingers. "They've given her a year. Maybe less."

His voice breaks. It kills me to watch the tears streaming down his wrinkled cheeks. The dam holding my own tears back fails, and I cry right alongside him.

I've watched and lived through grief stealing my dad's whole life and spirit. It breaks my heart to know this dear man, my friend and champion, will soon endure a horrific loss.

Charlotte has been like a favorite aunt to me ever since I started work at Skoolie's, and I can't imagine a world without her in it. How will Kirk manage this after spending his entire life living alongside her, building a world together? It's just too soon for him to have to say goodbye.

My thoughts go to my father and how he must've felt saying goodbye to my mother. *Did he feel this way too?*

Kirk bows his head, the pain on his face suffocating me.

I can't imagine him loving someone as long as he's loved his wife and knowing he's going to lose her. It strangles me, and I'm not really involved. *How awful must this be for him?*

"I'm going to be really honest with you, kid," he says, taking off his glasses. He wipes his face with the backs of his hands. "I'm not sure what I'm going to do around here."

"Kirk, don't worry about it. I'll do everything that I can. Between me and Burt and the guys in the shop, we'll run this place. You have nothing to worry about."

He forces a swallow down his throat before leveling his gaze at me. "I appreciate that, and I know you are capable of running the shit out of this place, Palmer. But I don't know if I even want to deal with it right now at all."

What? I rethink what he's just said, and it makes sense. I get it. *But what does that mean, exactly?*

Kirk puts his glasses back on. "I was up all night thinking about it. I might have another year with my girl. I've worked my whole damn life to provide this woman with the best life I could give her, and the only thing I can give her now is my time." He rolls his chair back in distress. "The thought of her home, dying, while I run in here to check things or having my attention distracted because of an auction . . . I can't do it, Palmer. I owe her the best of me—all of me."

"I understand."

I don't, because I'm not Kirk, but oh, to be loved as much as Charlotte is.

"I haven't made up my mind. This is a lot of information to process in a day. And I worry about you guys finding new jobs and all of that, but . . ." His voice cracks. "But I want to be home, feeding her soup and telling her how beautiful she looks."

Tears fill my eyes again. "As you should."

"You'll be the first to know when I make a decision. But I need to get home and figure out what we need to do now."

"Absolutely."

"Just do me a favor and start testing the waters for a new job, okay?"

I nod.

I'm numb, unable to grasp the enormity of what he's just said.

Charlotte is dying. *Oh, God. Please help them. Please help my boss, my friend, and his sweet wife through this.*

Tears wet my cheeks.

This is too much to process. My world has been turned on its axis.

How do I handle things at Skoolie's, provide support for Kirk's family, take care of Ethan, handle baseball practice, and look for a job and maybe a house? Because even though I know Kirk would never kick me out, what if he walks away from it all? What if he sells to someone who doesn't give a shit?

My lips tremble as I cry quietly, my heartbreak for Kirk bleeding into fear for myself and my son too.

My brain switches to the men in the shop, who will also lose their jobs. *How will their families survive?* There aren't a lot of jobs around here. It's not like they can just switch careers and make the kind of money that Kirk pays them. And that money gets filtered around town—to Fletcher's, to the gas station, to the bait shop, and to Bud's Sporting Goods.

I hiccup a breath, not sure if I can still breathe.

The weight of the situation slams onto my shoulders like a boulder rolling down a mountain. I think I might collapse.

If I don't run this place perfectly, if I don't make this work, we'll all suffer.

"I'm going to get going," he says, then picks up a briefcase off the floor and heads to the door. "I've already let Burt know that you're in charge while I'm gone. If I can't be reached, decisions are made by you. And if you're not sure what to do . . . do your best."

"I won't let you down. I promise," I say, hoping I can deliver on that. "Please, just go take care of Charlotte and tell her I love her. I'll organize a meal train, so please don't worry about food. And if there's anything else—call me. Okay?"

He stops in the doorway. "Thank you, Palmer. For everything."

"Of course," I say as he walks out.

The door slams shut behind him. I fall back into my chair, and when I'm absolutely certain he's gone, when I see his car pull down the driveway, I sob.

CHAPTER THIRTY-TWO

Cole

I sip my coffee and look down at the list I've been working on all morning. There are lines and arrows coming off each bullet point in every direction. The staggering amount of work that needs to be done to pull off a relocation is insane.

1. Decide what to do with my house in California
2. Get cars here
3. Have convo with Scott
4. Find a place to live here
5. Talk to Miigi

I relax into the chair at Mom's kitchen table, thankful that she and Dad went to Fletcher's for breakfast. The quiet and solitude are just what I need.

There are still so many things up in the air—from actually solidifying things with Palmer to tying up loose ends in my past so I can move on. To here. To her.

She's the only thing that's felt right since my retirement. *No, since before that.*

I work my shoulder around and straighten my legs. They're unusually stiff this morning. I'm picking up my phone to check my emails when it rings.

"Hey, Fish," I say, happy to hear from him.

"What's up?"

"Ah, nothing much. What about you?"

"Same thing, day after day. Actually, not really. I have news."

I sit up and lean against the table. "Do tell."

"Well, hold on to your hat, my man, because this one is gonna blow you away."

I laugh and remember the last time Fish *had news*. It must've been three or four years ago, back in his wild days before Nicole came into the picture. He'd been photographed in Mexico butt naked with three women on a boat.

"Hat is held," I say. "Give it to me."

"Well, I'm going to be a dad. Nicole broke the news to me when I got back to town."

My eyes nearly bulge out of my head. "What did you say?"

"Yeah, man. I know."

His tone is unreadable, and I'm not sure how to respond. I stand up, running a hand through my hair.

"Wow. Okay. Well, congratulations, first of all," I say, figuring that's a safe reply.

Fish laughs. "Thank you. I was a little spun out about it at first because it was obviously not what I was expecting. But I'm kind of excited about it."

A smile splits my cheeks, and a surge of happiness floods me. "I think it's great."

"I'm gonna be a dad, dude. Isn't that wild?"

"Wild as hell." I chuckle. "So, what's this mean for you?"

"You mean with me and Nicole? I asked her to marry me."

I walk to the sink and stare out the window into the backyard.

Although Fish getting married and having a baby wasn't something that I would've bet on happening in the near future, I wouldn't have put money down on me wanting to settle down with a single mother in Ohio either. But both things make sense in the most organic way.

"I better get an invitation," I say, grinning. "Even if you pull a stunt and elope—I better fucking be there."

"You know it. Now, what about you? You coming home or what?"

I turn away from the window and walk to the table. Glancing down at my to-do list, I exhale.

"Actually, I think I'm going to relocate," I say carefully.

"To Ohio?"

"Yeah."

I bite my lip and wait for Fish's response. Aside from my parents, he knows me better than anyone. If this idea is asinine, he'll tell me.

"That's fucking awesome," he says, catching me off guard. "Are you hitting it off with . . ."

"Palmer."

"Yeah, Palmer."

"You could say that." I laugh. "We're having a conversation tonight to make sure we're on the same page."

"Dude, you've been on the same page since the day at the restaurant."

"I have a few things to get together before I fully commit . . ." My phone chirps, and I pull it away just long enough to see an incoming call. "Hey, Fish? I need to take this call. Can I call you back?"

"Of course. Talk to you later."

I click over to the incoming line. "Hello?"

A voice clears on the other end. "Is this Cole Beck?"

"It is."

"Hi, Cole. This is Dr. Miigi. You are a hard man to get a hold of."

Sweat dots my forehead despite the cold chill racing down my spine. I move the phone from my right hand to my left.

"Yeah," I say, clearing my throat. "I'm sorry about that. I, uh . . ." *Didn't want to deal with this.* "Headed back east to see my parents for a while."

"Well, now that I have you on the phone, let's have a chat."

Fuck.

My stomach twists into a knot. I pace back and forth across the kitchen as the anticipation of the conversation gets the best of me.

I've intentionally put this off for much longer than is acceptable or responsible. It's the first thing in my life that I haven't necessarily met head-on, and that's because I don't know how to do that.

I don't want to do that.

I want to pretend like it's not a thing.

I grip the back of a kitchen chair. "All right. Let's chat."

"I'm sorry we're not meeting face-to-face for this confirmation, but I've had your test results sent to our partners in Scottsdale."

My chest burns as I try to drag in enough oxygen to keep me awake and alive. Whatever he says next—the diagnosis I've been avoiding—is going to change my life forever. My world will be separated into two parts: pre–this conversation and post–this conversation.

My fingers itch to end the call and never go forward, as if not hearing the words from Dr. Miigi will somehow make the facts he needs to deliver to me not relevant. Or real.

Yet they are real.

But for the first time since I started struggling to see a curveball and had unexplained muscle spasms that massage and sports therapy didn't cure, I have a plan. I have hope for a life that isn't centered around baseball.

I want to be with Palmer.

And if that's going to happen, I have to address this. I have to hear what he has to say and then move on—hopefully with her and Ethan.

Maybe it isn't as bad as I think. There's always hope . . .

I cling to that thought. "What did they say?"

I close my eyes. It's as though I'm in a movie scene where everything blurs around the main character, and the only thing that he can do is spin in a circle.

I'm spinning fast and wild, and the only thing keeping me centered is the kitchen chair.

"I'm very sorry to tell you, Cole. But your MRI, blood work, and the spinal tap you had a few months ago all point to multiple sclerosis," he says.

His words are careful and calculated, if not a little cold.

"But I feel fine. Aside from the vision issue that started all of this and some pain here and there, which could totally be from baseball," I say, trying to make a case for Dr. Miigi to be wrong, "I feel fine. I could still play. You know that. Maybe the results are wrong."

I say that, even though I know in the pit of my stomach that they're not.

Stiff muscles, tingling in my extremities from time to time, and cognitive issues like dropping things—I've been experiencing those too. I just don't want to admit it.

"I hear what you're saying, Cole. But I'm confident in the diagnosis. I think we caught it extremely early because you function at such a high level. The symptoms you were noticing—not being able to read the ball coming into home plate, for example—are things that might not have been noticed by the layperson."

I force a swallow and try to focus. *What the fuck does this mean?*

Just as I feared, my life feels like it's been ripped in half. This label, this diagnosis, is the delineator, and I want to scream and go back to before I answered this call.

Fuck, I want to hit something.

"What does this mean?" I ask him. "What does the rest of my life look like? What the hell do I do now?"

I haven't read much about MS, mostly as a way of ignoring it. If I didn't invite it into my world, maybe it would stay away. That was stupid, in retrospect, but it allowed me to survive not knowing, and I won't fault myself for that.

"We treat the symptoms as they arise—and there are a lot of treatments available. There are medicines you can take orally; there are injectables. We also have infusion treatments, and we'll work with you on selecting the right therapies as we battle this. Okay?"

I nod, nearly numb to the moment.

"Right now, it's important for you to keep exercising and eating right. Monitor changes, which, as you know, could be few at this point in time. It could be that way for a long time. Try to keep your stress level down."

That's ironic.

"You're in great physical shape," he says. "Let's work on keeping you fit and strong. When symptoms pop up, we'll figure out the best course of action. This will be a long-term game, Cole. We'll work together. I'm here to help you every step of the way."

"Yeah."

"But you're going to have to call me back a bit faster."

"I'll try."

He babbles on about making an appointment to see him again and insisting that I do a better job at keeping in touch. But all I can think about is Palmer.

My chest clenches as I imagine her pretty face awash in concern over this. *Do I have any right to do this to her?*

She's so strong, so nurturing. She's been through so much. What kind of a man would I be if I asked her to take this on too?

Palmer never turns away from the people she loves. She goes above and beyond for her child, for Kirk and Charlotte, for the community events like the nursing home picnics. She volunteered to be the team mom and deals with Jared in a way that's more than I could do if I were in her situation.

I think I'm going to vomit.

The thought of asking her to deal with this alongside me is nearly unfathomable. How do I just plop this on her lap—burden her with the prospect of a life that I can't guarantee? She doesn't need, or deserve, more issues in her life, and here I am, considering telling her that I love her but lacing it with this complication?

Fuck.

I say goodbye to my doctor and end the call. Then I drop my chin and attempt to regain control over my emotions.

"You knew this," I say to myself. "This is why you retired. You knew something was wrong."

I squeeze my eyes shut.

"But what do I do now?" I ask aloud. "What is the right thing to do?"

I open my eyes. They land on the to-do list from earlier today—just a few minutes ago, really. I was full of hope then and positive about my next step in life.

With Palmer.

If she were the one who had something like this to deal with, I would still want to be with her. Without a shadow of a doubt. There's nothing that she could say to me that would make me less interested in pursuing her than I am right now.

But does she feel the same?

She wants a husband, more kids . . . a family to love. And that's when I realize something vital. *I want to be a part of that family.* It already feels like my family.

"I'll tell her," I say, testing the words. "I'll tell her I have MS and see what she says. I'll give her the choice."

Even though the thought terrifies me, it's the right answer.

It's the only answer.

CHAPTER THIRTY-THREE

Palmer

I sniffle and grab a bottle of water out of the fridge.

My face is swollen. It hurts to touch anywhere near my eyes.

I cried off and on—every time I thought about Kirk's anguish and how terrified Charlotte must be—but managed to pull myself together enough to get through the day. I don't know when Kirk told the shop guys, but he must have. Burt came into my office to hand me a bunch of invoices and didn't make one smart-ass comment or insult. He just looked at me with a sadness that I felt deep in my bones.

Burt agreed to gather the shop guys Monday morning for a meeting. The only way we're going to survive this is if we work together.

But can we work together like we need to? That's yet to be answered.

I down most of the bottle of water. The cool liquid helps lower my still-heated emotions. Just because I survived the day and completed my typical daily tasks doesn't mean that everything is going to be fine. My workload is about to double, maybe even triple, and there's nothing I can do about it if I want a job.

My head pounds. Pain radiates from my temples through my skull. I'm headed to the bathroom to find a Tylenol when I hear a knock at the door.

Cole.

In the chaos of the day, I've forgotten he was coming over. And our date. And our conversation.

I yank the door open, desperate to see his face and feel his arms around me. His face lights up when he sees me, as if a joke is on the tip of his tongue. All it takes is one quick look for his humor to fade.

"Palmer?"

I'm not sure why seeing him on my front porch brings tears to my eyes, but it does.

He steps inside as I propel myself toward him and bury my face in his chest. He struggles to shut the door behind him before wrapping me up in his arms and squeezing me so tight that I think I might burst.

This is what I needed.

I breathe him in, letting the spiciness of his cologne cart me away from the troubles of my day. I lean into him and absorb the sturdiness of his body, which I appreciate today more than ever.

I pull back. He wipes my tears with the pads of his thumbs. His touch is tender yet intentional—just like his presence in my life.

"What's wrong?" he asks, his voice full of concern.

"I bet I look like a disaster, huh?"

He bends down and kisses me sweetly. "You couldn't look like a disaster if you tried."

It's a lie. I know that. But it's a lie I'm willing to take.

I take his hand and lead him downstairs. He sits on one end of the couch as I put my phone on the coffee table. Then he pulls me onto his lap, as if he knows I need the contact—that somehow having him here eases the stress of the day. *It does. It so does.*

"Okay," he says, getting us situated. "What's going on?"

"Kirk's wife, Charlotte, has cancer. He came into the office today to get a few things and told me."

"That's . . . that's horrible."

"They've been married forever, and now she has a year to live. How do you survive that?" I ask, my voice breaking. "I don't know which side would be worse—Charlotte's, because it's her life that's ending, or Kirk's? Because his life is ending too."

Cole's eyes flutter closed for a brief moment.

Tears spring to my eyes again. When Cole opens his and sees my emotion, he pulls me into his chest. I rest my head against him and feel the rhythm of his heartbeat.

We sit like this for a few minutes. Cole strums my back as I nestle against him. I wish I could pause time and keep things just like this—in a place where everything seems manageable. Where there's hope.

Cole pulls me tighter against him.

"Can I do anything?" he asks, his voice soft.

"Not really." My voice sounds distant, like it's not coming from me. "I'm organizing a meal train for them so they don't have to worry about food. And there's a church in town that will organize chores—like housecleaning and picking up groceries for families that are going through stuff like this. So I'm going to call them tomorrow too."

Cole refastens his arms around me.

"That's the saddest part of all," I say, my heart aching. "The world is so cold. It just keeps on spinning when tragedy strikes. Kirk and Charlotte are trying to spend their last months together, and the toilet still needs cleaning. The laundry needs washing. Life just goes on in the most unforgiving way."

"I know my mom would like to help you." His voice wavers. "If you need help getting this organized, I know she'd be happy to jump in with anything you need."

I fist his shirt in my hands and smile against him. "Thank you."

My adrenaline must drop because I shiver. Cole grabs a blanket off the back of the sofa and covers me.

I close my eyes as the exhaustion from the day's events seeps into my soul. Every muscle in my body hurts as if I've just run a marathon. I just want to sleep and deal with this later.

"How are things going to work for you at the office?" he asks.

Oof.

"Kirk might close the doors," I say, the words hollow.

I can't believe I just said that.

As much as I want to simply hide in Cole's arms, I can't. It's not how I roll. I don't operate like that. Besides, I'm sure Cole doesn't want me sitting here soaking his shirt all night anyway.

"Really?" Cole asks, surprise in his eyes.

I climb off his lap and sit next to him. He pulls my legs over his lap. Then he rearranges my blanket again.

"Yeah," I say, relaxing as best I can against the sofa. "I'm trying to keep things going. I just . . . I'll probably need to spend another three or four hours a day there to make sure everything is done. I'll try to redistribute some things because I can't be away from the house and Ethan all day and night."

"You can't just fix this yourself, Palmer."

"I have to try." I look him in the eye. "Kirk needs me, which is the opposite of the usual situation. He's never failed me, and I won't fail him now."

"Palmer . . ."

I pull my legs off him. "Look, he doesn't need the money. That place makes a lot of money—like, seven figures a year—which is surprising, considering we work out of a trailer, but it's true."

Cole's eyes widen.

"Kirk doesn't need to keep working, but he does it for us. For me and Burt and the guys in the shop. For Bloomfield." I take a quick breath. "But now it's us or his wife, and he'll pick Charlotte. He *should* pick Charlotte. But I have to think about saving my job and my house because he owns this place too. And if he shuts the doors, Cole, the whole town will feel it."

He doesn't reply. He just watches me warily.

"Those guys can't just go get another job—not making what Kirk pays us. There's nothing in this area for most of them anyway. For me either." I force the thought out of my head. "But all of the money we make gets pumped back into town. It keeps Fletcher's and King Pin Alley and Bud's all in business. If I fail, we all go down."

Cole takes my hand in his. "Sweetheart, this is not all on you. You have to rely on your community and the guys at the shop. This isn't your fight."

I wish he were right. I wish it weren't my fight. But Burt doesn't care enough to see this through, and the shop guys don't understand enough of the business to help. I don't have a choice here but to fight.

And it's not just for me that I'm fighting, something Cole wouldn't really understand. Everything I do is for Ethan, to keep a stable, warm, and loving roof over his head. *That's my job. That* is *all on me.*

He watches me carefully, as if he's not sure what else to say. It doesn't matter anyway. It's what I have to do.

"I'm done," I say, giving him my best smile. "You and I were supposed to have a conversation that I really wanted to have."

Cole's eyes avoid mine, and he blows out a breath. For a split second, a chill races down my spine. Before I have time to process it, my phone starts to ring.

"I need to get that because Ethan isn't home," I say, reaching for it on the coffee table.

The number is not one that I know, but I answer it anyway.

"Hello?"

"This is a collect call from an inmate at the Cuyahoga County Jail. All calls will be monitored and recorded. To accept the call and the associated charges, please press one now."

What the hell?

My jaw drops, and I turn and look at Cole. His eyebrows are raised like he's not sure what my reaction means. But then again, I'm not sure either.

I press one.

"Your call is being connected," a robot voice says.

The line clicks, and the sound of chaos drifts through the phone.

"Palm?"

My stomach drops to my feet as I hear Jared's voice. *This might just do me in.*

"What the hell is going on, Jared?" I ask.

"Hey, yeah, I need your help."

I squeeze my temples. "What did you do now?"

"Come on," he says, irritation thick in his voice. "I'm in a bind and could do without the attitude."

Is he serious right now?

I drop my hand . . . but not the attitude.

"You're the one calling me from jail," I say. "So I think you need to stop criticizing me and get to the point."

Cole jumps to his feet.

"I got picked up last night," Jared says, as if everyone gets picked up for a stint in the clink on a routine basis. "It's a bunch of bullshit, but my bond is eight thousand dollars. Ten percent, though. Could you float me eight hundred dollars and come get me out?"

I don't know whether to laugh, cry, or rage. Maybe all three. Any of them would be an acceptable reaction.

"First of all, I don't *have* eight hundred dollars, Jared."

"Can't you gather it? I'll pay you back. You know I'm good for it—"

"No." I grit my teeth. "I can't just *gather it*." *And he's not good for it either.* "Do you think I know people that have a few hundred dollars lying around to donate to your cause? Money that I'll owe them back because you'll never come up with the money. We've done this before."

"Palmer—"

"Do not 'Palmer' me." I run a hand through my hair and pace the room. "I've had the shittiest day of my life, and now you're calling me for help. You, the man that has *never* showed up for me when I've needed you."

He sighs.

Steam rolls from my head as my disbelief and sadness mold into anger. The fact that I feel better dealing with the anger than the alternative is probably a talking point for a therapy session.

Cole comes up beside me and rests his palm on the small of my back.

"What about your boss? Ask him. The man is loaded," Jared says.

"His wife is dying," I say, spitting the words at him. "Kirk is at home, consoling her as she deals with cancer, and you think I should call him? And say what, Jared? That my son's father landed himself in jail, again, and he needs to write me a check so you aren't inconvenienced?" I clench my hand at my side. "How about this? How about you sleep in the bed you made for once in your life."

"So what are you going to do? Let me sit here and rot? I'm the father of your son, damn it."

What. The. Actual. Fuck?

"I don't know what you're going to do. It's not my problem. I can't take care of another fucking person right now." I squeeze my eyes shut. "I can barely manage my own life at the moment. Between work, raising the son that we share that you seem to forget about until it behooves you, and trying to keep my mental health from tanking, I can't take care of anyone else!"

The fury feels good.

"I'm so sick of picking up the pieces of everything," I say. "When do I get to prioritize me? When do I get to be the main character of my life? Because I'd like to know."

I spin around, fueled by my anger. Cole's eyes are wide, and I realize that I'm shouting.

"Enough's enough," I tell Jared, my voice lowered. "Whatever you've done to get yourself in this mess . . . you're going to have to figure out how to get out of it."

I'm done. I can't take any more, and I refuse to break for anyone else's situation.

Jared doesn't answer. I'm sure he's shocked. I've never said this before—not so definitively and concretely.

I look into Cole's eyes and feel his presence radiating from a few feet away. I know he'll wrap me up in his arms as soon as I'm off the phone, and he'll hold me close.

The thought makes me smile.

"Good luck, Jared. But I have to go."

I end the call and blow out a breath.

I'm so angry, so freaking angry . . . but also invigorated, which sounds stupid. But I finally told him where to shove his selfish, puerile ass.

I take a deep breath and hope that Cole doesn't think I'm out of my mind and some kind of unbalanced banshee who cries one minute and rages the next.

Here's to hoping he doesn't want to run out the door.

"I don't want to talk about that," I tell Cole. "Let's talk about us."

He runs a hand down his face. "Why don't we sit down?"

Everything inside me stills, as if someone has halted the scene starring me and Cole.

I sit next to him, my confidence waffling, and look into his eyes. They tell me everything I need to know.

I'm fucked.

He doesn't want me.

He doesn't want us.

CHAPTER THIRTY-FOUR

Cole

I wait for the exhale.

My body, my emotions—they're all weirdly detached from reality. Maybe it's some kind of self-preservation mode that I've activated. If so, I'm grateful.

It's like I've forgotten how to breathe. I need to release the air in my lungs and fill them again or else I'm going to pass out, but the idea of blacking out and forgetting that I just heard her say all those things does seem preferable to dealing with reality.

"Between work, raising the son that we share that you seem to forget about until it behooves you, and trying to keep my mental health from tanking, I can't take care of anyone else."

"When do I get to prioritize me? When do I get to be the main character of my life? Because I'd like to know."

"I can't take care of another fucking person right now."

What the hell do I do with that? How can I even consider becoming another burden on her life?

Palmer sits beside me and curls her legs beneath her. I see the trepidation in her eyes, and I hate myself for it. Because I put that there. I gave her a reason to doubt me.

I know what she thought I was going to say when I got here. I practically told her that I wanted to try a relationship with her last night. And that's exactly what I was going to do when I arrived this afternoon. I was going to tell her about my diagnosis, tell her my plans to stay in Bloomfield, and tell her that I wanted to try something serious with her . . . and with Ethan.

That's all changed.

If there's one thing I hate more than anything, it's selfishness. It's the player on the team who tries to hit a home run instead of moving the runners around the bases. It's the guy who has one girl who thinks the world of him, yet he sleeps around with half the city. It's the guy who can't hold his temper and gets tossed for a few games, putting the rest of his team at a disadvantage.

If I tell her what I came here to tell her—that I'm falling madly in love with her—I would be doing that, knowing how she feels.

That she doesn't have the bandwidth to take care of anyone else.

I can't be that guy. I won't.

"I take it Jared got arrested?" I ask, needing an entry point into the conversation. Even though she told me she didn't want to talk about it, I don't know how else to break this awkward silence between us.

"Yeah," she says.

"What happened?"

She shrugs. "Hard to tell. I never got a straight answer."

The look she gives me is a plea to get on with it, to say whatever it is that I'm going to say.

If she only knew how I felt.

I shift in my seat and ignore the crack radiating down my sternum, splitting my chest into two. It's only a matter of time until my heart spills out and I bleed all over the floor. But it's inevitable. I know that now.

A wave of emotion starts in my core and erupts like a volcano through my body. I feel the sadness everywhere from my heart to my brain, down to the very fibers of my being.

"I had a call this morning," I say, testing the waters.

I don't know how much to tell her. But as I see the anxiety switch to concern, I know that I can't share my diagnosis with her. Not today. Not after Kirk. It's too much.

"What about?" she asks.

For a split second, I panic at the idea of walking away from her. It's the last thing I want to do. I want to be here and help her through the situation at work and this shit with Jared and whatever else life gives her along the way. But if I do that, life will be prepping to deal her the realization that I'm ultimately another problem she'll have to contend with.

At some point—maybe forty years from now but still eventually—I will likely need a caregiver. And although I know that's a part of life to some extent, my situation might look vastly different from the normal person's. It would be unfair to saddle her with that when it's what she's trying to avoid.

And, if I'm being honest, it's what I'm trying to avoid as well.

I take in Palmer's pretty face. She's so beautiful, so kind, so wonderful. The idea of asking her to take this journey with me fills me with so much embarrassment that I can hardly breathe.

Envisioning her taking care of me—helping me walk, eat, get dressed in the morning—it's more than I can bear. Shame sits so heavily on my shoulders that I know I can't possibly go through with this.

How can I be a teammate if I can't contribute? How can I live when she's wiping my ass and I'm ashamed of my existence? How can I look her in the eye and feel like a man?

I want to reach for her, to touch her, to hold her in my arms. My instinct is to protect her from the world and give her and Ethan everything good. But I won't be able to do that.

The thought alone has me ready to puke.

Even if I stay for a while, until she has things under control, it'll just make things worse. It'll be even harder to end things.

Somehow. Because I'm not sure I can do this now.

She watches me with a look bordering on distress, and I know I have to just get this over with.

I take a deep breath. My lungs stutter as I fill them. I hate lying. Especially to her. Especially right now.

"I had a couple of meetings before I left California," I say, which is at least the truth. "And, to make a long story short, some things have come up that require me to be in San Diego." I level my gaze with hers. "Full time."

I've never seen a bomb dropped, but I would imagine that this is what it looks like.

Her eyes widen, her lips part, and a look of unthinkable surprise sparks across her pretty face. The realization hits her that whatever she thought was going to come out of today is definitely not going to happen—and it definitely wasn't this.

My fingers itch to grab her and pull her into me. I want to hold her, to kiss away the fear and the sadness and the disbelief painted on her features.

I ache with regret. Knowing I caused her pain feels like being stung by a thousand bees, but there's no other way around it. I just pray that the irony of having to end things with her today is a blessing somehow. Maybe the other shit in her life will distract her from this.

But what is going to distract me?

Palmer's bottom lip trembles. "What are you saying, Cole?"

"I'm saying . . ." *I'm walking away, even when you need me to be your comfort and your rock. Even when I want to be both of those things.* "I'm going to get a hold of Ted and see if he can take over the team. I wasn't expecting this, and trust me, Palmer, I would do anything, *anything*, to make this situation different. But I can't. You have to believe me."

My voice cracks as I watch her struggle to not fall apart. She's too proud to do it in front of me, and knowing that she'll do it after I walk out is devastating.

I knew I wanted to be here in Bloomfield, to be with her, but I didn't realize how much until now. Until I can't.

"Palmer, I am so sorry. I am so fucking sorry."

She tries to smile, but her lips won't cooperate. It's just a flicker of movement that demonstrates the struggle that's warring inside her.

"So this is it?" she asks, her voice a few notes higher than it should be. "So this is goodbye and you leave?"

"I don't have a choice."

She looks at me in disbelief, and then slowly anger slides across her eyes. "No, you had a choice. *I* didn't."

She pulls away from me.

"You had a choice. I *didn't."*

That's what I wanted to do—to give her a choice. Am I wrong not to do that now?

"You had these meetings *before* you came to Bloomfield," she says, pain thick in her voice.

I hate this.

I mull the pros and cons as quickly as my emotional brain will let me. If I give her a choice, it would put her on the spot. She can't win. And even if she chooses to let me into her life, she'll clearly lose at some point anyway.

Damn it.

She just looks at me like I am now the enemy. It kills me; it makes me want to take it all back and just do what's easier right now—admit the truth.

But I can't. If I have to be the enemy to save her, I will.

"This was always on the books," I say. "You knew that."

Her brows shoot to the ceiling. "What was that shit last night, then? When you were saying that you liked it here or whatever? Or did I completely read that the wrong way?"

Fuck.

"No. I told you—today changed a lot of things," I say.

She swallows once, twice, three times. I wonder if she has a lump in her throat, too, and if it's strangling her like mine is me.

I reach for her hand, but she pulls away. It's like a knife through my heart.

"This is not what I want, Palmer."

"Really? Then you're not the man that I thought you were. Because that guy always gets what he wants. That guy got my number when I turned him down and finagled his way into dinner with me. He had me kissing him in a shed and inviting him over to my house, even though I knew this would end this way."

"Palmer—"

She points a finger at me. "I'm not blaming you. I'm blaming *me*. Because I knew better, and I let myself fall for a smooth-talking baseball player that acted like he gave a shit." She laughs angrily. "I'm sorry, Cole. I'm calling bullshit on your story."

Palmer gets to her feet. "I need you to leave."

What? I stand too.

"I need you to go," she says again, holding a hand against her forehead. "I can't deal with anything else right now."

"Let's—"

"Go. Now."

She drops her hand and looks me in the eye. The warmth that's usually there, the hint of a smile, is gone.

I step toward her. She moves backward as if she has to maintain some distance between us. Tears pool in my eyes.

Please don't hate me.

I don't want to do this. I want you—in every way.

I love you, Palmer.

She smiles sadly. "I just thought that you . . ." *Loved me.*

Her unfinished sentence rips through me, leaving a jagged edge behind it. I'm never going to recover from this.

"I'm sorry," I whisper, blinking back tears. "Be angry with me. Make this my fault. This has nothing to do with you, and you did nothing wrong."

"This sure feels like I've done something wrong."

Tears stream down her cheeks. I reach to brush them away, and she pulls farther back.

"Go," she says again.

"Fine. But can I talk to Ethan at some point?"

Her features soften, but she shakes her head. "No. I'll figure out something to tell him . . . like I always do . . . but he's going to be . . . devastated. *Please just go.*"

I can't argue with her because she's protecting her son, and that's one of the qualities about her that I love most.

"If you guys ever need anything . . ."

She turns away from me and huffs. "As if I'm ever going to ask a man for anything again. I've learned my lesson. Finally," she whispers.

I did this to her. I didn't just break her heart, but I also destroyed her dreams. All she wanted was a loving man and a family, and now, because of me, she's given up hope.

And that's the worst part of it all. I want to be her everything. And I hate that she'll never ask me for anything ever again.

I head up the stairs and let myself out before I break down in tears in my dad's truck.

CHAPTER THIRTY-FIVE

PALMER

I jump as a hand presses against my shoulder blade.

Lifting my head from the pillow, I spot Val standing next to my bed. I can barely see her through the fog in my eyes.

"Oh, Palmer," she says, sitting beside me.

My face is crusty from the tears and snot, and my hair is a matted mess. *"You couldn't look like a disaster if you tried."*

Cole's words ring through my mind like a ghost of perfection past.

"Are you okay?" Val asks.

"Do I look okay?"

She considers this. "No, you look like hell."

"Thanks."

She gets up and heads into the master bathroom. The faucet turns on, and various doors open and close. When she returns, she hands me a washrag and a hairbrush.

"Here," she says, handing them to me.

I scramble to sit up. "Why? What's it matter?"

"It doesn't, really. But it'll make you feel better."

I don't have the energy to argue with her. I barely have enough to wipe my face off and run the brush through my hair. But I eventually get the job done to her satisfaction.

She takes the cloth and the brush and returns them to the bathroom.

"Your call had me freaking out," she says as she comes back into the room. "I broke every speed limit between here and Forest Falls."

"I'm sorry."

Val climbs across the bed and flops beside me. "Don't be. That's what best friends are for."

I curl up next to her, saying a silent prayer of gratitude that I was able to get most of the story out over the phone so I don't have to do it now.

"I think I'm cried out. I've cried all day, and I hate crying."

She fiddles with my hair in much the same way I do Ethan's. We lie quietly together on my bed until the shadows from the trees outside slide from the top of the wall to the middle.

"I think I love him," I say sadly. "Loved him? Love him? Whatever."

Val sucks in a deep breath. "I think he loves you too."

I roll over to face her. "Are you out of your mind? Do you not see me here, caked in my own snot, because the man broke up with me?"

"You smell a little too."

I hit her, making her laugh.

"This reaction—this one-eighty he just pulled—this is an emotional response to something, Palmer. He's not a bad guy. He's not evil."

"Tell that to my heart."

She frowns. "Think about it. He would never hurt you on purpose. You don't believe that, do you?"

I consider her point. At any time before the last three hours, I would never have thought that Cole Beck would intentionally hurt me. *But do I now?* His words . . . his . . . *torment.*

"I'm sorry. Be angry with me. Make this my fault. This has nothing to do with you, and you did nothing wrong. This is not what I want, Palmer."

I think about his face as he told me he was leaving and the pain I think I saw there. The hesitation when he arrived and the way he stood by my side as Jared called.

"No," I say finally. "I don't think he would. But he did. I'm hurting right now, and he knows that. He did that. *On purpose.*"

"And he's hurting too. He has to be. You don't flip a switch like that without a big prompt." She turns onto her back and looks at the ceiling. "You didn't fight or anything?"

I shake my head.

"Something happened," she says. "I'm not saying this was right or good or that if he walked in right now, I wouldn't karate chop him in the balls."

I smile the biggest smile I can manage. She returns it.

"But there's more to this story. There has to be."

What does it matter if there is? It's not going to fix anything. Whatever he's committed to in California is going to be full time.

But what he didn't say was whether other factors were involved, and that says all I need to know. Cole knows communication is key in relationships. He told me that. So if he's choosing not to talk to me, then he's okay with our . . . whatever we had ending.

I close my eyes and try to find my happy place. At the moment, that would be anywhere but here. Just as I mentally begin to detach—ironically to a place that includes Cole and a bed—the sound of the front door opening rings through the house.

"Who is that?" Val whispers.

"Mom!" Ethan's voice arrives in my room just before he appears in the doorway. "Mom?"

Oh. No.

Oh no.

Please, no. Not yet.

I sit up and realize my worst nightmare: having to break my son's heart while mine is still bleeding.

"What are you doing here?" I ask.

"I came to get my baseball glove." He looks between Val and me. "What's wrong?"

Val turns to me. "Do you want me to . . ."

"Kirk's wife is pretty sick," I say, clearing my throat. "It's been a really sad day."

This explanation does nothing to assuage his fears. They're still written all over his freckly face.

What's left of my heart cracks. The raw edges slice my chest like a thousand knives because I know I have to tell him about Cole now. He begged me to stop protecting him by delaying news about Jared, and I think this is going to somehow hurt him even more. I can't make it worse by waiting and have him not trust me too—even though I'm going to wait to tell him about his father. At least until I have more details.

I cough. "Ethan, I need to tell you something else."

"Okay."

"Cole was just here . . ." I stop and gather myself just before my voice trembles. *Get it together.* "Something happened, and he had to go to California."

"For how long?"

I lace my fingers with Val's in the blankets. "For . . . probably forever, buddy."

Watching him process this information tears me apart. He shifts from one foot to the other. His brows rise, then furrow. His shoulders slump just before his head cocks to the side in confusion.

"What about the team?" he asks.

I shrug. "I think Ted is taking it back over."

His bottom lip quivers. "What about . . . you? And me?"

His hands come together in front of him as if he's in prayer. He shakes his head in disbelief.

I climb off the bed. But as I start toward him, he backs away.

"Honey, I know you liked him. I did too. And he liked us. A lot. He hated to have to go . . ."

He tries to speak, but something goes wrong and he coughs instead.

"I know this sucks," I say, my voice breaking despite my best efforts against it.

"Yeah." He bows his head. "I'm gonna go back to Sandbox's."

"Do you want me to get your glove out of the car?" I ask.

He smiles at me. It's not one of joy or happiness. It's one that crushes whatever I have left of my spirit.

"Nah, I'm good," he says. "Bye, Val. Bye, Mom. Love you."

"Love you too," I whisper.

I don't chase him down the hallway like I want to. I don't think that's in either of our best interests.

Damn you, Cole.

"Do you want me to go talk to . . . Sandbox's mom?" Val asks.

"I'll text her in a minute," I say, staring at the spot my son's just vacated. "I just . . . This is what I wanted to avoid all along."

"I know."

"And I failed."

I take my phone off the bed and type out a quick message to Sandbox's mom. Because my eyes are blurry and my head is a mess, I have Val double-check it and hit "Send."

Then I fall back against the bed as the tears form again and cry myself to sleep.

CHAPTER THIRTY-SIX

COLE

I hold my head in my hands. Either it's heavier than I've noticed or my hands are weaker. Either way, I sit on the edge of the bed in my parents' guest room and try to talk myself off a ledge.

How could things have been so perfect this morning and such a clusterfuck this evening?

The recent memory of making a list of things to accomplish so I could move to Bloomfield, and be with Palmer, stings.

God, why does it have to be this way?

This hurts more than any sports injury. It's more painful than any public humiliation of striking out in a big game. Losing Palmer is a hurt that I'm quite sure is never going to heal.

How can someone I just met mean so much to me in such a short time?

I never expected that it was possible, or else I wouldn't have gotten involved with her. Sure, she was pretty and sweet and feisty. Innocent with a slightly hardened edge. But I could've, I would've, overlooked all that if I'd known this would be the end result.

That I would bleed for the rest of time. That I would feel this sense of . . . failure, like I've never felt before. I've failed Palmer even more than I've failed myself or my parents.

I'll never see Ethan grow up to be the incredible man I know he can be—I know he will be. I'll never know Palmer as mine.

Fuck this world.

I stand up and pace the room, retracing the path that I've worn on the hardwood ever since I got back a couple of hours ago. The worst part—the only thing worse than the hole in my chest that feels like a fatal wound—is the pain in Palmer's face.

This disappointment. The anguish. The heartbreak.

The hope that she was misreading the situation because she expected more of me. Because I told her to, and she trusted me.

"This fucking sucks!" I say, but my words only rattle around the empty house.

My bags are packed and sit beside the door. I've booked a ticket from Cincinnati to Los Angeles, and all I have to do is head to Fish's apartment until my flight in the morning. It's the only place I can be guaranteed privacy.

But leaving feels like the end of my life as I know it.

I sit again. My head falls back into my hands. A stab of fire pierces my temples, making me wince.

I think I'm going to puke.

"Cole! Honey! We're home!" Mom's voice rings through the house. "Cole? Where are you?"

A wave of sadness swamps me as I listen to my parents' footsteps come up the stairs. I close my eyes and pray for help in telling them about my diagnosis.

"Cole?" A soft knock raps against the door.

"Yeah?"

My voice catches in my throat. It's hoarse, laden with so much emotion that the sound can barely get through.

Dad walks through first. He starts to speak but stops when he sees my bags. "Cole?"

If Mom sees the bags, she ignores them. Her gaze is fixated on me.

"I need to talk to you guys," I say, clearing my throat.

"What's going on?" Mom sits beside me. "Are you all right? Did something happen?"

I look at her sadly and reach for her hand. She puts it in mine and then presses her free hand on top of our joined ones.

Dad pulls a chair out from the desk and turns it to face us.

Being with them during the worst day of my life is a silver lining. It's not something I've had in my adult life—the luxury of having my loved ones around when shit hits the fan. Their unwavering support and the love radiating off them make me tear up again.

Fucking baby.

I sniffle. "So, this is a lot to take in," I say, stumbling over the words. "But I got a call today."

"From who?" Dad asks, his voice calm and steady.

I look at him. "From my doctor. One of them. Anyway . . . it turns out that I have multiple sclerosis."

Mom gasps. Her body stiffens, every muscle tightening as she searches my eyes for some hint that I'm kidding. Dad, on the other hand, sits resolute.

"Are they sure?" he asks.

I nod.

"That's why you retired." Dad's statement is that—a fact. It's not a question or a proposal but rather an understanding of a situation that's not made sense to him.

"I couldn't hit anymore. The ball was blurry. I couldn't read the nuances." I bow my head. "Everyone blamed the strikeouts at the end of the season due to the shoulder stuff, and that probably didn't help. But I was having issues before that."

Dad dips his chin too.

Tears slip down Mom's cheek as she squeezes my hand. When I look up, she's staring at the wall.

"What does this mean?" she asks. "Will you be okay?"

I shrug. “Okay” is such a relative term. This morning, I thought I’d be okay because I’d have Palmer and Ethan, and we’d have the excitement of facing a new day together. Now? I’m only okay because I’m not six feet under.

I’m alone, untethered from everything that’s ever made sense to me. But I don’t want to go there with my mom yet. I can’t even sort that in my own head at the moment.

“Yeah. I think so. I mean, I’m fit and healthy otherwise. And there are lots of treatments and things now that there didn’t used to be. The doctor said I just need to focus on staying strong, and we’ll deal with the symptoms as they arise.”

She turns to me slowly, her eyes glassy with the tears not yet fallen. “I’m scared for you.”

I wrap her in my arms and hold her against me. She shakes as she cries. I hold myself together until my father wraps us both up in a giant hug. Then I fall apart.

I squeeze my mom, and my dad squeezes me. We sit on the bed and hold each other for what feels like an eternity. I want to get up, to move, to tell them it’ll be okay—even if it might be a lie. But I sit and let them hug their child who’s just told them he’s sick. Because they need it. And maybe because I need it too.

It’s something I haven’t had time to really think about or prepare for—telling my parents about my new reality. I haven’t stopped to think how much this would hurt them.

I can’t imagine having an ill child. If something were wrong with Ethan, I’d—

He’s not mine.

Despite sitting with my family and physically being showered with their love and support, I’ve never felt lonelier. My heart and the innermost places in my soul, which I have just begun to feel, are empty. Cold. *Desolate.*

Mom and Dad release me. Both wipe their eyes as they sit in their seats again.

I want to run, to get away from all this as quickly as possible. *I need to for my own sanity.*

"What can we do for you, son?" Dad asks. "How can we help?"

"There's nothing you can do, Pops."

"Surely we can do something."

"At least let me make you dinner," Mom says. "How about a meatloaf?"

I smile at her as I take her hand in mine again. "I love how you think food fixes everything."

Dad chuckles.

"Well, it doesn't fix everything, but it makes it easier to think with a full belly," she says. "And it keeps me busy, and I need to be busy."

I take a deep breath. "I'm actually going to head back to California."

Mom's eyes widen. "When? Tonight?"

"I'm going to go to Fish's in Cincinnati since he's back in San Diego. I'll head out from there. I just . . . I need to be alone for a bit. I hope you understand."

"We do," Dad says, giving Mom a look to stay quiet. "You do whatever you need to do."

"Thanks."

Mom stands, unable to sit still any longer. "What about Palmer? Did you tell her? Is she handling it okay?"

Palmer.

What's left of my heart cracks as I imagine her tear-streaked face.

"I ended things with her," I say quietly.

"You did?" Dad sounds surprised.

I stand up next to Mom. "It was the only reasonable thing to do."

"How do you figure?" Mom asks. "Did you tell her? Did she not want anything to do with it? Surely she didn't push you away—"

"No, I didn't tell her. It would only complicate things between us, and . . ." I close my eyes. "Why do that to her? It's hard enough telling you guys and dealing with it myself."

"Oh, sweetheart," Mom says, her voice breaking.

I know, Mom. I know.

"Cole, this breaks my heart," she says. "You were so happy. She was . . ."

"Casey," Dad says, giving her a look before turning to me. "I hate this for you both, son. Is there anything we can do?"

I shrug helplessly.

Mom wipes her eyes. "I think if you'd told her, she would've understood. I mean—"

"Mom," I say, my voice strangled. "I can't."

Mom nods. "Okay. I'm sorry."

"When are you leaving?" Dad asks.

"Now?" I say, more like a question than anything.

"Well, let me make you a snack for the road." She looks at me, then Dad, then scurries to the kitchen.

Dad exhales sharply once we're alone and paces around the room. *Must be where I get the pacing thing from.*

"All shit aside, are you okay?" He comes to a stop. "Tell me the truth."

I look at him. "No. I'm not. Not even a little bit."

He sighs.

"I don't know what hurts more—the diagnosis or leaving Palmer," I admit.

He grips my shoulder. "You'll get some distance between you and her, and you'll know what to do."

"I already know what to do. I did what I have to do."

"We'll see. We'll see how you feel when you get a treatment plan locked down and it's manageable and the rest of your life isn't."

I shrug. "How? It won't change anything. Whether I can manage it or not doesn't mean she can."

"I'll tell you what, Cole. I couldn't live without your mother. And I know, beyond a shadow of a doubt, that she would rather walk through fire beside me than live on a beach without me. That's love. And if you figure out that you love Palmer Clark, you'll come home. You won't have a choice."

I wish he were right. But, for the first time in his life, Dad is wrong.

I love Palmer Clark, and *that's* why I don't have a choice.

CHAPTER THIRTY-SEVEN

PALMER

Keep going. Put one foot in front of the other.

I take a deep breath and plaster on a smile that doesn't read truthfully. It doesn't feel bright or happy, and my face is still swollen from crying myself to sleep. But hopefully it comes across to Ethan like I'm fine. Like everything is going to be fine.

Even if my heart might not be.

"Hey," I say, poking my head in his room. "Are you about ready?"

He looks over his shoulder with his gaming controller in his hand. Sandbox's mom dropped him off earlier this morning, and he went straight to his room. No retelling of the night's events, no request for chocolate chip pancakes. No anything except a smile that probably mirrors the one I'm giving him now.

"For what?" he asks.

"For practice."

He furrows his brows. "It's Saturday. We don't practice on Saturdays."

"Ted sent a group text this morning and asked everyone to be at the field at two this afternoon."

Ethan's face falls. "Tell him I'm sick." He turns back to his game.

I sag against the wall, defeated.

Every bone in my body aches. Every muscle yells for me to go back to bed. My head throbs and my chest burns, and fighting with Ethan over baseball, of all things, isn't what I want to do today.

But, then again, I don't want to do anything.

All I want to do is erase the last twenty-four hours of my life. I want to climb back into bed and close my eyes and pretend that Charlotte isn't sick and that Kirk won't lose the love of his life. That my—our—home, Bloomfield, might not be in jeopardy.

I want to pretend that Cole thinks enough of me to stay and that he'll be back through the door in a few minutes. And tonight, when I go to sleep, Cole will be beside me. *Loving me.*

I want to feel safe, like I did with him. I desperately need his smile to get me through this shit at work. I wish for the hope that he brought me, the light he shone on my life—the way things felt possible. Like there was something to look forward to.

Like there was something in this life just for me.

My eyes fill with tears as I look at Ethan, and I feel my heart break again for him. I want so badly to give him more, to be more for him, to attempt to fix all the things I've fucked up. But I can't, and whenever I try, things get worse.

Cole wasn't supposed to make them worse.

I stand straight and take a breath. *The show must go on.*

"You aren't sick," I say, my voice clearer than before.

"So?"

"Ethan . . ." I sigh. "Please turn off your game and look at me."

I think he's going to argue. For a moment, I think he's going to pitch a preteen fit and tell me no. But he doesn't.

He hits a few buttons on his remote, and then the screen goes dark. Slowly, he spins his chair around and faces me.

"What?" he asks.

We look at each other. How deep does our sorrow go? I know mine is bottomless—I'm certain that I'll never have someone in my life like Cole again because I'm certain he's a one-of-a-kind man—but I hope Ethan's isn't. *He's resilient. Kids bounce back.* But when I peer into his little green eyes, I see a grief that I know far too well.

What kills me is how easily he's accepted being let down. It's like he expected Cole to leave.

That's not what I want for you, sweet boy. You deserve so much more than this.

"This sucks," I say, the words wobbling. "I know it sucks and I'm sorry. But we're gonna be okay."

"I know we are. We're always okay."

"I'm glad you know that." *But I also hate that you've had so many experiences that have made you know that.*

He lifts his chin in defiance. "*We* are okay, but *this* isn't okay."

"Yes, it is. Cole has a whole life in California, and he had to—"

"Stop it!" Ethan gets to his feet. His hands are balled up at his sides. "Stop making excuses for him."

"I'm not," I say, carefully. "I'm explaining to you—"

"You are! You're trying to make it sound like it's fine that he left us, Mom, and it's not. If it makes *you* feel better to pretend like he had something more important to do than me and you, then fine. Tell yourself that. But it's a lie."

Tears fill his eyes. His face turns a bright shade of red as he wars against his emotions. The sight of him hurt and vulnerable slices me open.

I reach for him to hug him, to give him some kind of physical reminder that I'm still here, but he doesn't budge.

"Cole isn't like Dad," Ethan says, struggling to control his feelings. "Cole did what he said. He meant what he said. He wouldn't just leave us."

Oh, son. But he did.

"He's gone, Ethan. He's probably back in California right now . . . *like he was always going to do.*" I sit on the edge of his bed and pray for the right words. "Honey, sometimes things don't work out the way we want them to. Things change. Circumstances change. It happens."

"So that's it? You're fine with it? He's gone, and we just pretend like it's all fine now?"

"What choice do we have?"

He releases his fists. The heat in his cheeks starts to fade.

The reality of the situation hits Ethan full force. Cole isn't just a cool story to tell his friends. He can't take this breakup in stride like he thought he could. And reality hits me too—Ethan is still just a little boy. He's hurt and confused, unable to make sense of this mess.

But really, so am I.

As I watch my son come to terms with Cole's departure from our lives, I can't help but feel a touch of satisfaction. Not that he's hurting—I wish I could take that away. But Ethan saw what I saw in Cole.

It's a validation that I'm not out of my mind. What Cole and I had wasn't a casual fling like he's making it out to be. There was something there, something substantial. Something very freaking real, and Ethan felt it too.

"If you don't want to go to baseball, we can skip it tonight," I say softly. "I don't really want to go either. Maybe we can grab a sandwich and hang out instead."

Ethan stares at a poster that Casey gave him of the San Diego Swifts baseball team. Then he looks at me with a cold resolution that chills my soul.

"No, we're going," he says definitively. "I'm gonna go get my stuff together."

He marches past me into the hallway. I hear the front door open and shut.

I get up and start to leave but pause by the poster. Cole is in the back center. The photographer caught him in a mixture of a smile and a smirk. And even though I'm heartbroken and angry, I can't help but smile.

"I hate you," I say, despite the warmth that his picture gives me. "I hate you so much."

I reach out and let my finger touch his image. Then, with a heaviness in my heart, I walk away.

CHAPTER THIRTY-EIGHT

Cole

The sound of my cell ringing next to my head is the only reason I pull my face out of the pillow.

I bat around the sheets until my palm hits the device. I don't bother to look at who it is. It won't be the only person I want it to be. The only person who will never call me again.

"Yeah?" I say instead of a hello. *No sense in pretending this is going to be a polite conversation.*

"How are you?" Fish asks.

His words are measured, feeling me out. I'm sure he's a bit concerned since the last time I talked to him, I was working my way through a fifth of whiskey—something I never do. It was the only way I could numb the pain.

God, I miss her. I miss everything about her. Her touch, smiles, laughs—the way she's always upbeat and prepared with a comeback. I wish I were with her and Ethan this Sunday morning, maybe getting ready to go to Mom's. We could have dinner and hang out with them before going back to Palmer's for some trivia before bed. There would be no MS, no serious worries except how we look after her boss and his wife. *Together.*

I stretch out in Fish's bed and enjoy the moment of relative peace in my brain. It doesn't come often and arrives only when I'm thinking about being there with them.

My life has always been full of stadium lights and the roar of crowds. *So why did I love the peaceful life with a single mom in the middle of nowhere?*

Because that's where I am meant to be. I know it in my soul. I just can't have it without ruining her life, and that fucking blows.

"You there?" Fish asks.

"Yeah. I'm here." I sit up too fast, and my head starts to spin. I push my fingertips into my temples. "Fuck, that hurts."

"How much have you drunk?"

"I'm still awake, so not enough, apparently."

He sighs. "Do you want me to get you a plane? Given that it's midafternoon, you've missed your flight."

I drop my hand and look around the room. *I did. I missed my flight.* But instead of the panic I expect to feel, I don't. *Maybe I'm just numb?*

Or maybe nothing matters anymore.

I'm displaced, a man without a home. The only place that feels like I belong is the one place I can't go.

"I'll see about getting another ticket," I say, my voice devoid of any enthusiasm.

"Dude, let me make some calls. I can get you a private plane in the morning."

"It's fine, Fish."

He scoffs. "If Nicole wasn't sick as shit, I'd be on my way. I'd haul you over my shoulder and bring you back here and make sure you're gonna make it—which you will, by the way. But I gotta stay here with her."

I get up. My body screams at me to sit back down, but I ignore it. The pain feels good in a weird way.

"You're overreacting," I say.

"I hope I am," he mutters. "You're welcome to stay in the apartment as long as you want. But maybe you should get home and decompress a bit."

"But maybe you should get home." I wish.

I stumble around the room until I find my bag on top of a chair with its contents scattered all over the floor. *Great.*

"I'll check flights now and let you know," I say, kicking off my pants. "I'm gonna grab a shower."

"All right. You sure you're okay?"

"Yeah."

"Call me if you need me, Cole."

"Yeah. Thanks. Later."

I end the call and then toss my phone on the bed. There's no sense in looking for missed calls or texts.

There won't be any.

Checking for any communication from Palmer will result in me and the bottle of whiskey again.

That won't help anyone. Least of all my broken heart.

CHAPTER THIRTY-NINE

Palmer

"Just remember that old saying: 'You won't get more to deal with than you can handle.' Or whatever. Isn't that what they say?" Val asks.

"You know what? Fuck that person."

Val chuckles. "Sorry. I'm still getting used to ragey Palmer."

I rest the back of my head against the seat of my car and look at my office trailer. I usually sit in my car and finish my coffee, thinking about all the ways I'm going to slay the day. Especially Mondays. They're the first day of the week and a start to a new line on the calendar. The possibilities are endless.

But today? This Monday? The possibilities all lead me to the same place: more heartache.

The sky is as gloomy as my soul. The drizzle is as depressing as my thoughts. The wind is as cold as my bed was last night as I tossed and turned, missing Cole ferociously.

I gasp, my lungs stuttering as I struggle to breathe.

I miss Cole so much that it's hard to take in oxygen sometimes. My watch goes off with a light-blue screen and the word BREATHE printed across it, and I realize I've been holding my breath for who knows how long. It's like a band is wrapped around my chest three or four times and compresses me so tightly that there's no room to move.

No way to keep going on.

My spirit left when he did; my moxie and energy and freaking heart hitchhiked out of my life right along with Cole, preferring to spend eternity with him instead of the other half of my heart—the one inside my body.

That's how I know this whole thing is fucked. He's not just some guy I dated or slept with or was interested in. My reaction, my desperate need to connect with him in some form, any form, is visceral. I feel it everywhere and in every part of my life.

I ached when I saw a takeout container in the fridge at home, remembering how he got us expensive pasta for no good reason.

It pains me to take Ethan to baseball practice or see his cleats on the floor or smell the unmistakable smell of leather from his glove. I want to cry every time my phone rings because I know it won't be him.

He infiltrated every part of my life. I didn't even realize it was happening. I kept thinking it was manageable—and maybe it was as long as he was here. But now that he's not? I'm wrecked.

I open my car door and climb out. The cold air slams against my face.

"Well, as much as your little pep talk cheered me up," I say, "I've gotta go meet with the guys."

Val sighs. "Like this is what you need to be doing today."

"Yeah, well, the world just keeps going on despite the fact that I'm heartbroken and dealing with a heartbroken child that refused dinner last night. Again. And dealing with . . . everything else," I say, too tired to detail it out. "I'll just keep moving on and hoping that someday I'll look up and it'll be better. That's all I can do."

"I don't know how you do it. I don't know how you stay so optimistic."

I laugh halfheartedly. "It's all a lie. I just tell myself that because it's better than admitting it's probably going to always hurt."

"That's no fun." She groans and says, "I have to get into Fletcher's and help Jacinda through the breakfast rush. The ladies' church group is in today, and it's always a madhouse."

"Go. I need to get too." I climb the steps toward my office and try not to dwell on the fact that Kirk won't be here. "Have a good one."

"Call me if you need me."

I smile. "Thanks, Val."

"Of course. Love you."

"Bye."

I open the door and intentionally don't look into Kirk's office. I just march to my desk and toss my keys on it. But when I turn around to grab coffee, my gaze lands across the room.

Kirk's office is dark, almost haunting. I squeeze my eyes shut and remember his face as he met me at the door last night when I brought the casserole I'd made them.

God, please be with them.

I suck up my courage and grab my notepad. Then I head out the door again.

The walk to the shop is quick and muddy, and for some reason, I appreciate it. It would be wrong to feel this desolate on a pretty spring day. At least the universe is giving me that. It's giving me an overcast, shitty day to wallow in my misery.

The shop goes quiet as I enter. The scents of orange hand soap and grease meet me well before the stares of the guys do. I overlook the mountain of invoices on Burt's desk that should've been turned in last week and don't say a word about Fred's missing gas receipts from running parts last month. I just look at the gang of them and focus.

"Hey," I say with as much authority as I can.

I'm met with a round of grumbles and mutterings that I can't quite make out.

I practiced a speech on the way to work this morning before Val called. I gave a lot of thought about how to approach things and rally the troops, so to speak. But as I stand in front of my coworkers, all my preparations go by the wayside.

This isn't going to be as easy as I thought it would be.

Looking back at me are seven men who seem as nervous as I feel. The robust, capable men have a thread of anxiety about them that fuels mine. I pick at the hem of my shirt and try to hold it together.

Burt stands, crossing his arms over his chest in his trademark style. I can't read it. I can't tell what he's thinking.

"You guys . . ."

I lose sight of what I was going to say by the softness in their faces. What I see looking back at me isn't just concern for Kirk and Charlotte or for our jobs. They have concern for me.

Puzzled and unsure how to process this, I bow my head and wipe my eyes as discreetly as I can.

Fred ambles around the corner of the desk in the same blue and black flannel that he wore every day last week. He looks at me for approval. When I give him the slightest nod, he pulls me into a tight embrace.

He smells like Old Spice and tobacco, exactly what I think a grandfather would smell like. It's comforting and welcoming, and even though I told myself, promised myself, that I wouldn't cry, I find myself sobbing softly into his chest.

"This stinks," he whispers as he lets me go. "This really stinks, doesn't it?"

I nod, wiping my nose with the sleeve of my shirt.

"We've been talking," Burt says.

My insides flip-flop. "About what?"

He leans against his desk. Those big, burly arms of his flexing in the yellowish light. The others defer to him, their leader, as Fred makes his way back to his desk.

"Were you in here yesterday? In the office, I mean?" he asks.

"Yes. Ethan and I came by for a couple of hours after I went to Kirk's. I took them a casserole," I say, even though it's none of their business. "Shamrock always sends their orders on Sundays for some stupid reason, and Kirk usually is here to get them. I was afraid no one would think about it."

Burt almost smiles. Almost.

"What were you talking about before I got here?" I ask. "Me?"

He nods. "We were just saying how you'd be marching your ass in here and barking out orders as soon as you got to work. How you'll come over and tell us some big plan you have to save this place."

My jaw drops. *He can't be serious.*

"You're damn right," I say, my tears drying up at his brisk attitude. "I do have a plan. We have to try to save Skoolie's—not just for Kirk but for us. *For our families.* For the town."

I pause, giving myself a second to rid my voice of the wobble that was starting to surface.

"If he decides to close the doors, there's nothing we can do about that," I say. "But we can try to make things so easy for him that he doesn't want to."

Burt does it. He smiles. It's not an "Oh, go fuck yourself" kind of thing that I've seen from him before, but it almost has a hint of respect in it.

What's happening here?

He plants his hands on the desk and looks right at me. "You are not coming in here and telling us how *you're* going to save Skoolie's."

"Burt—"

"Because we are all going to try. *Together.*"

The room shrinks. The walls close in on the group of us as we stand silently in the shop office. The nasty orange smell subsides, and the acidity of the grease lessens. All I can think about are the people expecting me to respond . . . *to that.* To Burt's words.

"You aren't going to shoulder all of this," he says, his voice gruff. "You always just take over like if you don't do it, it won't get done."

"Well . . ." *Well, that's true.*

He grins in a slightly cocky way. "We are capable, you know."

I start to answer him but stop.

"Kirk put you in charge," Burt says. "Smart move, if I'm being honest. You're dependable and pretty quick on the computer. Customers seem to like ya too."

Gee, thanks.

"We're good with that because it's the best answer to our current problem, and we all just want to save our jobs. Right?" he asks.

I nod warily.

"All we ask is that you trust us a little bit, all right? Give us shit to do, and then let us do it. Don't go checking up on us or figuring we didn't do it or haven't done it and be ready to pounce."

My world stops spinning.

He's right. As much as I hate to admit it, Burt is actually right. The guys over here, Burt included, are capable. And if *I'm* being honest, I do tend to do what he's accusing me of.

I hope for the best, maybe, but I certainly anticipate the worst. My life has been filled with men who have let me down. Kirk aside. And I know that my knee-jerk reaction of expecting people to fail me—which I've unpacked in therapy over the course of my life—isn't one I should apply to all people. And, as Ethan said, if a situation isn't okay, I shouldn't simply pretend it is. *That's something I can control.*

Just because my father—and then Jared, then Charlie, and now even Cole—let me down every time I needed him doesn't mean that everyone always will.

How many times in my life have I been let down because I expected it? How many people have been willing to help me, to hold me up, but I turn them down, not allowing them to help me before I even give them a chance?

I think about this as I stand in front of Burt. I know it's true. Heck, it was even true with Cole. He had to break his way into my life . . . before he left it.

Forcing a swallow, I lift my chin. *One thing at a time.*

"You're right," I say, the words hot against my lips. "I'm sorry for not trusting you guys."

"Wow. That worked," Fred mutters, making them all laugh.

I look at him and smile. "I always knew you were a good egg, Fred. Don't blow it."

Their laughter gets louder, and I find myself surprisingly comfortable in their midst. Even Burt's arms uncross for once.

"All right, then," Burt says. "Let's work together. You figure out what you need us to do, and we'll get it done. You have our word."

I blink back tears. "And you have mine. I'll give you work and walk away. But if you don't do it . . ."

They all laugh again.

"I'm kidding," I say, relieved to have the pressure shifted off me. "Thank you, guys."

"We want to save our jobs, too, you know," Fred says. "I'm too old to find another one."

"We'll do our best," I say. "That's all we can do."

They all nod and, slowly, begin to go back to their tasks. Within a few minutes, it's just me and Burt alone in the office.

He comes around the corner and stands in front of me. Suddenly, he's not quite as burly, not as rough as I usually paint him to be. Seeing him like this—a bit softer and a touch vulnerable—paints our previous interactions in a different light.

"I know we don't always get along," he says.

"That's putting it nicely."

He chuckles. "But that's probably because we're cut from the same cloth. Now, don't get all violent about it," he says as I start to protest.

"I just mean we both like stuff done in our way and appreciate getting to call the shots. It helps us sleep at night."

I can't argue with that. It's true.

Maybe Burt isn't quite the jerk I had him pegged to be. Maybe he has a lot on his plate and a shop full of guys who rely on him, and maybe, just maybe, he's doing the best he can.

Like me.

He starts to walk to the door, and I follow.

"You'll hit an age, Palmer, when you realize that it's not all about the job." He holds the door open for me. "It's about the people you work with. It's about the freedom the job gives you to go home and enjoy your family because, believe it or not, my wife actually likes me. I think."

I giggle as we come to a stop at the path leading to my office.

"We'll get through this. But don't you spend all your time here. Make sure you're at home with your kid too. Those are the hours you can't get back." He nods. "Now get up there and shake off this feely shit and get back to work."

He tosses me a wink and walks toward the yard.

"Hey, Burt," I call after him, my voice floating in the wind.

He turns and looks at me.

"Does this mean we're friends?" I ask.

He shakes his head and grins.

"I need a friend, Burt."

"You need something, that's for sure."

I smile at him for the first time and head back to my office.

CHAPTER FORTY

Cole

Just pick one.

My computer screen glows in a level that's too bright for my hungover eyes. I don't know how some people drink all the time. I feel like complete shit.

I scroll through the flights from Cincinnati to San Diego, opting to avoid Los Angeles, and Scott, after all. There are various options to choose from, and I've perused them all day. I just haven't taken the plunge.

I'm operating in some weird state of limbo—unable to move forward, but I can't go backward either. I'm stuck in Fish's nice-ass apartment with nothing to do but field texts from my mother inquiring about my health and stability.

I lie to her. I tell her I'm fine. I tell her I'm out with friends and working on projects and making doctor's appointments when, in reality, I'm just lying around and trying to distract myself.

But everything—everything—reminds me of Palmer. Movies all apparently center around a love interest, which I find annoying. Music lyrics are downright disrespectful. Even rap lyrics touch on a woman they want to be with, and it's infuriating.

Can't a man just get a song without a woman?

I get up and stretch out. I've put off booking a flight for the last four days. *Why rush it now? What's waiting for me in San Diego but a different, sunnier version of this?*

My phone rings. I drop a hand and grab it, knowing it's Mom with another angle to try to check in without being obvious about it.

"Hello?" I say with a note of sarcasm.

"Cole?"

I drop my arm to my side and perk up. "Ethan?"

"Yeah."

His voice is rough. He sounds distant and hesitant, not at all like the boy I know him to be.

"What's up, buddy?" I ask, my stomach in my throat. "Is everything okay?"

My mind races with a million thoughts. *Is he hurt? Is Palmer all right? Did something happen?* I glance at the clock. *Who is with him?*

"I just went for a walk outside," he says, uncertainty riding in every syllable.

"Oh. Okay." I scratch my head. "How's baseball coming along?"

"It's okay. We had a practice Saturday and another yesterday. Ted says we'll probably lose a lot of games this year, but we can learn a lot."

He said what?

My head steams as I think of the asshole who just took over the team—*my team*. Even though it's not. *How dare he say that to them?*

"Who knows what will happen?" I say, trying to hide my feelings from Ethan. "Baseball is mostly about fun, anyway. Remember?"

"Yeah."

I pace the floor and have the thought that I'm suddenly my father, wishing my boy would talk to me. Wishing he'd just open up and tell me what's going on so I don't have to worry.

Oh, the irony.

"How's school?" I say, cringing as I really sound like my mother. *Next I'll be asking him about the weather.*

Just talk to me, kid.

"It's fine," he says like he's *not* getting to the point anytime soon.

"Ethan?"

"Yeah?"

I sigh. "What's going on?"

I stop walking near the window and gaze over the city. Cincinnati is beautiful. It looks like an amazing city to check out, and I think about telling Ethan about it—asking him if he knows any cool places we could go to if he and his mom were here.

But then I stop.

Because that's not happening.

My spirits fall to the floor, taking my heart right along with them.

"Do you remember telling me that it takes guts to tell people how you feel?" he asks.

"Yeah, I do. We were at your house playing trivia."

"You also told me that you and my mom had something special going on."

Fuck.

I grit my teeth to the point that I hear them grind together. The intense pressure in my jaw is much preferable to the state of pain in my chest.

"This is really complicated, Ethan."

"Why do adults just say things are complicated when they don't want to explain them?"

Damn kid. I smile sadly.

"Fair question," I say. "Sometimes there are tricky topics that adults might think kids can't quite grasp."

"Maybe. But sometimes there are things that kids have to think about, and they can't figure them out because adults won't explain them."

"Another fair point." I sigh. "My relationship with your mother is between the two of us. Okay? I mean that with all due respect. All I can share with you is that . . . is that something happened with me, not her—she's innocent in this—and I have to leave."

He groans, clearly unhappy with this answer. And then he takes in a quick breath.

Even though I can't see him and am a couple of hours away, I sense the change in him. I can feel the vibration of an upset little boy bleeding through the phone.

"You told me not to let my thoughts turn into worries," he says, his voice on the verge of panic. "And I'm worrying *because of you.*"

"Ethan . . ."

"You won't give me answers to my questions, but I'll give you one to yours—how are things? They're horrible, Cole. I'm on a walk outside right now because I'm tired of pretending like I don't hear my mom crying."

My vision of Cincinnati is blurred by the tears filling my eyes.

"She tries to hide it from me," he says, his voice wavering. "She's such a good mom. She doesn't want me to worry, but I do worry because I'm the only person looking out for her."

"That's not true. I—"

"It *is* true. You left." He spits the words out like they're a death sentence. "You're the only thing that makes her happy. You made our life so good because you were nice to us. You helped us. You were fun to be around, and you cared about us. We thought you did, anyway."

A frog sits in my throat as I try to blink back my tears. I've never felt as low as I do right now—all at the hands of a preteen.

"I do care about you," I say. "I care about both of you."

"Then how do I fix her? How do I make her stop crying? How do I fix this and go back to before we knew you?"

Don't. Please. Don't do that.

Remember me, Ethan.

"Buddy, I'm sorry," I say.

"We could go to California," he says, starting to ramble. "Did you think about that? Or you could stay here. You could go do what you have to do and come back."

"It's not that easy—"

"Or we could go somewhere in the middle. Would that be better? What about Colorado? It's in the middle. We'll go anywhere."

I smile sadly, wiping the tears off my chin. *If only it were that easy.*

"Where is your mom right now?" I ask him, needing to know she's safe.

"She's in the house talking to Kirk. Her boss. His wife is dying. It just makes Mom sadder and more stressed out."

A jolt of pain tears across my brain, making me wince. I think back to the last time I saw Palmer and her anguish over her boss. And I made it worse.

"I don't know which side would be worse—Charlotte's, because it's her life that's ending, or Kirk's? Because his life is ending too."

Her words echo through my brain. *"His life is ending too."*

Damn if I don't understand that.

I can't imagine having to watch the love of my life pass away. But on the other side of that coin, I know I wouldn't trade it for the world.

If I were lucky enough to have Palmer like Kirk has Charlotte, I'd feel blessed and honored to be with her through the last days of her life. I wouldn't have it any other way. I wouldn't care that it ended up with a miserable last month or that I had to see her sick or that I had to take care of her. It would be the only way I'd have it. Which makes me remember my dad's sage words . . . ones I didn't believe at the time.

"I'll tell you what, Cole. I couldn't live without your mother. And I know, beyond a shadow of a doubt, that she would rather walk through fire beside me than live on a beach without me. That's love. And if you figure out that you love Palmer Clark, you'll come home. You won't have a choice."

Something inside me stirs.

Holy shit.

I turn away from the window and walk to my computer. I close the lid.

My insides twist and turn, my mind racing through a series of unlikely events that just might be possible if I play my cards right.

"Ethan, can you do me a favor?" I ask him. "I know you don't owe me any favors, but I'd really, really like you to do this one for me."

"I guess. I'm still pissed at you, though."

"Whoa. *Language.* But, you know, thank you. Just don't let your mom hear you say that."

"What do you want?" he asks point-blank.

I run a hand down my face. My skin is hot and damp to the touch.

"I need you to trust me," I say.

"Why should I? My mom is upset because of you."

This kid and his fucking good points. The next thing I impart in him is going to be holding your tongue sometimes.

"What did I tell you about your baseball swing?" I ask him. "Do you remember?"

"Keep it level?"

I grin. "Yes. But also that it's a new skill for you, so you have to—"

"Practice." He sighs. "I don't care about baseball right now, Cole."

I can't help but laugh. "I know. But I'm heading somewhere with this analogy, so a little patience, please?"

"Well, hurry up because I gotta pee."

I shake my head and try not to laugh again. "You have to practice swinging because it's new to you. You'll make mistakes until you get it right, and then it'll become second nature."

"Yeah, yeah, yeah."

"Well, this thing with you and your mom—it's new to me. I've never, you know, done this before. And I'm gonna make mistakes."

"My mistakes don't involve someone crying their eyes out, so I'm not really feeling this analogy."

I snort. "Well, okay. I hear that. Just . . . trust me to fix this. I'm giving you my word. Man to man."

"All right," he says, his voice a little singsongy. "I like that. Man to man."

"Just don't say anything to her, all right? Give me a second. I have to get some things in order first."

"What am I supposed to do? Let her cry? Terrible plan, Cole. Terrible plan."

He sounds just like his mother. It makes me smile.

"I'll hurry," I say, laughing. I've missed this kid as much as I've missed his mom. I hope he—*and she*—will give me a second chance once I get my shit together. "But it might be a day or two."

"Make it one."

"I said I'll try."

There's a pause between us. It's not as contentious as before, and I don't think he's plotting my death, which is a plus. Instead, he laughs.

"Hey, Cole?"

"Yeah?"

"Just so you know, I knew you wouldn't just leave. I knew there was more to the story."

My smile is so wide it hurts. "You did?"

"Yeah." He laughs softly. "So go figure it out and come back. I miss you."

"I miss you, too, little man." *More than you'll ever know.*

CHAPTER FORTY-ONE

Palmer

"At least there's a little sunshine today." I peer through the blinds across the parking lot. "It might be a decent day after all."

I roll my eyes at myself. I don't believe for a second that it will, in fact, be a decent day. I haven't had a decent day all freaking week.

My desk demonstrates just how shitty of a week it's been. There are empty paper coffee cups, the kind Kirk loves and justifies because he can recycle them, all over my desk. My trash can is overflowing. Wads of discarded paper litter the floor and dot my desktop like errant snowballs that refuse to melt.

I'm as messy and chaotic as my workspace.

My hair is going on five days without a wash. I can usually pull three days pretty easily, but five is pushing it in a good hair week—a week when I'm not crying myself to sleep every night. But the tears have been getting a little better, and the cry headaches have eased a bit. I'm still overcaffeinating to make up for all of it, but I'm picking my battles in the Cole War.

The door pops open, and Burt sticks his head inside.

"Hey, we're all leaving for lunch except Fred. Want us to bring you back a burger from Fletcher's?" he asks.

"I'm good. Thanks for asking me."

"No problem."

He doesn't smile or wave or really offer anything in the way of friendliness except his offer—and I'll take it. It's progress.

The cinnamon rolls that I brought in this morning for the guys probably didn't hurt the progress either.

I sit at my desk and pick up my phone. My fingers instantly go to my camera app and click "All Photos."

I shouldn't do this. *Why do I do this?* But knowing it's a bad idea doesn't stop me. I need to see his face.

The scrolling stops at a photo I took the night Cole stayed over. His eyes are heavy and filled with sleep. His smile soft and tender. The light from my phone gives him a warm, cozy glow, and all I can see in his face is love.

And that's what makes this all so frustrating. This isn't about love. I know he loves me. This is about something else, and I don't know what it is—and I may never know.

My breath stalls as I press my thumb against his picture, wishing it were him. Wishing more than anything it was Cole in the flesh. But it's not, and it likely will never be again.

At least he's okay.

I sucked it up and called his mother on Wednesday. Val's insistence that something must've been wrong with him, that his behavior was so out of the ordinary, had started to bother me. So I called Casey and thanked her for being so kind to Ethan and me . . . then slid my way over to the topic of her son.

"I'm thrilled you called," she said. "Cole is going to be fine. I think he had a moment where some things looked pretty awful, but he's on the mend. It'll take a bit, but he'll be back on track soon."

Odd, but okay.

My phone buzzes, and Kirk's name is printed on the screen. I answer quickly.

"Hey," I say. "How are you? How's Charlotte?"

"Hi, Palmer. We're good. You busy?"

I look around the office. "No. You know how Fridays are. They're either swamped or dead, and today's dead. Which is good because this week has been a bit of a learning curve."

"I imagine it has." He pauses. "I need to talk to you for a second. I'm not taking you away from anything important, am I?"

Whoa. I get to my feet, my Spidey senses telling me something is off.

"I'm just doing paperwork," I say as naturally as I can. "What's up?"

"Palmer . . . I sold the business."

My hand flies to my mouth. *No. Please, no.* I squeeze my eyes shut and hold on as the bottom of my world falls out from under me.

"Already?" I squeak.

"It's fast, I know. The paperwork isn't finished, obviously. It's barely started. But I accepted an offer, and it's going to process. I'm sure of it."

I get to my feet. "So, what's that mean for us? I know you had to do what you had to do, Kirk, and I'm not upset with you at all. I'm just . . . you know, worried."

And scared shitless.

Every cell in my body shakes with trepidation and a fear of the unknown. *Will I hate my new boss? Will anyone be my boss, or will he hire all new personnel? Will he scrap the business and use the land for something else?*

"I'm not sure what he's going to do with it, to be honest," he says. "The offer was very fair, and I didn't even have to list it. I couldn't turn it down, Palmer. I hope you understand."

"Of course." *I just hate it.*

"The guy will be by this afternoon," he says. "He wants to look around. I told him that you'll be there and would show him around. You don't mind, do you?"

Yes, I mind. I don't want to show anyone anything.

I look into Kirk's office and frown. How on earth am I going to get this place cleaned up so the new owner doesn't think we're a complete disaster in here? *Ugh.*

"Sure. I'll do whatever you need me to," I say sadly.

"I'll come by next week and tell the guys. Please don't mention it to them. I want to have a bit more information from the buyer about his plans before we upset the guys for no reason."

"Understood."

"And, Palmer?"

"Yes?"

"Thank you for everything, sweetheart. You're one of a kind."

I smile, knowing that should make me feel better. But it doesn't.

"I'll let you know when he leaves," I say.

"That would be great. I'll be waiting."

"Okay. Talk soon."

"Goodbye."

I end the call and sit at my desk.

My head falls into my hands. I'm unable to cry anymore. I'm unable to really even be surprised by anything. It's just one thing after another.

I look up as a soft knock raps against the door. Then it opens. I expect to see Burt with a burger.

But it's not Burt.

And he doesn't have a burger.

I stand again, rolling my chair back so hard that it smashes against the wall. Tears fill my eyes as if they've suddenly remembered how to create moisture.

"Cole?" I ask, as if I might be hallucinating.

"Hey, Palmer."

What. The. Actual. Fuck?

CHAPTER FORTY-TWO

Cole

"Can you, um, breathe? Please?" I ask.

She parts her lips and drags in a huge lungful of air. The abruptness makes her choke, and she coughs for a couple of seconds, refusing to remove her eyes from mine.

I thought I remembered how beautiful she is, but I was wrong. Her eyes have lost a little of the luster I remember, and her face is blotchy—probably because of me. But she's still the prettiest woman I've ever seen, and all I want to do is hug the hell out of her.

To tell her it will be all right.

To tell her the truth.

And to tell her that I love her.

"What are you doing here?" she asks as soon as she's able to talk again.

I shift from foot to foot. "Did Kirk call you?"

"Yeah, but what's that . . . have to do . . . *oh shit.*" Her eyes go wide. *"Don't tell me . . ."*

I walk toward her but stop a few feet away. It's far enough that I can't quite reach out and touch her—for the good of both of us.

"We have a lot to talk about," I say gently.

"Do we?"

Her jaw sets. But the truth is buried in her eyes. She's hanging on by a thread. She wants to run into my arms as badly as I need her to. But the pride and dignity that I love about her so much keep her from it—and I respect that. Tremendously.

Make me work for it, Palmer.

"I have a lot of things to tell you, but I want to go at your pace," I say.

"Maybe this isn't the right time for me. I'm at work."

"And I cleared that with your boss."

Her eyes widen. "So *you* are the buyer? You bought Skoolie's?" She gasps. "Why would you do that, Cole? *Why?*"

I reach for her hand, but she pulls it away.

"You're the one that said that if this place fell, it would hurt the community," I say.

"I did, but that's a bullshit answer." She crosses her arms over her chest. "Is this some kind of game for you?"

Hardly, my love.

"Why, Cole?" she asks again.

I take a deep breath. "I know you have no clue, but I have a lot of money. Like, a mind-numbing amount of money, and it bothers me to some degree that I'm ridiculously wealthy from playing baseball. It seems wrong, and I have guilt about it. So I've been thinking I need to do something positive with it. I'll never spend it all anyway."

She blinks once. Twice. Three times.

"Skoolie's wasn't cheap, but it's a hell of an investment—not just for me and my plans, but for the town of Bloomfield that I've come to really appreciate."

"But how are you going to run Skoolie's from San Diego?"

"I'm not."

Emotions crash together in her eyes like a hurricane threatening the coast. It's a push and pull that's fun to watch but must be terrible to endure.

"I don't know how I'll actually manage it," I say. "Maybe I'll do it; maybe Dad will. I'd prefer it if you did it, since you run it now, but that's up to you."

"Cole . . . ," she says warily.

I force a swallow as my face heats. "You should know that I intend on buying it in a trust."

"Okay. Why do I care?" she says, still unable to process what I'm saying.

"Because I want the beneficiary to be Ethan. When he's old enough, of course."

Her eyes bug out. "What? You . . . you want to give this place to Ethan? Why? Why would you do that, Cole?" Her hands go to her hips. "What is going on here? You're starting to freak me out."

My heart pounds in my chest as I prepare to be the most vulnerable that I've never been with a person in my entire life.

What if she refuses to hear me out? What if she does listen to what I have to say and decides that I was right—she doesn't want anything to do with me? What if she feels like she can't take on caring for anyone else anymore?

I run my palms down my jeans.

"When I came to your house the other day," I say, starting slowly, "I came with the intention of telling you that I wanted to try things with you. I wanted a real relationship with you."

She looks at me with disbelief.

I continue on before she can say anything.

"I'd called Scott, my agent, and told him to turn down all of the offers that I'd received. I had a real estate agent come to look at my house in San Diego to put it on the market."

"Why?"

"Because I was going to move here."

Her bottom lip quivers. "Why?"

I take a deep breath. "I've never seen my parents so happy. They love it here, and you know what? I miss them. They're getting older, and it's my turn to be there for them. I didn't even really realize that until I came here."

She nods like that makes sense.

"Then I coached the boys," I say, smiling. "I love watching them and interacting with them and the way they all relate in a small-town kind of way that I've never seen before. And I want to be a part of that."

"Small towns are nice," she says, watching me out of the corner of her eye.

"And then I fell in love with you. And I fell in love with that little boy of yours." I smile at the way her shoulders slump in what I think is relief. "I just wanted to be with you. I want to share the home you've built. I want to build a life with you, Palmer."

Tears slide silently down her cheeks. "Then what happened? Why did you go?"

I walk to the chair across from her desk and grab the back of it. My exhale is harsh and full of the frustration and anxiety coursing through me.

"Palmer, I left because there's something I didn't want to tell you. I was going to, but then Jared called, and I decided maybe I wouldn't. Maybe it wasn't the best thing to do."

She quirks a brow. "Then why tell me now?"

"Because you deserve to make the choice yourself. And if I'm being honest here, I can't live knowing that I didn't tell you that I love you."

Her hand goes to her mouth. She lunges toward me but stops herself.

"I do love you, Palmer. I fell for you the moment I saw you. Is love at first sight real? If it is, I loved you then. If not, I fell for you as I got to know you and your son. I love both of you," I say, a laugh covering the hiccup in my voice. "But there's something you need to know."

My nerves almost get the best of me. I can taste bile at the back of my throat. I grip the chair and hope that it keeps me still long enough to say what I need to say.

"I found out—well, I've known for a while, but it was confirmed last week—that I have multiple sclerosis," I say. My voice is flat, unemotional, as if I'm telling her it's sunny today. "There's really no way to tell what my quality of life is going to be like going forward."

"Cole."

She flings herself around the desk and propels her body into mine. Her head nestles in my chest.

I wrap my arms around her and pull her so snugly against me that I'm not sure she can breathe. But I'm not sure I'm breathing anymore, either, so maybe we can pass out together.

This is right. This is the way it should be.

I close my eyes and feel her warmth, her energy—the way everything in my world seems to have snapped back together.

God, let this work out. Please.

She pulls back and touches the side of my face. "Are you okay?"

I smile at her. "Right now, I'm great."

"I mean it. *Are you okay?* Why didn't you tell me? I could've helped you process it."

Shrugging, I look at the ceiling. "It felt wrong."

"Cole . . ." She extracts herself from my arms and leans against her desk. "What do you do now? Is that why you are—were?—going back to California?"

I nod. "It felt easier to run away from my problems. And I'd convinced myself that I was doing you a favor."

She laughs. "Right."

"You were having the worst day of your life. And when I opened my mouth to tell you about my diagnosis, it felt like it, *like I*, could be the straw that broke the camel's back."

Palmer frowns.

"The last thing you needed in that moment was for someone else to tell you that they might have to need you to take care of them—"

"Cole—"

"And I couldn't do it to you, Palmer. I couldn't. I've lived my whole life with this baseball mentality of pulling your own weight and being a constructive member of the team. And to feel like a burden—that I would be a burden to you—was more than I could take."

"You could never be a burden to me."

Her words pull at my heartstrings.

"I swore to myself that leaving was in your best interest," I say, my voice softer. "But once I thought about it, really thought about it, I realized that I'd made a decision based on fear, not on love. Love stands through it all, and I knew I'd stand beside you if the roles were reversed."

A small grin slips across her cheeks.

"It took someone reminding me that true courage is being honest about your feelings," I say.

A look flashes across Palmer's eyes.

I smile. "Look, I can't promise you the future. I'm healthy. I should be strong for a long time, but you never know—"

"I know." She walks to me again and stops just inches away. "I know the only thing I've ever wanted is someone to do life with me. Whatever life is. Whatever happens. And then you came into my world and shook it up. For the first time, I wasn't scared for the future because I could imagine us together."

My God, I don't deserve her.

"Anything could happen, Cole. I could get sick. I could get into an accident on the way home and never walk again."

"Don't talk like that."

She smiles.

"I've missed you so much," I admit. "I went to Cincinnati and couldn't bring myself to get a ticket to California. Every time I thought about boarding a plane without you, I panicked."

She touches my cheek again, feathering her thumb over my face.

"I want to be beside you when we're celebrating and when things aren't great," I say. "I want to teach Ethan to play ball or chess or whatever he does. But let's hope it's not chess."

She laughs, her eyes clouding with unshed tears.

I grab her hand and bring her knuckles to my lips. I press a long, lingering kiss against them.

"I'm sorry I left you," I say. "If you'll have me back, I'll never leave you again."

She stands on her tiptoes and grins. "I can't have you back, Cole. I never gave you up in the first place."

I pick her up, making her squeal. Then I sit her on top of her desk.

"Don't mess up my stuff," she says, laughing.

I lean my forehead against hers. "I'm your boss now. I can do what I want."

She smacks my shoulder.

"I meant it when I told you that I love you," I whisper. "I love you, Palmer Clark."

"And I love you, Cole Beck."

I pull her close to me again, needing to feel her heartbeat against mine.

This is better than any baseball game I've ever played in, better than any home run or grand slam in the biggest games of my career. This, right here, holding my girl, is it. It's what I've always been looking for.

It's the sweet spot.

And I'm never letting her go.

CHAPTER FORTY-THREE

Palmer

"Burt's face . . ." I giggle as Cole drives me home. "At least we were clothed, I guess."

Cole snickers at the memory of Burt walking in with me sitting on my desk and Cole standing between my legs, kissing the hell out of me. He reaches across the console of my car and squeezes my thigh. "I need you unclothed as soon as humanly possible."

My blood heats, and it's hard not to undress in the passenger's seat and climb on top of him while we're going down the road.

"Is that what this is now?" I ask. "You think you can just undress me at any time?"

"You're damn right I do."

I lean back in my seat as his hand goes up my thigh.

Cole spent the entire afternoon at the office. Kirk ended up coming in for a few minutes while Charlotte was with her nurse and used that opportunity to tell the shop guys about Cole's purchase. They took the news well. Burt walked Cole around the yard after Kirk left, and I think they had a bonding moment over stale doughnuts.

"We have some things to figure out, though," he says, removing his palm from my leg.

"Like what?"

"Well . . ." He exhales. "Where do we live, for one?"

"What do you mean, 'Where do we live'? You know where I live."

Then it hits me. *He wants to live together.*

Butterflies take flight in my stomach, and I fight to keep them under control before I start dancing in my seat.

He glances at me out of the corner of his eye and grins.

"I know you're Mr. Moneybags and all," I say, laughing, "but I actually really like my house. Hey, by the way, do you own it now too?"

Cole chuckles. "Actually, I do. Or I will. It was a package deal."

I roll my eyes at his amusement.

"I do want to add quickly before we move on," he says, "that if you weren't cool with me owning your house—like, if you were pissed at me and felt awkward about it—I would've deeded it over to you. I never would've held that over your head."

"So you'll deed it to me now?" I ask, testing the waters.

He reaches for my hand and laces our fingers together. "Pretty sure when I marry you that you'll own half anyway."

I don't know whether to laugh, cry, or say a prayer that I don't wake up from this wonderful dream.

"I'm going to marry you, Miss Clark," he says, biting his bottom lip. "I'm going to marry you, put as many babies inside you as you'll allow, and dote on you until you're sick of me."

"Easy on the doting, sir. I like my own personal space."

He laughs in a way that makes me think he doesn't buy into the idea of personal space. *Oh dear. How will I ever manage?*

I grin at him. "Can we still live at my house? At your house? At *the house*?"

He squeezes my hand. "I know things have been really easy with us."

"Yeah."

"But some things are going to have to change a little bit, Palmer."

I furrow my brow. "Like what?"

"Like we can live at *the house*, but we'll need to get a security system. That's one example."

"Really?" I think about needing a security system in Bloomfield. It's unnecessary. Unless . . . "How much money do you have, Cole? Ballpark it, no pun intended."

"How much do you think I have?"

I shrug. "I don't know. A couple of million? That would be a lot."

He bursts out laughing.

"Don't laugh at me. I don't know how much athletes make!"

"Palmer, I'm worth many, many millions of dollars."

Many, many millions? Holy shit.

"That makes me super uncomfortable," I say.

"Then let's not talk about it. Let's talk about the possibility of remodeling the house and making it exactly the way you've always dreamed of. Maybe a big bathtub?"

"Ooh. And maybe a new dishwasher?"

He laughs again like I've lost my mind.

I sit quietly as we pull into the driveway. We climb out of the car when Val pulls in. Ethan jumps out of her car and barrels straight for Cole.

"You are here!" he says.

"I told you to trust me."

He did? "When?"

They look at me and chuckle.

"Call me!" Val shouts, winking.

"I will! Promise!"

"I'm holding you to that!"

She backs out of the driveaway, honking her horn in celebration.

My spirits soar so high that I'm not sure if I'll ever come back down.

I watch Cole and Ethan walk up the stairs to the house together, talking animatedly about baseball. My heart is so full that I think it's going to burst.

I've waited my whole life for this moment. Even when it felt impossible, even when I couldn't see the light at the end of the tunnel, I bowed my head and hoped that someday, good things would come my way.

And they did. They came in the best form. A six-foot, blue-eyed, smooth-talking baseball player who has a heart as big as California. A man who's willing to give up, who wants to give up, his beloved sunshine and salt water for a single mom and her little boy.

I think back to something Kirk said.

"The point is that you can't force fate, Palmer."

"With all due respect, I'm not sure that baseball is my fate. Let's hope not, anyway."

"Maybe it's not baseball. Maybe . . . maybe it's what baseball will lead you to."

You never know where life may take you. You just have to have patience and trust that it will all work out. You have to believe that the challenges, hardships, all the moments that will absolutely bend you in half are just making you stronger, more resilient, and absolutely more badass for life on the other side.

Because there *is* another side. There's always another season. For some, it's facing an illness and its many unknown variables. For others, it's learning to keep going when life looks bleak. But what makes it endurable is love. Messy, complicated, beautiful, and enduring love.

And for this household, that's probably going to include at least another season of baseball.

EPILOGUE

Palmer

Six months later

Did you use soap?" Cole's question rings down the hallway. "Get back in there and use soap, my man."

"But—"

"Ethan, please. It's soap. No one is asking you to do something wild like clean your room."

I giggle and turn back to the stove.

The meatloaf that Cole made cools on a rack next to a pot of mashed potatoes. Cooking is his thing these days. He says it gives him joy. *Who am I to take that away from him?*

Cole's arms come around me from behind, pressing his hands against my stomach, where a bump will be showing in the coming months.

"How's my little mama?" he asks, kissing me beneath my ear. *How I love when he calls me that.* "Hungry? Grab a seat and I'll make you a plate."

"When am I not hungry?"

"You're growing a future Hall of Famer in there." He grins. "Sit."

I learned quickly not to argue with Cole. It was one thing before I got pregnant, but now? He's nearly impossible to deal with.

The barstools were removed earlier this week in anticipation of the kitchen renovation, so I sit at the table. I'm not sure what we'll do next week, when the contractors begin work in this part of the house. I'm sure we'll figure it out.

Remodeling has been an experience. I keep forgetting that Cole, *we*, have money. I asked for a two-car garage. He had a space built to hold more cars than any two people will ever need. I suggested a walk-in shower. We have something that looks like you need a degree in electronics to operate it. And the day after I suggested a bigger closet to hold both of our things, a room was being built . . . on the other side of the soaking tub that I apparently mumbled about in my sleep.

I have to watch what I say to my husband—*even when I'm sleeping.* He knows no bounds and takes every opportunity he can to spoil me.

"Here you go," he says, setting a plate in front of me.

"This looks great."

"Mom's recipe." He sits across from me, having eaten earlier with Ethan while I napped. "I hope you like it."

The first bite melts in my mouth. The spices—Casey's *secret blend* that Cole won't share with me—are both aromatic and delicious.

"This is so good. It makes me want to fall in love with you all over again."

He beams. "Thank you, my lady. I've realized that hers are better than the ones I pull from the internet."

I laugh. "You're talking about the lasagna, aren't you?"

"Yup."

His laughter mixes with mine as we remember the lasagna that he made last week. It was highly inedible and resulted in corn dogs from King Pin Alley for dinner—something that didn't upset Ethan at all.

"Your dad called while you were talking to the contractor," I tell him. "He said your mom is on the way to pick up Ethan and that you have a closing tomorrow morning at eight. He wanted me to remind you because he's pretty sure you didn't write it down."

"Shit. No, I forgot. I'm glad he called because I was going to play golf with Bud in the morning."

I sit back in my chair and grin.

I've never been happier.

Sometimes I pinch myself to see if I will wake up from this life that feels like a dream. A handsome, kind husband who went from the big leagues to president of the Bloomfield Little League. From sand and salt water to rental houses and real estate.

He sits back in his chair. "The house we're closing on tomorrow is the one by the post office with the blue siding. Do you know the one I mean?"

"Yeah," I say, cutting a piece of meatloaf. "Val says she wants to transfer her lease to that one."

He shakes his head. "Does she think she always gets first dibs?"

"Yup. It's a best-friend thing."

He laughs. "I'm going to tell her she just needs to be grateful she's out of the funeral home."

"It's your fault. You're the one that basically doesn't even charge her rent and lets her get away with murder."

"What am I supposed to do? She's your best friend."

"Good point." I take another bite of the meatloaf. "Oh, *this is good.*"

He smiles proudly.

I set my fork down and reach for his hand. The wedding band that he placed on my finger five months ago sparkles in the light. It's a double halo with pink diamonds set in platinum and is absolutely over the top. It's entirely more than the simple band I suggested, but I love it because Cole picked it out for me. He said the color reminded him of the way I blush when I'm smiling. *How sweet is that?*

I'm caught off guard every single day by this man's attentiveness. The way he prioritizes me and Ethan is astounding. Watching him balance all the things on his plate—the real estate company he runs with his dad (which delights Lawrence to no end), the baseball league, helping at Skoolie's when I need a hand, and managing the house remodel—brings tears to my eyes regularly.

This is what love looks like.

Cole is forever asking for my input on things. He values my opinion, even if I don't have any experience in the topic at hand. He treats me with respect and won't stand for anyone not doing the same. He's involved in everything Ethan does—from school to baseball to *Fortnite*.

He even got his own game system so they can do it together.

My husband might not understand how much peace this gives me, but he's truly an answer to my prayers. Ethan has such a strong role model in Cole—both on the baseball field and off. He is shown every day what love, family, and respect truly mean. I now know that Cole modeled himself off Lawrence—a damn good man in his own right. A man I love, too, and a man who loves me and my son like his own.

"You're pretty incredible, do you know that?" I ask.

"Yeah. I know."

He winks as I try to jerk my hand away.

"I have something to ask you," he says softly.

There's a twinkle in his eye that makes my insides wobble. I've come to learn that this particular glimmer means that he's up to something—something he's not sure how I'm going to take.

"What?" I ask.

He shifts in his seat. "I didn't get to take you on a honeymoon because we were in the middle of the Skoolie's transfer and Charlotte's illness and the whole Jared debacle."

I roll my eyes at the last part.

"But now that everything with the business is finished and Charlotte is doing remarkably well and Jared is gone . . . for a while," he says, skirting over the plea deal that will keep Jared in prison for at least five years, "I was thinking we could take a babymoon."

I laugh. "A what?"

"A babymoon. I read about it online. It's like a honeymoon, but you take it before the birth of your baby. You know, like a final getaway before life gets super fun."

Oh, Cole. You sweet man.

I grin so hard that my cheeks ache.

"Where would we go? Who would watch Ethan? Can we really just get away like that with Skoolie's and your real estate company and the baseball league? You're in the middle of building an entire new Bloomfield Youth Sports Complex."

He grins.

"There's so much happening, Cole."

"And none of it is as important as *us*. Our relationship."

God, I love you.

"Okay," I say, sitting back and forgetting all about the meatloaf. "What do you have in mind? Because I can tell you've already been planning."

He smirks. "Yes. A little. Let's call it preplanning."

"Go on."

"Dad can handle Beck Properties. If he needs me, he can call. Bud's on board with monitoring the field situation. He's thrilled to be a part of the project. Burt said he could handle Skoolie's—"

"You've talked to Burt about this?"

He laughs. "Vaguely. Simmer down."

"What's with the two of you, anyway? You two are as thick as thieves."

"What? I like him. He can be a little difficult, but he's helpful. He helped me find the electrician for the house. Remember?"

I roll my eyes, more amused than annoyed, because Burt and I have worked out our own relationship. As long as I give him the space he needs and deserves, he gives me mine. It turns out that we're a pretty good team when we communicate. Go figure.

"Fine," I say. "Go on."

"And Mom is over the moon about getting to have Ethan to herself for a while. I think she's already been making a menu."

I laugh. "I bet she has."

He leans against the table and takes my hands in his. "So, what do you think?"

I think I'm so lucky that we found each other.

"Just tell me. I know you've already booked something," I say. "I can tell."

He chuckles. "Okay. Maybe."

"Cole!" I laugh. "What did you do now?"

"We leave for Auckland in the morning."

My jaw drops to the floor. *He has to be kidding me. He remembered that?*

Tears gather in the corners of my eyes. *Of course he did.*

"If you don't want to go, we can cancel it all today and it'll be fine. But I didn't get to take you on a honeymoon, and I'm still kind of pissed about that. I want to get you to myself for a while. You can't blame me."

"For how long?"

"Nine days." He bites his lip, searching my eyes. "Two of those are travel days. Plus, it's only really five days away from work, given the weekends. Right?"

I nod, my heart swelling in my chest.

"Palmer, I just want to make all of your dreams come true. I want to give you the world—everything you've ever wanted, no matter how big or small."

I get to my feet and walk to him. Cole pulls away from the table far enough for me to sit on his lap.

"So, no golf in the morning?" I ask.

He looks a bit sheepish at the question. But, before he can answer, I take his face in my hands and peer into his beautiful blue eyes—the ones that I hope our child gets—and smile.

"You are my dream come true, Cole Beck."

He kisses me, locking his hands around my waist. Before he can deepen the kiss, the doorbell rings.

"Mom must be here to get Ethan," he says, planting another kiss on my forehead.

"What if I'd said no?" I laugh. "I would've foiled all of your plans."

Cole winks. "You weren't saying no. I can be *very* persuasive."

This is true.

I stand, Cole following behind me, and walk to the front door. Cole pulls it open to see Casey on the other side. She looks at her son, then me, then Cole again.

"I told her," he says, smiling.

Casey squeals. "I'm so excited for the two of you. And for me. I'm also really excited for me."

The sound of rollers on the hardwood rings through the house. I look over and find Ethan pulling a suitcase into the foyer. He has a smirk that reminds me of Cole's earlier.

"You knew too?" I ask.

He laughs. "Everyone knew but you, Mom."

Casey pulls me into a hug. "Have fun. Enjoy yourselves and don't worry about us. I'll take care of my grandson."

Ethan hugs Cole and then me. "I love you, Mom."

"I love you, too, kiddo."

He pulls away and turns to Casey. "Let's go, Gram! Pap said I could help him build a picnic table today."

I can't help it. I tear up. It could be the pregnancy hormones, but it's really just an overwhelming gratitude that comes over me.

My kid has grandparents who adore him.

Casey waves over her shoulder, and then Cole shuts the door.

"I can't believe you did all of this," I say, the idea of flying to Auckland tomorrow just sinking in. "I need to pack. I don't even know what I need. What *do I need*, Cole?"

He chuckles and pulls me into his chest. It's his way of calming me down, bringing me back to the moment. And I love him for it.

"You need to bring yourself, your brand-new passport, and a smile. I got the rest," he says.

Even though that's not true—I'm totally going to have to pack—it is partially the truth.

For so many years, it was me and Ethan against the world. I had our lives on my shoulders every single day. Now, I have a husband who loves me with every fiber of his being—rain or shine, hell or high water. He proves to me over and over again that I don't have to carry everything anymore. He's got the rest.

And he does.

I hope this season of my life never ends. But if it does, and it probably will, that's perfectly okay. Cole and I have built a solid team that will face any season . . . together.

For the rest of our lives.

ACKNOWLEDGMENTS

First and foremost, thank you to my Creator. I'm so grateful for the opportunity to try again every day.

Writing an acknowledgments section without acknowledging the sacrifices and support my family contributes to each and every book would be ridiculous. Thank you to my wonderful husband, Saul; our four children; and our extended family. I know the dynamics of family life because of you.

A huge thank-you to the Montlake team—Alison Dasho, Anh Schluep, Jillian Cline, Patricia Callahan, Lindsey Faber, Bill Siever, and Kellie Osborne—for believing in me and this story. I'm so honored to work with you all again.

I would be remiss not to thank Tiffany Remy, Carleen Riffle, Marion Archer, Susan Rayner, Anjelica Grace, Mandi Beck, and S. L. Scott for their support, advice, and friendship throughout the writing of this book.

I have the best reader group out there! I'd like to thank Books by Adriana Locke for the endless laughs, encouragement, and fun. You are my readers, my friends, and my honorary family. Thank you for going on this ride with me.

And, last but certainly not least, thank you to each reader who chose to pick up this book. My goal was to provide you with a reprieve from daily life for a little while. I hope you enjoyed this story and walk away smiling and feeling a little lighter. I appreciate you. Thank you for giving this book a chance.

ABOUT THE AUTHOR

Adriana Locke is the *USA Today* bestselling author of *Like You Love Me*. After years of slightly obsessive relationships with the flawed bad boys created by other writers, Adriana created her own with such series as Dogwood Lane, The Gibson Boys, and the Landry Family. She resides in the Midwest with her husband, sons, two dogs, two cats, and a bird. She spends a large amount of time playing with her kids, drinking coffee, and cooking. You can find her outside if the weather's nice, and there's always a piece of candy in her pocket. Besides cinnamon gummy bears, boxing, and random quotes, her next favorite thing is chatting with readers. She'd love to hear from you! Visit the author at www.adrianalocke.com.